FISH SPRINGS

Beneath the Surface

Larry C. Timbs Jr is a former general manager and editor of community newspapers in Kentucky and Illinois, and has published numerous travel articles in the *Charlotte Observer.*

FISH SPRINGS

Beneath the Surface

A NOVEL BASED ON A TRUE STORY BY

Michael Manuel &
Larry C. Timbs Jr

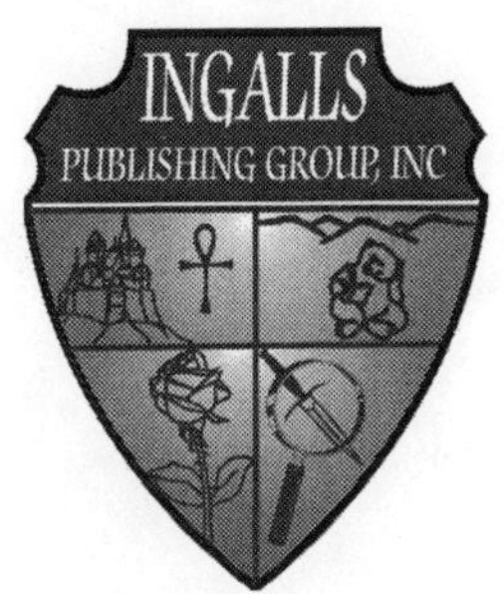

INGALLS PUBLISHING GROUP, INC
PO Box 2500
Banner Elk, NC 28604
ingallspublishinggroup.com
sales@ingallspublishinggroup.com
828-297-6884

Cover photo by Michael Manuel, Watauga River below the Wilbur Reservoir
Book design by Luci Mott

Library of Congress Cataloging-in-Publication Data

Manual, Michael.
Fish Springs : beneath the surface : a novel based on a true story / by Michael Manual & Larry C. Timbs Jr.
pages cm
ISBN 978-1-932158-47-2 (trade pbk. : alk. paper)
1. Mountain life--Tennessee--Fiction. 2. Tennessee, East--Fiction. 3. Watauga Lake Region (Tenn.)--History--Fiction. I. Timbs, Larry C., Jr. II. Title.
PS3613.A583F57 2014
813'.6--dc23
2014002574

Authors' Notes

My father, Lawrence C. Timbs, who originally self-published this story in 1981 under the title *Tragedy at Old Fish Springs*, died at the age of 90 in Elizabethton, Tennessee, on January 25, 2012. He was born in the Watauga Lake community of Fish Springs (now mostly under water), as was his father, James Avery Timbs, his mother, Mary Roberta Williams Timbs, and his grandfather, William Brownlow Timbs. My father said he was told this story, which he believed to be true, in 1938 from his maternal grandfather Robert L. Williams, who was said to be a cousin to the infamous John Williams.

— Larry C. Timbs Jr

When I moved to Watauga Lake in 2003, a neighbor told me about a little self-published book, *Tragedy at old Fish Springs,* by Lawrence C. Timbs. Being a student of screen writing, I adapted the story into a screen play. In 2009 at a screen writer's workshop, I caught the attention of movie producer Belle Avery with my screen play. Belle Avery loved the story and wanted to produce a movie of it, but thought a well-received book would help in the process, so she convinced me to write a novel of my screen play. Larry Timbs Jr, son of Lawrence C. Timbs, agreed to edit my book. A good choice for me as Larry was a retired journalism professor. Realizing Larry's talents I soon agreed to make him a co-author. Finding a publisher for unknown writers proved to be another challenge. Finally Bob Ingalls of Ingalls Publishing stepped up. While our novel is a work of fiction we still believe the core of the story passed down by Larry's great-grandfather to be true. We are excited that this story will move from page to screen.

—Michael Manuel

For more details about the authors and the story, see the Acknowledgments and notes in the back of the book, and the authors' website:
www.fishspringsnovel.com

Prologue

The workhorse whinnies and pulls desperately at his tether, terrified by his master's screams and the pungent odor of rattlesnake. The man gasps and hollers for help, then staggers away from the wagon, still screaming.

The timber rattler is wrapped around the man's neck and one arm, its fangs embedded in his hand. The freakishly thick reptile releases the hand and faces the man eye to eye, its slitty eyes focused on its victim. It rears away flicking its tongue, keeping its hideous head level with the man's, then strikes. The man screams in pain as he yanks the snake's head from his face. Blood flows profusely from the wound.

His strength fading, the man loses his grip on the snake's head, and this time the deadly rattler lunges for his neck, sinking its fangs into the ill-fated soul's jugular vein.

The victim stands rigidly while the huge angry snake uncoils, drops to the ground and slithers off into the brush. The man gasps one last time and falls face first to the ground.

Here was an unsuspecting Fish Springs farmer who had been toiling hard in his fields. He had taken a break to escape the scorching sun and eat his lunch under a sheltering shade tree. He had thoughts of the future, of growing old and reaping the benefits of a good life.

The venomous serpent, however, cut it all short—crushing his hopes and dreams and stopping the beating of his heart in a few moments of excruciating pain and misery.

Hardly anyone would have known how such a horrendous thing happened, had it not been for my grandfather. For you see, the community of Fish Springs, where I was born and reared now lies beneath the deep, blue waters of Watauga Lake. The lake, nestled in the mountains of northeast

He had been brought up in a household with little money, but with lots of hugs and laughter. Each member of the family had taken a turn every evening at Bible time. Wilfred White always remembered his father saying, "The Bible's God's letter to us, and we should read it."

Wilfred wanted Alfred to get a good education and had plans for him to go to college. "Why, our Alfred might one day become a doctor or lawyer," Wilfred often mused to his wife. "We've got to get him all the book learning he needs to get him out of this mountain holler and make something of himself."

It's not lost on Alfred that he's lucky to have Wilfred White as a father. Every night when he got down on his knees and said his prayers, he gave thanks to the Almighty for that fact, and, likewise, he prayed that his friend John Williams would have some peace and joy in his life. Not that he thought of himself as better as or smarter than John. It's just that the devil seemed to get hold of him on far too many occasions. There was that time in town that Alfred had thought it polite to make small talk with an elderly lady, but John said nothing.

Try as she might, the lady could not engage John in conversation. Instead, he just stared at the woman, not saying a word.

When Alfred asked him why he refused to talk, John shot back. "Why the hell should I? You know what? I ain't carin' if I never speak to another stranger again!"

But such sourness from John wasn't on Alfred's mind this day. For today was all about keeping the canoe afloat and having a rollicking time while navigating the white water of the roaring, beautiful Watauga River.

With the two adventure seekers, John's hound pup, Blue, was standing on the center seat of the boat with his front feet hanging over the side, barking ferociously at the bears. The man who gave John the pup said he was half pure blue tick hound and half pure beagle. The way John figured it, two halves made him one pure dog.

Alfred hollered, "John, did'ya see the bears?"

"Yeah, I wondered what Blue was barking at."

John pulled Blue back down into the canoe by his long droopy ears. "Shut up Blue! That mama bear'd gobble you up in one bite, and then she'd spit you out!"

Alfred screamed over the roar of the river, "Hold on! Rapids ahead!"

Both youths thrust their paddles deep into the rushing water trying to keep the canoe straight. A miscalculated stroke steered the vessel into a giant, moss-covered boulder protruding from the water. The canoe bounced off the big rock, almost throwing Alfred out. Then it splashed into a wide, deep pool at the bottom of the rapids.

"Ya hoo! What a ride!" Alfred yelled. "That was fun, wadn't—"

Alfred nervously glanced back, but only saw Blue. Worried now, he surveyed the water in every direction, desperately hollering, "John! John! Where are you?"

Alfred paddled the canoe to the bank and jumped out. He scampered above the boulder, searching, his heart pounding. Then, to his relief, he spotted John's hand clutching the jagged rock just above the water. Alfred waded into the river as close to the rushing rapids as he could get without being pulled under himself.

He grabbed John's hand and pulled as hard as he could, but his friend was held fast against the rock by the crushing water. He knew John would surely drown if he couldn't get his head above the surface. Then he felt John's grip tighten. Alfred summoned every fiber of energy in his body and yanked, and there, low and behold, was the top of John's head.

Alfred pulled again, and this time John broke free of the rushing water's death grip. Alfred pulled his exhausted friend to a sandbar. Totally spent, he fell to his knees. The fear subsided and he felt a rush of total relief.

Alfred asked his coughing, gasping friend if he was okay.

John grunted. "Yeah. Thought I was a goner. … I think I just seen Jesus. Like I'd died and was 'bout ta go ta heaven. But man I'm glad ta be alive!"

Stretched out now on the sandbar, John thought about what a close call he'd had with death. Too close, to say the least. *Why, I'm dang lucky to be alive. And if'n' it warn't for Alfred, I'd be dead as a cold stone. But I'd a done the same for him.*

Alfred dragged the canoe up the bank and tied its paddles to the seats. That way, it could be hoisted upside down and carried up the steep, winding path, to town.

"You sure you're okay?" Alfred asked. "I mean you can breathe okay and all?"

"Yeah, I'll live. Let's get the hell outta here. I've damn sight had enougha' this mean old river."

The bare-footed boys lifted the canoe above their wet heads and hit the trail. But they paid a heavy price for their ride down the Watauga. The winding path back to town was all up hill and full of obstacles like massive rock outcroppings, narrow ledges and fallen trees. Rattlesnakes and copperheads sometimes lay in the sun on the paths. Poison ivy, thorns and briars were also abundant, but the wildflower-lined path was also beautiful, especially in spring and summer.

Flame azalea, lady slippers, fire pinks and rhododendrons made this one of the most beautiful paths they'd ever walk. Right now, however, it's about not stepping on something that could make a good day very bad.

And while they walked, neither one spoke. It perplexed Alfred that John had not sufficiently thanked him for saving his life, but he tried not to dwell on it. *Still,* Alfred thought, *John don't know how fortunate he is. Why, if it hadn't been fer me, that ole boy would be just a dead, stiff body floatin' down the river. The fish'd be nipping at his nose and ears. And who knows if he'd have gone to heaven?*

Normally, Alfred loved following this path, despite what it threw at the walker to make it harder. But today, the enjoyment was taken away because of that twelve-foot canoe. When your head is inside a canoe, you can only see enough to keep from venturing off the trail.

Little Blue ran ahead, his nose to the ground. He stopped to study a butterfly and jumped at it when it took flight. He seemed thoroughly in his element with the sights, sounds and pungent scents of the woods. Every now and then, he wandered off the path, sniffed a wildflower or slunk to the ground if he'd spotted a lizard or some other small creature. Other times, he lifted a leg marking his territory.

Alfred replayed the day as he continued his hike along the trail. He knew his father didn't know that he and John were shooting the rapids and not paddling in the more calm areas of the river like they had promised. So in that respect he had betrayed his father's trust, and had almost lost his friend in doing so. He made a vow to himself. He would never try to deceive his father again.

When the boys arrived at Fish Springs, which had derived its name from several springs teeming with fish near the Watauga River, they were exhausted but glad to be almost home. Fish Springs had a feed store and a drygoods/general store on one side of the road, and a blacksmith shop and Bob's Barbershop on the other. Farther up the road was a one-room schoolhouse, Fish Springs Baptist Church and Fanny Ward's Boarding House, which catered to travelers, fur traders and salesmen.

To the boys, growing up in Fish Springs was just fine. There was fishing and swimming, hunting, exploring the woods and mountaintops, and of course canoeing the river. What more could a lad want?

John, normally quite talkative, still had not said a word. *Well, I guess if I'd have almost died, I wouldn't be saying much either,* Alfred figured.

Finally, John, his head still in the canoe, broke his silence. "Alfred, are we on the road?" he asked.

"Yeah, and I think we're getting close to the barbershop," his friend replied, relieved that maybe John was beginning to come around.

Alfred started to lift the canoe to check the road ahead when *Bonk!* The boys rammed into a red, white and blue striped barber pole protruding from the ground by the sidewalk in front of Bob Taylor's barbershop. They hit the pole dead center giving them a hard jolt.

John hollered, "God Damn, Alfred!"

"Sorry, John!"

They raised the canoe from over their heads and lowered it to the road next to the sidewalk. Then both boys forgot about canoes and bears and rapids and poles and everything else when they cast their eyes toward one of the prettiest sights they'd ever seen.

She was thirteen-year-old, cute as a button, Mary Clemmons. She had sparkling green eyes, and long blond hair in pigtails. Mary would be a head-turner for the rest of her life. Even at such an early age, her smile showed signs of growing kindness and sweetness to everyone she met.

The pretty girl in a long blue dress was pulled along by her aunt, prim and proper Caroline Hamby. Everything about Aunt Caroline spoke of a woman who wanted nothing to do with what she considered to be young heathens. She played life by the book—the Good Book, that is—and she believed that young boys were trouble—young men even more so.

After all, she herself once many years ago had dared to see what a young man could do to make her happy. And at first, things between them had been good. He had courted her, gone to church with her and bought her pretty things. Later, when she married Dudley Hamby, he provided for her, built her a house, put food on the table. In short, he did all the things a man was expected to do to make his woman comfortable and content. However early in their marriage, things in the bedroom had turned cold. Still, Caroline figured she had a good, Bible-believing, faithful, hard-working husband.

But her life changed radically the day she took her quilting group out to the barn to show them a litter of puppies. There Caroline and her lady friends found Dudley having his way with a young slave girl.

The marriage crumbled and Caroline sent Dudley on his way, never to be seen in Fish Springs again.

"I like your puppy. What's his name?"

Before either boy could speak, Aunt Caroline snapped, "Don't talk to those heathens, Mary!"

Alfred countered, "We're not heathens, Mrs. Hamby. We go to your church."

"Well, you talk like heathens. Only heathens would use the Lord's name in vain," Caroline said sharply. "Come along, Mary."

As they continued down the sidewalk, little Blue ran along behind Mary.

"Shoo, mutt!" Mrs. Hamby flapped her skirt at the pup.

"Blue! His name is Blue!" John hollered defiantly.

Mary gazed back at John and Alfred until Caroline jerked her hand, as the frolicking pup returned to John.

"That girl's ma is an old sour puss," John complained angrily.

"That's not her mother; that's her aunt," Alfred said. "Her mom and pop wuz killed when a tornado hit their house. They found Mary in a wash tub, without a scratch. She was only three years old when it happened. She's been living in an orphanage up until now. When she found out she had a great aunt, 'Mrs. Hamby,' living in Tennessee, she wrote to her. Mrs. Hamby went all the way to Arkansas and brung Mary back. My mom told me the whole story last week. I knowed she was here but this is the first time I seen her. My mom said Mrs. Hamby is a good Christian woman. Guess we ain't got no right to judge her, John. Ain't that what the Bible says?"

"Well if'n that ole biddy's a good Christian, then I'd rather be a heathen." John bristled. "Ya ever notice how them so-called God fearin' Christians don't care about nobody but theirselves?"

Bob Taylor, asleep in his barber chair, was jostled awake when the boys hit his barber pole. As Caroline and Mary were walking away, Bob came out to see that his pole was still firmly planted, and reminded the boys that they should watch where they were going. "Looks like you need a haircut, John."

"I like my hair this way." John snapped.

A fur trapper clad in buckskins rode up to the barbershop and dismounted. His foul odor announced his arrival. His sun-baked skin and scruffy beard made him appear older than his easy gait. He had a mule in tow with furs draped across his back. The mule rubbed his nose against the horse's rump to disperse the flies from his face.

"Howdy boys," the trapper said. "You tha barber?"

"Yes, call me Bob."

"Need me a shave an'a hair cuttin', and I'd like some'a that good smelly stuff you barbers got. Women folk're kind'a per-tic-ler bout how a man smells and a man's gotta get real close to a woman if'n he wants to really enjoy her. That there's something you boys need to know. Right, Bob?"

Alfred and John just looked at each other and grinned.

"That's right, sir. Come on in," Bob said. "Make yourself comfortable in that chair, and I'll fix you right up."

The trapper plopped down in the barber chair, and Bob draped a sheet over his body, below his head, tying it in back.

John, wrinkling his nose, said softly, "I hope Mr. Taylor's got enough'a that good smelly stuff."

Bob Taylor had opened the barber shop several years earlier, catering to the fur trappers who would stop and get a shave and a haircut on the way to the Trading Post in Elizabethton. Many of the trappers would hang out at Elizabethton's Black Bear Saloon, where competition to get a woman was tough—about ten men for every woman. So, as Bob always reminded his customers, it paid to look and smell your very best.

For twenty-five cents you could get a shave and a haircut. If you happened to get in a fight at the Black Bear Saloon, for another twenty-five cents Bob could bandage you up on your way back through Fish Springs.

Across the road, Daniel Smith exited the feed store and climbed up on the seat of a horse-drawn wagon parked at the loading dock. Isaiah, a young, muscularly-built slave, carried a sack of feed on his shoulder across the dock and dropped it into the back of the wagon beside several other sacks.

On seeing Daniel, Alfred called out, "Hello, Mr. Smith!"

"Hello boys! Nice day for a canoe ride."

"Yes sir," Alfred responded.

"Is that it, Isaiah?" asked Daniel.

"Yessa, masta Smith, dat it." Isaiah jumped into the back of the wagon and sat with his feet dangling off the open back end. Daniel snapped the reins and the handsome team of matched bays stepped smartly down the road.

Alfred, watching Daniel leave, spouted, "My father tole me Mr. Smith is the most respected man in Fish Springs."

"We'll, I ain't knowin' 'bout that," John says, "but my pa tole me he owns more niggers then any man in Carter County."

Alfred rolled his eyes but didn't respond.

"What'a you want'a do now?" asked John

"Let's go get a candy stick."

"I ain't got no money."

"I'll give you half," Alfred said as they picked up the canoe and crossed the road, Blue following.

"Someday, I'm gonna have me a big farm and some nigger slaves like Daniel Smith," said John as they set the canoe down.

Alfred just smiled and started up the steps to the general store.

"Me'n Blue'll wait here on the steps," said John.

Alfred entered the store while John sat, with Blue lying at his feet. John stared blankly, contemplating his day and his life. *It ain't fair. I work my ass off, and get nothin' for it. That no-good drunken father a' mine never gives me money. He spends every damn penny on 'shine, and the only money Mom gets, she has to sneak from his pockets. Someday I'll make my own damn money. If'n I want a damn haircut, I'll go to the barber shop and pay for it. Someday I'll have a big farm and nigger slaves…someday….*

John stroked Blue on the head. "Shit, Blue, I can't even buy my own damn candy stick."

CHAPTER 2
Surrender under the Stars

Spring 1862

John Williams leaned his sturdy frame against the hitching post, one foot up on the wooden sidewalk in front of the general store, flipped the moonshine jug upon his shoulder with a practiced shrug and took a sip. Tied to the hitching post was Charger, John's tall, black American Saddlebred horse. Blue, now matured into a much coveted coon hound, lay on the walk by his foot. Seated nearby on the edge of the rough boards, his friend Joshua Arnett and three rough scalawags shared another jug and talked about the ongoing war.

"Them damn Yankees got no business coming down here telling us we can't have nigger slaves!" John angrily declared.

The scalawags mumbled in agreement. Unshaven and foul smelling, as if they'd been sleeping in the woods for days, the three looked like they hadn't bathed in a long time. Their faces were wrinkled and sunburned, and their teeth, what ones they had, were snaggly and blackened. But they only cared, for the moment, about their jug of 'shine and the invading Yankees.

"Hell no, they don't," said Ben. "Them damn Yankee bastards come 'round here an we'll put'em in the groun'."

It was a pleasant, warm Sunday afternoon, and people dressed in their finest were walking on the sidewalk toward the upper end of the community to Fish Springs Baptist Church. Some crossed to the other side of the street to avoid a confrontation with the scraggly Confederate rooters.

Joshua injected, "You know, some 'round here 'grees with'em."

"Yep, here comes one a tha so'm bitches now," said another.

John took special note of the group coming up the sidewalk. "Hold ma jug, Joshua."

Five years had passed since John Williams was pulled from the river by his friend Alfred White. His broad shoulders and handsomely-chiseled face are now complemented by his dark hair kept neatly trimmed by Bob the barber. He's also a man who, though thinking of himself as God fearing, has never taken fully to religion. What few times he's gone to church he's heard preachers warn about the evils of sexual immorality.

And yet the higher-than-mighty preachers themselves, John has noticed, can't seem to tear themselves away from a good looking female. When such a creature becomes a widow or her husband goes off to war, it seems the preacher visits her home more and more. *They can bury themselves in the Gospel and claim they're walking with Jesus, but deep down,* John figured, *they're not much better than me.*

He also wondered, *Why in tarnation is makin' love such a sin? And why're folks askeered to death of goin' to hell 'cause they done it? How can anything that makes me feel so damn good be bad? The hell with all them preachers!*

Increasingly, he imagined what it would be like to bed a genuine passionate woman. Not just any woman but one that was good and upstanding and knew how to treat a man and make him feel like a man. She would need to cook and sew and keep the home fires burning, but she would also have to be eager to please and be pleased in bed. But where to find her? For sure, not among the bar maids he'd gotten up with at the local saloon. Those gals showed him a good, romping time upstairs, but they always had to be paid.

The irresistible Mary Clemmons was surely a candidate, *but she's such a goody two shoes, letting that Bible toting' aunt of hers rule the way she should live her life. And besides that, she'd want me to give up gamblin' and moonshine and no woman's going to tell me I can't gamble or drink.*

Walking toward them were Alfred White and Mary Clemmons. Alfred looked churchy and spiffy in his clean white shirt and striped trousers with red suspenders. Mary's blue dress displayed her aunt's love and handiwork, with tatted lace edging the collar and following the line of buttons down the front. Her teeth were perfect, her smile glowed and her green eyes sparkled. The envy of every woman in Fish Springs and the desire of every man, she cooled herself with a pleated silk fan as she and Alfred approached.

"Damn, she's a nice little thing!" Ben proclaimed. "Won't ever happen, but a man can dream whatever he has a mind to. God, If'n I could just get her up agin' a tree. Makes my loins quiver just to look at her."

"Shut your mouth, Ben!" John warned.

Mary was carrying a basket containing a cloth-covered pie. Seeing John, Mary took tall, thin Alfred by the arm and leaned into him.

"Good afternoon, Mary... Alf," said John pleasantly.

Mary nodded, flashing her stunningly beautiful green eyes at John.

"Afternoon, John," responded Alfred.

"What's the big occasion?"

"It's a pie social, John, at the church," Mary said. "If you come over later, I might save you a slice of my blackberry pie."

"I don't know, Mary. I need to pick some ticks off ol' Blue. But I'll try to make it."

John's cronies chuckled.

Mary, turning up her chin, said that she and Alfred would be on their way.

"See ya, John. Don't get tick bit," Alfred said.

"She's the prettiest gal in Fish Springs," Ben said. "I can't believe you're gonna let that damn Yankee sympathizer take her away from ya."

"He ain't takin' nothin' away from me." John reached for his jug and took a big swig. "Some things ain't what they seem."

John glared at Ben. *As if that ole nasty coot could have her!*

"You might think this old broken down geezer could never do anything with that young, sweet thing, John, but you'd be dead wrong." Ben stared John straight in the eye. "'Cause I can still lick the jar."

"You best shut your rotted mouth, Ben," Joshua said.

John pulled Ben up on his tiptoes by his overalls straps. "You gotta get shed a' them feelings, old man, 'cause Mary ain't never gonna let you touch her! And if'n you ever try I'll break your skinny chicken neck! Now, go on back to yore jug." John pushed Ben to the ground.

That evening in the church parish hall, alone at one of the tables, Mary and Alfred chatted while he savored his last bite of pie.

"Mary, I think your blackberry pie is by far the best pie here!"

While Mary took in Alfred's compliment, he crossed the room to where people were lined up for punch. Getting in line, he thought about what had been and what might have been. *God, I love that gal. She's the sweetest and most beautiful thing in the world! And to think that she could love me ain't nothing but a dream. What kinda life could I give her anyway? If only I'd been able to stay in college* … But things just didn't work out that way. His life had turned upside down and changed forever when his father, Wilford White, died half way through Alfred's third year of college. Wilford had suffered a fatal heart attack while cutting hay.

Devastated by the loss of the man he'd always looked up to and loved, Alfred made it back home to Fish Springs in time for the funeral. Then he had taken care of his father's business affairs and taken charge of running the farm. His grieving mother, her rock-solid husband gone forever, had moved to Johnson's Depot, Tennessee, to live with her sister.

And now, on top of everything else, I'm going off to a bloody war that's already killed thousands... And for what? Alfred stewed as he waited his turn in the punch line.

Alfred glanced back across the room and smiled at Mary, who smiled back. *Alfred is such a nice person—a real gentleman who knows how to treat a lady, and he's probably my best friend. I know he'd make me a wonderful husband.*

Tall, handsome Daniel Smith stepped into Mary's line of view. "Good evening, Mary."

"Good evening, Mr. Smith." Mary responded pleasantly.

"Nice turnout, but your aunt Caroline is missing," said Daniel, turning both hands up.

"She decided to sit this one out, but she's fine."

"Tell her we missed seeing her."

"I will. Is your Polly with you?"

"Oh, yes. She's at the hen table, talking recipes."

Mary chuckled.

"I saw Alfred with you, didn't I?"

When Mary said Alfred was in the punch line and nodded in that direction, Daniel told her he'd like to have a word with him, touched her shoulder and wished her well the rest of the evening.

"You have a nice evening, too, Mr. Smith."

Daniel and Polly Smith and their three children lived on a big, prosperous farm on the outskirts of Fish Springs. After Caroline Hamby brought Mary to Fish Springs to live with her, they figured it was hard enough for women living by themselves and even tougher raising a young girl. So the Smiths, well respected in the community, took Mary and her aunt under their wings. It was typical of how they lived their lives—being the kind of couple that people in Fish Springs came to when they had a problem.

Now there's definitely a real good Christian man, Mary thought. *Any woman would be lucky to have Daniel Smith as a husband. You can see that by the way he treats Polly and his children. He's even good to his slaves, never shouting orders or scolding them in public. And he loves this community and the Fish Springs Baptist Church. Polly's fortunate to have him.*

As Mary watched Daniel walking toward the line, she felt a hand on her shoulder and spun around, coming face to face with none other than John Williams.

"I come to get my piece of pie," he said smugly.

"You will *not* get a piece of my pie, John Williams, until you ask like a gentleman!"

"Well, then, may I have the privilege of tasting your pie, Miss Mary Clemmons?" John swept off his hat and bowed elaborately from the waist.

"You are so bad! I don't know why I waste my time with you."

"You just think I'm bad 'cause I don't act prissy like some men you know." John cut his gaze toward the punch line without moving his head.

"You can be a gentleman without being prissy, John."

From across the room, Alfred took in the puzzling little drama being played out by Mary and John. Puzzling to Alfred because Mary never said anything positive about John, and yet she always seemed to tolerate his bad behavior and then fuss about it. *Well, women can really be hard to figure out*, he reasoned.

"Did you lose your date, Alfred?" Daniel asked, staring at Mary and John.

"Only for one piece of pie, I hope, Mr. Smith," Alfred responded, shaking Daniel's hand.

"That's good! Mary Clemmons is a lovely young lady."

"Yes sir. She is."

"Alfred, there's word around town that when the call for volunteers to fight for the Union was extended, you enlisted."

"That's right, sir. I think it was the right thing to do."

"It was, Alfred. I thought about enlisting myself, but at forty-seven and with a house full of children—?

Alfred interrupted. "I'm surprised, Mr. Smith. I'd a thought you'd be opposed to the Union, being a slave owner."

"In the beginning, I was. I know economically speaking it's more profitable for farmers to be slave owners, especially the larger farms, but the more I studied about it, the more I came to realize that owning another human is just not right. Actually, I freed my slaves."

"I didn't know that Mr. Smith. Did they leave?"

"A few left. The others want to stay and work for me."

"That's wonderful, sir."

"Alfred, what I came to tell you is that I know recently you have taken over the responsibility of watching over Mrs. Hamby and Mary. I know you took them firewood last winter and did other things as well. Members of the church got together for a meeting and decided the men not enlisting, for whatever reason, will take care of the people left behind, especially the older folks. Just take care of yourself and we'll take care of things here."

"That's very kind of you and the other members, Mr. Smith."

"It's the least we can do as church folk. Good luck to you, son! Be sure to come back to us. Fish Springs needs good men like you."

"I'll do my best, sir."

Back at the table, John finished his pie. Pushing his plate forward, loosening his belt and rubbing his belly, he relaxed in his chair. He smiled at Mary very contentedly and sure of himself. "I'll be waitin' for you tonight. Come back out after Alf leaves," he whispered to her.

"I most certainly will not! What kind of a girl do you think I am? I'm not one of your floozies, John Williams!"

But John, drawing closely to her, was unfazed. "See ya later. I know you'll be there."

He departed just as Alfred appeared and handed Mary a cup of punch.

"I see John said something to make you mad again, didn't he?" Alfred said.

"Yes, he is such a scoundrel! I wish he was more like you."

"John'll never change, Mary. You just have to accept him the way he is ... or not. And remember, you don't even have to listen to him. Tell him to leave if you don't feel comfortable."

The couple gathered up their things, including the last uneaten piece of blackberry pie, which Mary saved for Aunt Caroline, and Alfred escorted his date home.

It was a balmy, summer evening with a chorus of crickets, tree frogs and whippoorwills filling the night as Mary and Alfred, holding hands, walked the dirt road to the other end of Fish Springs.

Feisty Caroline Hamby was in her porch swing, tired but determined to stay up until Mary and Alfred returned. Hearing voices, she cast her eyes toward the road and called out, "Is that you, Mary?"

"Yes, Aunt Caroline. It's me and Alfred."

"It better be Alfred! He's the one you left here with."

"She's still got me, Aunt Caroline," Alfred said with a chuckle.

"Auntie, you didn't have to wait up for me. I'm safe."

"I know that, sweetheart. I never worry about you when you're with Alfred." Turning to Alfred, Caroline said, "Did you have a good time at the pie social?"

"Yes, we did, Auntie; you should have come with us. Mr. Smith and others said they missed you."

"You didn't need some old woman dragging behind you," Caroline demurred. "Did you eat a lot of pie, Alfred?"

"I ate my share, Mrs. Hamby, but of all the pie I ate, Mary's was the best."

Mary shook her head in diffidence.

"I can believe that. Mary's a good cook. You need to remember that, Alfred."

"I will, Mrs. Hamby."

"Aunt Caroline!"

"I only speak the truth, Mary." Aunt Caroline gathered her robe around her and stood from the porch swing. "Well, I think I'll go on up to bed. I been sitting out here enjoying the whippoorwills, but it's time to turn in. Don't stay up too late, Mary. Good night, Alfred."

"Good night, Mrs. Hamby."

Caroline stepped inside, picked up a candle in a holder off a table by the door and lighted it from the oil lamp. In the glow, she ascended the stairs.

They moved to the swing and Alfred put his arm around the young woman of his dreams, pulling her close. She looked especially beautiful and seemed almost to glow in the moonlight.

"Aunt Caroline never goes to bed until I get home, and she hates whippoorwills. She told me they keep her awake at night."

Alfred laughed. "She's just protective of you, Mary. She loves you ... just like I do."

"That's sweet, Alfred."

He leaned into her and their lips met. "Mary, you know I love you dearly and I want to spend the rest of my life with you. I don't want to put pressure on you, but I'm just not sure how you feel about me."

Mary said nothing for a moment. She closed her eyes, opened them and then picked her words carefully. "Alfred, you're my friend and the nicest person I know, and I love you, but I'm not ready to make a commitment right now."

Alfred embraced Mary and they kissed.

"Mary, I have ta go away for a while."

"You're gettin' in the war, aren't you?"

"Yes. It's been bothering me and weighing on my mind for a long time. I've got ta do my part, so I volunteered ta fight with the Union forces. I have to go, Mary. But will you promise me you'll write me every day and that you'll answer my letters?"

When Mary gave her solemn promise, the two kissed again, as it would be the last kiss they'd share for a long time. But their bodies stayed politely and safely apart. Lips touched. Eyes glistened. Pulses quickened. And then the polite moment of intimacy ended. They said their good-byes. Man and woman separated—he to return to his home up the road and she to her bedroom.

Later that night, Mary, in her downstairs bedroom, changed into a long, soft-cotton sleeping gown. She knelt and prayed that she would somehow get her confused thinking about Alfred and John sorted out and for strength to resist her unseemly physical urges. While praying, she couldn't help also recalling a story she'd heard earlier in the evening at the meeting house. A woman, not so much older than herself, had shared that her own aunt, a widow, had prayed earnestly—and had even shared her fervent request in front of the entire congregation at church—that she'd get the Holy Ghost in her.

And then the widow's man friend had come over late one evening; the two had gulped a few shots of whiskey, had grown tipsy and fell into bed together; they enjoyed each other the rest of the night. "And that's when I got the Holy Ghost inside me! I could feel it all over!" the woman had recalled.

Maybe that the way it's supposed to be, Mary thought, fighting the temptation to go outside into the fragrant, starry night. But the pull was hard.

Now, I've got to be strong. I've promised myself I won't be taken advantage of. And I'm sticking to my promise. … When I give myself to a man, he'll be my husband and that's exactly what I'm going to tell Mr. John Williams. Mary tiptoed down the hall and slowly opened the front door just enough to peek out.

She half expected to see John, emboldened, wanton scalawag that he was, sitting on the porch, but he wasn't there. So she crossed the threshold and made her way, ever so slowly, across the porch and down the steps. The moon appeared from behind the clouds, casting light on her path. Night noises almost drowned out Mary's pounding heartbeat.

Suddenly the man she loved to despise was upon her, and he wouldn't be denied. "I knew you'd come out!" John blurted. "You cain't stay away from me. We're made for each other, Mary!"

"No, John, no! We can't, John. I promised myself! I even prayed about it. Please … We can't do this."

But her resistance dissolved when he cradled her in his arms and carried her, not kicking or screaming but with her delicate hands locked around his big muscular neck, into the wheat field below the house. Then he gently laid her down, and he teasingly raised Mary's gown above her breasts.

"John, I said we can't do this. We shouldn't—"

But then Mary, breathing hard now and her breasts pressed against his chest, lost her words. Her heart pounded in anticipation.

John could feel her fingers on his skin. They felt him, prodded him, in those private places on his body where a man craves a woman's touch. And they were full of desire, as were his, when he stroked her hair and back. Her soft, beckoning body seemed to glow in the moonlight.

They kissed, deeply and hungrily, and then it was impossible not to finish what they had started. Arms and legs wrapped around each other, and tongues became entwined. Words turned to grunts and groans of pleasure, enjoying each other, again and again, until neither could move.

Then they lay satiated in the soft grass in each other's arms.

Is what I felt' a gift from God or is it from the devil? Ravenous, wild lovemaking under the stars with a man I ain't got no business being with wouldn't meet the approval of the Almighty. Mary thought, *But so be it, at least for tonight.*

As John ran his lips down the side of Mary's neck and shoulder to her breast, he asked.

"Did I hurt you?"

"No, you didn't hurt me, John, but what we did was a mistake."

"Maybe so, Mary, but didn't I make you feel like a woman?"

Slipping back into her nightgown, she told him to be gone and to never, ever come back. And to never speak of what they had done.

John grinned, said he understood, kissed her good-bye and disappeared into the darkness as the moon slid behind the clouds.

CHAPTER 3
The Confrontation

"This is the day the Lord has made. We will rejoice and be glad in it!" shouted an early rising deacon of Fish Springs Baptist Church. It was a cool, refreshing morning in Fish Springs and most of the fog that covered the valley had burned away. It promised to turn into another long day suitable for working in the fields or tending to farm animals. The sunshine to the little mountain community seemed to have been sent straight from heaven.

And not only did he shout it from the steps of the sanctuary, the enthusiastic parishioner took it upon himself to run down the main street of Fish Springs and spread the good message throughout the community. "Give me a big loud Amen if you rejoice in the goodnesss of the Almighty!" he entreated all within earshot.

A few folks, inwardly irritated, perhaps, followed his lead.

"Amen, brother!" said one old gentleman from his rocking chair in front of the feed store.

Bob the barber happily joined in celebrating the verse from Psalms, and offered his own twist on it. "This is the day the Lord has made. We will rejoice with a shave and haircut!"

Wearing a wide-brimmed hat, work boots, an old cotton shirt and manure-stained pants, John was brushing his horse Charger in front of the barn behind his log cabin. John was not in range of any of the Amens, and if he had been, he'd have ignored them. He had a lot on his mind this crisp, beautiful morning, and he thought better when he was working. Blue, never easily excited, was lying lazily on the ground near him. Every so often, the dog swatted haplessly at a buzzing fly with his paw.

John had won Charger, a fine specimen of an animal, in a card game at the Black Bear Saloon. Normally John would brush the beautiful black American Saddlebred horse after a ride, but he had gone to the Black Bear after leaving Mary the previous night and downed a few drinks. The whiskey had relaxed and made him happy. He had playfully teased a few of the saloon gals, but that, last night, had been as far as it had gone. The women looked better as the night dragged on, but John kept his seat at the poker table. After his rendezvous with Mary, he had been almost too tired to lift a finger at the saloon, let alone pay to coax a female partner upstairs.

As he ruminated on it, he felt after last night he had a damn good chance of making Mary his own. When he set his mind to it, John Williams concluded that he usually got what he wanted, no matter the odds. Fact was, John had no choice but to fend for himself. He'd been doing that since he was sixteen.

Not able to tolerate any more of her husband's drunkenness, John's mother had left him, running off in the middle of the night with a cookware salesman. Then when their only son was in the tenth grade, he came home from school one day and found his father dead. Lying on his back in his bed, the low life had drowned in his own vomit.

While weaker types might have foundered or sunk into depression, his father's untimely death led John to drop out of school and take immediate charge of the farm. He had no choice but to become a diligent worker and a shrewd businessman. He had doubled the size of the farm and acquired a sizeable herd of beef cattle. The only part of John's ambitions not fulfilled was the ownership of slaves. But he knew, for him to be a slave owner, the Union would have to be defeated and run out of Tennessee. He would fight to his death to help make that happen.

But right now the determined young man's thoughts kept flashing back to Mary and the night before. At first, Mary had seemed hesitant and resistant. The young woman had professed to be an upright Christian who would NOT be tempted by the likes of John Williams. But her words had seemed, to John, a hollow protest. It had been as if a deep hunger within her would not let her be. As she spoke coyly of trying to be good and Godly and chaste, her pursuer had sensed a confusion raging within her.

He felt sure she would not be able to resist him, and this made him even more determined to have her as his own.

Yep, I don't always say or do the right thing when I'm around folks. And, yeah, I can be full of myself and even downright mean when I don't get my way. I drink too much, and I gamble too much and I love pretty women—all of them. But I'm a charmer, and I'm sneaky smart. And I damned well know how ta stand on my own two feet and get my way!

So maybe, he thought, *the best for me would be to live life my way and have Mary whenever I want her. Last night seemed to be working out that way, and she and I liked it a lot! Now I've just got ta finda' way to git' Mary to quit listening to that ole bitch aunt Caroline spewing lies about me. . . to quit stickin' her nose between us.*

John's ponderings ceased when Blue, his keen nose pointed up the road, barked and ran forward and then back to his owner. John noticed Alfred walking on the dirt road. He was approaching John's cabin when Blue, his tongue flopping from his mouth and his tail wagging, ran to greet him. Alfred patted the canine's head and reminded him that he was a good dog.

"What brings you over this morning, Alfred? I know it ain't just to pet and talk to Blue," John said.

"I'm volunteerin' to fight for the Union forces, and I'm askin' you, as a friend, to go with me."

John rammed the brush and curry comb together into a pail, causing Charger to pull back on his reins and shake the post he was tethered to. "Why in hell would I do that? I hate ever'thang they stand for! We wuz' doin' just fine down here. We don't need no damn Yankees tellin' us how ta live our lives!"

Charger sidestepped and tossed his head and Blue leaned his head against Alfred's knee.

"Slavery is dead wrong, John." Alfred stooped to pet Blue. "Surely you can see that."

"Says who? What'd them niggers have before they wuz' brought here? A straw hut and a spear, I reckon. And they all slept on the ground and had to fight off the snakes. Here they got good food and a warm and dry cabin to raise their pickaninnies in. They're taken care of, Alf."

Alfred paused, as if measuring his thoughts, then said, "I'll tell you what they had before they were brought here, John. Freedom! The same freedom you and I have. All slaves are not treated good, like Daniel Smith treated his. Some slave owners chain their slaves and whip'em. Some even hobble'em, they smash one of their feet, crippling'em so they can't run away. And a lot of the girl slaves get raped by their so-called masters.

"Did you know that, John? And did you know that when tha heartless white men brought them to America in those slave ships, a lot of'em slept below where there wasn't any fresh air or sunshine? And they were chained down there and laid in their own shit and pee? And did ya know some thought, on tha trip over here from Africa, that they'd be eaten. They'd heard white people were cannibals, so they jumped off tha ship and drowned. That's how bad they've been treated, John, and so it's time now for all of us to do tha right thing by 'em."

"So what if they had it hard!" John snapped. "They're niggers and God made'em go through all that for a purpose. And they're not s'posed to run away. They're slaves. And maybe it's good their owners have sex with'em. Interbreedin' ain't all bad. I hear tell it makes some right pretty light-skinned nigger babies."

Alfred held his ground. But he knew his efforts to win his childhood friend over had failed. "Word around town, John, is that you're enlisting in tha Confederacy. I was hopin' to change your mind, but I can see I'm wastin' my time here."

"Yes, you sure as hell are! I shoulda' figured you'd turn out to be a damn Yankee lover."

Alfred turned away, disgusted.

"That's right; turn your back on your own kind!" John bristled. "As soon as I get in this war, if you cross my path, I'll put a chunka' lead in your ass, just like I would any other Yankee son of a bitch!

"You hear me! You'll end up a piece a' dead meat!" John hollered.

Alfred, silent now, knew it was no use. *Shoulda known it all along. He's stubborn and hardheaded and he'd never change his mind about slavery or the war. But what kinda man thinks it's okay to own or chain another human being? I always thought John had somethin' wrong with him. Guess I knew all along about his mean streak.*

CHAPTER 4

The Lie

"This is the day which the Lord has made. We will rejoice and be glad in it!" Mary groaned and pulled the covers over her head at the shout from outside her window. She tried to go back to sleep, to escape back into the dream of last night, and maybe she succeeded for a while, but her guilt wouldn't go away for long. *What am I going to do? And what have I already done? How can I ever forgive myself?*

She kept thinking, but the answers wouldn't come. Somewhere they were buried deep in her heart, she knew. What was clear, however, was that she had a choice to make. She'd have to pick between Alfred White and John Williams.

Alfred seemed completely right for her—God fearing, a hard-working polite gentleman, surely a good provider and future father whom she could live "happily ever after" with. She and Alfred could have a good life together in Fish Springs, she concluded. They could work and worship together, make a warm, loving home for their children. And she was confident that Alfred would never, ever leave her or go carousing about saloons. He was the kind of sincere, honest, caring man any woman would cherish as a husband.

And then there was John Williams. On the surface, Mary knew there wasn't much to like about John. *He's ornery, given to drinking and gambling. He's too much of a carouser. Could I ever trust him? And all he wants is one thing.*

And yet there was just something beguilingly mysterious and attractive about that rascal. A devilish taunting voice inside her kept saying, *You're a woman with needs, and you know I can satisfy those, Mary. And what have you got, really, if you don't have what I can give you? I want you, Mary, and you want me.*

Mary took stock of herself in the mirror. It was easy to understand why men seemed taken by her. Her body, after all, was tempting—not too tall or heavy or thin, and her features—nose, face, lips and hair—stood out in a captivating way. She had once pined to be a redhead, but her blond locks shone from one hundred strokes of a boar bristle brush every night and her curls bounced seductively on her forehead. She wished that her eyes were brown instead of green, but so be it. And her breasts? John had told her they had ripened like two luscious melons and they had been made to help "pleasure a man." She had also noticed that Alfred seemed not to be able to take his eyes off them. Her bottom was "glorious and right smart full and plump" and "the answer to any man's dream," according to John. It was a head turner even when she wore loose fitting dresses. Her skin he described as "milky smooth" and made to be caressed. And her hips and thighs? John said he had drooled over those. He had confessed to her that he could not keep from becoming aroused in her presence.

Men. they're so silly and shallow, Mary reasoned, *as she took one last glance at herself in the mirror. But a man, even one I don't love, could make me feel so good! And that can't be right. Why can being with a man that way make it so hard to know your real feelings? What I need is a true partner, not just a lover...*

"Mary, you awake yet?" Aunt Caroline barked from the kitchen.

"Be right there, Aunt Caroline," Mary answered, putting her thoughts about her two suitors aside for now.

Her red-eyed, expressionless aunt had already finished her breakfast when Mary sat down at the kitchen table. It was apparent that she had been crying. Cradling a cup of coffee in her trembling hands, she finally faced Mary and spoke.

"I am very disappointed in you, young lady," Caroline said before her niece could take her first bite of a biscuit.

"Aunt Caro—?"

"I saw you from my window last night."

Mary's lips trembled. "But Aunt C—."

"Just be quiet! You broke my heart, Mary. I know it was you 'cause I checked your bed," said Caroline, her voice breaking. "I wanted to be wrong! God, I so wanted to be wrong."

"I'm sorry, Aunt Caroline. But I love him. I really do."

"That's no excuse! You could have waited. Now you'll both have to answer to God!"

"I didn't mean for it to happen, Aunt Caroline. It just did."

"It happened, because *you* let it happen," Caroline said sternly. "There had better be a wedding when this war is over or I'll march Alfred White down the aisle with my rifle."

"Aunt Caroline, it …" But Mary caught herself and held her tongue. If her aunt thought it was Alfred she was with in the wheat field and not John, then so be it. After all, Aunt Caroline was plenty upset already; no need, Mary figured, to make it even worse.

"It was wrong, Aunt Caroline! I'm sorry. I'm so sorry!"

"If I were you, I'd get down on my knees and ask God to forgive me."

Mary nodded, studying her clinched fists in her lap.

"You know what you and Alfred reminded me of last night?" her aunt, drying her tears, added. "I could barely see you 'cause of the pitch black dark, but I could hear plenty. And it was like a sow in heat rootin' 'round in the dirt 'n grass with a big ole boar. And that ain't a pretty thing to hear, Mary! It's a bad, nasty thing. You both have shamed yourselves before the Almighty!"

Aunt Caroline, looking upward, prayed. "Forgive them, God, for they know not what they have done!"

"I will give it all over to the Lord tonight, Aunt Caroline. I promise! And when we go to church next Sunday, I'll be the first one to sit on the mourner's bench. I need the Lord's mercy, and I hope that He'll forgive me."

While Mary's contrition didn't fully satisfy her aunt, it was a start. *The poor child is weak in the flesh,* her aunt concluded. *And we all sin and fall short of the Lord's will.*

Later that morning Mary made a visit to the Fish Springs feed and dry goods store; her aunt had dispatched her there to pick up some flour and coffee, but in the back of her mind, she kept dwelling on the penance she'd soon be doing on the mourner's bench.

Just outside the store, and drawing her attention, was an old Cherokee Indian. Folks said he was a "spirit man;" they called him Hunting Bear. He sat there in his deerskins and moccasins this warm dusty summer afternoon, with his legs crossed and arms folded, staring at something far away. He wore no war paint; nor did he have a tomahawk or spear, but a beaded necklace and copper armband caught Mary's eyes.

"O-gi-na-li" the old Indian shouted at her.

Now she couldn't take her eyes off him. *But what's he trying to tell me?* she wondered.

"It mean you friend," said Hunting Bear knowingly. "You come closer to me, please …"

Mary stepped closer, her curiosity battling her fear.

"You much feel bad today. I tell," he said. "You not sleep good. You worry."

He knows, Mary thought. *But how. Maybe he can tell by just looking at my face.*

"This what I say to you," the venerable Indian continued, shaking what appeared to be a long string of rattlesnake rattles. "This mighty snake spirit speak to me about you. He say you should not dive into river of lust. For you will not reach shore. It is deep, evil river without banks. With storms and killer winds. And current is strong."

Mary, speechless, turned to leave him.

But still he shook those rattlesnake rattles. And the old spirit man kept babbling.

Then, once again, he shouted. "O-gi-na-li!"

Over the next few days, and leading up to her encounter with the mourner's bench, Hunting Bear's message haunted her. *He was trying to tell me something. He knew! But how?*

And when she next saw Alfred, he was en route to the Great War.

"I'm on my way, Mary, but I couldn't leave without telling you good-bye," said Alfred, dismounting and holding the reins of his horse near where she sat on her porch. I tried convincing John to go with me but he is dead set on joining the Confederacy. I'm disappointed but I'll just have to accept it." Mary came off the porch and the two gave each other a little peck of a kiss and promised to stay in touch with one another—war or no war.

"I should tell Aunt Caroline goodbye," he said.

A lump formed in Mary's throat. "I don't think I would she's, she's … upset."

"Why? Because I'm leaving?"

"That must be it, Alfred. I'll tell her you said goodbye. We shouldn't get her more upset than she already is."

"Well, brace yourself, 'cause here she comes," said Alfred.

"Oh Lord!"

A grimacing, apron-clad Aunt Caroline ambled out the door and down the steps. Then she balled up her bony fist, yelled a few choice words and walloped Alfred with a roundhouse punch on the side of his upper arm. It stung and left his arm throbbing with pain.

"Ow!" Why did you hit me, Aunt Caroline?"

"You know exactly why I hit you, Alfred!" said Caroline. "You're a selfish, no-good scoundrel who just thinks of himself."

"I thought it was the right thing to do," he countered.

"You could have waited, Alfred!" she said, climbing the steps and slamming the door behind her.

"Doesn't she understand, Mary? I couldn't wait. They needed me now."

Mary, repressing a smile, said. "I know, Alfred. I'll tell her."

But Alfred knew that whatever Mary said wouldn't much matter at that point. Because he was now on Aunt Caroline's bad side. He had learned the woman could be hardhearted and unforgiving—even mean spirited—despite her continuous recitation of Bible-based instruction on how to live your life. And that—getting on Aunt Caroline's bad side—was the last thing he wanted on the last day he would see Mary for a long time. He clenched his teeth and rubbed his arm as he rode away. The pain kept throbbing. *Damn! That old woman hits hard. She could hurt a horse with that punch.*

CHAPTER 5

The War

Alfred rode to a designated meeting place across the river, where he met up with Captain Dan Ellis and five other Union recruits.

Captain Ellis, who would gain fame during the War Between the States, lived at nearby Valley Forge. Ellis, age thirty-four when the war erupted, was a successful Union scout and recruiter. Confederate authorities, constantly beleaguered by his campaign to help Rebel deserters, slaves and Unionist prison escapees, had a bounty on his head. But they could never quite corner the evasive, cunning Ellis, known throughout the mountains as the "Old Red Fox." The Unionist that Alfred joined up with was also credited with leading 4,000 men from East Tennessee, Southwest Virginia and North Carolina through Confederate lines and to the Yankee army.

Two days later John mounted an old work horse that he had retired. He had left his prized horse Charger, along with Blue, in the care of his friend Joshua Trent. Joshua, born with a club foot, tried to enlist in the Confederate army when the call came but was turned away. John knew that his trusted drinking buddy would take good care of Charger and Blue. He would turn the aging work horse loose once he got to the Confederate lines at the upper end of the Virginia peninsula.

John had been ordered to join a unit commanded by General John Bankhead Magruder. Shortly after he mustered in, Magruder's unit fought to delay General George B. McClelland's advance up the Virginia Peninsula, allowing General Robert E. Lee more time to prepare his defense of Richmond, the Confederate capital.

John soon found himself in the middle of a fierce battle on the peninsula at Dam Number One on Lee Hall Lake. Cannons blasting sent Confederate soldiers to meet their maker all around him. For the rest of his life, John would hear his fellow soldiers' blood-curdling yells and he'd see their horribly mangled,, bleached bodies floating face down in the water. Their valiant struggle and strong fortification held back the Union forces, at least for a while, but at a horrendous cost.

Thousands died, and many of those that survived did so with ghastly stumps for arms or legs. John thought, *What in the hell have I gotten myself into?*

The young man from Fish Springs, Tennessee, would be in other battles in this long war, the deadliest conflict in American history, but none as bad as this one. He would carry the memory of this first battle on the Virginia Peninsula with him to his grave.

And then, only a few nights later, he would skirt one of the most painful deaths imaginable. And this time, a bullet or cannonball would not inflict the damage. Instead, his brush with death came from an angry cottonmouth water moccasin. The snake had sunk its fangs into him. John, exhausted and blurry-eyed from battle and feeling his way through dark marshy, thick undergrowth, had put his left foot down in the wrong place in a cypress swamp near Richmond. He knew instantly, from the reptile's big, flat triangular shaped head and its solid olive color, that death could come within minutes.

He would survive only if a lethal dose of the snake's venom hadn't reached his bloodstream. And that, miraculously, seems to have been what happened. He still had enough of his wits about him, immediately after the bite, to slit the wound, push and suck as much poison out of it as possible and bandage it. The terrified soldier's lower leg became horribly discolored and blistered, and he had fits of vomiting, blurred vision and dizziness. But he survived. Three days later, after sipping soup and downing a few biscuits, his strength began to return and he resumed his hike through the treacherous swamp, but this time treading much more gingerly.

Two years had passed since John got into this war—one that by its end would kill at least ten percent of all Northern males ages eighteen to forty-five, and thirty percent of all white Southern males in the same age group. A survivor of fierce, desperate fighting at Richmond, Petersburg, Manassas and Bull Run, John huddled by a campfire with other soldiers during a lull in the warfare. Unbeknownst to the others, he sipped moonshine from his canteen. One of John's comrades had found a jug of the highly prized, smooth corn whiskey while rummaging through an abandoned farmhouse. He swapped it to John for a bag of tobacco. Not wanting to be caught with the brew, the sly man from Fish Springs stashed some in his canteen and buried the rest.

As he sipped he wrote to Mary.

March 15th 1864

Dear Mary,

I know I ain't wrote you in a while. My days are so crazy, it's hard to find the time. But I plum love getting your letters. Reading them helps keep me going. It seems this war will drag on forever. Old man Death stares me straight in my eyes every day, and it makes me know how precious life is. This war has made me take a good look at myself and I ain't liking what I've seen. Last Sunday a group of our troops gathered for a prayer meeting led by a preacher, and one of my friends drug me along. That danged preacher lifted me up. Things seem some bit clearer to me now. Things like, how bad I had treated you, how I'd done you so wrong. With God's help I vowed to give up drinking and gambling. I want to get active in the church, and right with the Lord, and when I get back, I intend to start treating you like the lady you are. And how I long to hold you in my arms, to feel your warm body, to taste your sweet lips!

John took a big swig from his canteen, wiped his mouth with the back of his hand, and signed the letter.

Love Forever,

John

He folded the dog-eared, yellowing paper, tied a string around it and carefully addressed it. Miss Mary Clemmons, Fish Springs Tennessee

John handed the letter to the overworked private in charge of collecting outgoing mail, who gave it to a courier who passed it along. The letter traveled by couriers on foot, on horseback and by railroad. Twelve days later Mary received John's correspondence. Elated with what she read, she immediately responded.

March 27th 1864

Dear John,

I got your letter yesterday. I think it is wonderful that you have received God into your life. I know I needed to do some growing up myself. I need to be more responsible for my actions. I loved you before, I love you even more now. I miss you and long for the day you are back in my arms. Aunt Caroline and I are doing okay. Daniel Smith and others from the church help us out with chores. I get mail from Alfred. He is doing okay. I long for the day when things can be like they were, and we can put this war behind us. I pray for you.

I love you.
Mary

Meanwhile, a few days ride by horseback away, Alfred wrote at a wobbly table set up in a spacious tent in the field headquarters for the Union army.

April 2, 1864
Dear Mary,

I received your last letter two days ago. It's wonderful to hear from you. I had the good fortune to see one of my former professors from East Tennessee University in Knoxville as I was delivering a message to headquarters. I had a nice meeting with Captain Tucker. That was a week ago. Yesterday I was reassigned to field headquarters; I will be writing dispatches and doing other paper work for him. I felt I had abandoned my comrades on the front lines. Even though they encouraged me to take the job, it still bothered me.

I talked to Captain Tucker about it and he made me realize how important my new job is. I pray this war will end soon. Our field hospital stays full of maimed and sick soldiers. The doctors and nurses, what few we have, are overwhelmed. So many men are sick and dying. It's heartbreaking. I pray for the day I can put this war behind me and again lose myself in your beautiful eyes.

All my Love to you.
Alfred

After washing her hair, Mary basked in the bright sunlight on the front porch. A hummingbird hung in the air just a few feet away. A cool breeze from the mountains felt especially good to her today. As her locks dried, she wrote.

April 15th ,1864
Dear Alfred,
I was glad to hear about your new job. You made the right decision. You are where you are most needed. Every Sunday at church someone will ask about you. You have so many friends in Fish Springs. Daniel Smith and others are watching over Aunt Caroline and me. It would be hard without their help. We all pray for the war to end and your safe return. Aunt Caroline sends her love also.
Love,
Mary

CHAPTER 6

The Living and the Dead

In Fish Springs, life goes on. Mary kept herself busy running aging Aunt Caroline's house and being an active member of the Fish Springs Baptist Church. She wouldn't let herself think about the idea that John or Alfred could be killed in the line of duty. But hardly a day went by that someone in the community did not receive such news about a husband, son or a friend.

A distraught Mary prayed extra hard when the wounded and sick and often barely alive amputees from the war arrived by horse drawn wagons back in Fish Springs. The wagons also occasionally carried a corpse, if the deceased had fallen beside a friend close enough to bring him back, but most of those killed from Fish Springs never returned home. Like tens of thousands of others who lost their lives in the war to bullets, bayonets, swords—or to the ravages of starvation and disease—their bodies were covered up in unknown battlefield graves or in shallow burial trenches. Many, in fact, weren't even buried. These unfortunate souls rotted into nothingness where they fell. Their enemy combatants, freezing in some instances because their supplies had run out or they were just plain greedy and had no respect whatsoever for the slain, did them the further disservice of stripping them of their shoes, boots and clothes.

Sometimes one of the wounded would bring home some token from a friend's body—letters most often or a tintype of a loved one, its leather case marked with blood. Small solace for heartbroken, grieving relatives who wanted to put their loved ones to eternal rest in a family plot.

Such was part of the lingering aftermath horror of the Civil War, for many of the young men from Fish Springs who died at Vicksburg, Manassas, Bull Run, Gettysburg, or elsewhere met their maker anonymously.

But even though their kin in Fish Springs couldn't be totally sure, in many cases, of who they were mourning, they grieved nevertheless. And it mattered not what race they were. Slaves, still scornfully called "niggers" by many of the townspeople, mourned alongside whites. They would hug and cry together and console one another. It seemed that the ravages of war brought some folks together when nothing else could. And while sympathizers of the South lived—neighborly enough—in close quarters in Fish Springs with those whose sons, husbands or other family members fought for the North, the neighborliness tended to be, at best, a surface friendliness. Deep down, a sort of festering open sore plagued the day-to-day relationship between those in Fish Springs whose loyalties lay with the South as opposed to those who supported the North. That sore would take many years to heal, and in some cases, while the war raged, would manifest itself in barns being mysteriously burned to the ground, livestock being stolen or laboriously cut and stacked firewood disappearing in the dead of night. Grieving, revengeful fathers of fallen sons, especially, could not forgive

Widows dutifully displayed their grief for their husbands or men friends by wearing long dark cotton dresses. They covered their faces with black veils, and professed to be devastated for months after they lost their loved one. However, a few of the "grieving widows" were overwhelmed with the challenges that each day brought. They prayed for strength and self-control but their entreaties to the Almighty seemed not to be heard. So, they discreetly pursued relationships with the few men available—and not that long in many instances—after their husbands had been put in the ground. It just seemed to some that, grieving or not, life was meant to go on, and, "sides," one of the widows professed privately to Mary Clemmons, "my Robert would never want me ta suffer so. He always did like Delbert anyways. He's alone and so am I, so it should be okay for him to help an' pleasure me. Ain't that the way the Lord means hit ta be?"

Against such a backdrop, Mary took one day at a time, trying to make sense, the best she could, of the meaning of life. She tried not to stew on troubling things or people she couldn't control, read her Bible daily, and stayed active in her safe haven, the church.

And it was there at a social on the church lawn, one beautiful spring morning in April of 1865 that Mary was serving tea. Suddenly, she heard thundering hooves and Daniel Smith appeared in a cloud of dust. An obviously elated Daniel jumped off his horse hollering, "The war is over! The Confederacy has surrendered! Our boys are comin' home!"

Aunt Caroline hugged Mary and shouted, "Thank God! It's finally over!"

Mary deceivingly responded, "Yes, Aunt Caroline, my man's coming back."

Then she thought about how sooner or later she'd have to tell her wanting-to-know-it-all aunt the truth. But first Aunt Caroline would have to see how John was changing his life now that he had found God. *She'll see how different he's going to be. So much more responsible and caring . . . a better man all the way around.*

BACK IN VIRGINA

John walked along a dusty road, a bed roll strapped to his back. Occasionally a wagon full of joyous troops, Confederate and Union, passed him. Commissioned officers and cavalrymen on horseback raced home to their loved ones and a normal life. As he plodded along, he focused on Mary and how he hungered to make love to her, to feel her body against his, to taste her lips. *But for now,* he thought, *I'll just have to bide my time and prove to Mary that I deserve her… I'll go ta church with her… I'll be speclly' nice to that ole bitch, Aunt Caroline. Anything to have sweet Mary as my wife! I can change my ways, but right now, oh, how I'd love to get her in bed, and cap it off with a swig of moonshine! A little shine ever' now'n then ain't never hurt nobody. And once we're married I can do as I please.*

A horse whinnying in a nearby pasture caught his attention, and as John approached the fence, two paint mares and a huge bay stallion stared at him. Seeing no one, John climbed over the fence. With his knife, he cut strips from his bedroll and fashioned a halter. He used the leather laces from his boots as reins and slipped the halter over the head of one of the mares, the calmest of the three horses. He removed the top two rails of the fence, then led the mare across, put the rails back, mounted and headed down the road. Stealing a horse was risky, even deadly. It could get you hanged. But he was willing to take the chance if it would get him home and to Mary faster. Besides, he reasoned, it wasn't really stealing if he turned the mare loose later.

Back at Union headquarters that evening, Alfred, not able to leave his post just yet, finished writing dispatches and other paper work for Captain Tucker. Tucker, smiling, entered the headquarters tent. "Sergeant White, our work here is finished."

"That's good to hear, Captain."

"Alfred, I know all the wagons have left, and it's a long walk to Tennessee. Take this voucher to the stable; they have a few extra horses. They'll saddle one up for you."

"I'm much obliged, Captain." Alfred managed a crisp salute. "That'll knock several days off my trip back home."

"It's the least I can do, Alfred. You've served this man's army well."

"It's been an honor, sir." Alfred gripped Tucker's right hand.

"Good luck to you, son. I hope things work out for you and the young lady you have been writing. What's her name?"

"Mary, sir. Mary Clemmons."

"Well, you tell Miss Mary Clemmons that your commanding officer thinks she should accept your marriage proposal."

"I'll do that, Captain."

"God's speed to you, son."

"Thank you, sir."

Early the next morning, while atop his mount, Alfred's thoughts raced. *This fine horse'll take days off my trip home. It's been three long years away from Fish Springs, my friends and of course Mary, my beloved Mary. Oh, to hold her again in my arms! To kiss her luscious, sweet lips! To feel her body against mine…*

He kept his horse at a canter as he entered a long stretch of road with fields on both sides, then heard a thud and a loud pop. His ride dropped under him. Alfred hit the ground hard and rolled. He lay there gathering his thoughts. *I'm okay. I think.*

He stood up, stooped over, glaring down at the horse. Blood poured from its neck. *But why?* Then another pop and he felt a sharp pain in his inner thigh like a jab with a hot poker. He crumbled to the ground. *Why is this happening?*

Two Confederate troops sashayed up from the bushes down the road in front of him. Alfred's rifle was in the scabbard under the horse, and he couldn't run.

He lay on his back, fear in his eyes, defenseless. The two Confederates approached him, aiming their muskets at his head. Hovering over him, one bedraggled soldier muttered, "I fine'ly shot me a damn Yankee."

"The war's over," Alfred said, his voice shaking.

"Bull shit!"

"It is, God be my witness. The war's over."

The other man responded. "Maybe he's right, Virgil. You know, we done been gone fer four days."

"I don't giva shit! I ain't goin' home 'till I've kilt me a damn Yankee!"

The scruffy Confederate aimed his musket at Alfred's head and pulled back the hammer. He had killed before but always in battle or in self-defense and never like this. This would be an execution, and it promised to be messy. With his helpless, wounded target being so close, it would be a devastatingly easy shot. And there would be no mistake about the kill. His ball would splatter bone, blood and brains.

Alfred, sure the end was near, took a deep breath and closed his eyes, trembling.

"Ain't he a coward?" Virgil said. "Jist like a yella belly damned Yankee! We oughta cut his head off 'stead of shootin'm."

As he lay there, prepared to die, Alfred thought about the quiet life he enjoyed at Fish Springs before becoming a soldier. He had never wanted to kill or be killed, but somehow found himself in harm's way. He wondered how this could have happened to him. And why was he going to die so badly—shot in the dirt, like a miserable, stray dog, and probably not even going to get a decent burial? He figured they'd leave his body right there, and the buzzards and other varmints would pick his bones clean. No one would say any words over him or give him a Godly sendoff. No one would weep. To the contrary, his dastardly, heartless killers would dance with joy and brag about sending another Yankee soldier to Satan. He'd even heard that in some instances Confederates, taking a cue from Indians, had scalped and peed on their prey. *Why did it have to end this way?*

Then, as he stared at his smirking executioner, only a few feet away, he tried to get at peace with himself. He didn't want to go to eternity, or wherever it was that slain innocents went, wallowing in fear and dread.

It hasn't been such a bad life, and if God wants to take me, so be it. I did the best I could. I've served my purpose. I prayed. I read my Bible, I worked hard and I honored my parents. I made mistakes. Forgive me, oh Lord, where I've fallen short...

"Lookee there at him shaking so!" his murderer laughed. "Why, I bet he messes his pants before I shoot his head off!"

"Virgil, Virgil."

"WHAT, Dub? Can't cha see I'm 'bout to kill a man? You best shut up and take this all in. Ain't ever' day we get to send a Yankee bastard to hell."

Dub pointed down the road at five riders, in tattered gray uniforms, approaching quickly. They were yelling something inaudible as they slapped their horses with the end of the reins. Two of the ones in front waved their swords to catch the Confederates' attention.

"It's okay," Virgil said. "They're Confederates. You let me do th' talkin'."

The five riders came to an abrupt halt, their exhausted mounts stumbling and snorting, as if pleading for some sort of respite. Dust swirled in around them. Captain Gallagher, leading the group, spoke.

"What in the Hell's going on here, private?"

"I shot this here damned Yankee, Captain. He could be one'a them dispatch runners."

"The war's over, private. Didn't you know that? General Lee surrendered two days ago at Appomattox Courthouse. The only thing he's got left is his sword and his old stallion, Traveller. He's told his army to pack up and get back to their families. So that's where you should be right now, private—on your way home. … 'Cause this fightin's come to an end. Now, I'm ordering you to shoulder your muskets and go home where you belong! There's been enough dying and sufferin' for two wars."

Knowing he could have easily been arrested for desertion and that the sudden end of the Civil War might have saved him from prison—or even a worse fate—Virgil humbled himself and breathed easier. "Sir, me an' private Dub here ain't heard nary a thing. We got sep'rated from our unit. Been lost for, going on four days now, and we almost starved ta death."

"It's an unlikely story, private. I think you're a bald-faced, gutless liar. And, like I said, you best head back to whatever home you came from. You're not a soldier any more! Go back and take care of your family, if you have one, or I'll have you both arrested for desertion!"

"Yes sir," Virgil sheepishly replied. "I've been proud to serve as a son'a the South, but if you say the war is over, I'm leavin'. So them damn Yankee boys won?"

"Nobody won. President Lincoln is wantin' the nation to bind up its wounds, and the bloodshed and senseless dying's over. Now leave this poor, defenseless man before I have you arrested."

"Yes sir!" Vigil shouted, snapping a salute. "Me and Dub'll be on our way right now."

"Sergeant Combs, put a tourniquet on that man's leg, give him some water and something to eat and take him to Richmond. There's a Union field hospital there."

"Yes sir, Captain."

"Haygood, you go with him."

"Yes sir."

"Thank you, Captain," Alfred, barely able to raise his head, said with a grunt.

The Captain did not speak. He just nodded and rode off with the other Confederates.

Meanwhile, many miles away, but with the same goal of getting back to Fish Springs and to Mary, John carefully guided the mare through the woods, thinking it would be best to stay off the road for a while.

To help keep his sanity and take his mind off of his precarious situation—navigating with very little food and no fresh water through a snake and mosquito-infested marsh in Virginia— he thought about Mary. Always, it came back to the same thorny question. How to win her over as his bride and to get past Aunt Caroline? *That ole' bitch of an aunt. Why's she always stickin' her nose in my business? She don't know me. I ain't a bad man.*

John crossed a wide, rocky creek and kicked the mare in the ribs when she hesitated. He heard the roar of a big, crashing waterfall downstream. It reminded him of when he and Alfred would explore the mountain wilderness near Fish Springs. They had found a huge waterfall with a deep pool at the bottom—full of rainbow trout. *God almighty, I wanna get home soon's I can. But I'll never fish with that Yankee sombitch agin.*

He rode into a field where a primitive log farmhouse had stood but had been burned down, probably by the Confederates. An ancient weather-beaten barn was still there. It was getting dark and starting to rain, so he decided to bunk down in the barn. John put his ride in a stall and scraped up a hand full of hay for her to munch on. Later, lying on a thin makeshift bed of straw and surveying the field in the dim light, he saw a doe.

"Just my damned luck," John muttered. "I'm starvin', there stands my damn dinner, and I ain't got powder or shot. And if that ain't bad enough, I ain't been paid my lousy sixteen dollars a month for the last three months. The only damn good thing I know for sure is that when I get back, I'm fixin' to marry the prettiest girl in Fish Springs, and nobody's gonna stop me. And I'm gonna make love to her every day and night for the rest of our lives."

That thought made him ravenous. John devoured the last soggy biscuit from his knapsack. It was cold and rainy and he was sleeping in a barely standing barn in a drafty loft tonight, but he took some comfort in knowing the end was in sight. *They's better days ahead. No more damned fightin an killing. No more getting' up at five ever' mornin' for God-forsaken reveille. And never agin' havin' to scrounge, like a dog, for somethin' to eat and drink. No more sickness and disease and goin' without sleep.*

And then he wondered which side had actually won the war. Had it been the Yankees, like he'd heard? Or had the Rebs stood their ground and kicked those blue bellies all the way back to Pennsylvania—or wherever they came from?

For all the fighting and suffering and disease he'd been through in Virginia, it now really didn't seem to matter. All he knew was he was going home after living in a treacherous, snake ridden, mosquito infested—except in the winter when he almost froze to death—swampy, wilderness. And he'd had to endure all this misery for three long years. Going home, after somehow surviving the drudgery and horror of a long, painful, ravaging war, to his sweet, divine Mary.

He couldn't wait.

CHAPTER 7
Almost Home

It was late morning as John, on his mount, approached Joshua Arnett's farm on the Doe River. He had ridden out of his way to fetch his horse, Charger, and his best friend—his old hound dog, Blue. John was proud of his horse and fancied how folks looked up to him when he rode Charger through Fish Springs. But it's his dog Blue that he missed so badly. Blue offered him unconditional love, and nothing could change that. Not even when John, drunk at the time and too pathetic to let the dog out when he barked, kicked him for defecating in the cabin. When the loyal animal whimpered, lowered its head as if it had lost its master's affection, John had regretted the kicking. And he swore to himself that he'd try to hold his temper after that.

Not wanting his friend Joshua to know about the *borrowed* horse he was riding, the former Confederate soldier dismounted out of sight of his house. He took the halter off his ride and slapped the animal in the rear, sending it galloping in the other direction. John figured if the mare didn't make it back home it wasn't any skin off his nose.

A half mile walk later, he could see Joshua's farm house across the swift flowing Doe River, and, if his eyes weren't playing tricks on him, he thought he had spotted old Blue.

Yep there his loveable hound was—lazing on the porch with a few other dogs. With his blue-gray coat and long droopy ears, you couldn't miss Blue.

"Blue!" John hollered, a big grin breaking out on his face.

He had definitely gotten the attention of the other dogs, their tails wagging and their barks those of animals that had been aroused. They paced to and fro, like they couldn't decide whether to run toward John or away from him—but not Blue. He just stood up and stared curiously at the stranger. It seemed the dog then realized it was his master's voice; he sliced the air with his tail, danced with his front paws and smiled with his eyebrows. Then the faithful canine leaped from the porch and hit the ground in a flat-out race to the river. He dove in and began swimming across.

But very shortly the dog seemed to be struggling against the strong current. He began thrashing about, not able to keep his head above water. For all his fighting to survive, Blue seemed destined to drown.

"No!" John hollered. He bolted to the roaring river, kicked off his boots and dove into the cold water. "Please, God, don't let my dog drown! I cain't lose him now!"

He swam furiously, fighting to keep his head above the rushing water, and catch up to his floundering best friend. It would probably be the only time in Blue's life that he didn't mind being grabbed by his tail; its tip had been barely above water when John managed to grip it. John pulled his endangered four-legged companion to the shore, laid him on the grassy bank and pushed on his chest. Water gushed from the dog's mouth and nostrils, and he seemed not to be breathing. Panicking and near tears, John began thinking the worst.

"Please God, help me. Don't let this happen. Don't let Blue die. He ain't never hurt nobody in his life. He's ma best friend, Lord."

John pressed again on the dog's chest. This time, less water spurted from Blue's mouth, and then none. He frantically put the end of Blue's muzzle into his mouth and blew hard, forcing air into the dog's lungs. Then he pushed on Blue's chest, forcing the air back out. He did this again and again. John, wet and near exhaustion from swimming and tugging, got into a rhythm of blowing and pushing, blowing and pushing... And then Blue started taking short, labored breaths. Cold and totally spent, John sat in the warming sun on the river bank, his friend's head on his lap. A desperate, undeserving man had begged God to save his dog, and it seemed to John that his prayer had been answered.

"Thank you, Lord! Thank you!

"And, Lord, please don't let me ever mistreat my friend again!"

Then total exhaustion overwhelmed him, and John lay his head next to his dog on the river bank and slept a deep dreamless sleep. But after a couple of hours, Blue had had enough. Time to awaken his slumbering boss and get on with life with the one person he loved more than any other human in the world.

Blue ran his wet sloppy tongue all over John's face.

"Blue, looks like you're ready to go home," John said, paying no mind at all to the dog slobber on his mouth, nose and cheeks.

John's friend offered his signature bark as a reply.

With that, man and dog, once again inseparable, John retrieved his boots and headed to Joshua's house. It wasn't until then that John realized he and Blue had been carried about a quarter mile downstream.

When John and his dog got back to Joshua's weather beaten log cabin, Joshua was nowhere to be seen. Same with John's horse, Charger. The animal was not in the barn lot or the barn so John figured that Joshua had probably ridden Charger to The Black Bear Saloon.

He probably goes there ever' other day, John figured. It seemed likely that his friend would not return before dark, if not tomorrow.

"Blue, let's get outta here, boy. What say we hightail it to Fish Springs?"

Blue, back to his old self and eager for any kind of adventure, barked again, as if to say "What're we waitin' for?" Then he began wagging his tail and he darted slightly ahead of his master. John swore the dog was trying to entice him to get moving toward Fish Springs.

As dog and man began walking, John wasn't thinking about food or Blue's close call. Instead, his mind was on Mary again and what it would be like to once again hold her, to feel her soft, curvy body against his own. But how to handle Alfred? *I've got to play it plum' smart when Mary mentions his name, and not speak ill of 'em, 'cause Alfred's her friend, but I know he ain't her lover. And life, for this ole mountain boy is about to get better. Jist got to bide ma time. It"ll be hard to not show hatred towards that Yankee son of a bitch, but I'll not do it, for the love of Mary.*

Then suddenly, out of the corner of his eye, he noticed something unusual about the ground cover in the shade of a big tulip poplar tree. He bent down for a closer look, and, low and behold, it was ginseng! His heart beat faster, knowing he had lucked upon this prized rare mountain plant, with its five tell-tale green leaves and clusters of red berries. There it was—*just waitin' for me to dig it up and sell so I kin have a little more money to buy somethin' nice for Mary. Some say that 'seng'll cure just about anything that ails ya—includin' colds, coughs and headaches, and others say it'll make ya a better man in bed.*

As he dug in the moist dirt with his pocket knife and carefully pulled each sprout of ginseng up by its roots, he wondered why someone else hadn't stumbled upon this money growing out of the ground. *Maybe my luck's turnin'.* Then he reminded himself to ask Mary to brew them a cup of hot ginseng tea. *She can put a little honey in there and we'll both git in tha mood real fast… I've heard that ole root makes a woman sa hot she jist wants to love on ya all night!*

Later that evening relaxing in a swing on the porch, Mary read Harper's Weekly by the light of a lantern. It was the illustrated newspaper Daniel had picked up for her on his last trip to Johnsons Depot. The paper, chock full of pictures of what life was like beyond Fish Springs, kept Mary spellbound. She imagined herself being among all those tall, majestic buildings, fine and up and coming young gentleman … of living in some faraway romantic place like New York or California.

I could be one of those ladies, I'm pretty, I'm smart. Why can't I have some of the nicer things in life?

"Mary," a familiar voice whispered.

Mary immediately thought that perhaps it was God. *And he's going to scold me, 'cause I'm dwellin' too much on riches and such.*

She gazed into the darkness but could only make out a faint silhouette of a person. She was fearful but then realized a human being had spoken her name. Blue trotted into the light and up onto the porch, brushing her on the leg with his cold wet nose. She bent down and stroked him on the head and then she her heart began racing. Where Blue was, John had to be near. She could feel his presence.

"Mary, you come here right now!" John said as he stepped into the light.

With that, she jumped from the swing, ran down the steps and into his arms.

"John, oh John! Oh God, how I missed you! I can't believe you're finally back!"

"I love you, Mary."

Clinging to each other, they kissed.

"Don't you ever leave me again," she said. "Don't even think about it!"

"God as my witness, I will never, ever leave you!"

John pulled Mary up on her tip toes, and their lips were inseparable. They kissed, and then kissed again and again, each time a little longer and deeper.

Meanwhile, back in Virginia at the Union field hospital, Alfred's wounds were attended to. The field doctor told him the lead shot passed through his inner thigh as well as part of his scrotum. The good news was he could still perform as a man—to an extent. But the downside, according to what he learned from the doctor, was that his injury could possibly cause him to be sterile. Also, there could be some small lead fragments still embedded near his manhood, but, be that as it may, the doctor said, it would be best just to leave them alone.

Alfred was bandaged, given two makeshift crutches and a cot in the war-ravaged recovery tent along with several other soldiers, kept warm and fed three times a day. The rations—ground beef, potatoes and turnips and eggs for breakfast—weren't half bad. *Beats cold biscuits and salty dry meat.* Alfred figured, *and at least I'm not sleepin' on the ground.*

And the longer he stayed at this regimental hospital, the more he was thankful for his condition. Because the hospital, a series of tents with wheat-straw covered dirt floors, was crammed with sick and severely wounded or dying soldiers. Many of the injured had come there from bloody Antietam, where the Union lost more than 5,000 men.

Alfred's wounds, though serious, seemed relatively minor compared to those of the poor unfortunate souls awaiting amputation of their limbs. Some of them would die from shock; others wouldn't be able to stand the excruciating pain, and their hearts would simply stop beating. Their only hope was the surgeon's scalpel and saw that removed infected skin, muscle and bone, but it was a dreaded fate at best. For when he was first brought in and waited for hours in the surgical tent, Alfred witnessed soldier after soldier screaming deliriously for mercy and God's help. From their stretcher, already near meeting their maker, they were lifted up and placed on the crude operating table—a sheet-covered wide plank supported by two barrels. The grisly procedure usually took only a few minutes. If the soldier was getting his arm amputated, a tourniquet was applied far up the arm to stem the inevitable profuse bleeding. If there was no chloroform, the patient was allowed to gulp whiskey or brandy and to gaze one last time at his soon-to-be hacked off limb. He might also bite down so hard on a bullet that his teeth cracked.

After the cutting, sawing and wiping up of the blood, Alfred noticed that the patient, bandaged and wrapped in a blanket, was usually in one of three states—unconscious, alive but in unspeakable agony, or dead. If fortunate enough to be alive and to escape infection or disease, the wounded warrior would live to return to his home and loved ones. But Alfred also knew that the amputees' lives would never be the same. *How could they ever return to life—as they knew it before the war—with a "stump" for an arm or leg. They'll go home as sickly, miserable, pathetic men, and some'll commit suicide when their wives desert 'em for "whole men."*

The next day, pain or no pain, Alfred felt he had to write Mary, so he asked a nurse if she could bring him a pencil and some paper.

"I could do that, soldier," said the no nonsense nurse, her graying hair closely cropped and a small silver cross dangling from her neck. "But you need to get out of that cot, and walk a little. Take your crutches but only use them when you have to. They have paper and pencils in the commissary.

"Where is the commissary?"

"It's the tent next to the surgical tent with the big red cross on the side—where they took you first."

The stocky woman helped Alfred to a standing position, then handed him his crutches. Light headed at first, Alfred regained his balance and made his way slowly, acknowledging other recovering soldiers as he hobbled along.

As Alfred progressed up the hill toward the surgical shelter, he again became aware of men screaming. He tried to block the agonizing cries from his ears but it was hard. And on top of that, with every step, a sharp pain shot down his leg. But he endured it.

Alfred noticed a small, frayed tent near and toward the back of the surgical tent and ambled unsteadily to it. Pulling back the flap and trying to step in while holding his crutches, he lost his balance and fell to his knees inside the tent. Then a sickening odor overwhelmed him. *What the hell? What could that be?*

He found out soon enough, for the scene inside was a chamber of horror. There, just a few feet from where he leaned on his crutches, was a macabre pile of sawed off arms, hands, legs and feet. And the putrid smell made him gag.

Alfred only glanced at the grisly stack of human limbs, but what he'd seen and smelled would be etched in his brain till he died. Nightmares of that encounter inside the medical tent would haunt him, and each night before he dozed off he would constantly touch his arms and legs—just to be sure they were still there.

Rumor had it in the hospital camp that some lost their arms and legs needlessly. It was suspected that the overworked, exhausted, exasperated surgeons had too many patients and too little medicine and chloroform. So they just butchered, as it were, knowing full well that some of the soldiers would die anyway—if not from the effects of gangrene, then from other maladies.

And here's the proof, Alfred thought. *Proof that too many men—far too many—had their bodies mutilated at the hands of those they trusted. May God have mercy on all of us!*

Alfred couldn't turn his head away fast enough. As he stumbled outside, a wave of nausea overtook him. He dropped his crutches, crouched to the ground and puked violently.

"What are you doing here, soldier?"

Alfred raised his head to see a Union captain in a blood splattered white apron holding a severed arm, the precious red liquid of arteries and veins dripping from the sawed end. Alfred struggled to his feet and saluted the officer. The tired officer did not return the gesture.

"Well?" asked the captain, tossing the arm onto the pile inside.

"I was trying to find the commissary, captain. I wish I hadn't of stumbled in there."

"It's a ghastly, hellish thing. That's for sure, soldier. I guess I've become insensitive to it. I'm sorry you saw it. The commissary's on the other side."

"Thank you, captain."

"At least this damn war is over and I'll eventually run outta patients. … If I last that long."

"God bless you, sir. I hope your work ends soon," Alfred said, offering another salute. This time the captain saluted back. As Alfred did a ragged about face, pivoting on his crutches, a bedraggled, battled-worn private pushed a wooden wheelbarrow inside and began loading the grisly pieces of bone and flesh.

"Private."

The disheveled soldier faced the captain. "Yas-sir."

"The next time I'm here, I better damn not see a big pile of body parts in this tent. It's not that far to the area where we bury 'em. Do I make myself clear, private?"

"Yas-sir, captain," said the private, saluting and grudgingly resuming his ghastly task.

Hobbling back to the recovery area from the commissary, Alfred stopped to take a deep breath. When the pain had become too intense, he had used his crutches for the last half of the trip, and now his armpits ached. Too tired and emotionally distraught to write, he laid the crutches aside and crawled into the cot. Then he closed his eyes and tried to recall something pleasant—anything but hacked body pieces—to put himself to sleep.

A hard rain pelted the tent. Any other time, that would be a sleep inducer, but not this night. After tossing and turning for hours, he pushed the army blanket off him and sat straight up, envious that the other wounded men seemed to be resting peacefully. But Alfred remained wide awake. If was as if someone kept jabbing a knife in his side; only this was worse than any physical pain. He couldn't get past the horrendous scene of blood and sawed off flesh. He even took a few swigs of whiskey that a nurse slipped in to him to dull his senses, but it had only a minimal effect.

A few times, he cried out for the nurse to come soothe him. The woman checked his wounds. Then she kissed him nurturingly on his forehead and held his trembling hands. When he told her about the pile of bloody limbs, she whispered, "Hush up, soldier. You shoulda never seen that. … Now don't you have a sweetheart back home you need to write? Might do you good to write her tonight."

So, after the nurse fetched his writing paper and pencil and lit a candle next to his cot, Alfred collected himself and set about sharing his thoughts with Mary. He decided first off he would NOT write about bad things. *Because Mary don't need to read anything about that. It'll just cause her to fret and lose sleep herself… No, I'm just gonna tell her where I am and write about somethin' cheerful.*

But what on earth would that be? Alfred wondered. *What could possibly be good or uplifting in this man's war?* And then he had an idea.

April 12th 1865

My Dear Beloved Mary,

How I've missed you! I thought about you today when the most glorious rainbow I've ever seen suddenly appeared above our camp. Its colors made me want to dance with you and hug you! It was red, orange, yellow and green.

You know, Mary, only God can make a rainbow, and only He could have made you. You're the most beautiful and amazing woman in the world. I can't wait to be back in Fish Springs and wrap my arms round you!

And I'd already be home if it hadn't been for a rogue Confederate deserter who shot me in my upper leg. The coward ambushed me on the road. Shot my horse from under me, then shot me. The liar claimed that he didn't know the war was over. I would be dead, love, if it hadn't been for a Confederate officer—a good, God-fearing man—who came to my rescue.

So here I am—licking my wounds and recovering in a field hospital in Richmond. It's not all bad. I have my own cot and the nurses look after me. Plus, the food's hot and good. I'm on crutches but I've still got my arms and legs, and I'm healing and gettin' stronger.

Please wait for me and keep praying for me. I'm getting better every day.

I should be back in Fish Springs in a few weeks. Can't wait to see you! Get ready for me, Mary! Give my love to Aunt Caroline.

Love, Alfred

If Alfred wanted his letter to make a favorable impression on Mary, and to reaffirm his affection for her, he definitely succeeded. For days later—after being picked up by a courier on horseback and relayed to several other couriers over the course of hundreds of rugged miles, the love note arrived intact in Mary's hands in Fish Springs. And when she eagerly opened and read it, she squealed with delight.

"He's wounded but he's alive, praise God, and he's coming home!" she hollered, wrapping her arms around John. "I just knew he'd be all right! He says they're taking good care of him in a field hospital in Richmond, and he'll be back in Fish Springs in a few weeks."

"Well, bless his little Union heart, Mary," John grunted, relieved that his rival wouldn't be home for a while. *It'll give me more time alone with her, and I know one damned thing. I'm gonna make the most of it. Just wish Alfred would stay away! I don't need that damned Yankee complicatin' things.*

His embrace with Mary and his feigned sympathy were quickly interrupted by Aunt Caroline, who pointedly reminded them that tomorrow would be Easter Sunday. If they weren't in church, they wouldn't be walking with Jesus, she warned.

When Mary asked her aunt if it would be all right for John to sit with them during Easter service, she reluctantly nodded yes.

Then she wondered. *What'll people think? Me and my Mary sittin' with a ruffian, a moonshine drinkin' gambler who's been seen with painted women. But then again, if he's been saved, what choice do we have?*

Sunday morning, John made good on his promise to Mary about being ready for church. Even Aunt Caroline had to admit he looked spiffy—practically like a new man—when he rode up to the sanctuary on Charger. John wore new boots, a dark suit with a black vest over a white shirt, all purchased in Elizabethton after returning from the war. Even Charger looked renewed. He had been thoroughly curried and sported a new bridle.

Well, he does look right smart handsome. I like the way he's got his hair combed straight back and how it glistens an' all, Aunt Caroline conceded to herself as John dismounted, tied Charger to a hitching post and offered Mary his arm. At least, he's tryin' to be a gentleman.

"Mornin', John," Caroline said curtly.

"Mornin', Mrs. Hamby," he replied. "Mary can I do one thing 'fore we go into the buildin'?"

"Why, what would that be, John?" Mary asked.

Without replying, John removed his suit jacket and carefully handed it to Mary.

Aunt Caroline's brow furrowed, and her eyes squinted. *What the devil is he up to now?*

John parted the gate and entered the little church cemetery—located only a few steps away from where they would worship. With Mary and her Aunt glaring curiously, he followed a makeshift path winding through and around the dozens of headstones. Tall, magnificent oak trees, their branches full of leaves, shaded this final resting place for so many of Fish Springs' war dead.

John respectfully knelt down next to one marker at the head of a freshly dug grave. The marker and a small American flag had been overturned and broken whiskey bottles littered the grave. He bowed his head briefly and seemed to mumble a silent prayer as he set about removing the broken glass and righting the marker and flag.

Then, casting his eyes upward, he walked slowly and solemnly back to Aunt

Caroline and Mary, used a handkerchief to wipe the sweat from his forehead, dusted off his britches and put his coat back on.

"I ain't standin' for no desecration of no grave. And makes no diffrence to me if it's a Yankee or Rebel layin' there," he said. "Hopefully the sheriff'll catch whoever's doin' this and put'm in jail."

Glad that her aunt had now seen an apparent redeeming side of John, Mary squeezed John's hand as they then entered the sanctuary. But she couldn't help but notice, as they walked down the aisle toward the front of the church, how members of the congregation had their eyes riveted on them.

"Why, that there's Mary Clemmons. I thought she was sweet on Alfred White, so what's she doin' consortin' with that devilish John Williams?" one frail little know-it-all, in a blue print dress, sweater and red bonnet, whispered to her bespectacled, confused husband.

"You don't s'pose Alfred White's been kilt in the war do you?" her husband responded.

"Welcome and what a wonderful Easter Sunday morning it is!" a beaming Preacher Ike Redford shouted from the pulpit. Balding and with piercing blue eyes, a stern face, square shoulders and a belly sagging over his belt buckle, the Bible-clutching man of the cloth asked everyone to stand and sing the opening song. "Christ the Lord is Risen Today."

Members of the congregation opened their hymnals, rose and responded enthusiastically.

"Christ the Lord is risen today, Alleluia!
"Sons of men and angels say, Alleluia!
"Raise your joys and triumphs high, Alleluia!
"Sing, ye heavens, and earth reply, Alleluia!"

When they were done singing, Redford bid everyone to be seated. Then, his booming voice filling the church, he proclaimed that there would be no Christianity but for the resurrection of Jesus.

"And because of that amazing Easter event," Redford preached, "even as we ourselves break down and die, we can be assured as Christians that we have new life in Jesus Christ. When our physical bodies decay, we will join the angels in heaven!"

From the congregation, "Amen!"

"Yes, Amen!" Redford answered.

"And also because of the divine grace that Jesus has given us as righteous, Bible believin' Christians on this beautiful Easter Sunday, we shouldn't a been on anybody's side of this war in the first place. Today, as we praise God that this war is over, Christ calls us to be there when our warriors come home. … Be there to heal and comfort them. We Christians don't shoot or tear down our wounded and hurtin' others from the war. We embrace 'em, pardon 'em, help 'em anyways we can."

When one tobacco chewing Yankee sympathizer in the front pew frowned and whispered to his wife that he'd rot in hell before he forgave or forgot what any Confederate soldier did, Redford paid him no mind.

The preacher continued. "Throughout this long, bitter and horrible conflict, thousands of men died. Brothers and sisters, some of 'em were killed in battle, and some died of wounds, or they got sick or they starved. But they died, just the same, and it was for a cause they fervently believed in. One that divided families and friends … pitted blood against blood. And regardless, we need to remember 'em as good Christian souls who had different ideas about the way things should be.

"But all the fightin's over now, praise the Lord!"

From the congregation. "Praise the Lord!"

"And our young men'er comin' home! Men who fought for the Confederacy. Men who fought for the Union. Equally good men. Do not judge them!

"Remember what we are instructed to do in Matthew 7, 'Judge not, that ye be not judged. For with what judgment ye judge, ye shall be judged. and with what measure ye mete, it shall be measured to you again.'

"Love 'em all and wrap your arms 'round 'em! Love 'em for what they sacrificed. Love 'em for their valor. Together we can heal Fish Springs.

"Can I have an Amen?"

"Amen!!" came a thunderous roar from the congregation.

Mary squeezed John's hand. His eyes met hers and he returned the squeeze.

Preacher Redford, picking up a hymnal, instructed everyone to "turn to page two-o-one. 'Amazin' Grace.' Please stand."

The congregation rose and sang. But Mary had a difficult time focusing on the hymn. Instead, her mind was on John. *I'm so proud of him … I guess, truth be told, I've always been infatuated with him—even back when we were in school together.* Even when he was disrespectful to Mrs. Beasley, who at times could be a bit overbearing herself. Mary didn't understand why, but for some reason she was attracted to his bad boy ways. *Perhaps,* she rationalized, *it was because I was only thirteen at the time. What could a thirteen-year-old girl possibly know about boys or life or anything?*

John guessed by Mary's expression that he was making headway with her.

This church thing might be workin' after all . Now, if only I can change Aunt Caroline's opinion of me, I can get Mary as my wife. I can do it, but first I've got to win over that old bitch.

He closed the hymnal and offered the dreaded aunt his most endearing smile.

Before Preacher Redford could speak, the doors to the sanctuary burst open and in barged a man wet from perspiration and out of breath. The congregation stared spellbound as the man ran straight to the pulpit to the preacher and whispered into his ear. The preacher listened, then dropped his head and closed his eyes to gather his thoughts.

He faced the worshippers.

"It pains me greatly to pass to you the shocking news I have just received," Redford said somberly. "But President Abraham Lincoln has been assassinated. He was shot Friday night and died yesterday from the wound."

Cries of anguish filled the church. Wailing and screaming seemed to come especially from the older folks in the flock—doubtless some of them blood kin of Fish Springs' war casualties.

Meanwhile, Mary found John's arms for comfort, and Daniel's wife Polly, like a nurturing mother hen, pulled her children together.

One man shook his fist and hollered. "Them damn Confederates! May they burn in hell!"

"They kilt my boy too!" a woman shouted.

"Please! You are in the house of the Lord!" Preacher Redford, holding his right hand high above his head, reminded them.

Other men ranted against the Confederates and those who supported their cause.

"The no-good, cold-blooded killer!" one old geezer yelled. "It's 'bout time we put all them Rebs in the ground!"

Redford called for calm but to no avail. The mumbling and threats and curses continued.

On seeing Daniel stand up, John seized a golden opportunity. His shout startled Mary.

"Now y'all stop!" he commanded.

And suddenly the congregation grew silent.

"Have some respect for Reverend Redford and this sanctuary," John added.

"He's a Confederate!" a scruffy old man, pointing at John, objected.

"To the contrary sir, I *was* a Confederate but that ended when the war ended. I'm a citizen now jist like you and all the others in this place of worship. President Lincoln was my president too, and I hate it he was kilt. I pray the Lord'll heal the hearts of those who harbor hatred because of this war."

"Amen, brother! You're preachin' the grace of Easter!" Reverend Redford declared.

"Yes, Amen!" a man in the back of the church concurred.

"Reverend Redford," John interjected, "could you please lead us in a prayer to comfort Mrs. Lincoln and 'er family and to bring us all tagether as Christians?"

"Yes, brother John. "I certainly will. And praise the Lord for having you with us here today!"

"Amen!" responded a few parishioners.

Aunt Caroline forced herself to rethink her position. *Maybe John's been saved after all. Time'll tell.*

John Williams has become a man I could spend the rest of my life with, Mary thought, swelling with pride.

Later, as they left the church, Mary told John how proud she was of him. She said she'd never forget the way he'd gotten the congregation to calm down.

Even Aunt Caroline flashed John a subtle smile of admiration. "That was a Godly and manly thing you did in there, John," Caroline opined.

"It wasn't such a big thing. I only said what I felt. Folks have ta learn howda' get along with one 'nother, 'specially at Easter."

"Will I see you tomorrow, John?" Mary asked, as Caroline walked away. She had not let go of his hand and had hardly taken her eyes off him from the time they rose to exit the sanctuary.

"Nothin would please me more, darlin', but me and Joshua's got plans tomorrow. We're goin' ta Butler ta bring back a couple'a steers. But I'll see ya Tuesdey' fer sure my love," said John, as he mounted Charger.

"I love you," Mary mouthed.

Early the next day Mary and Aunt Caroline sat on the porch talking about the assassination of President Lincoln and the war ending.

"What I can't get out of my mind, Aunt Caroline, is how terrible it musta been at that theatre in Washington where our President was murdered. They say a man shot him in the back of his head—with his wife sitting right next to him. And it happened on Good Friday! Can you imagine? "

"It must have been horrible," Aunt Caroline mumbled, not raising her head from her knitting. "But Mary, your man Alfred'll be home soon enough."

"Yes," said Mary, feeling pressure to tell Aunt Caroline the truth. But while she tried to muster up the courage, Daniel and Polly arrived in their buggy.

"Good morning, ladies."

"Good morning, Daniel, Polly."

"I have some business to attend to in Elizabethton, and Polly is going along to do a little shopping. Would you ladies like to go with us?"

"Come with us dear hearts," said a smiling, upbeat Polly. "It's a beautiful day for a carriage ride."

"Okay, Mary?" Aunt Caroline asked.

"Sure, Aunt Caroline. I always love to go to Elizabethton and I need a few things."

"Then I'll get my bag."

The ride to Elizabethton on the old dirt road was not too bad. Daniel's new buggy absorbed most of the holes and bumps. Speaking loudly over the sound of his trotting white horse Millie, he confided to Mary how surprised he was to see John Williams in church with her Easter Sunday.

"He's a changed man since the war, Daniel," Mary said. "John said he has been saved and he wants to be a good Christian."

"That's wonderful, Mary. It's for sure the war changed a lot of men, some for the better, some for the worse. I'm happy for John. He certainly made a favorable impression in church Sunday."

Daniel leaned back and glanced over his shoulder. "But you're being awfully quiet back there, Caroline."

"Not much to say."

"Aunt Caroline is not convinced John has changed, Daniel," Mary said.

"We'll see, child. We'll see," Aunt Caroline replied.

"What about your good friend, Alfred White?" Polly asked. "Have you heard from him?"

"Yes, I have Polly. I got a letter from Alfred two days ago. He was on his way home when he got shot by a rogue Confederate.

"But Alfred'll be okay. He got shot in the leg. He said he'll be home in a few weeks."

"I know Mary doesn't show her excitement, but she can't wait to see Alfred," Caroline announced.

Polly's face lit up. "Oh! Is there something here we should know?"

Mary, facing Caroline, answered with a stern "No!"

CHAPTER 8

Roast Duck and a Glass of Wine

Rhododendron, Mountain Laurel, Canadian Hemlocks, Tulip Poplars, birches and wildflowers of all colors lined their road. The winding route cut through a dense, green forest that filled the cool mountain air with the scent of pine needles. The road also wound through acres of rolling Tennessee meadows. Cattle, horses and sheep grazed on some of those stretches. They also noticed swaths of rich cropland, much of it freshly plowed.

Nature's wonders in this part of beautiful, rugged Tennessee always dazzled. And when they crossed an icy cold trout stream, Daniel yelled out to an old man fishing with a boy—probably his grandson, Daniel figured—standing knee deep in the creek with his pant legs rolled up.

"Y'all catchin' anything?"

"Nope, ain't caught nothin'," the old fisherman replied.

"They just ain't a bitin' today!" the shirtless freckle-faced boy yelled back.

Daniel tipped his hat to the two anglers and gave them a friendly wave.

As they continued their journey to Elizabethton, Mary pledged to herself that she would try to do right and never again fall short of God's commandments, *because, it's not what you've got. It's what you do, the path you follow.*

Maybe, she figured, one of these days she could get some time alone with Daniel and ask him for guidance. For it seemed to Mary that the stringent, straight-laced Aunt Caroline, though she loved her deeply, wasn't of a mind to hear her niece out when she asked her for advice. Instead, she'd quickly condemn or chastise. Aunt Caroline meant well, Mary knew, but maybe the kinder Daniel would be a better listener and not so quick to judge.

When their buggy pulled to a stop at the General Store in the center of Elizabethton, they were almost sad their scenic ride had ended. But, as they stretched and dusted off each other's clothes, they also looked forward to shopping and taking in the sights and other things of interest in the county seat.

"Polly, I'll be back here at two o'clock. That's about two hours from now. Do you have your watch?" Daniel asked as he took each of his passengers by the hand and helped them down.

"Yes, dear heart."

"Okay, ladies, have fun."

He reminded them that he had business to conduct at the nearby bank, post office and courthouse. He promised he wouldn't be late in picking them up. With that, Daniel climbed back up on the buggy and headed off.

Before their ride was out of sight, the three ladies entered the Elizabethton General Store, and they immediately took in the smells of sweet onions, apples, cider, candy, cabbages, gingerbread and candy.

They feasted their eyes on the wall of colorful bolts of cloth and other items—spools of thread and rolls of ribbons and lace. Filling most of the store were dry goods—animal feeds, hoes, plows, shovels, vegetable seeds and barrels full of dried beans. Next to those barrels were burlap bags, useful for customers who scooped out and weighed whatever quantity of beans they wanted. The store also sold all manner of boots, salves and ointments, soaps, pocketknives, rifles, handguns, ammunition and fishing supplies.

And if you didn't have the money to buy what you wanted, the owner of Elizabethton's ever-accommodating general store had been known to let you trade a chicken for a sack of flour or a piece of fatback for a five-pound bag of sugar, or a bushel of corn for a few toys.

But folks also came here for more than just buying food or supplies, because the general store in Elizabethton had long been a community-gathering place, where you could catch up on the latest news, gossip and rumors.

Most of that catching up occurred around the store's potbellied wood stove, even in the summer, because that's where folks sat. It was in the middle of all the dry goods, and today a group of men—a farmer, a blacksmith, a livery stable owner and a few old men—conversed in the caneback chairs facing the unused stove.

Near them was a small table with a checkerboard. But no one was playing; instead the men were engaged in a lively exchange about their favorite subject, other people.

The stable owner, smelling of horse manure, asked if they remembered "that young fella that lived 'tween here and Valley Forge? Ya know, the one that fought fer the Confederacy and said he whupped all them Yankees? The one that seemed kinda skittish when he came here ta tha store? I heeyerd tell his name was Rufus."

When the listeners, their curiosity piqued, nodded they indeed remembered, the storyteller continued. "Well, a'body never knows when tha Good Lord's gonna call'm home, 'cause that very fella was burreed yesterdey' at tha' Colored Church Cemetery. They didn't have no place else to lay'm ta rest, and he wuddin' a member of any house'a God, so the colored said they'd burry'm."

Mary, standing within earshot, inched a little closer so she could hear the rest of the tale. She had just pulled a book from one of the store's dusty shelves and she pretended to be browsing through it.

"Well, ain't that'a thang ta happen to a white man that up an' dies," the blacksmith groused. "Guess a man better never git briggety. Elsewise, they'll lay'm to rest with with a bunch'a niggers."

"But that ain't tha half'a hit!" said the farmer, his voice rising and his eyes widening. "Cuz they wuz two women there at his grave a mournin' and each of 'em cradled a baby. One said he wuz the daddy of the child in her arms, and when she commencedt ta cryin' an' carryin' on so, ta other one claimed the same thang—that he'd daddied *her* youngun!

"But that ain't all.... Both a them wailin' women said they wuz married to him, and one of 'em didn't know nary a thang 'bout tha other one! Seems they lived 'bout ten miles apart from one 'nother. This Rufus fella was a trapper and he wuddn't home much, 'cause he wuz out in these here mountains trying to trap bears and mountain lions and beavers and such. Least wise that's what he said he wuz'adoin'. "

"You ain't told us what kilt him," the blacksmith objected.

"Ain nary a'body knows," the farmer said. "He jist up and died, but somes a'sayin hits 'cause he wuz married ta two ladies at the same time and he'd lied to 'em so much it got tha best of him ... Made his heart stop a'beatin."

"Suits'm that he's a layin' down there 'mong the canker worms with them coloreds!" one eavesdropping shopper at the General Store yelled. "I heeyered that same tale and hits true. He done them women wrong and now he's left 'em with his babies. He shoulda' kept his britches on ... May his soul burn in hell!"

Mary was amused by the story but also wondered, *could somebody really love two people that much or was the man who fathered those two babies just a scoundrel? It's true that I love two people. I've loved Alfred as long as I've known him, but it's not the same kind of love I feel for John. I feel excitement and passion when I'm with John. It is all I can do, to keep my promise to myself and God, to save myself for him. I know John has a questionable reputation, but he's changed so much. I love the man he's becoming since being saved.*

"Have you not found anything, child?"

Mary, startled into reality, turned to face her aunt and Polly.

"Oh yes, Aunt Caroline, I've found myself a book." She had chosen one with a red buckram cover, its paper wrapper lost in the months it had been in the store. Checking the title, she added, "I've heard tell of the Overmountain Men since I was a girl. Maybe I can learn some more."

Aunt Caroline had in hand a bag full of licorice and hard candy.

"Polly, what did you buy?" Mary asked.

"Well, I found Daniel a pearl-handle pocket knife!" Polly boasted. "Ain't never seen one like it. Daniel broke the blade on the one he had."

Then, as regular as rain, Daniel was there to pick the three women up.

"Looks like you ladies found some things," he said, pulling back on the reins to stop Millie and the buggy. "Climb back aboard and we'll be on our way."

"Did ja' get all your business taken care of, Daniel?" Polly asked.

"Well the man I was spose' to see at the courthouse wasn't there. They said he'd be back at four-thirty so I reckon I'll half'ta go back there later."

When the women asked him where they were going now, he said they'd find out soon enough.

As they approached the Carter Mansion on the outskirts of Elizabethton, Mary was struck by the beauty of the plantation's tree and flower-covered grounds. And as if the grounds weren't stunning enough to hold her attention, there was the house itself. Built by John Carter and his son Landon in 1780, the legendary home was said to be the oldest mansion in Tennessee. Mary had always wondered what it had been like for Landon and his wife Elizabeth, for whom Elizabethton was named, to raise their family in such an elegant, stately place.

"Daniel, you ever been inside the Carter Mansion?" Mary asked.

"What's that, dear?" Daniel, cupped his right ear with his hand. "A man cain't hardly hear a thing with these trottin' hooves."

Mary, more loudly this time, put her question to him again.

"As a matter of fact, I *have* been in that house, Mary. I knew Samuel Carter and his brothers as younger men. Today they own the Carter Mansion. They're good folks, and they've not forgotten where they came from. Their grandfather and great grandfather built it."

"It must be really, really old," she said.

When Daniel informed her the mansion had been built late in the previous century, Mary asked him what the inside of the house was like.

"It's right elegant. Hand-hewn panels, murals on the walls, fine oil paintings of mountains and wildlife, two fireplaces, nice high-dollar furniture."

Daniel is a smart and scholarly gentleman. I wonder if Polly knows how lucky she is…

"Did Samuel Carter live there?" asked Mary, dying to see the inside of the old home.

"No. He and his brothers lived in a house up the road a piece. His father, Alfred Carter, grandson to John Carter, built that house. It's also a magnificent home. We'll come to it in a few minutes. And, I might add, Samuel Carter is now a brigadier general in the Union army."

"Child, you're gonna wear Daniel out with all your questions," Aunt Caroline said. "It's not lady-like to be so nosey. When I was your age, I wasn't allowed to ask so many questions.

"Leave her be. She's an inquisitive young lady, Caroline. I don't mind her questions one bit. Matter a'fact I like 'em. That makes for an intelligent woman."

Mary felt relieved she hadn't misspoken after all.

"This, Mary," Daniel said, pointed to the Alfred Carter home, "is where Samuel and his two brothers lived as young men. It's a really big house. And right up here is our courthouse. It's by far the largest building in Elizabethton. I still have some business to tend to here. But first Polly and I are treating you and Caroline to a meal."

"Daniel's taking us to the Snyder House! It's my favorite place in all the world!" Polly said. "I hope you're hungry 'cause you'ns is fixin' to eat the best vittles ever!"

Daniel, nodding and smiling, snapped the reins on Millie, and his feisty horse pulled the buggy faster. Their buggy passed the courthouse—a three-story red brick structure with impressive white columns built in the 1850s.

But Mary couldn't get her mind off the Carter Mansion. *Oh, to have lived there in all that finery. And I bet it had tapestries hangin' on the walls and silver candle holders an' red-velvet covered chairs.*

Minutes later, Daniel's buggy pulled up in front of the Snyder House, the first hotel in Elizabethton. Built in the 1850s, it consisted of four good-sized houses connected by passageways. Mary had heard of the Snyder House being the hub of activity in Elizabethton and catering mostly to top shelf people, travelers, and well-heeled locals. She also had heard of the beautiful hotel's reputation for delicious food. But she and Aunt Caroline had never been able to afford to eat in such an establishment.

"Af'ta noon Mista Smith. Mizzus Smith. Is you goun' eat with us taday?" asked the tall, lanky brown man in a red coat with white pants and a black top hat.

"Yes we are, Abraham."

"Fine! We takes good care of yo' hose and buggy whiles yo eat."

"Thank you. I'm sure Millie is a mite thirsty, Abraham," said Daniel.

"Ok, Mista Smith, yo fokes has a nice meal," said Abraham.

Inside the Snyder House, the hungry sojourners were led to a spacious, ornate room, with white tablecloth-adorned tables, fine silver place settings and exquisite white china trimmed in gold. A dazzling, crystal chandelier hung from the ceiling in the center of the room. The maitre d' greeted them, escorted them to a table and seated them. At a nearby table sat two businessmen in gray suits. One had a gold watch on a chain suspended from his vest. The other, removing a blue derby from his balding head, smoked a big cigar. The swirling, pungent aroma of the cigar smoke found its way to Daniel's table, where it had the effect of transporting Mary to a magical, faraway place of romance and mystique.

Maurice the waiter, a slightly built man with jet black hair and a handlebar mustache, addressed Daniel. "Afternoon, Mr. Smith.

"Afternoon, Maurice."

"May I suggest a fine bottle of cabernet sauvignon while you look over the menu?"

"Good choice, Maurice, and four crystal wine glasses."

The thought of imbibing alcohol of any sort, however, hit an uneasy nerve with Caroline. "Daniel, you *do* know that Mary and I won't drink the devil's brew?" she said, a tone of reprimand in her voice.

But Daniel, smiling subtly, didn't flinch. "Now Caroline, do you really think that Jesus would serve the devil's brew at the last supper?"

"Well, I hear tell that was just grape juice, and besides, what would Reverend Redford think if he got word of me an' Mary drinking booze? Why, he'd be a thinkin' awful poorly 'bout us for sure."

"Caroline, it's your decision. But I want you to know that I've shared a bottle of wine at this very table with none other than my friend Reverend Ike Redford. And I can tell you he enjoyed it immensely."

Caroline eyed Daniel for several seconds and couldn't help but notice an anxious Mary grinning from ear to ear. The Fish Springs foursome seemed to relax when Maurice returned with the bottle, popped the cork and poured a sample for Daniel to taste.

"That's fine, Maurice."

"Caroline?" Daniel asked softly.

"Okay, but only a teeny bit for Mary and me. One of the things that'll get you to hell faster'n anything is to take pleasure in what the ole' devil tempts us with."

Daniel ordered his favorite meal—standing rib roast, a specialty of the house. Caroline and Polly had the baked rainbow trout, and Mary feasted on a serving of mouth-watering roast duck with sautéed mushrooms and asparagus tips. When she finished, she dabbed her mouth with her napkin and sipped the last few ounces of wine from her crystal glass. *This may not be New York City but it's sure a big step above Fish Springs,* Mary thought.

Mary laid her silver across the top of her plate, like she had been taught by Aunt Caroline. Then she smiled, remembering something from her childhood. If she had one end of her silver on the dish and the other end on the table, her mannerly Aunt would admonish her. *Mary your oars are in the water.*

And it was to be expected that Aunt Caroline would be ever hovering over how her niece conducted herself, for she had prided herself in teaching Mary all the social skills befitting a proper young lady. Much of that etiquette Mary learned from books her aunt had ordered, including *The School of Manners, Decency in Conversation Amongst Men, General Rules of Etiquette* and many others. Mary struggled to get through some of this supposedly "instructive" but mind-numbingly dry literature. But she stuck with it, and emerged, her aunt insisted, a more refined lady.

That sort of polishing suited Caroline just fine, for she herself had been brought up in a social setting. The daughter of a well-to-do doctor and a socialite mother, she had been raised as Caroline Bartholomew in Boston. Sheltered and a bit in the dark about matters of romance, she had let her defenses down—had in fact swooned—when Dudley Hamby, her first love, kissed her.

As fate would have it, Dudley turned out to be a roving man in search of an easy dollar, and Caroline would become his bank. They married, and Dudley, on hearing about cheap land in Tennessee, brought his gullible wife to Fish Springs, where they used Caroline's dowry to purchase an 800-acre farm.

Caroline, naïve about love, had been smart about money, so she made sure the farm was in her name. Once she sent Dudley on his way, Caroline sold the farm and bought a small house in town. She feared that her disgraced husband would return to claim a part of her estate, but she breathed easier upon later learning he was gunned down by an enraged father of a fifteen-year-old debutant; the scoundrel had tried to elope with her.

A fittin' demise for the mesogynizin' bastard, Caroline thought.

"More wine, Mary?" Daniel asked.

Mary deferred to her aunt.

"Oh, go ahead child! We're already boozers! We might as well enjoy it."

"Yes please, just a tad," Mary, smiling, said.

Daniel, shaking his head and laughing, poured Mary's glass half full. "That's what I love about you, Caroline. The good Lord gave you strong morals but you've still got a sense of humor."

"Well, it ain't me. It's more like the booze talking."

Polly covered her mouth with her napkin to keep from giggling out loud.

As Daniel, Polly and Caroline bantered, Mary's mind focused on the present moment. She almost had to pinch herself to make sure all this was real. *Here I am in a fine hotel. I've just finished my first meal of roast duck, I've sipped my first glass of wine and I've witnessed a true miracle--seeing that same wine pass between the lips of Aunt Caroline. Only Daniel Smith or Jesus Christ himself could've convinced Aunt Caroline that it's not a sin to have a glass of wine. This is surely a day I'll never forget. I only wish I could've shared it with my beloved John.*

Little did she know that her life was about to change.

CHAPTER 9
Caught at the Black Bear Saloon

"Thank you so much for the lovely dinner, both of you." Aunt Caroline hooked her cape against the early evening chill as they left the Snyder house and headed back into the heart of town.

"Yes, thank you for the wonderful experience of—," Mary began.

"However," Caroline said, lowering her voice, "the wine drinking part had best be kept amongst ourselves."

"Well, I reckon we can agree to that, just as long as we can keep'a doin' it," said a grinning Daniel.

"Hang on Lucifer, I'm a'comin'," said Caroline, looking down from the buggy.

Everyone except the serious Aunt Caroline laughed. Then even she, too, broke out in a giggle.

Daniel reminded them that he needed to be at the courthouse by about four-thirty. "My business'll take 'bout a hour. Do you want to do some more shopping?"

"If it's okay with Polly, I'd like to go back to the General store and look in some pattern books," Caroline said.

Polly agreed that was fine with her, and a few minutes later Daniel pulled to a stop in front of the General Store.

"I'll pick you up here at five-thirty. That'll give us plenty a'time to get back to Fish Springs afore dark," he said. As they listened to him, the three women straightened their long dresses. "Now y'all run along and we'll meet up again directly."

"Aunt Caroline, I'm going to that little dressmaker's shop down on the corner. Okay?"

"Sure sweetheart. Now you try not to get your dress dirty, dear, 'cause this street's a might muddy ta day.

Mary gave her aunt and Polly a curtsey and began walking, on the wood sidewalk, toward the dress shop.

Along her way, two grizzled old men sitting on a bench tipped their hats to her.

"Good afternoon, Miss. You're a purty little thing. Betcha' wouldn't hug an old feller's neck, would ya?"

"Afternoon," said Mary, without breaking stride.

At the corner she gazed at the window of the dressmaker's shop. A long pink dress displayed on a wooden frame caught her attention. *I wonder if John would like that on me. Maybe I should try it on.* Money she inherited from her parents, held in a trust until she turned eighteen, could help her pay for that beautiful garment, she reasoned. *I've just got to have that dress! John'll love it.*

But as Mary started to enter the shop, she noticed a reflection in the window. *That looks like Charger—John's horse. Is he in Elizabethton today? What on earth would he be doing here?*

Turning back, Mary noticed the horse was tied to a hitching post along with others across the street. *Surely there's other big black horses like John's. He told me he wouldn't see me today 'cause he had to go to Butler and bring back two steers, so it can't be his. Now this is plum' crazy, but I've got to be sure.*

She crossed the road and inspected the big black horse. Gripping the saddle and nudging the stirrup to the front, she saw, on the bottom corner of the saddle, the carved initials "J.W."

"It is Charger, but why's he tied up here—next to the Black Bear Saloon?"

She began intuiting the worse, but then reminded herself that John was a man, and sometimes a man, even the best of the gender, gets thirsty. *He's probably just in there having a beer. I guess I can't fault'm for that, after all, I just drank wine … but he said he'd be in Butler and that's in the other direction.*

Her mind churned. She wouldn't be satisfied till she saw for herself what John was up to, but, then again, Mary had never been inside a saloon. She had always heard they were filthy dens of sin, lust and drunkenness. *So do I dare set foot in the Black Bear? And, what if John's in there? What then? Maybe it's best I just get away from this place right now an' leave 'em be.*

Curiosity got the best of her. She slowly opened the door and stepped in. In the dimly lit room there sat John, his back to her at a large round table with Joshua and three other men, holding cards.

A bottle of whiskey and a half empty glass were on the table in front of him. A cheap looking woman in a low cut dress, doubtless a lady of the night, Mary figured, sat at the bar on a stool near John, her glistening eyes, ruby red lips and painted face focused on him.

Mary didn't know anything about poker, but she instantly understood that she had caught John in the midst of some serious gambling.

A man with slicked back hair and a goatee was dealing the last of five cards to the other players, and it seemed that John, judging from the pile of chips in front of him, had already done very well.

Her eyes tearing up, Mary stood in the shadows near the saloon's swinging double doors taking it all in.

John took the last card and put it in his hand. "It's gonna cost ya 'nother dollar to see what I've got," he brazenly said, tossing a silver dollar into the pile of coins in the middle of the table.

"Too rich for me," said the goateed dealer, folding.

"Me too. I fold. I think I'm already hurtin' right smart," said the other.

"I call," said Joshua, putting a dollar in the pot.

John, cracking a smile, laid his cards down face up, revealing three queens and two fives. "Full House," he said, chuckling.

"Damn you, John Williams! You can't lose today!" Joshua yelled.

"It's 'cause my sweetheart's bringin' me good luck. Come here, Madge. Gimme 'nother kiss."

Mary had heard and seen enough and she wanted to leave, but couldn't force herself to do that, just yet. Madge, jumped off the bar stool and planted fervent kisses all over John Williams' face and neck.

And he reveled in her advances. It seemed forever to Mary before he shooed her away.

"Now, Madge, you just calm down and get control of ya'self, 'cause ya know I done made you a happy woman … You do right and we'll take kindly to one 'nother 'agin, but not now."

But Madge wouldn't be deterred. She kept showering him with affection interspersed with complaints that he'd ignored her for too long.

"John, you said we'd go back to the room after that last hand," she whined.

"Hey, let's give the boys a chance to win their money back, babe. We have all night. I'll make you feel like a real woman later—I promise. Now, go back ta the bar and get yourself 'nother drink."

With that brush-off, John raked his winnings toward him and ordered his competitors, blurry eyed from drinking whiskey and feeling cursed that they'd lost so much money, to "ante up."

Mary had taken it all in. She had stood, frozen and unnoticed—she thought—in the dim light, her heart breaking, tears streaming down her cheeks. She began sobbing uncontrollably.

"There's a lady standin' by the door, John, and she ain't a bit happy," one of the players grunted.

"It's Mary, John!" Joshua said.

"Can I help you, Miss?" Madge asked

Mary didn't respond; instead she bolted out the door.

John's glare froze at the entrance. In a matter of minutes, everything he'd hoped, planned and schemed for had just walked out of his life, and there didn't seem to be a damn thing he could do about it.

"Who's Mary, John? You knew her, didn't you? You bastard, you!" Madge screamed.

"Shut your damn mouth, you little tramp!" John said, pushing the saloon woman away.

"Sorry, John," Joshua said.

"It ain't your fault." Then John, feeling emboldened and shaken at the same time, poured his glass to the top with whiskey and chugged it down. "Deal the damn cards!" he demanded, slamming the glass to the table.

Mary fled from the saloon, the back of her skirt dragging through the mud. She ran all the way back to the General store and plopped down on a bench near the front entrance. She must have been a dreadful sight to behold, because a young, handholding couple walking by seemed to take pity on her. The gentleman tipped his hat and asked, "Are you, okay, Miss?"

Mary distraught and weeping, whimpered, "Yes, just leave me be, please."

What she had witnessed back at the saloon tormented her. *Aunt Caroline's been right all along 'bout John. Why didn't I listen to her. Why've I been such a fool?*

Mary sat on that bench, despondent and in anguish. She just wanted to get out of Elizabethton and back to Fish Springs but her Aunt and Polly were nowhere in sight. *How can they be shoppin' so much? I want to leave NOW!*

Within a few minutes, her aunt appeared. "Mary, dear, you don't look so good. And you've gone an' 'pert near ruined your petticoat! Look at yourself!" Caroline scolded. "Here comes Daniel now so you gather your muddy skirts right this minute, young lady, and get up on that buggy!"

On the other hand, Daniel and Polly held their tongues. Mary obviously had been crying; something had upset her and they would let her tell them all about it in due time, the couple reasoned. Besides, Caroline's sharp rebuke of her niece had done nothing but upset her more. Her arms folded tightly, her eyes shut and her shaking finally beginning to subside, Mary sat there suffering in silence in the buggy.

When Daniel asked her if she was okay, she said she just wanted to go home. She pleaded with him to get the buggy moving.

"Sure. Giddyup!" Daniel exhorted to his white carriage horse as they began the journey back to Fish Springs.

This time, a somber Mary paid no heed to those same magnificent mountains, rich river bottomlands, and virgin forest with century-old towering trees and spectacular wildflowers. She kept her head down and her mouth shut. Each jarring hole in the road, each bothersome rock butting against the wheels of the buggy, making the ride rougher, made her wish she'd never gone to Elizabethton in the first place.

About an hour into their ride, while rolling through a dense, overgrown area of the forest, Daniel yelled. "Good Lord! Lookover there!"

To their left, off the road a piece, a pack of red wolves devoured the carcass of a deer. They paid the travelers from Fish Spring no mind, but one of the animals, his long, bushy black tipped tail wagging with excitement and blood dripping from his mouth, barked and howled, causing Millie to neigh and shuffle nervously.

"Easy girl, now ain't that a sight ta behold," Polly observed.

Any other time, Mary would have been amazed at the sighting, but not today.

"There used to be tens a thousands of 'em in these parts, Polly," Daniel said. "They roamed this land like'n they owned it. But the injuns and trappers have 'bout done 'em in.

"They's still a few of 'em left, however, and if you came out here late at night you'd see 'em howlin' at the moon. I think they're some of the wildest, prettiest creatures God ever created."

"And they kill sheep and cattle and chickens," Caroline retorted.

"Maybe so, Aunt Caroline, but I still like 'em. Listen to that howlin'. It's spiritual, like they's aimin' to own the night. I just wish folks wuddn't hunt 'em."

The buggy kept rolling, and the rest of the trip the four tired people said little. But Daniel wondered what had happened to Mary. *She was so happy and full a life and then begged us to get outta town and go back home. Something or somebody back there hurt her, but what or who? Maybe Aunt Caroline'll draw it out.*

And that's what the always curious aunt set about doing later that night when she and her niece sat on their porch swing.

Something's eatin' away at that child and I'm gonna' find out what or who it is, Caroline thought.

"I think I deserve some explainin'. What the devil's wrong, Mary? What happened in Elizabethton?"

At first, Mary held her tongue, but her determined aunt wouldn't settle for continued silence.

"Now you go ahead and spill it right this instant, young lady!"

Her mouth and throat dry, Mary gathered her wits. Then she forced herself to talk. Her story came out slowly and raggedly. "I saw him in the Black Bear Saloon. He was drinking whiskey, gambling, and he was consortin' with a whore! He lied to me, Aunt Caroline! He's been lying to me all along!"

"John Williams?"

"Yes."

"Well, didn't I tell you? I ain't a bit surprised! But why waste your time on him? Alfred'll be home soon. Don't—

"I loved him, Aunt Caroline! I truly loved him!"

"John Williams?"

"Yes. It was John you saw me with in the wheat field that night, Aunt Caroline, not Alfred!" Mary confessed, sobbing.

Stunned but saying nothing, Caroline got up and left her angry, heartbroken niece bawling with her feet up on the swing, her arms wrapped around her legs, her face on her knees.

Not knowing what to do or say, she lingered inside the house for a few minutes but could stand it no more. *Well, the child's made a mistake an' fallen short of the glory of God, but who ain't done that? She's still deservin' a second chance...*

Only a few minutes passed before she wrapped her arms around Mary.

"Now, Mary, you just get over all this right now. You're not the first woman to get fooled. You been lied to and done wrong, but it won't be the last time that happens to you, child. Now you just get ahold of yourself and put all this behind you. I still love you, and I'll help you through this."

Dabbing her eyes with a handkerchief handed to her by Caroline, Mary managed a tiny smile and whispered, "I'm sorry I lied to you, Aunt Caroline."

"I am, too, Mary, but I suppose I had you too scared to tell the truth. Things'll work out. They always do. Just be glad you found out now instead of after you did something really stupid, like marrying that scoundrel."

The two women, both of them now tearful, embraced each other, but their tender moment was interrupted by the unmistakable, night-piercing sound of a trotting horse. They squinted to see John on Charger—hanging to the saddle horn as he approached, swaying from one side to the other.

"Speaka' the devil," Caroline whispered.

"I don't want to see him, Aunt Caroline," Mary said, hurrying into the house.

John, obviously inebriated, stopped and slid unsteadily off Charger, almost falling as he hit the ground. He straightened up and tried to stand without swaying, but had to keep taking steps to stay upright.

"I n-need to see Mary, plee-zz, Aun-car-line," John said, slurring his words.

"She doesn't want to see you, John Williams! Furthermore, you're drunk and I want you to leave right now!"

"I'm not gonna leave till I see Mary. So get'er! O-kay?"

A disgusted Caroline retreated into the house.

"O-kay than-k yoou.

"Yoou see, boy. Yoou hav to be fir … firm with a woman," John said to his horse.

But then he lost the power of speech. The sight of Caroline, brandishing a rifle, angrily cocking the hammer with her right thumb and aiming it at him sent shivers down his spine.

"Now, now, Aun-Car-line, I thought ya', you and me was getting to be good friends. Yooou wouldn't sh-shoot a good friend now, would ya?" John implored her, shielding his face and head with his hands.

"You and me ain't friends, John Williams! Get on your horse and head up the road, now!"

"Now Aun-Car-line."

BAM! Caroline fired a shot a foot to the right of John's boot.

She had definitely gotten his attention.

After two failed attempts to remount Charger, he managed to pull himself up and stormed away, quickly escaping the fury of his attacker..

"No, Aunt Caroline! You didn't shoot him, did you? " Mary hollered. She had run out the front door on hearing the gun shot.

"No, child, I didn't, but I should have for what he done to you! He wronged you!"

Mary hugged her aunt, who put the gun down and escorted her to the swing. "Sit down here with me, dear. I want to talk to you."

"Child, I've raised you like my own. I love you dearly and I only want what's best for you. You and I plainly know that John Williams ain't the man for you. If he talked you into marrying him—and he will try—you'd be doomed to a life of misery. Believe me, I know about the likes of him. You may think you can change him, but men like John Williams never change. Don't waste your life on him! You have too much to offer.

"And I want to remind you that your best friend Alfred'll be home soon. I know, as sure as a wolf howls at the moon, that you care for Alfred. Spend some time with him. You ain't seen him in three years. You may find that you feel differently about him now. I know you had passion for John Williams, Mary, but passion'll fade. Love from a good man grows stronger. Alfred White's a good Christian man, and he'd make you a fine husband. Just take your time. You have your whole life ahead of you."

The two women embraced. Then they held hands.

What on earth would I do without my Aunt Caroline? How could I have lied to her? How could I have been so wrong about John? How does a woman know when a man's telling the truth? What is love, anyway? All night long Mary tried to make sense of what had happened to her till finally she drifted off to sleep.

The next morning after breakfast, Caroline, thinking the best thing for her niece was to be kept busy so she wouldn't sit around moping, sent Mary to pick up some things at the Fish Springs dry goods store.

But as fate would have it, while there she came face to face with the one person she most wanted to avoid.

"I need to talk to you," John said curtly.

"There's nothing you can say! It's over."

"At least hear what I have to say."

"No, please leave!"

Aware that people there were staring at him, John reluctantly left the store.

But Mary, not to be deterred, continued her shopping and didn't leave until she'd bought what her Aunt sent her for—a bag of corn meal, a sack of beans and a jar of molasses.

Mary left the store and walked along the wood sidewalk to the lower end of the scattering of buildings, then along the road where the sidewalk ended. Suddenly she heard a horse whinny behind her.

And there was John in the saddle on Charger.

"You need to hear what I have to say!" he demanded.

But it was to no avail. Mary didn't respond.

"I wanted to treat you like a lady, but men have needs, Mary. That saloon girl doesn't mean a thing to me. I promise you. And that's the first drink of whiskey I've had since I went off to war."

"We all have *needs*, John and it was not about the whiskey. It's about respect and being able to trust each other."

"I'm not perfect!" John angrily declared. "I know that, but I'm not a bad man, Mary. And I'm damn well sure your old aunt's been making up lies about me. You need to stop listenin' to that old bitch."

John's sarcastic comment struck a nerve. She swallowed hard and tried to control her anger, but her words still came out cutting like a knife.

"Aunt Caroline does not lie unlike *some* people I know! And I will never stop listening to her! It's you that's the big fat liar, John Williams!"

"Well, Mary," John shot back, "we could've had a danged good life tagether. We coulda' made each other REAL happy, and you know what I mean by that ... but you're fixin' ta throw it all away. It's yore decision. And remember this, that old bitty of an aunt of yoress is half crazy and she'll run your life just as long as you let her. I heeyerd that Aunt'a yores was such a terrible wife that she lost her husband to a nigger girl."

Mary, red-faced, would have none of his contrition or backtalk. "I have no idea what you're talking about and frankly I don't want'a know! You should go to Hell for the things you've said!"

"Damn' it ta hell," John muttered to himself as he rode away. "I jist cain't get nary a break a'tall in this life."

As Mary continued along, she wondered how she had begun changing. It hadn't been like her to be so outspoken and honest with her feelings, and she'd never in her life tried to hurt anyone. But John had it coming. *I'll have to ask for forgiveness for my hateful language and that outburst of anger. But it sure felt good.*

CHAPTER 10
Alfred's Homecoming

"Don't be melancholy, my dear," Aunt Caroline said. She gave Mary's shoulder a pat as she rose from the porch swing. "Be grateful you found out so quickly. It would have been a true tragedy had you tied yourself to such a scoundrel. Believe me, I know."

"I know you're right, Aunt Caroline," Mary said, turning sideways in the swing and tucking her skirts around her. "I'm trying not to brood, truly I am. But I just don't understand how a man who swore he loved me could be such a liar. And not only did he lie to me, he lied to everybody. And how in God's name could a man lie about being saved? Seems to me that would put you on the steep slope into Hell."

"Give up on him. You can't change a liar, Mary. Excuse my language, but you can't make horse poop smell good and hes one of the stinkinest ones I ever smelt." Aunt Caroline could make you smile even in the worst of times.

"Guess you had it right all along—once a scoundrel, always a scoundrel!"

Typical for early May, a morning rain filled the creeks and rivers around Fish Springs. Then the sun came out and with it a slight breeze that seemed to refresh the little mountain community. Just a few weeks earlier, you couldn't go outside without feeling the sting of the cold wind blustering in from the snowy mountain peaks. Today, however, the breeze caressed and revitalized instead of stung. It felt downright good.

A perfect day for reading and to get John Williams outta my head, Mary thought. Then she took out a book—one that she had discreetly gotten by mail order from a store in Knoxville—and moved to the rocker on the porch.

She didn't dare read *The Secrets of Womanhood* in front of Aunt Caroline or anyone else. *No, this is my private book.*

She stared again at the book's cover. It featured a drawing of a beautiful, bosomy woman, her long frilly skirt pulled up above her knees and her eyes full of excitement, being embraced by a muscular, bare-chested man. The veins in the man's neck seemed to be bulging with passion.

Confident that no one would see her, Mary opened the cover and began reading. The words on page one assured any young woman that the way to a man's heart and soul rested to a great extent with pleasing him physically.

> **You should cultivate an understanding of the mysteries of your own body and realize that any man delights in seeing you in all your natural God-given splendor. That means the two of you—you and your young man—should undress slowly before you put out the candle. Make sure that he sees you unpinning your gown and removing your silky undergarments. You, likewise, should bear bold witness to his stripping off his shirt, britches and underwear. And there, both of you will be—you with your breasts exposed in all their glory, he in his nakedness, his breathing quickened, his manhood swelling, aching for you. But do not let him immediately have his way, entirely, with your body. You should entreat him to touch and squeeze and fondle you tenderly. He will beg to enter you and experience the full, unimaginable pleasures of your warm, welcoming flesh. But you must tease your gentleman. Make him wait to fulfill his raging need. Soon, however, the fires of desire will overtake both you and your man, and the instrument of his manhood will be denied no longer. And you will not want to deny it. You will want him, and he you. … And you will no longer be able to govern his lust. Nor will you want to! This time, you will be doing the begging—for him to satisfy the urgings at the center of your womanhood. …You will let him have his way, he will delight in your wantonness, and you will not be able to get enough of him!**

Mary wiped the beads of perspiration from her forehead, closed the book and took a deep breath. The sultry prose had quickened her heart, and a strange, delicious heat seemed to be welling up in her body. The narrative had been almost more than she could stand, and she felt guilty, even slightly ashamed, for indulging in it. *What would Aunt Caroline think?* But the more she read, the more she wanted to, and the harder it was to put the *The Secrets of Womanhood* down.

Then a bothersome clanging noise, coming from somewhere in the distance, broke her concentration. The more closely she listened, the louder it got—like pots and pans hitting together. She vaguely remembered hearing the sound from months ago. When a peddler's wagon rolled to a stop in front of her aunt's house, that same annoying sound had aroused her from a nap.

And sure enough, when Mary strained her eyes, she spotted him. A short, elderly, gaunt man in a wrinkled brown suit and with a derby tilted to one side of his head at the reins of a peddler's wagon. *Can't a woman ever find time to read?* Mary thought, hastening to conceal her sensuous book as the cluttered wagon—the sign on it boldly proclaiming JOE'S SKILLETS—clattered to a stop in front of the house.

"Good afternoon, Miss." The little man tipped his derby and smiled.

"Afternoon," Mary replied, trying to hide her irritation.

"Might you need a fine cast iron skillet, Miss?"

"No, thank you," Mary replied curtly.

"Well then, would you be interested in a worn out Union soldier by the name of Alfred?"

Mary gasped with joy at the sight of Alfred, dressed in his Union uniform, climbing off the other side of the wagon with a cloth travel bag.

"Oh yes!" she squealed. "That, I would be interested in!"

Alfred—exhausted, wounded and limping with a cane—fixed his eyes on his beloved. *Can it actually be her? God, she's more beautiful than ever!*

Mary dashed down the steps and hurled herself into his waiting arms. It had been years since they'd last seen or touched each other, but it didn't matter. Nothing—not a war, not another suitor, not even a lingering bullet wound—could now keep them apart.

He wrapped his arms around her and clung to her tightly—he never wanted to let go of her. He could feel the full length of her body crushed up against his. It aroused and tantalized and made him want to hug her more closely. He had dreamed about her *And now, I have her in my arms!* But Alfred restrained himself. *Mary needs time to get to know me again. I have to be patient.*

"I missed you, Mary," Alfred said.

"Oh, my dear Alfred! Do you know how much I've missed you?" Mary clasped his hands and looked him up and down. "You've been hurt worse than you let on. You're limping,"

When he assured her that his leg would get stronger every day, Mary smiled. Deep down, however, she suspected that Alfred suffered more than he admitted.

"Thank you for the ride, Joe!" Alfred hollered to the itinerant peddler, who had delighted in bearing witness to so much happiness.

"Youuns is welcome, young man! And you and that young lady have a good life and go about enjoyin' yourselves as much as ya can! 'Cause you're both mighty lucky to have one another. As the good Lord says, cain't no man be nothin' iffen' he ain't got a good woman!" Joe snapped the reins and headed toward the center of town, where he'd spend the rest of the day peddling his wares.

Alfred wondered if the Bible truly did say anything about a man not amounting to much unless he attached himself to the right woman. He had read the Good Book a lot at the field hospital, and even before that during long, dreadful nights while camped with his unit, and never had run across such a verse. But now that he thought about it, what the peddler had said made total sense to him. Mary would complete him—make him whole and make life more fulfilling.

"You know, Mary, I've been thinking about this day for a long time. And I kept prayin' that it would happen, and now here we are. You're even prettier now than when I left for the war!"

"And Alfred, you're handsomer than ever!"

After the two had professed their mutual love again and again, and worn themselves out with hugs, talk turned to Aunt Caroline. Mary assured Alfred that her aunt was doing just fine, and that while she was napping, it would be a perfect time for a cup of tea.

"Now just sit yourself right down on that porch swing, Alfred, and I'll fetch us the tea. I made it this morning."

Alfred smiled, but then, when Mary left and he eased himself into the swing, he repressed a grimace. Something, the more he mulled it over, just didn't seem right, or maybe things seemed too good to be true. *Did she miss me as badly as I missed her. And what about John Williams? Did he make it back, and if so, is he courting Mary? I wouldn't trust him as far as I could throw a horse.*

But be that as it may, Alfred reminded himself that John, for all his orneriness and shortcomings, had once been his friend. It had always been an uneasy, awkward friendship—from their early days as rambunctious boys playing in the woods or canoeing down the river. But they had nevertheless been close, and he'd never wish John any harm, regardless of what the future would hold—or not hold—between Mary and himself.

Still, however, Alfred worried. There was just something about him—some quality that Alfred DIDN'T have—that drew women to John. For if he set his mind to it, John always got what he wanted with the fairer gender. Women for some unexplainable reason found Alfred's adversary handsome and interesting. They even seemed, oddly enough, to be drawn to his wildness, unpredictability and brazenness.

Whatever happened to being courtly and a gentleman? Alfred wondered. *And you'd think that a woman could get past a man's physical appearance ... I know Mary's always thought of John as handsome, but surely she knows I'd be the better husband. She knows I'd have more to offer her. Or does she?*

When Mary returned with the sweet tea, Alfred was staring numbly out at the mountains. She sensed he had something on his mind but did not question him.

"This is really good sweet tea, Mary."

"Ain't nothin', Alfred. Aunt Caroline showed me the secret to brewing it. … Now, tell me, how far'd you ride with that peddler."

"Just from Elizabethton. Joe drove his horse and wagon from farm to farm, so it took a while for us to get here, but it all worked out. Before that, I caught a train from Richmond to Johnson's Depot. Then I rode on a farmer's wagon to Elizabethton."

"Well, I'm glad you made it back home to Fish Springs," Mary said, sipping her tea. "So many didn't and some that did came back with limbs missing. The stories we heard …The carnage … Oh, it was all so horrible! I understand, Alfred, if you never, ever want to talk about the war. Maybe some things are best left unsaid."

Alfred thought about the grisly pile of limbs at the field hospital. He remembered the sawed bones and flesh … the screams on the operating table where legs and arms were separated from human torsos. A wave of nausea swept over him.

"Alfred, you all right? You don't look so good."

He pretended not to hear her question. Then he got hold of himself and changed the subject.

"So what's happening around Fish Springs? John Williams make it back from the war?"

"Yes, he's back and just as ornery as ever," said Mary. "But right now, I'd rather not talk about him. Let's just talk about something else."

"Ok—how are the Smiths?"

"They're fine. They worried somethin' awful about you, though, when I told 'em you'd been shot. They made sure you got put on the prayer list at church."

"They're mighty good people, Mary. And just knowing Daniel Smith was watchin' over you an' Aunt Caroline meant the world to me. God made two angels in Daniel and Polly Smith."

Mary appeared to be in deep thought, her eyes locked onto his.

"What is it, Mary? Tell me." Then he noticed a big tear running down her cheek.

"Mary, are you all right?"

"I'm just so happy you're safe and home that I don't know what to do. I feel like I'm the most blessed woman in Tennessee!"

Maybe I DO have a chance with this woman, Alfred thought, hugging her closely. *And glory be, she's hardly mentioned John. Maybe he's history…*

In the months that followed Alfred gradually became able to shed his cane. He still walked with a slight limp, but otherwise he had no visible injuries. He had been one of the lucky ones. So many of Fish Springs' war veterans were amputees, or they had lost their eyesight or hearing, even their memory from the trauma of what they'd had to suffer. The limp, it seemed to Alfred, was a reminder from God—and the war—of what he had gone through. *And I can still be the man Mary needs and deserves. I can make her feel like a woman, and she can make me a whole man—limp or no limp, if she will only have me.*

He would show her how hard he could work. But he had come home too late in the year to prepare his farm for the growing season. So when he wasn't making repairs on his old log house or the barn, he spent time with Mary. Through the fall and winter, the couple had become inseparable, and Mary's love for Alfred intensified every day. They would take long walks in the woods, and sometimes Mary would prepare a picnic basket. Always, she had a tasty treat for him in that basket. If it wasn't her irresistible blackberry pie, it was her delicious chocolate cake. Alfred got so he couldn't wait to see what she would surprise him with from her kitchen.

On Christmas Eve night, in front of a fire after Aunt Caroline had gone to bed, their chairs pulled close and their knees touching, Alfred could wait no longer. "Mary, I love you more than words can say. Will you marry me?"

"What took you so long?"

At that moment, Alfred was ecstatic.

"Yes, Alfred, I'd be honored to be your wife—till death do us part. You know that!"

Alfred stood up pulling Mary to her feet and wrapping his arms around her, pulling her warm, slender body to his. They kissed passionately for several minutes. He held her so close that he could fill the sinuous place of her slender shape with the swell of his own. He had never wanted her more than now.

Mary kissed him longingly, then leaned back. "Alfred, you know I love you and I want you as badly as you want me, but can we please wait? It's a promise I made to myself and to God."

When Alfred said he'd do or honor whatever made her happy, she kissed him again— even more passionately, and it was all she could do to keep her promise. That night they made plans for a June wedding. They also talked about children. Mary confided in him that she'd always dreamed of having a large family.

"Is that all right with you, Alfred? Can we have lots of children?"

"Just as many as you want, Mary. And when you have enough, just holler stop," Alfred, chuckling, said. Then they both burst out laughing.

Mary put her fingers to her lips and whispered into his ear. "Let's not wake Aunt Caroline because she'll make me go to bed."

Alfred, glancing out the window, noticed, for the first time that night that snow was falling. "Look Mary, it's snowing."

"Isn't it beautiful Alfred? Look how hard it's coming down."

"My father once told me if the snow was heavy and fell straight down from the sky you were in for a deep blanket of the white stuff. It could be as much as two feet or more.

"Looks like I'm gonna be treading home through a lot of snow."

While Alfred was looking out the window, Mary turned and disappeared into the darkness. Then his bride-to-be returned with two pillows and two thick quilts. She placed them on the floor by the fire.

"I'm not lettin' you go out in this weather. You're stayin' here tonight."

"Yes, ma'am," Alfred replied, grinning.

They lay down on the floor, their heads on the pillows, their bodies between the quilts. Then they turned on their side and Alfred wrapped his arms around Mary. Like two spoons pressed together, they snuggled in the warmth of the fire.

Mary felt perfectly content and happier than ever. *I wish I could just freeze this moment in time. This is the way life's supposed to be. God wants us to be happy—to enjoy each other. And, you know what? Aunt Caroline was right all along. I want to marry Alfred and have his babies and keep him happy till I die. How'd she know he was the man for me?*

CHAPTER 11

The Wedding

They had prayed for a picture perfect wedding day and they got it that Saturday in early June. The cloudless blue sky and a big yellow sun, made even more pleasant with a cool mountain breeze, put everyone in an joyous mood. All of Fish Springs seemed to be smiling for Mary and Alfred's special day. And the turnout for the wedding couldn't have been better. In Fish Springs when someone got married everyone was invited, and almost everyone came. There was no need to send out invitations. Women decorated the church and brought covered dishes for the reception, which would be held in the church yard.

Mary and Alfred stood in front of Reverend Ike Redford as the packed church listened to the wedding vows. Mary was stunning in her blue dress that had been especially created for her by the dressmaker in Elizabethton. With the dress accentuating her womanly curves, and with just a hint of tempting cleavage peeking out from her top, Mary turned heads when she entered the sanctuary. Alfred, too, was quite handsome. He wore a dark suit with a gray vest and a white tie. *How could I not love and adore this man?* Mary thought. *What woman wouldn't want to have a gentleman like him as a husband—to make beautiful babies with him?*

"Mary, do you take Alfred to be your husband?" Reverend Redford asked. "Do you promise to stay by his side in sickness and in health, for richer or poorer…"

"I do."

"Alfred, do you take Mary to be your beloved wife?...To keep her as your wife 'till death do you part? To always love, honor and cherish her…?"

"I do."

The ceremony had been short and simple—exactly what they wanted. And the congregation applauded heartily when the happy couple were pronounced man and wife. The applause in the little white frame church grew louder when the bride and groom kissed and hugged.

One old man in the back of the church elbowed his wife of 50-plus years. "Takes me back to when you and me tied the knot, Maggie," he whispered. "And I ain't gonna ever forgit our weddin' night. Why, you wuz rarin' to go… You plum wore me out."

"Shut up, you ole coot," his wife, holding two fingers to her lips, sternly said. "You and me wuz just foolish younguns way back then."

"Maybe so," he said. "But we wuz somethin' wild and rompin' on our weddin' night."

"I said shut up," she shushed him.

Caroline confided in Daniel's wife at the reception. "Polly, I honestly think Mary avoided a lot of misery when she ran John Williams off."

"I'd say that's the God-fearin' truth. And you didn't help her, did you?" a slightly smiling Polly said.

With that, the two of them burst out laughing.

But Polly's eyes suddenly got big and she gasped, "Oh my God!"

"Wha … what's wrong?" Caroline asked.

Then she saw what had so alarmed Polly.

It was John Williams, cool as you please, matter-of-factly tying his horse to a hitching post at the road. Others at the reception began stirring uneasily. The community knew full well about the bad blood between Alfred and John. As John walked slowly across the church yard, looking for Alfred and Mary, he nodded to people that lived in and around the community. Men he had fought beside and men he had fought against, in the war, acted like they were the best of friends.

But John knew better. *How could' a man pretend ta be friends with a lowdown Yankee bastard that just tried to kill'em. It makes no sense.*

Only a few spoke to John and some even turned away as he passed.

"Ignore that low life, Luther. He'ins got no business b'in here," said a wrinkled-faced, grudge-holding little woman to her husband.

Prodded by their nervous wives, two men approached John to try and stop him from coming any closer after he spotted the newly weds, but they were held back by Daniel Smith. "Hold up a minute fellows; don't assume too much."

When the men, despite the entreaties of their wives, backed off, John tipped his hat to Daniel, thanking him, and continued walking toward Alfred and Mary.

"Mary, I wish you all the happiness you deserve," John said, tipping his hat.

When Mary thanked him and shook his hand, John turned his eyes to Alfred.

The two former competitive suitors shook hands and smiled uneasily at each other. For several seconds, neither said anything. Then John spoke.

"Alfred, I know we didn't agree 'bout the war, and I know we both wuz trying to git Mary, but I reckon the best man won. She'll make ya' a wonnerful wife. And I 'gratulate ya' and wish you'n her all tha happiness in tha world."

Seemingly at a loss for words, except for an awkward "Thank you," Alfred extended his hand again to John who this time shook it even more vigorously.

Then, John, seemingly satisfied he had accomplished what he set out to do, waved to the crowd, mounted up and rode away.

"Now there goes a changed man. He done lost the most precious thang in the world to him and he's 'cepted hit and'll make the best of hit," one woman, shading her eyes from the bright sun, told her husband.

"We ain't seen tha last'a John Williams," he snapped. "You jist mark my words ... I knew his daddy an' his daddy's daddy, and they's bad blood runnin' through that fam'lee."

Once John was out of sight of the wedding reception, he slowed his horse down to an easy amble. It had always seemed to him that with Charger in such a gait, he did his best deep thinking. And reflecting on it now, he couldn't help but remember all the smiles, back patting and hugging at the reception. He'd been there only for a few minutes, but it was enough to take in how polite, happy, kind and friendly folks had SEEMED to be to one another.

John reminded himself, however, that he knew better. For some of those very same, outwardly joyous, Christian well wishers fought their own demons. John knew that not everything and everybody in Fish Springs was as wonderful and content as met the eye.

Why they ain't no better'n me, he concluded. *And some of 'em's shorely worse.*

John recollected that Jacob Jenkins, one of the wedding reception revelers, had punched his wife, Ramona, so severely when they'd argued over money that she'd suffered a skull fracture. It was common knowledge around Fish Springs that Ramona Jenkins, a faithful churchgoer and mother of the couple's three children, had almost died. But there, at the celebration for Alfred and Mary, they had been—smiling and outwardly acting very much like a happily married couple.

And John had also noticed Russell Johnson, a deacon and Sunday School teacher at Fish Springs Baptist Church. All that worshipping and praying hadn't stopped the always suspicious and jealous Russell from threatening to shoot his wife Ruth for hanging out a nightgown with lace trim on the clothes line. Russell, who a few weeks ago at the feed store had sneered angrily at John when the latter cast a lecherous glance at his wife, never took kindly to her public airing of that which hugged most closely to her naked skin; the always on-the-lookout Russell took that as a sign of a wayward woman. He didn't believe his wife for one minute when she swore otherwise. But there at the reception, Russell and Ruth had been—laughing, and making merry to their hearts content, as if they'd never had a cross word with one another.

The shapely and beautiful Millie Rogers and muscular and handsome Ben Cox also stood out to John at the reception. They were both married, but not to each other, and they'd been caught red-handed, only partially clothed and in a compromising position, on a picnic blanket in a thick patch of woods just outside of town. That little embarrassing escapade had been, for a few weeks, the raging talk of the community, but Millie had nevertheless stayed married, as did Ben. There they had been at the wedding reception—Ben in his fancy, dancy suit and Millie flaunting herself in a low-cut print dress—chit chatting and circulating, with their own spouses, through the crowd—as if the blanket episode had never happened. And unbeknownst to the roaming couple, John had entertained his drinking buddies at the Black Bear Saloon with the story of their escapades.

They's lots 'a folks puttin' on airs in Fish Springs and actin' awful purty, but deep down, they's slinkin' 'round an' sinnin' atryin' ta git what they can git, John surmised.

The more he mulled about all that hypocrisy, and the way he was shunned by some at the reception, the angrier John became. It seemed everybody was against him, and the supposed do-gooders themselves had no business judging him. But that's what they seemed to be up to, and, the more he thought about it, the more John Williams despised it.

To let off steam, he put his horse in a full run, viciously whipping Charger's flank with the end of the long reigns and hollering a stream of profanity—all directed against Caroline and Alfred and all the other do-gooders.

"I'd be marryin' Mary taday if that damn old bitch Caroline had stayed outta it! It was her fault, tha old, mizzerable hag!"

Back at the reception, people continued having a good time. Mary was an even happier—and relieved—bride now that John had accepted her wishes and had publicly made amends with Alfred. Even if John had some lingering jealousy he kept to himself, Mary could live with that as long as he didn't try to ever again come between Alfred and her. Still, she vowed to say a prayer for

John that night. She would ask the Lord to send an angel to protect John, not as her past or future lover, but as a troubled, saddened, defeated human being who needed all the divine help he could get.

She put such thoughts aside when Daniel, Polly, their two boys and their daughter, Izzy came up to Alfred and her and congratulated them. Her hug with little Izzy lasted the longest because Mary had a special fondness for her. One day, she hoped to have a daughter of her own, and, if that happened, she wished she could be just like eight-year-old Izzy—happy, curious, rambunctious and smart. The blue-eyed, pigtailed Izzy, a picture of innocence and sweetness, was at that stage in her life when she wondered about everything and everybody. Some grownups became annoyed with all her questions and exploring, but not Mary. She thought of it as perfectly normal and cute.

When Polly told Mary she made a beautiful bride, Izzy, not to be outdone, gushed about how much she loved Mary's dress. And, indeed, Mary's beautiful blue dress with its delicate lacy trim accentuated her natural beauty. She had also pinned in her hair a rare Gray's Lily that a friend had brought her from Roan Mountain, one of the few places they grew, and a wreath of roses encircled her waist.

"I want a purty dress like Mary's when I get married, Mama."

"When're you gettin' married, Izzy?" Mary, smiling, asked the little girl.

"Maybe when I'm sixteen."

"Let's make that twenty-six!" Daniel said with a laugh.

Meanwhile, all around them, the wedding celebration continued—even as daylight began to fade. It was as if folks at Fish Springs had been bottled up all winter and spring and craved having a good time. Some of them couldn't get enough of the fun. Eligible single men, a few of them still nursing their war wounds, did their best to be charming. Single women, seeking affection and romantic love, sized them all up as potential suitors. Some of these men and women, "found each other and it won't be long afor they rush ta the altar," one grandma at the reception predicted.

Even Daniel's handsome son, sixteen-year-old Charlie, came under scrutiny by the younger teenage girls who competed for his attention by flirting and flaunting their natural attributes. But Charlie seemed more interested in jawboning to his buddies about fishing and hunting and such.

A few newly matched couples were noticed walking closely, arm in arm as they called it a day and began, reluctantly, to bid each other farewell. Some single women, who'd lost their husbands to the war, became envious and emotional when they realized that without a partner, their lives would never be as fulfilling. They had known that emptiness for some time, but seeing all the happiness at the wedding reception just drove home the sad reality even more.

As the mandolin music began to wind down, Alfred addressed Daniel. "Mr. Smith ..."

"Call me Daniel."

"Okay, Daniel. I want to thank you for tendin' to Mary and Aunt Caroline while I was away, and I appreciate what the other church members did, too."

Daniel responded that he'd relay the thanks. Then, he assured Alfred that all he and others in the church had done was precious little compared to the years of service Alfred had sacrificed for his country.

After a few minutes of small talk about the wedding, Polly looked up at the sky, causing Daniel to follow suit.

"Well, we best start home, folks, 'Cause it looks like some dark clouds'er movin' in," said Daniel. "It was a beautiful weddin',"

"Yes, it was," Polly added. "We love you both, dear hearts; see you in church."

"Bye, Miss Mary," said Izzy.

"Bye, Izzy. You come and see me."

That evening, a roaring wind with hail pounded the wood shingled roof of Alfred's farmhouse. Mary and Alfred had arrived there around dark, and they feared that the hail would break their windows or that the roof would be blown off. But the sturdy log cabin, built by Alfred's father and two uncles when Alfred's father and mother were married 27 years earlier, held its own. Constructed of hand hewn chestnut logs, dovetail notched and chinked with clay, the cabin had withstood many a ferocious killer storm. Even when a tornado, a rarity in this part of mountainous Tennessee, struck Fish Springs, the log cabin had stood as a lonely sentinel of shelter and as a lasting testament to what man could build if he really set his mind to it.

And not that it was that big or impressive. Compared to some of the fine homes in Elizabethton, for example, the cabin struck the casual passer-by as not much more than a place to lay your head.

But with one large room opening up to a kitchen and a fireplace and two small bedrooms, it was more than sufficient for Mary and Alfred. The dwelling also had a big porch on the front and a small one on the back—perfect for catching up on your reading on a sunny day or for enjoying yourself in a rocking chair. Alfred's father had added a wood burning cast iron stove for heat and a cookstove in the kitchen.

As the storm thrashed against the farmhouse, Mary lay excitedly in a featherbed, a sheet the only covering for her body. Clad in a brightly colored robe Aunt Caroline had given him as a wedding gift, Alfred sat nervously on the side of the bed.

"Alfred, I would love for you to touch me. I know we've both been wantin' this and waitin' for a long time. Please put your hands on me, but be gentle," said Mary, thinking her shy, fidgety husband might need a little encouragement.

"Just give me a few seconds, Mary," he said.

Startled by his reticence, she pulled the sheet back up over her body and tried to make sense of what was happening. *Maybe he's just afraid he'll hurt me, or that he won't make me happy,* she thought. *After all, men can be strange.*

"Alfred, darling, was there something you wanted to ask me before we make love."

Still in his robe, Alfred tried to collect himself. And then, try as he might, he just couldn't get John Williams out of his mind. For he had long felt in his bones, and couldn't seem to get past the suspicion, that Mary had lost her virginity to John.

Damned that persistent John Williams! Even when he ain't here, he's here and he's left his mark on my Mary, and she ain't never gettin' over'm. But I can't change that, and after all, I'm not lily white myself cause I've had my share'a willin' young gals when I was away at college.

"Alfred? You all right? Talk to me, Alfred."

He looked her straight in the eye and held her hands. "You know, Mary, when you love someone with all your heart, the physical part don't matter so much. And there's some folks that even believe sex ends up making it hard to know your real feelings. Well, I don't know about that, but I do know this. There's nothing in this whole world that you could do or tell me that would lessen the love I feel for you tonight and for the rest of my life. I want you to be my lifetime partner, Mary.

"And I think we both know we've done things that are best forgotten," Alfred added to his wife—now sitting up in the bed and clutching the sheet to her neck. "We've all sinned in the eyes of the Lord, but tonight we're new and pure to each other and that's all that matters."

"That's the way I feel, too, Alfred."

"Now I know, Mary Clemmons, you're gonna make me a Godly wife and I promise you, as God is my witness, I'll live up to my end of the bargain. I want to be with you forever."

Alfred took Mary's hand and put it to his lips. "On the very first day I saw you, being pulled along by your Aunt Caroline, I knew I wanted you in my life. I was sixteen years old and you were only thirteen, and if a boy could be prosecuted for his thoughts, I'd still be in a dungeon.

"But I didn't think of you in a bad or unchaste way. I promise you that, Mary. I just dreamed of loving you and being loved by you. And the older you got—and you getting' even more beautiful and all—I couldn't help but love you even more. And today, this is how I always dreamed and hoped it would turn out. With us being together for once and for all … and with me loving you 'till the day I die. Even if you upped and left me right now for another man, and I pray that never happens, I'd love you forever. I'd give my life for you, Mary."

Mary didn't know what to say. *Is he saying that if I got dressed right now, left this bed and went straight to John Williams, he'd still be my husband? Men can be so strange!*

"Is there anything you want to say to me, Mary?"

"Alfred, I think you already know how I feel. What you just said makes me love you even more, if that's possible. You're God's gift to me and I'll make you a good wife and a happy man and give you all the babies you and I want. What else can I say?"

"I thank you've said all you need to say, my love."

"Now, Alfred, I really want you to—"

Alfred kissed his new wife tenderly. "I love you, Mary White."

Alfred loosened his robe, let it fall from his nakedness to his feet and pulled back the sheet. His heart pounded, and his loins rose to the occasion when he saw Mary's beautiful, panting body. She was ready. She desperately wanted him, and he her. Nothing— not John Williams or anyone or anything else, and definitely not a summer storm—would impede their lovemaking. Alfred at first gently lay on his new wife and slowly made sweet, passionate love to her, being careful not to hurt her or do what she didn't want him to do. In just a few minutes, however, their lovemaking became wilder, more uncontrollable, more raucous and infinitely more pleasurable. While the rain pounded and thunder echoed through the mountains, Mary and Alfred took each other's bodies to places they'd never been. Then they slept deeply in each other's arms until the wee hours of the morning when they awoke and made love hungrily again. It was a night of romance, whispering and unabashedly exploring their most intimate, physical selves. And it was a night that neither of them would forget for the rest of their lives.

The next morning, feeling thoroughly rested and not the least big guilty for indulging herself so deeply and lovingly with Alfred, Mary awoke to the delicious smell of bacon frying in the kitchen. She slipped on her robe and strolled up behind Alfred, who was dressed but barefooted. She wrapped her arms around him below his waist and felt her husband becoming aroused as she fondled him sensuously.

"Mm … I'll try to finish cookin' your breakfast before I respond ta that gesture," said Alfred.

"I guess you're right. We do need to eat, don't we?" said Mary, reluctant to stop, but sitting down at the kitchen table.

"You made me a very happy man yesterday and last night, Mary. Matter'a fact, I'm the happiest and luckiest fella' in Fish Springs!"

"You know who else I made happy?" Mary asked.

"Who?"

"Aunt Caroline. She really loves you, Alfred."

"Well, I love her too. She's a sweet lady."

"I'm a little concerned about her, though," Mary said. "Th' other day I had ta lift a bag of potatoes ta th' table for her. That's not usual for Aunt Caroline. She's always been strong as an ox, but I'm afraid she's losin' her strength. I guess that's ta be expected. She'll be eighty years old this November."

Then Alfred and Mary agreed that being seventy-nine and living alone was risky. They pledged to check on Aunt Caroline every day.

For the rest of summer and into the fall, they adjusted to married life. Mary soon learned that Alfred had a strong work ethic. Through the growing and harvesting season, he worked the farm from sun-up to sundown, every day but Sunday, when they would pick up Aunt Caroline and go to church.

Alfred also realized he had a hard working wife—not afraid to break a sweat or get her hands dirty. Mary fed the livestock, gathered the eggs and tended the garden, and that was after preparing breakfast and before house cleaning, lunch and supper. Alfred and Mary checked on Aunt Caroline every night, walking the half-mile to her house, using a lantern to light the path, except when they found their way by the light of the moon.

Mary loved the long walks especially on warm, starry nights filled with the fragrant pines and spruces in the mountain air, the night noises of tree frogs and crickets, the barking of little foxes and every once in a while the howl of a red wolf. As they walked, they shared childhood stories, their dreams, their fears, even their most intimate thoughts.

Often, Mary would bring children into the conversation, her desire to be a mother and her concern about not being pregnant yet. Alfred always assured her that it would happen soon enough. "When the Lord thinks we're ready, he'll give us a baby," Alfred said time and again.

But he also had a lingering fear. *What if I can't father children? After all, that army doctor told me I might not be able to because of my injury.*

One balmy summer evening, Alfred arrived home from working his crops to the smell of chicken frying in a skillet. After putting his workhorse in the barn lot, filling a trough with hay and another with cool spring water, he pushed his tired body toward the cabin. Once inside the back door, he knew instantly that dinner would be a treat.

He hugged and kissed Mary as she took sizzling, golden-crusted chicken from a frying pan with a long pronged fork and placed it on a platter.

"Hi, sweetheart! Your fried chicken smells wonderful!"

"It's ready now, so wash up," said Mary, pushing him gently away.

"You're the boss, woman. You tell me anything and I'll do it."

Alfred then poured water from the blue enamelware pitcher, given to them as a wedding gift by Aunt Caroline, into a washbowl and cleaned his hands and face. And his wife took a pie from the oven out to the back porch railing to cool.

"I love fried chicken," said Alfred, drying off and sitting down at the table. He attacked the big, crusty breast with a knife and fork, but Mary grabbed his hand.

"Aren't you forgettin' to return thanks to tha Lord?"

"Lord almighty, forgive me for not sayin' the blessing, but we're truly thankful for this meal and for all the blessins' and bounty you've provided us taday," said Alfred, his head bowed. "And forgive us our sins, as we forgive those who sin against us. Amen."

With that ritual out of the way, the happy couple set about devouring a delicious meal of fried chicken, mashed potatoes and gravy, green beans, tomatoes and biscuits.

"Here's your honey, Alfred. Just got it taday from ole man Miller who's got all those bee hives down by the river. He gave me a quart jar for nothin'. Called it a weddin' present. Said his honeybees is plum tired out from makin' honey all summer and 'bout done with their work for 'nother season. Said, too, we'd better squirrel away all the food we can 'cause ole man winter's gonna be somethin' fierce this year."

"That so?" Alfred, his mouth full of food, said. "But isn't that Miller man kind'a quare?"

Mary only shrugged and noted that Miller had also said that he had to be twice as vigilant in recent weeks to keep the deer and bears out of his crops—even standing guard at night with a shotgun over his corn, beans and tomatoes.

As Alfred piled another helping of mashed potatoes and gravy on his plate, Mary cautioned him to save room for dessert. "I made you something special for your sweet tooth."

"What?"

"You'll see."

"You made me a pie didn't you?" said Alfred, reaching for a chicken leg and noticing his wife's mischievous smile. *Mary's always givin' me the best surprises!*

As the couple talked about their day and finished supper, unbeknownst to them, things were happening out back. A huge female black bear stood at the edge of the woods behind the cabin. She sniffed, holding her head high, catching the aroma of Mary's blackberry pie cooling on the porch railing. She huffed and her two cubs scurried up a nearby pine tree as she cautiously lumbered toward the back porch.

"Are you finally ready for your dessert?" Mary asked as she got up from the table, took off her blue print apron and headed toward the back door to get her blackberry treat.

"I'm always ready for one of your pies! You know that!"

But no sooner had he told her that—and thought again about how fortunate he was to have such a beautiful, loving wife who also happened to be a wonderful cook—than Mary let out a piercing scream.

"You bring that right back here! Now! You put that down!"

Alfred ran to the back door and looked out. To his amazement, there stood his wife—angrily shaking her fist and demanding that the mother bear give her pie back.

"You put my pie down and get out of here!"

Mary stopped about twenty feet from the bear but kept fussing.

"For God sake, Mary, come back!" Alfred hollered as he ran to put himself between his beloved wife and the bear. "She'll eat ya' alive! Let 'er have the danged pie!" Alfred grabbed Mary by the arm and pulled her toward the house.

But Mary wouldn't be deterred. She kept shaking her fist at the bear and pulled against Alfred to get closer to the large menacing animal.

"Mary! The pie ain't worth it! Git'way from 'er!"

Bear and woman stared at each other for several seconds. And then, to Alfred's horror, the bear dropped the pie and charged toward Mary, who hightailed it and ran screaming—past Alfred and onto the porch before gazing back.

Alfred knew from experience that you had to stand your ground. No human could outrun a bear. To try could be a fatal mistake, so Alfred stood firm—raising his hands above his head to make himself look more formidable. The big, ferocious, furry animal stopped about eight feet short from where Alfred held his ground, growled loudly, then did an about-face and went back to her pie. Alfred, his heart pounding and sweat dripping down from his forehead and nose, backed away slowly to the porch, then pulled Mary inside the cabin, shutting the door. He took a deep—I'm glad we're still alive—breath and faced Mary. She was crying.

"I'm sorry Alfred. I know I put us in danger. But I worked all morning long on that pie! I even picked the blackberries so I could make it for you. I knew it was your favorite . . . ," Mary said, bawling and wringing her hands.

"You can't take food from a bear, Mary."

"But it was our food!"

"It became hers when she took it. And she would kill you if you tried to take it back." Alfred put his arms around his wife.

"Promise me, Mary. You'll never try to take food away from a bear, again."

"I promise, Alfred."

He peered out a back window of the cabin to see if the big bear had left. "Come here, Mary. Have a peek."

There, near the edge of the woods, were two playful little bear cubs with their faces buried in Mary's blackberry pie. Their mother watched over them.

"Guess I was tryin' to take food away from'er babies. That'd make me mad, too," said Mary, smiling. "Guess I don't blame'er one bit."

With that, man and wife put their arms around each other, gazed into each other's eyes and headed back to the kitchen.

"Do we have to do the dishes just this minute?" Mary, a twinkle in her eyes, asked. "I myself am a little tired from all that excitement with the bear. Besides, we don't have any dessert to eat. Wonder what we can do?"

Alfred, grinning, held her hand and led her to the bedroom.

The dishes didn't get done 'till the next morning.

And that typified the rhythm of their marriage in their first few months together. Dinner most every night would be followed by a bath, followed by making love before a night of deep slumber.

However, things eventually began to change. Mary at first thought she was just imagining that Alfred's desire was waning. But then she became mildly alarmed when several days would pass before sexual hunger pulled them back to the bed. Alfred seemed fine with this arrangement, and Mary tried to convince herself that she, too, could live with it—to an extent. For she fully knew it took more than a sexual bond to keep a marriage alive and vibrant. But then again, she also thought, why should she, of all women, be deprived of one of life's most ecstatic pleasures? She had friends who were newly weds and had been told it was nothing at all for husband and wife to make love at least once every other day, and even twice daily or nightly, if that's what the couple mutually desired.

And then there was the matter of becoming pregnant. It weighed more and more heavily on Mary's mind as she and Alfred's sex life grew colder.

Mary even turned to instigating more lovemaking, prodding and tempting Alfred any way she could to be a man in bed. But very little that she did in this regard seemed to be working. In fact, her becoming the instigator had seemed to have the effect of making Alfred feel pressured to get Mary pregnant. It was as if, from Alfred's perspective, he felt more like he was providing a service, rather than making love to his wife.

Then on a cool, rainy Sunday night, perfect for lovemaking, a scantily clad Mary flirted and teased with Alfred until he willingly followed her into the bedroom and lay down beside her in the feather bed. But even though he desired her mightily, he could not perform. Embarrassed and frustrated, he sat on the bed holding his wife's hand.

"I'm sorry, Mary. I failed to fulfill you. I feel terrible."

"You shouldn't feel bad about it, Alfred. I'm sure this has happened to most men. Besides, what's one little night? We have the rest of our lives together."

But in the weeks that followed, it seemed the harder Alfred tried, the worse it was. Nothing seemed to be working, in a sexual way, from his waist down.

Finally, he decided that in time the problem would probably correct itself. Perhaps in a week or two, he'd try again.

Judging from what she said and her behavior, Mary couldn't have been more patient and sympathetic of Alfred's problem. She tried not to pressure him, but at the same time she worried. It was bad enough to be missing out on having sex but her greatest fear was that she might never have a child.

Through the fall and into winter, a more idle time after the growing season, Alfred and Mary had an otherwise normal life. Alfred kept himself busy doing repairs around the farm, putting up hay, mending fences, clearing fields of rocks and stumps, cutting firewood for the winter.

Then there was the farmhouse that always needed something repaired, like the chinking between the logs that occasionally fell out. When that happened

Alfred would dig out some clay near the spring and mix in horsehair that he kept after trimming or currying the horses. He'd work the mixture in between the logs where it would harden like mortar, keeping the log house tight and snug in the winter.

And the roof always seemed to need a few shingles replaced. To do that, Alfred would saw out a block from a cedar log about ten inches square. Then he'd take a hatchet and split off singles about a quarter inch thick to replace the bad ones on the roof. Cedar worked best because it split easily and held up better to the elements.

Mary stayed busy inside the house—cleaning, cooking, darning, even making dresses for herself. Together, the couple spent time with friends and attended church functions. They also took Aunt Caroline wherever she needed to go. They were very discreet about their sex life and kept the problem to themselves. However, on one occasion Mary asked her increasingly nervous husband if he had ever talked to anyone about his problem.

"No, I have not."

"Would you consider doing that? Maybe you should see a doctor. Other men must have had this problem."

"I absolutely will not! It's my problem and I'll take care of it myself!"

"It's *our* problem, Alfred!" Mary shot back, trying to contain her own anger and resentment.

Alfred stormed from the room and didn't talk to her for the rest of the night.

The next day he apologized for getting so angry. "Just give me some time Mary. I'm sure this'll go away."

"I'll try to be more understanding, Alfred, but what if the problem doesn't go away?"

"The problem *will* go away, Mary. I promise."

CHAPTER 12
Death and a Funeral

It was a hard, bitter cold winter for Fish Springs. Snow covered the community five times between mid-December and February, with the last white stuff staying on the ground for two weeks. The chest-deep snow drifts and high winds brought all outdoor work to a grinding halt; the bone chilling icy wind kept people bundled up inside and huddled around their fireplaces. Then in the last week of February there was a break in the snowy weather. It was as if the sun and a few rays of warmth had been stored up for weeks and now had finally found a way to break through and give folks a welcome respite from so much harsh weather. A lot of the snow had melted away, making Fish Springs accessible by road.

A mile down the road from Alfred and Mary's farm, the Smiths were starting to stir. Polly was cooking a big breakfast of eggs, smoked sausage, biscuits and gravy. It was a Monday and Daniel would be dropping Peter, eleven, and Izzy, nine, off at school after a two-week shutdown because of the last snow. Daniel needed to go to the dry goods store anyway so it wasn't a wasted trip.

Sixteen-year-old Charlie had his dad's permission to do a little squirrel hunting, using his new Henry lever action rifle, at least new to him. Daniel had acquired a new Winchester model 66, which evolved from the Henry rifle, from a gun dealer in Johnson's Depot. So after a day of hunting and training with Charlie on gun safety, Daniel passed his old Henry rifle down to his son. He cautioned him once again to be careful and to remember that the rifle had only one purpose—to kill.

After breakfast, Daniel and the younger kids took off for town in the buckboard, and Charlie, after promising his mother he would be back before dark, began his trek through the woods for Pond Mountain. Most of the snow had melted except for the deep drifts. Charlie reasoned the squirrels would be active trying to gather as much mast as possible before the next snow.

Making his way through the dense, dark woods, he noticed how fast the clouds were moving. *Not necessarily a bad thing, maybe it's going to warm up*, he thought. Charlie was glad he had encouraged Turnup to stay in the warmth of the house, because the dog, who always seemed to be happily wagging its tail, would chase more squirrels away than he could bag. Turnup could help you find your way home, if you got lost, but he wasn't much help when it came to hunting.

Mary had asked him a while back if his dog actually ate turnips.

"No M'am."

"Then why do you call him Turnup?"

"'Cause that's where we got him. He just turned up."

Charlie couldn't help laughing again—to himself—when he remembered that exchange. But the dog actually had turned up out of nowhere. He may have been abandoned or just gotten lost, but Charlie had instantly taken to the bedraggled little animal. And since that first day when he scampered up, seemingly out of nowhere, onto the Smiths' porch, dog and boy had been practically inseparable.

As he continued through the woods, the terrain got rockier and steeper and the air colder. A spring-like day had suddenly grown crisply cold, and the wind picked up slightly. Charlie noticed the four to five-foot drifts of snow lining his path, and he was glad he had dressed warmly. He had on his long johns under his coveralls and a heavy denim coat with a stocking cap. He also wore a pair of leather gloves with a slit for his trigger finger, and all this was good because his trip to the area of Pond Mountain, where he had seen a cluster of hickory trees, was farther than he remembered—probably two miles or more from his house. But the walk, now getting colder and more difficult by the minute, was worth it, because as he eased up to the hickories, he could hear squirrels chattering.

One sat, making a racket, on a jagged limb about a hundred feet away. He shook his tail and fussed at Charlie for being there, but not for long. The boy quietly eased his rifle into a shooting position, drew a bead on him and squeezed the trigger. When the animal plunked to the leaf-covered, frosty ground, Charlie proudly put his first kill into a burlap bag he had tied to his belt.

Now he didn't feel the cold as much as before. Boy and squirrel had met, and boy had won. *This hunting stuff is going to be fun,* Charlie thought. *And 'sides, I can hep put food on our table. Mom and Dad'll be proud'a me!*

After Charlie bagged three more furry creatures, the area went still. All the surviving squirrels had gone into hiding. But Charlie knew, if he sat quietly and long enough, his bounty would return. He wanted to return home with six squirrels—just enough for him, his dad and Peter—so he sat, leaning against an ancient oak facing the stand of hickory trees.

Charlie's mom wouldn't eat the squirrels. She said they looked too much like rats, so naturally Izzy wouldn't eat them either, but the guys loved them. *What could be better'n a big ole plate of fried squirrel, with a big cat-head biscuit, split open an' smothered in squirrel gravy? Makes my stomach growl jest to thank about it,* Charlie thought as he reached into the bag and pulled out his last kill. While eying the rodent's bulging yellow buck teeth and beady black eyes, he had to admit it did bare a slight resemblance to a rat.

Charlie also studied his Henry rifle. Very few sixteen-year-old boys had such a sought-after rifle. His father had told him that a Henry rifle could be fired eight or ten times while a Confederate reloaded his musket. And the troops that could afford them bought one, because they were not issued to most Union foot soldiers. The Henry repeating rifles were not available to the Confederates for the most part. And even if they got one, they couldn't find ammo for it.

After a long wait, the illusive rodents came out of hiding and started gathering the few hickory nuts remaining on the forest floor. Charlie had loaded the 10 cartridges he had left into the breach of his rifle after he departed from the house. Missing twice, he had fired six rounds. It took two rounds to make the next kill because he was so far away. Then Charlie headed home because his father had always told him, "Son always start home with at least two cartridges, because ya' never know what you might run into along tha way."

As he made his way down a steep, slippery incline in the woods, the biggest, fattest squirrel he had seen all day taunted him. Charlie needed one more for his planned meal. He had to take the shot. The icy wind began to pick up even more, making it hard to hold his rifle steady. But, bearing down on the brazen animal, he took aim anyway. The bushy-tailed, loudly chattering rascal paid him no mind, as his shot seemed only to graze the target.

"God d—!" but he held his tongue and steadied his firearm. The next shot ended the chattering. He let out a cry of celebration, but his joy was short lived. He knew he had better make haste, for, as he put the last kill into his bag, the wind whipped up so hard that small ice-laden limbs were torn from the treetops. And the temperature continued to drop rapidly. Then as Charlie upped his pace toward home, he saw what appeared to be a crushing white wall closing on him.

He was quickly immersed in the heaviest, most dangerous snow he had ever seen. His visibility went to zero. He couldn't even see the ground as he stumbled along trying to find his way. *Surely this ain't gonna last very long*, he thought. But it did and an hour or so later, when his hands and feet started to go numb, and it began to be a struggle just to breathe such cold air, he had a horrible thought. *I could damn well freeze ta death out here. It ain't lookin' good a'tall. God, if I'd just brung ole Turnup along, he'd get us back home.*

Back in town Daniel cast his eyes toward the dark, low-level clouds that seemed to grow darker and more threatening by the minute. Then it started. The sudden, crippling snowstorm caught everybody off guard. Daniel was half way home with the kids in the buckboard when the bad weather hit. *Thank God, I picked the kids up and they worn't walkin' home,* he thought. He had been in blizzards before but this was the worst he had ever witnessed. It was a nor'easter and the combination of freezing wind, sleet and snow threatened to kill, shut down or downright horrify. He covered the kids with a tarp and encouraged the shivering horse, Millie, to keep moving with his whip. The mare, her eyes covered with a glaze of ice, sensed where the road was and found her way.

Then, as he hustled the kids inside the house, which seemed to be holding its own in the fierce storm, he found out that his son had not returned and he became even more worried.

"Please, Daniel! Find my boy," Polly pleaded. She was hysterical and crying, and Daniel's reassurances did nothing to make matters better.

"Now, Polly, you know he'll be home soon enough. Charlie's got a nose for how ta get back home—blizzard or no blizzard. Besides, Turnup'll lead him back."

"But Turnup didn't go with'm, Daniel! He's layin' over there by the fireplace!"

Now why in God's holy name didn't that boy take the dog with him? Daniel wondered. But the more he dwelled on that troubling question, the more unsettled he himself got. And the last thing he needed right now was to alarm Polly even more with his own fear of the worse. "Well, he's probably in a cave huddled to a fire 'bout now," Daniel said, but he knew that was just wishful thinking.

"Get Isaiah and some of the others to help you," Polly said.

"It's at least a mile to his homestead, Polly. It'd take too much time. I need to go now. You just get on over there by the fire and keep warm. I'll bring Charlie home."

When his wife seemed to begin to calm down, Daniel hugged her and beckoned Turnup to join him. The dog, ensconced in a warm cozy place next to the fireplace, yawned, opened his eyes slightly and raised one of his long, floppy ears but then lay back down.

"Turnup, I said get out here!" said Daniel, standing in the doorway.

This time, the canine scampered to his feet and trotted outside in the freezing snow and wind. Turnup came up to Daniel and wagged his tail, as if saying *Let's go get Charlie right now and bring'm home!*

Then Daniel, with Turnup following him, took the mare to the barn and saddled Burney, his rough-riding quarter horse and headed toward Pond Mountain. But he couldn't see to guide the horse along in the worsening blizzard. He himself seemed to be losing the battle against the devastating weather. His breathing grew more labored, the howling wind almost blew him out of the saddle, and his rabbit-fur gloved hands quickly got numb. Every movement degenerated into a struggle. The blizzard would surely kill him, his horse, the dog and Charlie, he knew, if he didn't find his son soon.

Daniel frantically hollered at Turnup. "Find Charlie, Turnup! Find Charlie!"

But the swirling, blinding snow was already too deep and the short-legged beagle mix could hardly move more then a few feet. Daniel began to feel hopeless. *Please help me, God. Please save my boy.*

Meanwhile, about a mile away, Charlie had almost given up. He could normally hear the river and find his way to it, but the wind was too loud, and the snow had transformed a once familiar haunt into an icy, foreboding whiteness hiding all landmarks. After trudging in circles for what seemed like hours, he stumbled into a large rock outcrop and crawled underneath. That offered some protection, but Charlie knew it would only delay his death. He was so cold that he thought maybe he should just go to sleep and get it over with. But then he focused on his mom and dad and his younger brother Peter and little Izzy. *I've got ta keep fightin'. I cain't let 'em down. Please help me, Lord.*

With icy, stiffening lips, he mumbled, as best he could remember, the first few lines of the Lord's prayer. "Our father—you bein' the one in heaven. Hallowed be thy name. Your kingdom be comin'. An' your will be a doin'. On earth, as you're havin' it be done in heaven. And fergive us our trespasses, please, as we fergive them that trespasses 'gainst us…" But that's all of the prayer Charlie could recall. *All them days a settin' in church,* he thought, *and I can't even 'member a danged little prayer.*

Daniel was making little progress. He did well just to keep moving, and the snow had gotten so deep that Turnup was of no use at all. So he dismounted and scooped up the little dog under his arm, remounted and let the mare find her way back home. He would set out again as soon as the storm let up. First, however, he, the mare and the dog had to get home to safety and shelter—no easy task in such a deathly storm. The horse trudged in the direction she figured she came from, and a few hours later, man and animals arrived safely back home.

Putting Turnup in the door, stomping the snow from his soggy boots and brushing it from his coat and hat, Daniel felt utterly defeated when he went inside. But he wrapped his arms around Polly and tried to reassure her.

"You're so cold, dear! Your arms are like ice!" Polly said between sobs. "Is he dead? Oh pray God, tell me our boy's still alive!"

"Don't give up, Polly. Not yet. Just pray this storm stops. You know our son. He's pretty danged smart and he's probably somewhere safe and dry. If I know Charlie, he'll stay hunkered down there till this blizzard blows over."

"But we don't know that! We can't know it!" she cried.

"I feel it in my bones, Polly. Charlie's alive. Just you wait and see. Me and Turnup'll go back out there and find him soon as this blizzard blows itself out. By then I can get Isaiah and the boys to go with me. We'll find him, Polly."

Meanwhile, in the cold, foreboding whiteness, Charlie, shivering and fighting off sleep, had crawled along under the rock outcropping, searching for a more protected spot. Then he spotted an opening under the rock. It was about two feet high and two and a half feet wide. Lying on his back, he eased himself in, feet first, leaving his rifle near the opening. He slid slowly down a steep incline into the darkness, hoping to find the bottom. He knew he could be launched into a cavern, where his body would never be found, but he felt he had no other option. Anything beat being outside, where nothing could possibly stay alive for very long.

He thought about his short life—birthdays, Christmases, hugs and kisses from his family, swimming with his friends in a mountain river that he thought of as so very cold at the time. *But no way I knew what COLD really wuz back then. How the cold could make ya' feel numb all over and come close to freezin' your brain. How it could make ya' want to die jist so ya' could go to heaven and git warm with Jezus.*

Then about eight feet down the incline his feet touched bottom. *Thank ya, Lord, for gettin' me ta safety.* Praise gave way to amazement at how warm it seemed to be inside. Still, it was pitch black dark so he couldn't tell the size of the hole or cavern—or whatever it was—that he'd landed in. Nevertheless, he had a feeling it was a small chamber. He slid to the bottom on his rear, his feet pressed against the wall in front of him. He seemed to be up against something firm and soft, maybe somethin' covered with heavy moss, Charlie guessed. He pulled a glove off and leaned out and touched the soft wall in front of him.

Instantly Charlie's realized his safe haven was anything but. And he got really scared. This time he wouldn't freeze to death. Instead, he'd be mauled and eaten alive by the hibernating bear he was wedged against.

Charlie sat frozen in fear, trying to decide what to do next. When his eyes finally adjusted to the dim light, he could see the bear was curled up on his side facing the other way. The sleeping beast was huge, filling the entire bottom of his den.

His first thought was to flee, but outside he'd die for sure. Inside, he wasn't real certain. He thought about his rifle, but then cursed himself using up all his ammunition. He'd known better than to not save any bullets. *Damn! I cain't shoot tha bear cuz I ain't got no cartridges left. Dad was right. You jist never know what ya might run into.*

Studying his options, Charlie thought, *maybe I can hold myself up on tha rock incline and that ole bear'll never even know I'm here.* But when he tried to clutch and hang onto the steep, slippery incline, Charlie would always slide back down, resting against the bear. He prayed it would not rouse.

Knowing that he'd freeze to death if he went back outside, Charlie played out a scenario of what might happen if he stayed in the cavern and if the sleeping bear woke up.

Will he flee, like they always do, when I come upon one in the woods? But what iffin' he don't do that? If the bear wakes up, he might kill me, but maybe he'll jist keep a sleepin'. Dad said he'd hyeared about a man findin' a big ole hibernatin' bear under a pile'a hay in his barn. And he'd had a devil of a time wakin'm sos he could run'm off.

Then again, if he wakes up but don't feel threatened maybe he'll jist leave me be. Dad said bears ain't natrully aggressive lessen you try to get thar food, like I hyeard 'bout Mary doin', or get one cornered, like I'm problee doin' right now. Damn! I wish I warn't 'tween tha bear and his way out. At least they ain't no cubs in here. Dad said the God awfullest worst thang you could do was git between a mother bear and her cubs.

Charlie spent anguishing hours trying to stay off of the sleeping beast and checking on the still howling storm outside. Throughout it all, he kept praying for a break in the weather. And then, giving in to total exhaustion, he gingerly lay down against the warm bear's back.

With his left ear pressed against the soft black fur, he heard nothing for a while and then the slightly audible shrill sound of air entering the hulking animal's lungs. After a few seconds, the slumbering beast exhaled. Charlie heard the bear's heart beat and counted off six seconds before it thumped again.

He harkened back to what his dad, who had read about hibernating black bears, had told him. Now he sorely wished he could recall more from that father-son chat, but he did remember that the bear's functions slowed down—by three fourths. His breathing slowed and his heart would only beat nine or ten times a minute when he slept deeply. *God, I jist pray he sleeps deep and don't wake up till I git outta here.*

Charlie also remembered his dad telling him about the bear eating things that would plug his bowels; to avoid pooping or peeing when he hibernated. *That's why it don't smell sa' bad in here. Maybe jist a little musty,* he thought.

Then in the spring when the bear came out of his den, he would eat a herb called squawroot to unplug or loosen his bowels. His dad also told him that female bears with cubs slept more lightly, so as to protect their young. Charlie didn't know if he was cuddled against a male or female. All he knew was that his body was pressed up against a soft, warm, potentially deadly beast. And even though he lay there hopelessly in mortal fear, he was not able to hold his eyes open another minute.

Back at the Smith house, Daniel dozed in a rocker by the fireplace, getting up often to gaze out the door and check for a break in the storm. Persuaded by her husband to take a big swig of moonshine to calm her nerves, Polly had long since gone to bed, but she slept fitfully, calling out to her husband several times during the long winter night for updates on the weather.

Finally, a break came just before daylight. It continued to snow, but much more lightly now, and the wind, unforgivingly brutal for so long, seemed to have almost died out.

"Polly, I'm a goin'. The storm has broke," Daniel said to his grieving wife—now bent over in the warmth of the fireplace. "But we need to prepare for the worst 'cause I don't think Charlie could've survived outten weather like this."

As Daniel spoke to his wife, his voice broke and he struggled to keep his composure.

"Oh Daniel! My poor Charlie! Our first born! He froze ta death!"

With Daniel and Polly standing there and holding and trying to console each other, the front door suddenly opened.

And in walked their long lost—given-up-for-dead—son.

"Mom, I'm starvin', " Charlie blurted, flashing a big grin.

After the crying, hugging, and a short, shocking explanation of how he had survived, the prodigal son sat down to a delicious breakfast of bacon and eggs, grits, biscuits and gravy. Then Charlie and his parents relaxed by the fireplace, where he shared with them all the details of his survival.

Charlie said the most frightening time, by far, came that same morning.

"I jerked when I woke up, kneein' the bear in tha back. My face was agin' his back and I hyeard his heart abeatin'. It started beatin' faster and faster and his lags started twitchin', like Turnup's do when he's dreamin' 'bout chasin' rabbits. "

"So what did you do?" Polly, wringing her hands, asked.

"That's when I skedaddled. An' low and be-hold when I crawled out, tha storm had petered out. I hyeard the river and that helped me find ma way back.

"Pa, Ma, I'm sorry you wuz sa' worried 'bout me."

"You survived, son. You're alive 'cause you used your head and we're very proud of you," said Daniel, his voice breaking from emotion and tears welling up in his eyes. "The Lord must'a had other plans for you, Charlie." Then father and son held each other like neither one wanted to let go.

"Amen to that," Polly said.

"One thing's for sure, I prayed alot," Charlie said through his own sobs. "And I promise ya' I ain't never gonna' fall asleep in church agin."

About that time, Peter and Izzy scampered down the stairs and smothered their wayward, lucky brother with hugs and kisses. Then he told the story all over again, this time sparing the young ears the parts where he thought he would die. They sat rapt by the fire as Charlie recounted how he'd taken refuge under a rock outcropping from the ferocious storm—only to find himself slipping into the pitch black dark cavern home of a hibernating bear. When little Izzy pushed him to tell him more about the bear, Charlie only offered that it scared him but he ended up sleeping peacefully in the end of the ordeal.

"Bears ain't sa' bad iffen' ya' know thar nature and don't git sa' skeered. They's as skeered of us as we is a' them."

"But what iffen he'd woke up and wanted to eat you?" Izzy, wide-eyed, persisted.

"Well, he didn't, did he? That big ole sleepin' bear ain't gonna bother any body a'tall. Why, we'll problee run across'm in tha spring, and he'll want some'a Mary's blackberry pie."

Izzy and Peter laughed and hugged their brother. Then they made him promise to tell more about what he'd been through.

Daniel had no doubt about the veracity of Charlie's story. Neither did most people in and around Fish Springs. But a few skeptics, those who knew absolutely nothing about bears, weren't convinced.

"That there ferocious bar wudda' et his lag off soon as he touched'm," said one geezer, who swore he'd been around bears all his life.

"That man eater wudda' kiltem soon es he smelt'm," said another doubter. "That lad's a bald face liar. He problee' done spent tha night with'a gal so's he had to make up a good tall tale ta tell his pa."

The engaging story of survival under such dire circumstances—in the midst of a killer storm and sharing a rock cavern with one of the most feared animals in the mountains of Tennessee—eventually reached the editor of a hunting magazine in Nashville. The editor wrote Charlie, wanting to come with an assistant to Fish Springs and photograph Charlie and the den where he had found refuge with the bear. When Charlie balked at the idea, the editor noted that only "photographic evidence" would deem the story true to his readers.

Shy by nature, Charlie told his dad he didn't want to reveal the whereabouts of the den, especially to a hunting magazine.

"I know it's just a bear, Pa, but I don't want any harm to come to'm, and 'sides, they's folks would still think I'm lyin' no matter what that magazine man wrote. Ain't nothin' he could write that'd change thar minds."

Daniel said he understood completely and left the decision of whether to accede to the magazine's request entirely up to Charlie.

"I'll stand by ya' whatever you do, son."

"Then I'll write that editor man and tell'm not to come."

"So be it," said Daniel.

A mile up the road, Alfred and Mary dug out of the six-foot deep snowdrifts that blocked the entrance to their cabin. They had stayed hunkered down and cozily warm inside while the howling, fierce winds and heavy snow—the worst wintry blast to hit Fish Springs in years—blanketed everything in sight, piled up, froze and then, at last, had begun to melt. Through it all, Mary fretted about her aunt. Had she stayed warm? Had she enough wood for her stove? Sufficient food, water and blankets?

"Alfred, we've got to go check on her," Mary said when the storm had finally subsided.

Alfred dreaded getting out in all the drifts so early, but he knew his fidgety wife wouldn't stand still 'till they checked on Aunt Caroline. So he got the wagon ready in the barn, making sure the horse that would pull it was watered and fed. Satisfied they and the horse could make it through the icy, snowy—but now calm and peaceful—wilderness, he set out on the trip with Mary beside him.

Patches of dirt had begun to show but a blanket of vast whiteness still enveloped most of the terrain. Icicles, sparkling in the sun, hung from cliffs along the road. The sky was clear and the sun on the snow blinding, but it was still very cold. Because of the snowstorms hitting one after another, it had been three days since Alfred had last checked on Aunt Caroline. But he and Mary pledged that they'd get there through the deep snow and around the giant fallen trees blocking the road—come hell or high water. They'd taken the wagon, loaded with firewood and other supplies for Aunt Caroline.

The half mile ride aboard Alfred's wagon, from the couple's cabin to Caroline's house, didn't take long. The horse knew the route well. The horse's breath in the cold air looked like steam blowing from a tea kettle, but onward he trotted.

Warmly dressed and huddled on the frozen wagon seat, Mary had covered herself with an old blanket.

"Are you warm enough, Mary?"

"I'm fine, but it's nice we ain't got so' far to go."

"True. Now, when we get ta Aunt Caroline's, you get on in and warm yourself by the fire. I'll be in soon as I unload this firewood."

"I can help ya."

"No, I'll do it."

As Alfred pulled the wagon to a stop at the front of Caroline's house, the horse threw his head up and blew out one long breath. Alfred then set the long-handled brake on the wagon. After that, he climbed down and helped Mary, taking her hand.

"I'll be in, in a few minutes. You go ahead and see to your aunt."

Alfred got back on the wagon, unset the brake and coaxed the horse to pull him to the back of Caroline's house. There he began stacking wood on the back porch. Although some of the snow had melted, the air was still cold; his boots soon got soggy wet and his joints stiffened.

Mary, with some trouble, got the icy, stubborn knob of the front door to turn. But even then the door resisted being opened.

Mary had a haunting feeling. *It's as if everthang here's frozen an' lifeless. How's Aunt Caroline stand it? Why doesn't she just move in with us? We might as well all live tagether anyway. It ain't as if she'd be interruptin' anything.*

Mary forced the door open. She could see the top of Aunt Caroline's head, her hair pulled back tightly in a bun like she always wore it, just above the back of her favorite resting place, a large maple rocker. Her aunt loved to sit in that old rocker and read or knit. Sometimes she would fall asleep. The fireplace, only a few feet away, kept her warm.

"Mary!" Alfred yelled. "Do you think I should bring in more wood before I do any more stacking?"

No answer.

"Mary! Can you hear me? Should I fetch more wood?"

Still no answer.

"Burr, Aunt Caroline. It's cold in here."

" Did your fire go …?"

"Aunt Caroline! Aunt Caroline!" Mary screamed. "Wake up!"

But her aunt didn't move.

And when Mary touched her hand, she was icy cold.

Her aunt's lips were blue and her face an ashen gray.

"Alfred! Alfred!" Mary yelled. "Something's happened to Aunt Caroline!"

Alfred dropped his armful of firewood and tried to open the back door but found it locked, so he ran to the front.

"What's wrong, Mary?"

"It's Aunt Caroline!" Mary blurted. "I think she might be dead!"

Alfred felt Caroline's chilled neck for a pulse, but detected nothing.

"I'm so sorry, my love, but she's gone."

"Oh, Alfred! She died alone! Without a soul with her. She probably froze to death. She suffered!"

Alfred tried to console Mary. He held her as she wailed. He gently patted her head and back when she blamed herself for not making Aunt Caroline move in with them.

"We tried that, remember. She wanted to be independent."

Then he spotted a few glowing embers in the fireplace.

"This fire's not really completely out, Mary. I don't think Aunt Caroline was cold. I bet she died in her sleep by a warm fire."

"Bless her heart. She was a good, Christian woman and a good mother to me. I'll miss her so much, Alfred. I loved her. . ."

"I know, Mary. I know."

As soon as the ground began to thaw, a resting place was dug for Aunt Caroline. Preacher Ike Redford conducted a graveside service that was short but inspirational. Family and friends said their good-byes, and each of them proclaimed that Aunt Caroline had been "called home to be with the Lord." And because it was still winter and nothing was blooming in Fish Springs, mountain greenery and red holly berries framed Aunt Caroline's grave. A small rock marker with a simple cross on it, with the words "Caroline Bartholomew Hamby, 1786—1867" reminded folks that Caroline Hamby had been born, had lived and then had left this earth for a better place.

Ike hugged Mary first and then Alfred.

"My heart goes out to both of you. Please call on me if you need anything," the preacher said.

Mourners gathered themselves, said their last farewells, and filed out of the little cemetery.

"We're so sorry for your loss, Mary. Are you okay?" Polly asked.

"I'm makin' it, Polly. Thank you."

"Let us know if we can do anything, please," said Daniel. "Aunt Caroline was one in a million."

"Thank you both," Mary said.

"We'll miss her," said Polly, fighting back tears. "She'd become my dearest, most precious friend."

"She loved you both. She often told me you were her favorites," Mary said.

"Well, we loved her too," said Daniel. "It was a beautiful service, Mary. I think everybody in Fish Springs was at the church."

"Except maybe your neighbor, John Williams," Polly interjected.

"Now, Polly," Daniel countered.

"Well, you could say Aunt Caroline and John didn't get along very well," Mary said.

"The way I heard it, she made John get along up the road one night," Daniel said.

Everyone smiled except Alfred, who seemed puzzled.

"John came to the house drunk one night," Mary said, "and Caroline ran him off with a rifle shot, close to his foot."

"You never told me that story," Alfred said, laughing.

"She was a pistol all right," Polly said.

Daniel put his hand on Alfred's shoulder. "Alfred, if you need any help with anything, you just give me the word."

"Thank you, Daniel. By the way, I understand your boy Charlie had a close call. That was quite an incredible story. Is he okay?"

"He's fit as a fiddle, and right now he's home watchin' the younguns. He told me to tell you how very sorry he was for your loss."

"You thank Charlie for me and tell him I want to hear all about his amazin' night in tha bear den," Mary said.

"We will, dear heart. And we'll see you in church. We love you," Polly said.

Not far from the church cemetery, two old men sat on a bench whittling, taking advantage of the sunny winter day. One had a thick wad of chewing tobacco in his cheek, and, turning his bald, mole-blotted head slightly, he'd spit a heavy stream of the ugly brown juice every few minutes. The other, in frayed, faded clothing and wearing heavy work boots, seemed riveted on his task at hand—mindlessly whittling a small chunk of wood into absolutely nothing.

The whittlers noticed the crowd coming from the cemetery.

"Who'd they plant taday?" one asked.

"Caroline Hamby."

"So, who was she?"

"An old bitty who folks said read'er Bible right raglarly and hovered over her pretty li'l niece like a mother hen."

"That same cold, prune-faced woman whose man took up with a slave girl."

"Yep, that's the one."

"Wonder iffen' she ever 'lowed a fella to touch her?"

"Doubtful. She wuz in church ever' time the doors opened and they say she kept'er skirts clean after her old man was run outta town.

"Well, she shore ain't havin' no fun now, is she?"

The men stared at each other and nodded to acknowledge they both had Caroline Hamby rightfully pegged for a sexless, feelingless creature. But folks close to Caroline Hamby—like the Smiths—knew her as a good Christian woman who loved life and had gone on to her just reward.

Then the old codgers resumed what they'd do for the rest of the day in still cold Fish Springs. Someone had died, and some folks grieved, but others, far as the two old whittlers were concerned, were just putting on airs.

"She's got dirt on'er now. Too bad the ole stiff neck didn't 'joy life while she could," one of the knife wielders offered as a note of finality.

CHAPTER 13
Hard Work and a Bath

Aunt Caroline's will provided that all her earthly belongings be left to Mary, including her house, all its contents and a little money Caroline had in a bank in Elizabethton. Mary wasn't sure what to do with the house, and thought she might sell it. Alfred's house was more conveniently located to the farm so they would not move. As for the money, that would come in handy for farm improvements.

Winter turned to spring and Alfred stayed busy getting the farm ready for the planting season. The couple had gotten into a daily routine. They would rise in the morning at first light. Alfred would go to the barn and feed the stock while Mary made breakfast, usually biscuits, eggs, ham or bacon, grits and coffee. After breakfast Alfred would load everything he needed in the work wagon, and hook up one horse to pull it. The other would trail behind. If Alfred worked at the other end of the farm, he would take his lunch, which Mary prepared. After Alfred left, Mary fed the chickens and gathered the eggs.

It was as if keeping busy helped her forget about the deeper, sadder parts of her marriage. Work became an escape, a way for her to think about how good she had it. After all, so many other women had it worse.

I'm married to a God-fearin', hard workin' good man. He loves me. He does all he can to support us. He's here for me every day and night. He puts food on our table … No need for me to be so obsessed about our laying down together.

But her body ached to feel whole. Her physical desires had been pent up, and now they wanted out. Something had to give. Mary couldn't just go on pretending that life was perfect.

Mary put such ruminations aside and straightened her blue apron when she heard the sounds of Alfred's wagon and horse. Ready for another long work day, Alfred yelled. "Mary! You there? Got anything for a man to eat? "

"Here you go, Alfred," Mary said, handing him smoked ham and biscuits wrapped in a clean dish towel. She also included an apple and a jug of sweet tea.

Alfred tucked his food inside a sack of horse feed he had on the seat beside him. "Thank ya, Mary. I'll be back before dark and I'll be plum tired and hungry agin'."

"Okay, Alf. Be careful."

Alfred headed toward the other end of the farm. His 100 acres of land, about 70 of it cleared and the other 30 in hardwood, lay between the road to Elizabethton and the river. It was some of the best soil in Carter County. He felt he was born to work this fertile ground—to make it surrender its bounty to Mary and himself.

I'll prove to her that I'm worthy ta be her husband. I can outwork any man in Fish Springs, and I'm a pretty good provider, if I do say so myself. I'll buy her fine things—clothes, jewelry, furniture, that sweet smellin' stuff she likes to put on her neck, books 'cause she loves to read.

He guided the horse down a familiar narrow, primitive road toward the river and stopped in the shade of towering oak trees framing one side of the 10-acre cornfield he'd be plowing today. Then Alfred untied the trailing horse from the wagon and walked him to the plow at the edge of the cornfield. It had rusted from sitting out all winter, but the plow's heavy steel blade would be bright and shiny by the end of the day.

Alfred hooked up the work horse to the plow and began his task. He would plow until noon, eat lunch, switch out the horses and plow until late in the afternoon. He would plow a row down and a row back, and every few minutes, his throat parched from the hot, unforgiving sun, he gulped water from a jug he had on the wagon. It all made for a long, grueling day's work.

Not every man would sweat like this for a woman, Alfred thought, as he fetched another jug of water, stripped off his shirt and splashed himself and continued plowing. A row down. A row back. The sun burned even hotter. The work horse kept pulling the plow steady and straight. Gnats and mosquitoes and other insects attacked Alfred's arms and face. And yet onward he toiled for hours until the light faded and his work horse tired.

Finally, horse and man were spent. Time to call it a day, to go to the house. For the man, that meant going back to sweet, loveable Mary. For the horse, it was fresh hay and rest in a clean stable that Mary had prepared for the loyal work animal while her man labored all day in the field.

He could hardly wait. Mary'd surely have him a delicious supper and it'd be nice, later, sitting on the porch swing, enjoying the cool mountain air. Even her scent beckoned him to her. She had definitely sprinkled that "sweet smellin' stuff" all over her before he got home. But then he also thought about how she'd gotten more and more restless of late. She kept brushing her body up against his, kept massaging his back and running her fingers down his neck and to the top of his chest, seeming to crave something that he just downright could not oblige her with right now.

When he got home, and as soon as he had stabled the horses, Mary called her exhausted, sweat-stained husband for supper. She had fried chicken, mashed potatoes with gravy, green beans and biscuits.

"Aunt Caroline sure had it right when she said you could cook! Your chicken's the best and a fella'd die for that gravy and mashed taters."

"Thank you, Alfred, but I'm just tryin' to be worthy of bein' your wife. And by the way, I filled the tub for you."

"Sounds like you think I need a bath."

"Well, whether you need one or not, the warm water'll soothe your tired muscles."

"Well, if you say so, Mary. A man don't want ta stink his home up ..."

While they ate, Mary shared with him how she'd been reading her Bible extra hard in recent days and that an "old fashioned Holy Ghost feelin" had seemed to come over her. She said she'd taken a renewed interest in those parts of the Word that showed anything and anybody could change, if only they'd follow the will of the Lord.

"Ya know, Jesus didn't come for them that were perfect, Alfred. He didn't come for tha up and uppers. He came for tha down an' outers. Those with problems and 'flictions and sores and leprosy and demons in 'em. And he cured 'em. He made 'em well and beautiful, just like a caterpillar goes through a change and turns into a beautiful butterfly. We just have to lay all our sins an' aches an' physical shortcomin's at the alter and give 'em all over to Jesus and pray 'bout it."

Alfred kept chewing and swallowing his food, but the phrase "physical shortcomins" bothered him. *What's she hintin' at?* But he said nothing, figuring Mary would tell him soon enough.

After supper, Mary served her fretting husband a slice of apple pie—the perfect dessert for their dinner. Then she put two kettles of water on the wood-burning stove to heat for his bath. It was about dark, so Mary lit a lantern, and then she unwrapped a huge, thick, red candle she'd bought at the general store in Fish Springs. She lit the wick and the candle gave off a fresh pine odor.

"Lord, that smells good," he said. "Are we celebrating something?"

"Maybe, we'll see. Now eat the rest'a your pie an' get outta them filthy clothes."

Alfred, smiling, finished his pie, and then stripped while Mary emptied the hot kettles of water into the tub.

"Now you just enjoy a good long soak. I'll be back in a minute," said Mary, a mischievous twinkle in her eyes. "I've got to make the bed with fresh sheets. I'll turn 'em down while you start your soak."

Once he eased his tired, aching body into the tub, Alfred found the warm water utterly relaxing; so much so that he had to fight to stay awake. He took the big, fragrant bar of soap and began scrubbing the plowed ground off himself.

"I'll wash your hair for you," Mary said tenderly, as she returned.

"Thank you, love. You're better'n any red-blooded man deserves. I'll do my dangedest ta stay awake."

"Maybe I can help you," she said seductively.

Alfred noticed that his wife had changed into a lacy nightgown. She had untied her long, beautiful hair, and the top of her gown seemed to strain to contain her full, luscious breasts. The bottom of the gown covered only part of her smooth, silky thighs. Alfred knew any man would die to have her.

It's as if she's ripe for the pluckin' and I cain't do a damned thing, he thought.

But if Mary wanted him then and there, she had not yet said so. Instead, she did her best to comfort and reassure her husband—not through words but through her hands.

She palmed the soap and lathered Alfred's hair. Then she slowly and sensuously massaged Alfred's scalp with her fingertips from front to back and down the back of his neck to his back. She sudsed up his back and then she reached into the water and ran her hand gingerly along the outside of Alfred's leg to his knee, and then on the inside of his leg to his thigh.

He leaned back, took a deep breath and moaned as his wife stroked him. His body seemed to be responding, and Mary, her heart quickening and sweat breaking out on her forehead, sensed it. She took a pan of warm water from the stove, tested it with her hand and poured it over Alfred, rinsing off the soap. Alfred had a hard time containing his excitement.

"Ya' know, dear, I believe I'm feelin' somethin'. Can I dry off now?"

Mary nodded, and smiling, patted her husband with a soft towel.

"I'll be waitin' for you in bed," she said. "Don't be long."

And there his beautiful, wanton wife lay as Alfred, now clean and dry and smelling like the fragrant soap he had used, entered their bedroom. She was naked and breathing rapidly, panting with anticipation on their cozy featherbed.

"Come here, Alfred!" she beckoned. "I want you in the worst way! I've got ta have you, Alfred!"

Alfred nuzzled up to his wife. He put his arms around her and kissed her. Her body, deprived and hungry for so long, met his, ached and arched for his.

But it was no use.

Alfred could do nothing, try as Mary did to make it happen.

For several minutes, they kept trying, but to no avail.

Mary sat up in the bed, her eyes looking downward. She pulled a blanket over her voluptuousnesss.

Alfred cupped his head in his hands. "God must be punishing me. This must be my cross to bear. I'm not a man! I can't even make love to my wife."

"Don't say that, Alfred. Maybe there's somethin' I can do."

"There ain't nothing you can do, Mary."

"I just want to help you."

"Well, you can't, Mary! Can't you get that through your thick head? It's that damn war!"

As he pulled on his trousers, Mary leapt from the bed and grabbed him by the arm.

"Wait, Alfred! Please! We need to talk about this!"

But her husband, now feeling like a cursed eunuch, spun and slapped Mary across the face. "Leave me be, God damn it!"

Mary slumped to the floor in shock. She couldn't believe Alfred had turned against her. She curled, sobbing into the fetal position. Her face was beet red where her husband had struck her.

Alfred was ashamed. He had never hit anyone in anger, much less a woman. He had completely lost his temper with the woman he adored and she'd never feel the same way toward him again.

"Mary!" Oh my God, Mary! I'm so sorry."

He kneeled down and touched her on the shoulder, trembling and pleading for her to forgive him. "I'm so sorry, Mary. Mary I—"

"Go away, Alfred. Just go away. Leave me alone."

He forlornly dropped his head and left her. Then he sat depressed and alone on the front porch steps. He replayed Mary's shocked expression when he struck her. He cried. He couldn't shake the shame he felt. *Oh my God what've I done?*

He brooded there on the porch until past midnight. A cool breeze coming off the river did nothing to calm him. The situation seemed hopeless, desperate, cursed.

"Lord, I know I've gotta good an' beautiful wife, and I hope she still loves me but how's a half man like me keep a woman like Mary? She needs a whole man, Lord, but I can't seem to be that for her. Please, Jesus, don't let me lose her!"

The sound of a horse clopping on the road interrupted his self-pity. It was John Williams riding behind Madge, the saloon girl. She had the reins, and he held tightly onto her in a drunken stupor.

"Ma-Madge, dige I tell you how nice it was for ya' ta ride me ho-home?"

"John Williams, is that you? " Alfred shouted.

"Yeah. It's m-me, Yankeeman," John said, his words slurred.

"Your cattle'er comin' through your fence onto my property!"

"Don'cha y-ya' worry 'bout hit. I'll f-fix my f-fence, Yankeeman," John blurted.

As they rode toward John's cabin, John said to Madge. "I'd l-like to whup that Yankee man's ass! That's what I'd like ta do."

"Hush up. You couldn't whup a flea's ass now. You damn drunk."

"Ma-Madge, dige I tell you how nice it was f-for you t-to give me a ride ho-home?"

"Yes, dammit—about five times."

"Ha Haaa, O-Okay, then," John slurred.

The following day, Alfred, still tormented for striking Mary, tried to talk to her. He begged for her forgiveness. But still emotionally taken aback by the incident, she wasn't sure she could ever forgive him.

Then, after what seemed hours of awkward silence, Alfred made up a story and told Mary he was heading out to pick up some supplies.

"Then why're you still here?" Mary asked. "Just be gone, Alfred."

He thought, as he hitched the wagon up, *Maybe the devil had a hand in all this. He's wickedly tricked me into believing I could fulfill my role as a husband.*

And then, another thought—this one lurking and threatening. In his mind's eye, he could well imagine Mary and another man, screaming with pleasure, begging for more of what each was giving the other, enjoying themselves immensely in his bed, while he toiled in the fields trying to make life better for her. He couldn't shake the hurtful idea that that other man in their marriage bed was one John Williams—ready, able, cunning and more than willing to assume Alfred's husbandly physical duties.

No! It can't be. It ain't nothin' but my damned imagination! Alfred pulled his horse to a stop in front of Fish Springs Baptist Church and went inside to the front near the altar. About to go down on his knees and pray, he heard his name called out.

"Alfred, my boy, what brings you?" Ike Redford asked. The jovial preacher had just entered through the back door.

"I've got the devil in me, Reverend Redford."

"Well, Alfred, maybe it's not as bad as you think. May be he's just passin' through."

The preacher's insensitive statement startled and depressed him even more. So much so that the only thing Alfred wanted now was to be gone from there. He headed toward the door.

"Wait, Alfred! I'm sorry, son. I shouldn't'a made light of your pain."

Alfred solemnly looked the preacher in the eye.

"Betty always warned me that someday I'd hurt somebody's feelings tryin' to be funny, and I can see that I just did that. I'm sorry, Alfred.

"Now let's start over. How can I help you, son?"

"I hit Mary." Just saying it made Alfred ashamed and tearful.

The preacher tried to console him by putting his arms around Alfred and patting his back.

"My son, prayer works when nothin' else don't, and this is when you need to give it all over to the Lord."

Ike Redford prayed for Jesus' grace, understanding and forgiveness, and he beseeched Jesus to have the Holy Spirit give Alfred White some measure of solace.

"Alfred, if anybody else'd told me you'd hit Mary, I woulda' called'm a liar. That's so unlike you. What brought this fightin' on?"

"Well, I'm ashamed ta say."

"Let it all out, my son."

"It's just that I've been frustrated tryin' to be a man to Mary, reverend," Alfred confessed after a pause for a few deep breaths. "You see, I have this war injury and I didn't think it'd cause me any problems and at first it didn't.

"But now I can't do hardly anythin' in bed with her. I can't be the husband she thought she's was gettin'—far from it. I can't do nothing, and here she is, all set on havin' children and keeps puttin' pressure on me.

"We were fussin', and I guess the devil got to me, and I just lost myself. I hit the person I love most in the whole wide world. How could I do that, Reverend?" Alfred buried his face in his hands and closed his eyes.

"Back up, Alfred. You mean you haven't been able to consummate your marriage?"

"No, no! I was fine for a while. Then things down there," Alfred said, pointing to below his waist, "just quit workin'."

The man of the cloth told Alfred he wasn't the first former Civil War soldier to suffer from a battle injury and he wouldn't be the last—not by a long shot. Then he shared with him that other young men in the community—men whose names he promised he would never reveal—had physical problems similar to what Alfred's sounded like.

"They're havin' to work through it ta keep their marriages alive, Alfred, and you will, too. You'll learn soon enough that life's not easy, but I guess you already knew that, didn't you?"

The revelation that others in Fish Springs had war injuries that threatened their marriages did make Alfred feel better. Yes, he had a frustrating, embarrassing predicament, but he wasn't the only one, according to the preacher, and maybe others had found out how to conquer it, Alfred reasoned.

"Alfred, I can help you heal your heart, I can talk to Mary for ya. I can pray for ya, and with ya, but I can't fix your body. Nary a soul in Fish Springs can do that. Only the good Lord or a good doctor can help you. Have you talked to one, son?"

"No sir! I don't rightly want some doctor pokin' aroun' and cuttin' on me. What good would it do? If I could be a man before, why can't I now?"

"That's something you need ta ask a doctor, Alfred, and don't assume he's gonna' cut on you. Now, I know a good doc —"

"I ain't gonna' see a doctor 'bout my privates!" Alfred protested.

"But you need to, Alfred."

"Thank ya, reverend," Alfred said, "but I don't think you can help me."

Alfred started to leave.

"If it's forgiveness or pity you're lookin' for Alfred, you'll have to ask Mary for that."

"I tried that. It's ain't workin'."

"Well, keep tryin' and prayin' and please consider goin' to a doctor," Ike Redford said emphatically.

Alfred stalked out the sanctuary's open front door.

"I'll pray for you, son! Jesus don't give up on any of his sheep!"

"Thank you for that, but I think this sheep is lost," Alfred mumbled.

Cursing himself for getting so mad at Reverend Redford, Alfred climbed in his wagon and left the church, his head hung, and feeling even more depressed.

CHAPTER 14

A Glass of Cool Lemonade

A few days after he sobered up, John got around to mending his fences. The harsh Tennessee ice, wind and snow, along with termites, had taken their toll on the aging structures. Even the chestnut rails had begun rotting. Barbed wire, what little there was of it, had rusted. In short, the aging split rail fences needed a lot of repair.

But John, with his faithful dog Blue by his side, set about the task. He strung new wire. He replaced rails. He dug holes for new fence posts.He lifted, hauled and nailed. And gradually, the fence began to improve.

Now the blamed thang looks like it might hold for 'nother five years, John thought as he wiped the sweat and grime from his brow, took a deep breath and admired his labor. He tried not to think about his aching hands and back or the bloodthirsty chiggers that had been biting him for the last few hours. Because while the fence was better, John was not. He was embittered that Yankee Alfred White, *a hen-pecked man if I ever seen one*, had somehow brought all this work on him.

No way that Yankee bastard Alfred can complain 'bout this damned fence agin'. Why, he ought'a be glad I'm his neighbor. Corse iffn' I wanted to cause'm trouble, well, I could do that, and then some…

John tried to shift his thoughts. *Best I git on back to this cotton-pickin' fence. 'Cause if I keep at it, I can gitter' all done befer' the dog days'a summer set in.*

So he resumed walking along the fence line, checking for more breaks or holes, and making mental notes of how much he could accomplish tomorrow. Because today he had done all he could; his bloody, sore hands—full of splinters—hurt too much, and the chiggers had taken their toll on his sweaty frame. Plus, he was getting hungry and weak. Nothing would do him like a good cool drink and maybe cornbread, fresh tomatoes and beans.

What I need's a good meal, a good chew of terbacker and a good woman.

Iffn' only sweet Mary an'me had gotten married.

She'd be feedin' me and makin' me feel like a man, and she'd be a' reapin' some good thangs, too. Iffn' only I hadn't a got caught at the Black Bear. If only Alfred waddn't around , I know I could get Mary back, 'cause now I don't have ta deal with that crazy Aunt Caroline. She's in the ground. And maybe that's where Alfred ought'a be.

While he meandered forlornly along the fence line, John hadn't realized he suddenly was upon Mary and John's house. John had noticed Mary many times before while working on his own land but he had only waved. She always politely returned his wave, but that's as far as it ever went. *After all, she's a married woman. An'a man could git killed foolin' aroun' with somebody else's wife, but then agin', I sure as hell ain't afeared a' that son-of-a-bitch, Alfred.*

He came out of it when he spotted Mary across the road on her porch. A picture of loveliness, she sat there snapping beans, pulling strings off of them and putting them in her skirt that she had pulled up to her knees. John had a hard time taking his eyes off her. *What I'd give jist to caress'er and make'er feel like a woman. That's what she was made fer. And wouldn't I be doin' Mary a favor if I made'er feel good?*

Three days later John sashayed into the Black Bear Saloon at noon and found his friend Joshua. There he was, sitting by himself at a table, drinking a tall brew.

"Where th' hell did you go last night?" Joshua asked."Bring us another brew, Ted.—Have'a seat, John. I'll buy ya a beer."

John didn't respond. Instead, he just plopped down in the chair with a big, sly grin on his face.

"John you asshole, you spent th' night with that redhead that was in here last night didn't you?"

"She dragged me to her house. What am I s'posed to do, turn'er down?"

"Good thing Madge didn't catch ya."

"She went ta visit her folks in Knoxville."

"Boy, it must be nice ta have any woman you want. I s'pose the only one you cain't have is Mary White."

John said nothing for several seconds; he just stared at Joshua.

"What makes you think I ain't had Mary White?"

Joshua's eyes widened. "What? "

John, still grinning, chugged his beer.

"What'im bout ta tell you stays at this table. You done got that, Josh?"

"Shor'."

"Three days ago I was repairin' my fencin', across the road from Mary's house, and glory be, there sat beautiful, purty-as-a-fresh-mountain-daisy Mary, alone, on her porch. So I waved ta her. She waved back and motioned fer me ta come over.

"So me an' Blue crossed the road ta pay Mary a visit. After all, we bein' neighbors an' all. She said I looked like I could use a cool glass of lemonade, so she brought me one and I set in tha swing ta drink it. Then we talked a bit 'bout Blue and how I was doin' and other stuff. And she was playin' with that little button at the top'a her blouse, and that 'bout drove me crazy! All of a sudden, Mary looked at me with her big green eyes and done told me Alfred was workin' at the other end of the farm and wouldn't be back 'till 'bout dark. Then she told me she'd thought about the night I'd made love to her … had made her feel like a real, gen-u-wine woman. And while she was talkin', she commencedt ta breathin' right fast. That right there was all I needed! I done picked her up and carried her into the bedroom and I don't rightly know if she wiggled out of her blouse and skirt 'fore I got my pants off, but I couldn't wait no longer! I threw 'er in thar big feather bed and that thang rocked and creaked. I pleasured her and she me, and we couldn't get 'nough'a each other! Our lips and our tongues and legs was ever'where … She kept tellin' me to do'er agen and I kept obligin'.

"She kept askin' me ta pray for her an' Alfred's marriage, and so I did. I yelled 'Halleluia' and 'Amen' sa many times while we was gettin' it on in that feather bed that I thought I was some kinda' preacher.

"She screamed and hollered so loud, I was skeered' Alfred'd hear her. I did'er three or four times. I ain't even sure how many. But by then it was gettin' late in the evenin' and I sure as hell didn't want Alfred to catch us, so I left. She made me promise ta come back real soon."

"You lucky son-of-a-bitch. So when you goin' back?"

"I ain't rightly knowin', but I reckon when I feel the hunger. I gotta go, Josh. I ain't been home in two days. I got some farming ta do. Thanks fer the suds."

"Sure, but I still say you're one lucky son of a bitch."

"It's ain't luck, my friend. It's my charmin' ways." John, grinning smugly, chugged down the rest of his brew and left the saloon.

He then thought as he mounted Charger. *Damn I told that tale sa' good I almost believe it myself.* He knew Josh likely would spread the story around *but that's okay, 'cause Mary'll be mine sooner or later. And 'sides, if Mary hadn't a gone inside when she saw me, it could'a happened that way.*

Mary stood at the dry sink in her spotless kitchen cleaning a bread pan she had used that morning. She thought about Alfred's reluctance to do anything about their problem. Her married life was so lacking. In the bedroom, it hadn't lived up to her expectations at all. Lately, for example, Alfred had seemed to resist touching her, and even the most innocent peck on the cheek no longer marked their day. They slept together, but that's all that happened in their feather bed. No excitement. No arousal. No wantonness. The bed had become a cold, barren place for rest and nothing more. Mary suspected that Alfred had lost all feelings for her—if indeed he had ever had any in the first place. *Maybe he just fooled me and hisself from the start. He just had the idea he wanted a woman, but never really did. Or maybe he just wanted to spite John and prove he could get me instead of his ole rival.*

Mary tried NOT to think about being unfulfilled in her marriage. She concentrated on other things—her flower bed, her recipes—many of them passed along to her by Aunt Caroline—keeping her house in good order and clean, reading her Bible.

A few hours later she sat barefoot on the porch repairing holes in Alfred's socks. A few feet away, almost within touching distance, two hummingbirds hovered in mid-air. Both of the brightly colored little birds glittered and darted here and there—first forward a few feet, then backward. Mary, who figured her flowers had attracted them, thought she could detect a sound like the buzzing of a bee. The birds had evidently come out of the mountains—or maybe from heaven, Mary mused, to remind her that today was sunny, beautiful and full of promise and wonder.

The sounds of Alfred's horse and wagon caused her to glance away from the tiny buzzing birds with the long, sharp beaks and to drop her darning needle.

What's wrong? He's home early today? I wonder what's happened.

Alfred gave Mary a hint of a smile as he pulled his work wagon past the porch on his way to the barn. After he unhitched, fed and watered the horses, he joined his wife on the porch.

"Alfred, you okay? You're early. I ain't even started supper."

When he assured her he was fine and just had a few things on his mind he wanted to talk to her about, his anxious wife felt a slight tinge of relief, but she was also uneasy and said nothing. She continued her darning, while her husband sat facing her.

"I know I've been a big disappointment to you as a husband."

"Don't say that, Alfred!"

"Let me finish," he said softly, looking directly into his beloved's emerald-colored eyes.

Mary stopped darning and her eyes met his.

"That's bad enough, but worse'n that, I didn't consider your feelings. Your frustration, your fear of not havin' younguns'. All I thought about was me. This problem's made me depressed and irritable and I ain't been treatin' you very nice. I don't know if what's wrong with me can be corrected, but tomorrow I'm goin' to see a doctor in Elizabethton.

"Reverend Redford recommended him. His name is Dr. Jim Godfrey. If he can't help me, maybe he can send me to someone who can."

Mary said nothing, but her heart pounded. *Maybe he's finally gettin' it that we cain't go on like this.*

"Mary, when I was shot in the leg, a bit of the lead fragment from the bullet pierced my scrotum and got into one of my testicles," Alfred said, dropping his head. "The Union doctor that treated me said it was better to just leave it be. And while he was sewin' me up, he said my wounds wouldn't cause me no trouble with my manhood. I shoulda' told you all this before we married, but I was so danged sure that everything'd be okay. I'm sorry, Mary. I just didn't want to lose you.

"I don't know if this'll help, but even if I can't father children, we'll have 'em. I know that's not—"

"Thank you, Alfred! You don't know how much I've been prayin' 'bout this! And we don't need ta worry right now 'bout havin' babies. God'll take care of that part. First, let's see if we can get you some help, and I'll do everything I can to help you."

The idea that she could still be a mother made her so excited that she cried tears of joy. She had about lost hope that Alfred could make her truly happy again. Now, however, that didn't seem so far-fetched.

"Thank you, Mary! God, I love you! I was so afraid you might be leavin' me. I even imagined that you and ..." His voice broke between sobs before he could finish his sentence.

"I won't leave you, Alfred. I'm your wife forever—'till death. Remember what we promised on our weddin' day? With the Almighty's help, we'll get through this together."

The next morning, Mary cooked her husband a mouthwatering breakfast of biscuits, gravy, eggs, ham and coffee. The two chatted about maybe adopting children if Alfred couldn't father them. Then Mary made Alfred a lunch of smoked ham and biscuits and a jug of sweet tea for his trip to Elizabethton.

"I'm off Mary. I've got a danged good feelin' about this. I'm just sorry I put it off for so long. I love you!"

Mary, standing pretty as could be on the porch, blew him a goodbye kiss.

Alfred knew more than ever before that he was a lucky, blessed man. He believed with all his heart that he had married the most beautiful and caring woman in Fish Springs and he intended to keep her. He would do whatever it took.

"I should be back before dark. Bye, darlin'!" Then he mounted his mare and rode away.

Mary said a prayer to herself as she watched her husband disappear over the hill. He would soon be riding through a mighty gorge on his way to Elizabethton, and she'd heard tales about mountain lions attacking humans and horses at that juncture. *Lord, please watch over my Alfred and deliver him from harm. And I pray for your pow'r in puttin' our marriage back on the right track. Alfred and I love each other, and that's all that matters.*

CHAPTER 15
The Diagnosis

Alfred held his trusty mare in a trot as he made his way along the road to Elizabethton. It was a beautiful day for a ride, and ordinarily he would have lingered at some of the scenic cliffs, waterfalls and valleys. Today, however, he just wanted to get where he was going, and the sooner the better.

As the mare kept a steady pace, Alfred had a tough time staying calm. He was full of questions. For sure, he couldn't live with himself if he didn't try to work on his marriage. *But how's a man to talk about that kind'a thing to another man, even if he's a doctor? And what can Doc Godfrey do for me? What if someone finds out that I'm less of a man for Mary?*

Then Alfred reminded himself that he had no choice. *If things don't change, I could lose Mary and I couldn't blame'er for wantin' a whole man. I know she says she'd never leave me, but she deserves better. So I've got to do this. There's no way 'round it.*

As he tied his mare in front of Dr. Godfrey's house where he maintained his office, Alfred dreaded baring his soul and body. He had arrived at an average sized home on a busy road not far from the courthouse. As Alfred entered, a slender white-haired woman, in her mid-sixties, greeted him. A pair of spectacles hanging from her neck, she sat prim and proper behind a desk.

"Good afternoon, sir. Are you here to see Dr. Godfrey?"

"Yes m'am. I have a one o'clock appointment."

When Alfred identified himself, she glanced at a list on her desk and told him to have a seat. Then she left the room. Alfred reckoned it was to tell the doctor that his one o'clock patient had arrived.

Sitting there alone in Dr. Godfrey's waiting room, Alfred took a handkerchief from his pants pocket and nervously wiped the sweat from his forehead. He noticed a wooden sign on the desk, carved with the name Blanch Godfrey. Alfred reasoned that Blanch must be Dr. Godfrey's wife. Then, pacing back and forth, he surveyed the room more closely. Its walls had a fresh coat of white paint. Only one wall, the one directly in front of him, had a picture on it. It was a painting of Jesus, with a soft glowing light behind him, cradling a lamb. A small-paned window of wavy glass, with red curtains, offered a distorted view of the outside. The seating area had four chairs. In the center of the room was a table with a Bible and a few old newspapers. The floor was all wood and creaked when you walked on it. In a corner was a wood stove with a flue pipe routed to the chimney. Alfred saw that the ceiling seemed a bit black, no doubt from soot or smoke coming from the stove.

When it's cold in here, he keeps his patients warm. So that's a good thing. He cares about 'em, Alfred thought.

The anxious patient from Fish Springs sat back down and was about to doze off when the door burst open and a young boy ran in.

"I need the doctor! Where's the doctor? "

On hearing the commotion, Blanch Godfrey hurried into the room.

"What on earth's the matter, young man?"

"My daddy done broke'es leg! He needs to see the doctor! Now! He ain't doin' sa' good!"

"Ok, now just calm down. I'll get Doctor Godfrey."

Moments later Blanch came back with her husband, a slender, gray-haired man in his early seventies. He had a mustache, thin-framed glasses that hugged his ears and nose, and a neatly trimmed beard.

"Where's your Dad, son?"

"He's out front in the wagon with my Mom! He's hurtin' somethin' awful! Please help 'm!"

Before the physician could say anything else, the boy frantically pulled him out the front door. "We ain't got no time ta talk! My Dad's hurtin' somethin' terrible!"

A couple of minutes later the doctor reentered and passed through the office, then came back with a flat wide board.

"You must be Alfred White?"

"Yes sir."

"Alfred, would you mind helping me bring in a patient? He only has his wife and little boy with him."

When Alfred said he'd be glad to help any way he could, the doctor and his patient from Fish Springs sprang into action.

Writhing in pain, gritting his teeth and clenching his fists, the injured man in the back of the wagon definitely had seen better days. He groaned and grunted and covered his contorted face with his fists as Alfred and the doctor lifted him onto a wide sheet-covered board. He was tall, and so thin he hardly seemed heavier than the boy. Then, with his worried wife, toting his jug, and son following, they carried him through the office and to the examining room, where they set the board on an oak table.

"I thought you'd a been hollerin' by now with all the movin' you 'round we were doin,'" Godfrey said.

"I'm'a savin' it up, doc."

"Blanch, would you please take this young man to the waiting room? Missus, you may stay here with your husband. And Alfred, would you mind helping me with Jake's leg? That your name?"

"Yes, sir. I'am J-Jake Shoun and that thar's my wife, Ruth. My boy's n-name is Luke."

"Well, then, I'm Doc Godfrey and this good man that's going to help me set your leg is Alfred White.

"Ok, Alfred?'

"Okay Doc, but I don't know nothin' 'bout settin' legs."

"Alfred, all you have to do is hold him firm and tight around his arms. It takes a lotta strength to pull a leg straight. And when I yank on it, he'll scream and try ta move like the devil. Now you just get ready to hold 'em real close and steady like, just like a bear'd hold onto its cub that almost slipped off a cliff . . ."

As the doctor cut Jake's pant leg all the way to his hip, revealing the crooked leg below the knee, Alfred wondered how in tarnation he'd gotten himself into any of this. *Why'd I have to come here for an appointment today, of all days. . . ?*

"How'd you break your leg, Jake?"

"Tree I was'a cuttin' down kicked out on me."

"I see. I could give you some chloroform for the pain, but I need to ask you somethin' first, and I want the honest-to-God truth. How much'a that jug you had?"

"Well, doc I done d-drunk bout half it, on ma' way here." Jake, still writhing in pain, slurred his words.

"Or more," his wife Ruth added.

"Well, that should be enough," Doc said as he pulled at a rope tied to the table leg beneath Jake. "But I'm gonna loop this rope around your other foot to keep it outa the way while we work."

"It's the only time, s-she didn't f-fuss at me fer drinking that much, Doc. The pain was real bad, Doc."

"I see. Can't rightly say as I blame ya', Jake."

Jake looked at his wife with a validated grimace.

"Now are you ready? This'll hurt."

"I reckon, doc," Jake mumbled, still clenching his face with his hands. Standing at the end of the table, Alfred ran his arms under Jake's, and planted his feet against the bottom of the table legs.

"You ready, Alfred?"

"Ready, Doc."

Jake, who evidently had bottled up his hollering, screamed "OH! SHIT!" loud and shrill enough to be heard all the way to Fish Springs.

"Ow! Owww!" he yelled.

"Now you just stay still as you can. Try not to move," Doc Godfrey ordered. "Alfred and me's almost done."

Alfred, memories of all of the pain and suffering from the war filling his head, held onto Jake as hard as he could.

"Don't let'm move an inch, Alfred. We're gettin' it straightened out."

"Oww!" Jake screamed again.

But Alfred, amazed at how much strength it took to set a leg and how determined the old doctor was to get it back to its right shape, figured that was the last of the patient's excruciating pain. Because right then and there Jake flashed a big toothless grin and breathed a huge sigh of relief. His rough, dirty fingernailed hands dropped from his sweaty, grimacing face and he opened his eyes.

"I'd really like a chew'a 'baccer right now or a shot a good Tennessee moonshine! I ain't never felt such! And I pray ta God I don't never feel such agin!" said Jake, reaching for his jug that his relenting wife handed him.

Jake's boy Luke ran in when he heard his dad scream, but went back out with Blanch after his dad convinced him he was okay.

"You done right good, Jake. And so did you, Alfred," said the relieved doctor, stretching and wiping the sweat from his own head. Then he methodically felt all around the break.

"Whata ya think, Doc? Will it m-mend p-proper?" Jake asked.

"It should," said the doc, still feeling the leg. "It's a clean break."

Then he asked Alfred to return to the waiting room and stay a little longer while he splinted Jake's leg.

"Couldn't a done it without you, Alfred. Thank you. And if you don't mind, tell my wife to bring that boy back here so he can be with his dad. It'll put his mind at ease."

"Sure, Doc."

Jake reached out to Alfred, squeezed his hand and thanked him. "It was a p-pleasure to meet'cha, Alfred. Would'ga like'a hit on this jug? Thar's a bit left?" Jake then again shook hands with the total stranger who'd helped him get through one of the most wrenchingly painful times of his life.

"No thank you, Jake. You just take good care of that leg."

Another hour lapsed before Jake, helped along by his wife, hobbled out the front door on crutches—his injured leg wrapped and splinted with strips of wood all the way around.

Least ways, somethin' good's come of this trip. Maybe if nothin' else, I helped a man get back on his feet, Alfred mused. *Guess the Lord DOES work in mysterious ways.*

Blanch Godfrey escorted Alfred back to the examining room and told him Doc would see him shortly. As Alfred waited, he noticed aspects of the room. There was another pair of crutches leaning in one corner and a long shelf, at about eye level, stretching from one end of the room to the other. The shelf contained boxes of bandages and swabs, bottles of medicines and pills. In one corner was a black leather bag with a handle that Alfred figured the doctor carried with him on house calls. In the other corner was a large box, open on top, half full of splints like the ones used on Jake's leg.

And most intriguing to Alfred was a life-size picture of a human skeleton. The skull seemed to be smiling, and the skeleton's bony hands and fingers dangled to its sides as if it were standing at attention. Alfred wondered what its eyeballs, now just empty sockets in the skull, would have looked like. *And what about its privates? Wonder if it had been a man or woman?*

"Sorry ta keep you waitin' so long, Alfred. How was your trip from Fish Springs?" asked Godfrey, amused that his patient, like so many others before him, seemed captivated by the six-foot tall image of the skeleton.

"Well, doc, I have'ta be honest. I've been mighty nervous about this whole thing. I almost turned right around and went back home. And I wouldn't be here at all if it wasn't for my wife, Mary. I guess you got my letter explaining what's ailin' me 'bout my nature?"

"Yes, I did, and you said in your letter that Preacher Ike Redford gave you my name, so I reckon you go to his church?"

"Yes, Fish Springs Baptist. How'd you know him?"

"Ike pastored a church here in Elizabethton years ago that me an' Blanch went to. He's a good man, knows his Bible like the backa' his hand. He tries to be funny. Ike told us he was tired of so few folks comin' to our mourner's bench, and so he accepted an offer to preach in Fish Springs."

"Yep, that's him," Alfred said laughing

After more innocuous conversation, Dr. Godfrey, nudging his eyeglasses to the top of his head, got down to business. The first thing he told Alfred was that he'd done the right thing by coming to see him.

"So give yourself a pat on the back, Alfred. Lots'a men try to sweep somethin' like this under the rug. Or they're too embarrassed to talk about it. But this kind of problem, about your 'nature,' as you call it, Alfred, is more common than you think. I'll tell you this. You're not the first man and you won't be the last to come in here complainin' about not being able to have or keep an erection.

"And yes, young man, I read your letter about how you'd been shot during the war and what that's done to your marriage. Thanks for sharin' all of that with me. I know that took a lot of your time to write down, but you gave me all the details." Dr. Godfrey, reviewing Alfred's letter, nodded his approval.

"So what do you think, doc? Can I be fixed? Can I save my marriage?"

"Well, Alfred, from the way you described your injury, I think I'd a'come to the same conclusion as your Union doctor. However, I've had patients who fathered children with one testicle, so that shouldn't be your problem unless your wound was worse than it sounds. I can refer you to a doctor that specializes in this kind of situation, but first let me ask you something."

"Sure, doctor."

"You said in your letter your wife thought you'd been shot only in the leg, and you hadn't told her about the injury to your testicle yet. So have you told her now?

"Yes sir," Alfred replied, puzzled by the doctor's question.

"And when did you actually tell her?"

"Just yesterday, doc."

"Have you and your wife tried to have sex since you told her?"

"No, sir."

"Well, Alfred, it's entirely possible some, if not all of what's goin' on with your nature, could be in your head."

"In my head?"

"That's right, Alfred. See that skeleton over there? If you could see tha' brain, you'd know what I'm talkin' 'bout. It's one'a the biggest organs in the body, and once somethin' shakes it up, a man's whole body's affected—the way he thinks, what he does or don't do, how he sees the world, how he gets along or not with his friends and family, his nature…

"What I'm sayin' is your brain has a lot to do with your erections, Alfred. Not 'fessin' up to your new wife with the whole truth 'bout your injury made you anxious, added to your worryin' and frettin' over tryin' to please your wife in bed. Then her wantin' to get pregnant just caused more anxiety, making everything worse.

"Lower your trousers for me, Alfred, and let's have a look."

Alfred nervously took a deep breath, unfastened his belt and dropped his pants.

Dr. Godfrey chatted amiably with his patient as he examined his testicles and penis, cupping them in the palm of his hand. He told Alfred to turn his head and cough strongly as he held one testicle, then the other.

Alfred flinched slightly as the doctor did this procedure.

"Am I hurtin' you, Alfred? 'Cause I don't mean to. I'm almost done here."

"That's okay, doc. I guess I'm a might skittish about getting' examined down there..."

Seconds later, Alfred breathed a sign of relief when Dr. Godfrey rose from his examining chair and told his patient to pull his pants back up.

"So you're saying that a lot of this might just be in my brain, doc? That maybe since I told Mary the whole truth I might be able to have sex again? That my problem could be caused by anxiety?

"Yes I think that's a possibility, Alfred. Now mind you, I don't claim to be that knowledgeable about this kind of thing, but over the years I've had men patients with sexual troubles, and all that stuff went away after they got their head straight.

"Let me ask you something else, Alfred. Have you felt a lot of nervousness about this whole thing? Uh, about not being able to get hard and satisfy your wife, that is?"

"It's about all I've felt and thought about, doc. I can't get my mind off of it."

"I understand completely, Alfred. You're a human. You're a young man, and you're in love with your wife, but you're frustrated and worried. Am I right about that, Alfred ?"

"Dr. Godfrey, you couldn't be more right about anything in the world."Alfred confessed that he had agonized over losing Mary because he hadn't been able to make her happy in the bedroom.

"Here's what you should do, Alfred," Dr. Godfrey said. "I want you to relax and make love to your wife. But not tonight because you'll be tired after your long trip home. You and Mary make plans for a romantic evening. Don't force it. Just have fun and enjoy each other. Take your time, be playful with each other and see what happens. Then come back and see me and let me know how it went. And remember. you ain't the first man, and you won't be the last, to have trouble gettin' or keepin' an erection.

"Now get on back to Fish Springs and make you and your wife happy! Oh, and by the way, thank you again for helping me."

Alfred thanked the doctor, shook hands with him and promised to keep him informed. He seemed reassured by what Dr. Godfrey had said about taking it easy and slow and having fun with Mary. On his way out of the office, Dr. Godfrey said. "Oh, one more thing. do you have a picture of your wife?"

Alfred showed him a picture that had been taken on their wedding day. Mary looked as lovely as ever, with her long, lovely hair, sparkling eyes, perfect teeth and curvaceous body.

"Oh, my! She's a peach, Alfred, and I'll bet she's waitin' for you to come home right now! You're a lucky man! Now get back home with her where you belong. And remember what I told you about not trying too hard to make it happen. Just be patient and have a good time. You'll see..."

"Thank you, Dr. Godfrey. Thank you very much."

Once in the saddle and on his way, he thought about what Dr. Godfrey had advised him. *Relax. Take it slow. Have fun. Be playful. Enjoy each other. It'll happen soon enough...*

But then again, what if I fail. What if it don't happen? What then? Will Mary turn to someone else? John...?

When he got back to Fish Springs, it was after dark. Stars twinkled brightly from far above the highest Tennessee peak, and the moon, partially hidden by clouds, was a pale yellow. It had been a long, stressful, eventful day. But Alfred, exhausted and trying to make sense of it all, was also upbeat when he told Mary about Dr. Godfrey's diagnosis.

"Dr. Godfrey said my problem could be in my head."

"I don't understand, Alfred."

"It means what happened to me when we tried to make love could have been caused from anxiety. Dr. Godfrey said I was anxious because of not telling you the whole truth about my injury."

"Really? Well, what do you think?" Mary asked.

"It makes sense to me. Look, how 'bout I come home early tomorrow evenin' and we'll see?" He took Mary in his arms and pulled her close.

"I like that idea. How about I fix us an early dinner of fried chicken, mashed potatoes, fried okra and a blackberry pie for dessert? I'll give you a warm bath. Then we can get in the feather bed that I will have ready with the new sheets I've been saving. We can cuddle by the light of a candle and see what happens. Okay?"

Alfred held Mary tightly as she laid out the plans for the next night. His heart started pounding and his excitement grew as she talked about it.

"Mary."

"What Alfred?

"I want you now. I can't wait till tomorrow."

"Well then, why don't you take me, Alfred? What are you waiting for? The chickens to come home to roost?"

Alfred cradled Mary in his arms and carried her into the bedroom. Giggling, they couldn't get their clothes off fast enough, dropping them to the floor, and fell into the bed.

This time Alfred was the man he had prayed to be. It was like their raucous wedding night all over again. Mary's nostrils flared as she arched her back to have as much of Alfred as she could get. Their bodies meshed like they had been hungry for one another for far too long, and were, at long last, being fed. She buried herself in a pillow, dug her fingernails into Alfred's back and screamed, loud as she could, with pleasure, as she and her reinvigorated, uninhibited husband reached that ultimate level of sexual bliss. Later, their satiated bodies sweaty and spent, they lay contentedly in the dark holding each other.

"I love you, Mary."

"I love you, Alfred. And I always will."

She thanked the Almighty *for such a good man who loves me and'll take care of me. He provides me a home and food. He'll give me children, or adopt them with me. And thank you, Lord, for making Alfred whole again, and for keeping me strong, not being tempted by unchaste thoughts, and not giving up on my husband.*

Mary thought that a little encouragement might make Alfred want to have her again, but just as she reached down to touch his manhood, he started snoring. And then, smiling, she herself fell asleep.

The next day, before heading off to work in the fields, Alfred picked a plump chicken from the coup and rung its neck, a job Mary could do but didn't care for. He also helped his wife gather some fresh vegetables from their garden. Then he hitched the horse to the work wagon and pulled around to the front of their house.

There stood lovely Mary, his lunch in her hand, her short plain skirt riding temptingly a few inches above her ankles. Dirt from the garden had stained her clothes, and when she tried to swat the dirt off, her skirt rode up. Alfred's heart quickened, as he thought about making love to his beautiful, sensuous wife again, and again, and again…

"I'm sorry I fell asleep so quickly. I was just plum wore out," he said.

"Alfred, last night was wonderful. Besides, we have tonight and tomorrow morning, and—"

"I'll see you about four o'clock, sweetheart, and I'll be ready for you! I promise!" he said. Then he leaned down from the wagon seat and kissed her.

"I will count the hours! Be careful. I love you," said Mary, handing him his lunch.

"I love you too," Alfred said, putting his lunch in the feed sack and snapping the reins to head out.

Meanwhile, across the road and not far from their home, John Williams stood menacingly and shakily on his porch. It had been another long, rough night of drinking and carousing for him, and now, in the aftermath morning, he was paying the price. Waves of nausea wracked his body but he had to get past this. That was because today, he reminded himself, he had things to do.

His only hope was to get some hot coffee in his system and stay away from alcohol for the next few days.

John steadied himself on his porch and took another swig of coffee from his tin cup. Then he watched as Alfred White, who seemed oblivious to him, passed his house.

"Have a nice day, Yankee man," John mumbled.

CHAPTER 16

A Bad Day

Mary was optimistic about the day ahead and her future with Alfred. Shortly after he left, she went to the fence row along the road and picked enough blackberries for a pie. The big, juicy, ripe berries were plentiful, thriving in the wild among the hickory, oak and black gum trees. They also seemed to do especially well along the split rail fence. Within about half an hour, she easily filled her basket.

Her hands red from the berry juice, she returned home where she made the dough and put the pie together. She would bake it in the oven later when the wood-burning stove was hot for cooking supper.

Then she went to the spring behind the house and brought back a bucket of cold water. Their water at this time of year was as cold as ever because of the ice melt from Pond Mountain. It seemed the more severe the winter, the colder their water was in the spring.

She plucked the chicken that Alfred had caught and killed for her, cut it up and put the parts in the cold spring water to keep fresh. She wiped all the chicken blood off her, as she hated that freshly killed animal smell and mess. Then Mary got everything ready that she would cook later.

She put her hands on her hips, looked at herself in the mirror and began imagining how she and Alfred would enjoy each other after dinner. Mary undressed and inspected herself closely in their bedroom dresser mirror. She liked what she saw. She ran her hands softly over her curvy breasts and gently played with the inside of her thighs. She imagined that it was Alfred fondling and tickling her womanly private parts, and that image excited her.

Then she took a bath and washed her long blond hair. The tub of warm water, heated on the wood stove, relaxed and soothed. Mary immersed herself in suds and dreamed of holding her husband's body close to hers.

For the longest time, she just lay luxuriously there in the tub, focusing on how she and Alfred could get their marriage back on the right track. She thought of the past weeks and how unhappy her life had been. *I'm gonna' prove to Alfred that I'm a worthy wife. We're 'afixin' to make our marriage stronger then ever!*

When the water began to lose its warmth, Mary got out of the tub and dried herself with a towel. Aunt Caroline had made it for her as a wedding gift. The towel, which she kept in a special place in her bedroom, had embroidered hearts and pictures of Cupid on it. Sewn into it were these words. Mary and Alfred.

Dried and powdered, with a talcum that Alfred had gotten her for their anniversary, Mary basked on the back porch steps in the warm sunshine, waiting for her hair to dry. She fluffed it with her hands to speed the process. The sun's warmth energized her body.

She lingered there for an hour—baking in the sunshine, letting her hair dry and then combing it. And occasionally Mary let her hands drop to her breasts. Had anyone seen her, they would have thought that she was a young woman in love with herself. But what she really cherished was this God-given feeling of how wonderful it was just to be alive, clean and vibrant on such a spectacularly beautiful day. The only thing missing was her husband, and he'd be home soon enough.

Suddenly, she realized that time had almost gotten away from her. It was past three o'clock, and she had not finished cooking dinner, and there she sat day dreaming on the back porch!

Mary focused on their dinner. Her blackberry pie cooled on the porch railing, and the fried chicken was kept warm on the stove. But the other fixings had to be finished. Earlier she had spread a blue and white trimmed-in-lace tablecloth, reserved for special occasions that Polly Smith had made for her, on their hand-hewn, kitchen table.

She quickly finished the rest of the dinner, then went out and picked some wild flowers, placed them in a vase with water and sat the burst of color in the middle of the table. She arranged the dishes, forks, knives and spoons in their proper places. Aunt Caroline, she knew, would be proud that her niece had learned correct kitchen table etiquette.

As the old grandfather clock in the main room chimed four times, everything was ready, except for her missing husband.

Where is he? He shoulda' been here by now? He wuddn'ta forgot about what we planned, would he? No! That just ain't possible. Alfred was as excited as me when he left this morning. He couldn't wait ta get home!

Mary sat on the porch a bit irritated that she had worked so hard and diligently to have everything ready for her absent husband. Around four-thirty, she stoked the wood stove in the kitchen, then returned to the porch. As the clock chimed five times, the anxious young wife began wringing her hands, and pacing. Finally, she could stand it no more, she pulled her apron off and walked to the road. She squinted, hoping to see Alfred's wagon in the distance, but the road was vacant. The longer she stood there, the more she worried.

God, please bring 'em home to me!

Finally, she heard a horse and wagon approaching—but from the other direction. It was Daniel Smith, with his son, Charlie.

"Good afternoon, Mary."

"Afternoon, Daniel. Charlie."

Noticing her anxiety, Daniel asked her if everything was okay.

"Probably, Daniel, but I'm just a mite worried 'bout Alfred. He's workin' at the other end, in the lower field, and he said he'd be home 'bout four o'clock, and it's after five. It isn't like him to lose track'a time."

Daniel told her he and Charlie were going that way and would be glad to check on Alfred. Mary thanked him and said to say hi to Polly for her.

As he drove off, Mary returned to her porch swing. *Somethin' ain't right here. He's really, really late! Alfred should be home by now!*

And then she remembered the food she had left on the stove. It would be getting cold unless she put another stick of wood in the fire. So she donned her apron again and went back to the kitchen.

Meanwhile, Daniel and Charlie headed down the road.

"Mary shore' is a purty thang, ain't she, Pa?"

"Oh, starting to notice women, are we?"

"Pa!"

Daniel laughed as his son blushed. "You're right, son. She's right pretty."

Daniel noticed a kettle of vultures hanging in the sky. They weren't exactly flying away. The scavengers were circling over the area that he and Charlie were headed to.

"I wonder what them're after," Charlie said.

"I don't know, son. I hope it's a dead animal, maybe a deer. I guess we'll know soon enough." Daniel prompted his mare to a faster pace.

"I see Mr. White's wagon, Pa."

"Yeah, that's his wagon."

As they drew closer, Charlie saw the huge, ugly birds standing on something in the path. Every few seconds the scavengers would peck at what they stood on, then look nervously from one side to another and continue their feast.

"Pa, is that him?"

"I hope not, Charlie. I hope not."

Two vultures were chomping at a body lying face down, their sharp beaks dripping blood.

"Scat! Scat!" Daniel hollered as he climbed down from the wagon. "Stay here, son!"

And with that, the big, grisly birds flapped their wings and lifted off.

Daniel cautiously approached the corpse on the path. He dropped to his knees and turned the lifeless body over.

"Oh my God, you poor soul!" he gasped. "No! No!"

"Is it Mr. White, Dad?"

Daniel, spellbound with horror, only nodded.

Charlie started to scamper down from the wagon.

"Stay there, Charlie! Don't come over here! You don't want to see this!"

Daniel remembered when he was thirteen years old he'd seen a man's corpse dragged from a cabin that had burned down. The image of that poor soul's horribly charred face haunted him for years.

Alfred White's looks were at least as disturbing. The huge, carcass-gorging birds had already started devouring his back. His face, neck and one hand were grotesquely swollen and were blue-black. Puncture wounds on his head, face and neck underscored the gruesome sight.

His face wore a hideous expression of terror and panic.

He looks frightened, like he'd encountered somethin' terrible. But what on earth could it'a been? Daniel wondered.

Could Alfred have been beaten to death? But looking more closely at Alfred's swollen discolored neck, Daniel focused on two unsightly puncture wounds. He also saw the same kind of wounds on the side of his face and one on his hands.

"Charlie, fetch me that old army blanket that's under the seat!"

Charlie, got the blanket from the wagon, and keeping his distance from the body, waited as his father grabbed the blanket from him and covered the remains.

Flies were already depositing eggs in the open wounds on Alfred's corpse, the last thing Daniel wanted Charlie to see.

"Son, I want you to stay where you are! Sit under that tree. Don't come near this body! I'm going to see Mary White. Then I'm going into town to tell Sheriff Nave about Alfred."

"Okay, Pa, but what happened to'm?"

"Snake mighta got'm, but we'll let the sheriff decide that."

"A snake?" Charlie gasped.

"Just keep your eyes open son. And Charlie ..."

"Yes, sir."

"Stay away from the body! Whatever bit him had fangs, and who knows? That snake, if it was a snake, still might be lurkin' 'round here somewhere."

As Daniel rode away from the death scene, he couldn't shake the idea that a venomous snake had filled the last seconds of Alfred's life with terror. *All those bite or puncture wounds or whatever they were… all over his neck'n face and arms…!*

And Alfred, he also guessed, had died without a chance in the world of even yelling for help.

Daniel knew that deadly rattlesnakes and copperheads shared the Fish Springs mountain community with their human neighbors, but bites, while they did occur from time to time, were rarely fatal. Especially with copperhead bites, herbal and country doctor remedies had saved many a life.

Every so often, however, someone dying after being hit by a big rattler would remind folks to keep their distance.

Daniel had heard that a rattlesnake-handling holiness preacher—a few miles up in the mountains from Fish Springs—got bit on his face. The preacher had hoisted the reptile above his body, at an evening church service, while he recited words presumably uttered by Jesus and recorded in the Book of Mark. "They shall take up the serpents; and if they drink of any deadly thing, it shall not hurt them."

"This is a testimony of my faith in the Almighty!" the preacher, so sure of himself, had boomed.

And at that very moment, Daniel had been told, the angry, writhing rattlesnake slithered from the preacher's grasp and sank its fangs into his face.

Guess that snake hadn't read the Bible, Daniel mused as he continued his ride toward Mary's house. *But that holiness preacher, when he got bit, lived for ten hours before his heart and breathin' stopped. And Alfred seems to have been dead in just minutes, because he was still close to where he was workin'. Lord God, how could that'a happened?*

CHAPTER 17

Suspicion

Mary ran to the road when she spotted Daniel approaching.

Grim faced, he set the brake and climbed down from his wagon. He avoided eye contact with her and said nothing as he tried to gather his wits. But it was no use. She knew something terrible had happened.

"We found Alfred, Mary. I'm so—"

"Is he dead?"

"I'm afraid so, dear." Daniel dropped his head, measuring his words. "It was bad, Mary, real bad."

Her arms clinched tightly, balling up her fists and closing her eyes, Mary collapsed to the road on her knees. She began wailing and rocking back and forth, as Daniel tried to comfort her.

"What happened to him, Daniel?" She sobbed. "How'd he die?"

"It looks like he was bit by a snake, Mary."

"Oh my God, Daniel!" Mary's body convulsed as she rocked to one side, then another. Tears had somehow worked their way into her mussed hair. Her eyes remained tightly shut, as if she were afraid to open them and see the truth.

Daniel kept trying to comfort her—reminding her that Alfred was in a better place now because he was a Christian and had gone home to be with the Lord. But she was too devastated to hear his words, and continued to bawl.

Over and over, Daniel expressed his sorrow to her. Then he pulled her limp body up from the road and held her tightly. Like an affectionate father would hold a grieving daughter.

"We were gonna' have children and spend a long life together!" Mary spoke brokenly between sobs. "We were makin' plans! Oh, my poor Alfred! Why'd this happen? Alfred was a good, decent, hard workin', God fearin' man."

Mary wiped her eyes on her apron. "God must be punishing me. I'm a sinner."

"We are all sinners Mary—I know you loved him more'n anything in the world. And Alfred loved you, too, I'm sure. But we just don't know why or how these awful things happen. We have to take it to a greater power'."

"Alfred hated snakes more'n anything in the world! He told me he once dreamed 'bout a rattlesnake crawlin' in bed with him when he was a boy. He never got over that nightmare. Oh Lord, his worst fear!" Mary cried and rocked in anguish and grief to one side and the other.

Gradually, however, she opened her tearful eyes and gently pushed Daniel away.

"I'll be okay," she said, trembling and taking a deep breath. "I want to be left alone just now, Daniel. I'm sorry but—"

He cut her off. "I understand, Mary. You're grievin' and hurtin' really bad. You need some time by yourself. I'm gonna give you that 'cause I've got to go fetch Sheriff Nave. But I'll have Charlie bring Polly here to watch after you. Will you be all right 'till then?"

Mary didn't answer and seemed to be in shock as Daniel walked her to her porch. She sat down in the swing.

"Will you be okay, Mary?" he asked.

"Yes. You just go about your business, Daniel. Don't fret about me. I want to pray for my husband's soul." Mary took a deep breath and dried her eyes. It was as if a sense of acceptance began to set in, and she was preparing herself, steeling herself, to cope with her husband's unspeakable death.

Alfred had been the love of her life, and now he was gone, never to return to her arms or home and bed—imperfect as that may have been in recent months—and Mary told herself she was just going to have to get used to it. There would be a wake, a mourning, a funeral, a burial, and she would somehow have to get through it all. *Now, I've just got to get my faith back an' see my way through all this. Alfred would want me to lean on th' cross'a Jesus.*

On his ride to get Sheriff Nave, Daniel himself grieved and tried to make sense of Alfred's terrible demise. Mary, far as he knew, had always been a sweet, loving, Christian, woman, devoted to her husband. She'd been brought up right and proper by her Aunt Caroline. Why would Mary have to suffer so?

Daniel had always been told, and he had told others, that no one knew God's divine plan. But he was always troubled, and puzzled, when someone like Alfred—a good Godly person—or an innocent child, met an untimely death.

As Daniel urged his horse onward toward the sheriff's office, he heard a honking overhead. About fifty geese were flying in a V-formation. He stopped to take in one of nature's most fascinating spectacles—the huge, squawking birds seeming to fly in perfect rhythm, first tilting to the left and then to the right—but always together in formation.

Daniel, always of the mind that nature had lessons for people, thought that too many folks in Fish Springs, despite their church-going ways, secretly harbored bitter grudges. And instead of working with and helping one another, they did just the opposite. *Would that human beins could be like those birds—workin' and flyin' together and movin' in the same direction so that they wouldn't be alone in gettin' through the twists and turns of life.*

And would that Mary, so deeply hurt right now, would have folks walking and working and worshiping with her and comforting her in her darkest hours. 'Cause if birds can stay together and flap their wings in the same direction, people ought to do the same, 'specially when one of their neighbors is grievin' somethin' awful.

When Daniel arrived, Sheriff Nave was yelling at a strapping fellow who seemed, as folks around Fish Springs put it, "a might tetched in the head."

As Sheriff Nave tried to handcuff the man, who reeked of moonshine, he would have none of it, resisting arrest, flailing about and screaming.

To the sheriff's consternation, a small crowd began to take notice.

"Now, Ben, you just behave and come on right calm like. I ain't wantin' no trouble from you, hear me? " Nave implored his inebriated captive.

And, facing the crowd, the obviously aggravated sheriff let it be known that the arrest was none of their business and that they best scat.

But one onlooker wouldn't be so easily deterred.

"What'd he do, Sheriff? Why you puttin' 'em in jail? Everbody knows old Ben ain't right'n his brain!"

"All I d-done wuz b-blow in a hoss's nose so's he'd like me and be a better h-hoss!" Ben, fighting the sheriff's every move, protested. "And I jist l-love hosses and m-mules! They's my fave-vert f-friends!"

Finally, after a lot of tugging and pushing and muscling him into submission, Carter County's chief law enforcement officer cuffed Ben, grabbed him under his left elbow and dragged him, kicking and bawling, to jail.

And when that happened, a chorus of hearty boos came from outside the jail.

"Ben ain't never hurt nobody! You caint just lock'm up for drinkin' a little shine an' blowin' in a horse's nose!" one of the rabble-rousers complained.

"I done told ya'all! Now git 'fer I arrest ever lastin' one of ya!" the sheriff snapped. "I'm lockin'm up 'cause he's drunk as a skunk and I don't want'm hurtin' hisself or nobody else!"

The sheriff as he turned to see Daniel standing on the wooden walk outside the jail. "Mr. Smith, what brings you here?"

"I found Alfred White dead in his field. I'm not for sure but he could've been bit by a snake."

Nave asked a few questions and assured Daniel he and at least one of his deputies would immediately come look into the situation.

The news of Alfred's death spread like wildfire from their conversation in the jail. Nave especially hated big crowds at death scenes, as they got in the way of his investigation.

"Now you all just keep your mouths shut 'till I git ta the bottom of this!" an aggravated Nave ordered onlookers at Alfred White's death scene a short time later.

The stocky man who regularly won re-election to his coveted office wore a black felt hat, had a big thick mustache and kept an impressive silver revolver holstered on his right hip. A tin star with the word "SHERIFF" in the middle of it was pinned on the left side of his leather vest.

Nave went about his work on the case in his usual, methodical, no-nonsense fashion.

"Ain't this somethin'," said Nave as he examined Alfred's body. "I ain't never seen nothin' like this. It's like some kinda' serpent got ahold of'm and just bit'm ta death. But I cain't say for shore. How in tha world did he git them fang marks, or whatever they are, way up on his neck? If it was a damned snake that bit him, its venom shot straight to his heart."

As the sheriff speculated, a curious crowd of wide-eyed Fish Springs residents moved closer and bent their ears.

"Now ya'all get on back!" he demanded. "For all we know, there coulda' been a crime here, and I cain't have no fool disturbin' this area! I cain't tell ya' nothin' yet 'cause I don't know nothin' yet!"

The gossip and rumor mill in Fish Springs went into high gear. The bystanders reluctantly retreated, but not before they had seen plenty. A few of them practically ran to their own homes or to their neighbors' homes and spread the juicy news. "Sheriff Nave thinks Alfred White done got bit by a big ole rattlesnake and died, and it coulda' been throwed on'm!" said one.

"They say a snake bit'm an' he puffed up and started rottin'!" another rumormonger said. "And not only that, they think it wuz a rattler big 'round as a stove pipe that sank its fangs into poor ole Alfred…"

As darkness neared, and a cold fog moved in, most of the crowd—weary that the sheriff was keeping information about the case under such a tight lid—dispersed from the death scene. The place where Alfred White had apparently taken his last breath became practically deserted, and that suited Sheriff Nave just fine. For he could now go about his work without worrying what anyone would say, or, more specifically, claim that he said. *Damned stupid gossipers. You say one thing and they git it totally wrong. I wish they'd just keep their mouths shut!*

The sheriff explained to Daniel that he had sent for Moss Campbell, an expert on snakes, so that he could rule out any possibility of foul play.

"But what do you think, Sheriff?" asked Daniel. "The only thing I could figure was a snake bit him."

"Well, that probably happened, Daniel," said Nave, pushing his felt hat back a bit on his head and stroking his mustache, "but the thing that puzzles me is how Alfred got bit sa bad in tha neck an' face. The hand I can understand, if he was reachin' down for somethin'. His lunch is still on the wagon seat in that feed bag, so he didn't sit down on the ground ta eat. Anyway, maybe Moss Campbell can shed some light on what happened. I'll be back in the mornin'. And Daniel, I'm much obliged that you've gotten your men to watch over this death scene and the body tonight. We don't want no critters disturbin' the corpse."

"Alfred was my friend, Sheriff. It's the least I can do."

"How is Mrs. White?"

"She's terrible upset, of course. Polly's stayin' with her."

"Understandable. Are you goin' to her home now?"

When Daniel said he thought he'd be paying Mary a visit, the sheriff instructed him to pass his own condolences onto Alfred's widow. He also told Daniel to mention to Mary that he might need to ask her a few questions later "but first we'll see what Moss Campbell has to say."

"Okay, Sheriff."

Later, at the house, Daniel hoped that he would find that Polly had somehow managed to comfort Mary, but that wasn't the case. She broke down again when she heard that Sheriff Nave was suspicious of how Alfred died. Polly and Daniel had to remind her that Alfred was in God's hands. That divine reassurance, along with some soothing hot tea that Polly got her to drink before she went to bed, helped her some.

When they were sure the distraught widow was asleep, which wasn't until after midnight, Polly chastised her husband. "I wish you hadn't told Mary what

Sheriff Nave had said. She don't need no more pain."

"Well, I wish I hadn't either, now," said Daniel. "But at least it won't take her by surprise if he has to ask her some questions."

"What do you think happened, Daniel?"

"I just don't know, Polly. We'll learn more tomorrow. Right now, I'm going home to check on the kids and hit the sack. Do you need anything?"

Polly said she would be fine and then kissed her husband good night. It had been a long stressful day and night for her, for Mary and for everyone who had tried to help Mary. Polly, now in her night gown, said her prayers, including a few lines for Alfred. Then she blew out all the candles and doused the house's oil lamps except for one in the kitchen. She listened to hear if Mary was sleeping. She was. All seemed okay, so Polly stretched out on the floor, in the bedding she had brought from her own house, and fell asleep.

Earlier that night, as one of the messengers returned to Elizabethton, the shocking news fell on eager ears at the Black Bear Saloon. "A snake killed Alfred White!" shouted the man as he burst through the saloon's swinging doors.

Inside the Black Bear, men were laughing, singing, clapping and stomping their feet to music banged out on an old upright piano. But upon hearing the news, they stopped wetting their whistles with whiskey and beer and fell silent—almost solemnly so. The bartender stopped wiping the long paneled oaken bar. Madge, wearing too much makeup and dressed in a brightly ruffled skirt with a low-cut bodice, withdrew her hands from the shoulders of a man playing poker at the round table and focused on the courier.

The man she had been massaging as he played poker was John Williams.

"What'd you say 'bout Alfred White?" John asked the gossipmonger. "Come agin' with that."

"I said he been kilt dead—bit by a snake! But Sheriff Nave is spicious'. That's straight from Nave hisself. I hyeered it with my own ears!"

"When?" John asked, trying to ignore the pall that had fallen over the saloon. The place had become as quiet as a funeral parlor.

"They don't rightly know yet," the eager messenger said. "Funny, quare thang, though.They say he wuz bit on his neck and face. They cain't rightly figure out how it happened, so Sheriff Nave sent one of his deputies to fetch that snake man in Butler. You know, ol' Moss Campbell. He's sposed' ta be a snake expert. Daniel Smith got two of his darkies to stay with the body down in Alfred's field all night to keep critters away. Moss Campbell's a comin' in the mornin'."

"Poor Alfred," responded John, laying his cards down, stuffing his winnings in his pockets and standing up.

"Deal me out fellers. I'm headin' back ta Fish Springs," John said.

"When I seed ya' in here, I figgered' you might not'a heered it," said the news purveyor, now facing John.

"Well, you done figgered' right."

The pianist started playing again and the loud, raucous talk and laughter resumed. As John turned to leave, he came face to face with Madge.

"He be the one that lived across the road from you?" Madge asked. "The one who married that woman you wuz sweet on? What now? You gonna' run back home so's you can comfort her?"

"That was a long time ago, babe. You know you're the only woman fer me."

"Yea, and you damn well best leave it that way, John Williams!"

"Don't get your panties in'a knot, Madge. I'll be back in a day er' two. I jist need ta pay my respects."

Then John kissed Madge, whose eyes dared him to stray from her, and left the saloon.

Back in Fish Springs, hours later, John Williams paused in the moonlit, tree-lined road. He wanted desperately to visit Mary, but it was very late. *In the mornin', I'll just come and visit her and pay my respects like everybody else. Let Mary grieve fer'm. Give her some time. She'll forget about the son of a bitch soon enough. Then I'll make my move. I'll make her Mrs. John Williams, and I'll show her what it's like ta be married to a real man.*

Early the next day, Polly brewed some coffee and offered to cook breakfast for Mary, but she said not to bother because she couldn't eat it. Instead, she thanked Polly for everything she'd done.

"I'm strong enough to be by myself," Mary said. "You need to be with your own family. Go on home. And you don't need to come back here, Polly. I'll be fine. God'll take care of me."

"I'll see you in a little while, dear heart. I ain't leavin' you fer long."

"I love you, Polly," said Mary, giving her caretaker a hug.

John, lingering on his porch as Polly passed in her buggy realized that he could at long last go to Mary's, house, so he wasted no time.

"Mary, are you okay?" John asked.

She opened the door when he knocked and backed away, crying.

"I have to ask you, John Williams. Did you have anything to do with Alfred's death?"

"My God, Mary! How could you ask me that? Do you really think I could kill my friend, somebody I growed up with? 'Sides I hyeered' he was bit by a snake."

"He was, but Sheriff Nave's suspicious of how it happened."

"Well, I guess I rightly know what you think of me now," said John, lowering his voice and hanging his head as if humiliated. "How could you hurt me like that, accusin' me of sich a thang, Mary? As God is my witness, I ain't had nothin' ta do with Alfred's death."

"I'm sorry John, I just—"

"I know you're in a heapa' pain, Mary, and I'm sorry 'bout that, but I just wanted to pay my respects. Alfred was my friend."

Mary didn't know what to say. And a part of her felt ashamed. *Well, it's true they did grow up tagether' and they was friends for a long time.*

Then she spoke. "I'm sorry, John. I know in my heart you never could have done such a horrible thing. I'm just tryin' to make sense of it all, and I ain't doin' so good. Thank you for paying your respects."

John hugged her respectfully and said he understood. Then he told her she could depend on him to be a good friend.

"I'm goin' ta see if the sheriff or that snake expert comin' from Butler knows anymore 'bout Alfred's death," he said. "And I'm sure the truth'll come out, Mary. Meanwhile, if they's anythang' I can do fer you, remember I'm just across the road."

She nodded and said she was sorry again for accusing him.

"It's okay Mary. You're under a lot'a stress right now. You're still suffrin'."

Once outside her house, John, gloating, smiled inwardly. *Mary'll soon be mine again. It's just a matter of time.*

CHAPTER 18
The Snake Man's Theory

People had again begun congregating at the death scene by the time Daniel returned. As he rode up, he waved to Isaiah, his muscular, tall ex-slave whom Daniel had pressed into duty to stand vigil overnight with the corpse. Standing, as if at attention, at the base of a huge oak tree that shaded the area, Isaiah waved back. Another of Daniel's workers, Mo, lay flat on the ground, sound asleep. Isaiah kicked Mo, also an ex-slave, in the foot, and he woke up.

Daniel put the apologetic Mo at ease, then asked Isaiah if everything had gone well throughout the night.

"Yes sa', we had'a run off'a couple'a ol possums an'a coon, but dat's all."

The darker skinned Mo, still stretching awake and revealing big ivory white teeth, added. "I know, I sho' was glad to see dat ol' sun come up!"

"Well you'all go on back and get some sleep," said Daniel, thanking them for watching Alfred's body. "But don't stray too far. I'll probably need you this evenin' ta dig a grave."

"Yes sa'," Isaiah said. "Sho' is bad 'bout poor Mista Alfred. He be a good man."

As Isaiah and the sleepy-eyed Mo carefully weaved their way through the growing crowd of curious onlookers, Sheriff Nave and the county coroner arrived and ordered everyone to move back.

"Now folks, I ain't gonna' tell you no more! This here's an investigation and you best be on your way!" the irritated sheriff growled. "Some of you's gonna' end up behine' bars iffn' you refuse my orders!"

Then he faced Daniel and Doc Rueben Bowers, the coroner who was stepping down from his buggy.

All three men shook hands and exchanged greetings. They also deliberately kept their voices down—so as not to tip off the ever-more-curious and restless crowd—as they discussed Alfred's death.

Doc Bowers, dressed impeccably in a suit and wearing small-framed glasses that seemed almost to slide off the tip of his thin long nose, nodded to Daniel, laid his medical bag on the ground near Alfred's body and pulled a handkerchief from his pants pocket. Removing his glasses, he blew his nose loudly, then began wiping the 'sweat from his face and spectacles. "Well, well, well. Let's see what we got here," said Bowers, removing the old army blanket that had covered Alfred's body.

Members of the crowd gasped.

"Look at that!" one man screamed. "He's 'bout black!"

"That there riggamorgus done started rottin'm away!" another yelped.

Sheriff Nave, who'd heard about all he could stand, angrily raised his hands and demanded silence. "Now y'all just hold your damn tongues and let Doc Bowers do his job! This here's a death scene and you ain't got no reason to be here noways."

"But why cain't we give our opinions, Sheriff?" a brazen fellow at the front of the crowd asked.

"Because I said you cain't! That's why!"

The coroner smiled, as if somehow amused by all the commotion. And then, as a hush finally fell on the crowd, he proceeded with his examination.

Doc Bowers began by shooing away the flesh flies that had begun collecting on the rapidly putrefying body. Alfred's grossly swollen mouth and bulging lips, yellowed eyes, along with his distended tongue and blackness, made him almost unrecognizable.

"Poor soul! Hit looks more like a rottin' carcass than abody!" one onlooker blurted out.

"Which one? Alfred'er Doc Bowers? " another snickered.

"I'm placin' you under arrest!" an exasperated Sheriff Nave proclaimed. He grabbed the smiling comic, muscled him to the ground and handcuffed him.

With his prisoner in tow, when the sheriff again warned everyone to hold their tongues, no one said a word.

Meanwhile, the coroner, still coughing and fighting an ugly cold, had taken his time meticulously examining the bloated corpse. He had cut off Alfred's shirt and bent over and looked closely at the victim's hair, nails and skin. Then he had carefully inspected the puncture wounds, flinching as he absorbed the expression of utter terror, still discernible on Alfred's darkened, rotting face. With help, Bowers turned the cadaver over.

"Did vultures get to him?" Bowers asked.

"Yep. I shooed 'em away," Daniel said.

"I don't see any other marks on tha body other'n these pecked holes an' fang punctures," Bowers said. "And it does appear that he died from snakebites, but like ya say, I don't rightly see how he got bit on his face and neck. I never seen a case just like this. But I'll go with a snake bein' the cause. That's my conclusion.

"And the poor fella musta died really fast 'cause when that ole snake got ahold of him, it most likely dog-bit'm, judgin' from the puncture wounds."

"Whatcha' mean by dog bit?" the sheriff asked.

"I mean that big ole' snake bit inta tha soft flesh a Alfred's throat an' face with its fangs and wouldn't let go," the coroner said. "It locked onto'm with its fangs even as poor, suffrin' Alfred shook 'bout somethin' awful. Musta been a horrible way to die. A man ought never to take his last breath like such."

The sheriff thanked Doc Bowers for his report and asked him to stay a little while longer.

Then he took Daniel aside. "Daniel, I hear tell there was bad blood between Alfred and John Williams. Can you shed any light on that?"

"Sheriff, I think that got resolved after Alfred and Mary got married. Leastwise that's what I thought."

The sheriff, rubbing his chin, studied this for a moment and thanked Daniel for offering his opinion.

"Now, folks," the sheriff said, "Maybe some a you'd like ta go over there and git in the shade a that oak tree. You know it's about too hot for anybody here in tha' sun."

But the sheriff's attempt at dispersing them didn't work. No one left, and, in fact, the numbers in the mass of mumbling onlookers increased in anticipation of the arrival of Moss Campbell, the snake expert, who was approaching on his mule.

Word throughout Fish Springs was that Campbell knew more about snakes, especially poisonous species, than anyone else in East Tennessee. Legend even had it that the balding, grizzled man with a big hairy mole on his nose had been bitten by rattlesnakes dozens of times. That had happened, the stories asserted, as he handled them in church services or as he caught them with his bare hands in the wild. He had many old crusty fang marks on his hands, arms and legs, but somehow the serpents' poison had not killed him.

Where others had done all they could to stay out of the way of what some declared were God's lowest, most feared and dreadful creatures, Moss Campbell had done exactly the opposite. He had eagerly sought rattlesnakes and copperheads out, and even, on one occasion had handled a cottonmouth water moccasin, snatched from a swamp in Virginia, and stared it straight in its beady eyes. The deadly snake had coiled itself around his upper arm but had not bitten him; instead it almost seemed to relish contact with Campbell's body. The "snake man" had actually befriended one of the world's most venomous and feared vipers.

Moss Campbell, whose little, slit eyes themselves resembled those of a snake, climbed down from his ride and pulled his cane off the saddle horn.

"Thanks for comin' over, Mr. Campbell," said the sheriff.

The venerable "snake man" wore an old tattered suit and limped with his walking stick. He made eye contact with no one, and seemed instantly obsessed with searching the scene.

"Where is he? Where's the body?" Campbell asked.

Nave guided him through the throng of people to Alfred's corpse.

"I'd like for you to tell us what you think happened here, Mr. Campbell."

The snake expert got down on his knees next to Alfred's body and commenced his inspection.

After painstakingly studying the bite marks, he spoke. "Yep, snake done this. From the size of these bites, most likely a timber rattler. A big fella'. Problee 'bout six foot with fifteen to twenty rattles. We got copperheads in these parts, but not big enough to do this here kind'a damage."

"Moss, we can't figure out how he got bit so high up on his body," the sheriff said. "His lunch is still on the wagon and he wouldn't have laid it down before he ate. You thinkin' the snake could've been on the wagon?"

"Maybe, but that big ole snake would'a warned'm to stay away by rattlin'."

"Well, what the heck did happen here?" asked a frustrated Sheriff Nave, removing his hat and scratching his head.

"Let me study this a bit, Sheriff."

"Sure, Moss. Take all the time you need. I'll get back to tendin' this crowd."

"What's tha snake expert think, Sheriff?" one of the onlookers shouted.

"That ain't none'a yor business!"

The sheriff noticed that John Williams had joined the fray.

Well, now's as good a time as any to question that young man about Alfred White's death, Carter County's chief law enforcement officer surmised, discreetly summoning him from the crowd. He walked with John to the shade of the big oak tree, still watching Moss Campbell near Alfred's wagon. The snake man was hunched over and picking up a piece of blue egg shell. He nervously rubbed the mole on his nose as he turned the shell over and over.

"John, I'd like to ask you a few questions about Alfred White," the sheriff said.

"Poor Alfred. Was it a snake bite?" John asked.

"Yes, but they's a lot we don't know about how it happened. John, where were you 'round noon yesterdee'?"

"Damn you, Sheriff! Why're you askin' me that? "

"Now, John, don't go gettin' all contrary on me. I'm just tryin' to do my job here. I know they wuz' bad blood between you an' Alfred White."

"Sheriff, we might notta 'greed on the war, but Alfred White wuz' my friend. Me an' him growed up and played tagether as younguns.'"

"Yeah, and ya' both wudda' done anythang to git Mary," Sheriff Nave sourly responded. "Everbody knowed you 'bout lost it when Alfred married'er."

"I did hurt some, Sheriff, but then I 'cepted it. I went ta Mary and wishted her and Alf tha best. Ask'er fer yoreself."

As they spoke, the sheriff glanced over his shoulder. He watched Moss Campbell, still near the wagon and holding the eggshell, but this time he was gazing upward.

The lawman pressed on with his questioning. "John, I'm gonna' ask ya agin. Where wuz you 'round noon yesterdee?"

"Same damn place most ever' man in Fish Springs is this time'a year! Workin' my crops outin' the hot sun! Now I ain't answerin' no more questions 'till you ask everbody else here the same thangs."

As the sheriff said that would be all, for now, Moss Campbell, a sly grin on his face, boomed. "I figered it out! I knowed what happened here!"

Suddenly re-aroused, everyone at the death scene gathered around the snake man—eager to hear his theory.

"Alfred White was in tha wrong place at tha wrong time," Campbell declared. "It's 'cause snakes love baby birds and bird eggs, an' they'll climb most any tree to get at'em. They's good climbers goin' up. Trouble is they cain't climb down, 'cause a way their scales is facin'. Oh, they'll try, but they'll most apt ta fall. I've seen many a snake fall out'a tree tryin' to come down, and I ain't never seen one that couldn't slither away after hittin' the ground. Now if'n you look right up yonder, you'll see a bird nest which is 'bout over the end of this wagon."

As every pair of wide eyes in the crowd glared upward to where the vaunted snake man pointed, he continued. "That thar' nest had baby birds in it. A big, hungry rattler clumb up thar an' swallered the birds and then was tryin' to slither down. But it fell, landin' on Alfred White's head as he was reachin' for his lunch."

Mumbling and gasps came from the crowd, and one old timer trembled as he screamed, "It wuz an act a' God! Oh my! Poor ole' Alfred musta wronged the Lord somethin' awful, 'cause the Good Book says, 'Vengeance is mine, saith the Lord!'"

Weary of so much drama, the sheriff winced but took no action against the offender of his orders to keep silent. "Go on, Moss. Keep talkin'."

The snake man, now sure that he'd solved the mystery, chawed down on his wad of tobacco, spit an ugly brown stream of juice to his side, and continued. "When tha snake landed on'm, Alfred tried to pull it off'm. That's when the rattler struck his hand. When he pried it off his hand, it bit'm in his face. If'n he could'a throwed'm off then it might not'ta kilt'm, but it weren't to be. That big ol' mean rattler was wrapped 'round Alfred's squirmin', sufferin' body, and it weren't a gonna' turn loose. It struck agin, clampin' down on Alfred's neck, squirtin' pisin into his main blood pipe."

"Carotid artery," Doc Bowers interjected.

"Right," said Campbell. "I reckon Alfred only took a step'er two befer' he went down. Prob'ly dead 'fore he hit the groun'. That's what happened here. I'll stake my repertation on it."

Sheriff Nave stared at Doc Bowers. "Doc?"

"It makes sense to me, Sheriff. I sure can't come up with a better answer."

The lawman addressed Daniel. "Off the record, Daniel, what do you think?"

"It's the best explanation I've heard, Sheriff."

"Well, then let's make it official. Since you agree, Doc, write it that way in your coroner's report, and I'll do the same in mine. I'm releasin' the body to you, Daniel, so you can go on and git' it buried. It's gonna' get hotter today, and that smell's gettin' worse by the minute. I'd get him in a box and covered up in a grave as soon as you can."

"I will, Sheriff."

When John Williams, inwardly breathing a sign of relief, asked Daniel if there was anything he could do, Daniel asked him to take Alfred's wagon back to his house and put it in the barn, "and tell Mary, me and my wife'll keep checkin' on her."

John said he'd be much obliged to do that and anything else to help the widow.

Then Sheriff Nave asked if he could have one last word with him.

"Yeah, Sheriff?"

"I guess all this makes you innocent."

"I s'pose you wuz' jist doin' your job Sheriff. I guess it's hard when your victim ain't got no enemies."

"Well, unlike Alfred, most of 'em have at least one. See you later, John. I need to see Mary White to tell her what we came up with here, and I'll tell her you're bringin' Alfred's wagon back."

"Okay, Sheriff."

As John prepared to mount his horse, all he could think about, just then, was Mary—no doubt grieving but also sweet and lonely. *She's gonna feel bad 'bout the way she done me after she gits the verdict from Sheriff Nave, but I'll fergive'er. She'll get that Yankee bastard in the ground soon enough … And then…*

John Williams at that moment was the happiest man in Fish Springs. For him, Mary's time for healing and getting past her husband's death couldn't pass fast enough.

CHAPTER 19

Obsessed

Carter County's chief law man knew what came next. As he rode slowly on the narrow road through the dense green forest toward Mary's house, he thought of how he'd describe to Alfred's widow what caused her husband's death. *Ain't no need to give her the gruesome details. She's done suffered enough.*

He stopped next to a dark gurgling creek in the woods and dismounted. Then he removed his hat, leaned against a moss-covered boulder and stared upward. As his horse gulped from the creek, the sheriff rubbed his tired eyes and reminded himself that sometimes things weren't as they seemed in outwardly peaceful, presumably God-fearing Fish Springs. On occasion, such as just last month, Sheriff Nave had been summoned to a scene, just outside of town, where a man had nearly bled to death. The injured gentleman's wife had insisted that her then unconscious husband had cut his hand off while chopping wood.

But that had not been the case. In fact, far from it.

When the man came to and could talk, he told a grisly tale of his wife bashing him in the head with a shovel to within an inch of his life and then tying his hand and forearm to a low-hanging limb of a giant pine tree. Ignoring his pleas for mercy, the self-professed Christian woman commenced to cut his hand off with his union saber. She intended to take his head off but he ducked at the last second.

Sheriff Nave had been beside himself when he learned about this mutilation—stemming from the wife's jealous rage. She had found her husband a day earlier in a compromising position with her own sister, who happened to be married to the injured man's best friend.

He had charged her with attempted murder, and today she awaited trial from a cell in Elizabethton. She would almost surely be found guilty and sent to prison for a long, harsh sentence.

"There's a special place in Hell fer what she done ta her husband!" one close friend of the family had declared. "'Cause what she done is what the devil's work is all about."

But another relative, on the wife's side of the family, took exception to such condemnation, proclaiming that "the damned scoundrel orta knowed better than ta fool 'round with his wife's own blood. She shoulda' cut something else off 'stead'a his hand!"

And as for her unfortunate husband? He barely survived, but was now regaining his strength at his mother's house.

A brook trout broke the surface of the creek, causing Sheriff Nave to wish he could have taken the day off and gone fishing.

He kept coming back to the haunting fact that evil lurks everywhere and that below the surface in Fish Springs—and no doubt all through the rugged, beautiful mountains of East Tennessee—things often weren't as they appeared. *Terrible, unspeakable things happen in these mountains and it's jist like Preacher Redford says, "Life'd be sa' much better if there wuz no devil, but long as you're on this side'a the river, you're gonna' be doin' battle with'm, 'cause ole' Satan don't never rest."*

The well-spoken preacher, Sheriff Nave concluded, had summed it up perfectly. Yes, plenty of so-called upstanding folks went, regular as rain, to church here and professed their love for the Lord and for each other, but be a lawman long enough and you'd see a lesser known and uglier, darker side of the community. An undercurrent of greed, lust, thievery and lying was all too common. *But could be it's like that ever' wheres, and it ain't jist here.*

When another full-of-life brook trout, this one about two feet long and speckled with a golden underbelly, broke the surface of the clear, cold stream to catch a water bug, Sheriff Nave put his hat back on and petted the nose of his horse.

"Best we git on our way, boy," the sheriff whispered. "Alfred's widow'll be frettin' somethin' terrible, waitin' fer the news 'bout her man ..."

The seen-it-all law man wasted no time completing his trip. When he got to the White's house, as he expected, there stood Mary, worried, anxious, fearful, anticipating the worst.

When he shared his final report with her, Mary, listened intently but said nothing. She stood stoic like, as if numb to the core or in some sort of trance.

After a few moments of awkward silence, the sheriff spoke. "Now you just feel free to ask me anything, Mary. Bless your heart ... You have a right to know as much about this case as me."

But Alfred's widow, tortured that her husband had suffered such a horrible ending, was nonetheless relieved that he was not the victim of a murder. Weak from shedding so many tears, she had no questions. "I just want to turn it over to the Lord."

Tipping his hat, the sheriff bid her good-bye and promised to let her know if anything new came up. He felt remorse for Mary but also a sense of relief, for now she knew as much as she needed to about how Alfred died. It had not been an easy conversation but a necessary one, and Mary had somewhat surprised him with her lack of curiosity. In fact, she had said hardly anything. It was as if the sheriff had had to pull words out of her mouth. *She didn't have nary a question, but the poor woman's grievin' and hurtin' somethin' terrible,* he thought.

As Sheriff Nave left, he waved to John Williams who was fitting a collar to the mare he would use to retrieve Alfred's Wagon.

"I'm on my way, Sheriff," John hollered. "I've 'bout got this here work horse fitted. And soon as I git that done, I'll be on my way to git his wagon. That wagon'll be back in Alfred's barn by this afternoon. I promise you that, Sheriff."

"Thank you, John."

John Williams—what a rascal, the sheriff deduced. *Always gamblin' and hangin' out at the Black Bear Saloon with that gal Madge. Truth be known, he probably hated Alfred White and he's lickin' his chops to have a chance ta git Mary White in bed. A Johnny rebel who ain't never took a likin' to black folks not workin' as slaves. A liar and a scoundrel if ever there wuz one.*

As the sheriff rode off, John figured that if he wanted to see Mary alone, now would be the best time. Because, over the next few days, well-meaning friends and neighbors, and a few nosey ones, would be dropping by to offer their condolences and to bring the grieving widow baskets of food. They'd also be praying with her and offering to help her any way they could. There'd be little, if any time, over the next week or so, for the two of them to be together.

But he was determined to steal a few minutes alone with her right now, before fetching Alfred's wagon. So John quickly tied his horse and the work horse to the hitching post near Mary's house. He splashed water from his canteen into the palm of his left hand. Then, with his right hand dabbed his fingers in the water. He ran his wet fingers through his jet black hair. He also tried to straighten his shirt collar, and, with those same damp fingers, rubbed the scruff of his neck quickly.

Satisfied with himself, with his hat in his hands, John knocked, and Mary opened her front door.

"I saw Sheriff Nave leaving.'"

"Yes and I'm so sorry, John."

"So he told you how it happened?"

"Yes, I feel awful for even thinking what had happened to Alfred had been anything but an accident. Please forgive me."

John assured her he accepted her apology and was there only to offer to help her. Mary smiled faintly. She dried her tears, straightened her body, thrust her shoulders back and took a deep breath. "Thank you, John."

"You need time to grieve fer Alfred," he said. "But I can still be a good neighbor. You an' Alfred have a right nice farm here, but you cain't take care'a it by yourself. You'll need a strong back, and I can be that fer you. You want me to do anythang 'round here, just leave me a note on my door.

"I'll pray for you, Mary."

"Thank you," she said, again tearing up. "He was a good man. It ain't fair he died so young. And it was so horrible what happened to him!"

"I know, Mary. I know. God bless his soul."

As John said farewell, he almost couldn't take his eyes off her. For Mary looked as lovely and tempting as ever, even at her worst time. Her blue print dress hugged her curves—her shape the desire of any man. And John had considered, just for a few moments, taking her in his arms and kissing her and running his hands all over her and making her forget about grief and death and misery. He could have done that, of course—would have relished doing that—but knew the time was not right. *We'll be tagether soon 'nough, he reminded himself.*

Alfred's funeral was held two days later on a Saturday morning. It was a hot, windless, humid day, with the sun in the cloudless sky baking everyone relentlessly. Most came in their best clothes. Many of the women, dressed mournfully in black skirts, wore hats or dark veils, but some of the men looked like they'd hurriedly arrived at the funeral from their work fields. A few wore dirt-stained clothing and muddy boots. Human sweat and grime, coming from those who had rushed from their fields to the church at the last minute, could be smelled in the back of the sanctuary. But even that could not compare to the smell of corruption from the flag-draped casket that waited beside a freshly dug grave in the small cemetery. This would be Alfred's final resting place.

The wooden pews at Fish Springs Church were so packed that many folks stood shoulder to shoulder in the back. The first few pews were reserved for family and close friends. Seated next to Mary on one side was Polly. On the other was Alfred's mother who had made the trip from Johnson's Depot to be at her only son's funeral. Almost everyone tried to ward off the heat with their hand held fans.

A contingent of Civil War veterans, who had fought on the side of the Union, provided the honor flag.

Preacher Redford stood beside the altar decorated with wild flowers, rhododendron and mountain laurel cut from the young couple's farm, as he delivered Alfred's eulogy.

"Alfred White, brothers and sisters, was a good and honorable man. And today, we're all here to pay our final respects to him. And while we're all sad, for Alfred and for his widow Mary, we ought not to forget that he's in a better place. He's with our Lord and Savior Jesus Christ."

The preacher went on to extol what a fine soldier Alfred had been during the Civil War. He noted the sacrifices he had made for his country and that Alfred had come home to Fish Springs after the war—wounded and weak, but happy to be home.

Then Preacher Redford seemed to lose track of what he was supposed to be doing at the funeral. He paused, took a gulp of cold water from a Mason jar on the altar, wiped his forehead and raised his voice.

"And brothers and sisters, while I'm at it, I think Alfred would want all of us ta come clean with our sins . . . to confess what we've done wrong and ask Jesus for forgiveness! So if there's any man or woman here today who'd like to come up ta the altar rail and lay their heart on the Lord and tell us how they've fallen short of following God's commandments, Alfred White would want you to come on up here to the altar."

A few of the people quit fanning themselves, closed their eyes and bowed their heads. Others whispered to one another, or elbowed the person next to them and grimaced.

"Be sure your sins will find you out!" Preacher Redford thundered, seeming to be pleased with himself that he had made the congregation uncomfortable. "So if you've done wrong by the Lord, Alfred White wants you ta bare your soul here today!"

Mary winced. She hadn't expected that her husband's funeral would turn into a call for confession and redemption.

And in the back of the church, a fidgety, sweating John Williams eased himself toward the back door. *What's that idiot preacher a doin'? Why's he tryin' to get under my skin? God, I need a swig 'a whiskey!*

The passage of time, as some say, heals and makes things better, but not so with Mary. Because three weeks after Alfred's funeral, she was still depressed, and she began feeling fatigued and nauseous. She at first chalked it up to the shock of losing her husband. She had begun to resign herself to always feeling sad and forsaken. But when her breasts started to swell and seemed overly tender to the touch, she suspected that what was happening to her had nothing to do with Alfred's death.

It had been a little over three weeks since she and Alfred had been able to have sex, and she missed her period. *Can it possibly be that I'm going to have Alfred's baby?*

A knock brought Mary out of her rocker and to the door.

"Hi Mary. I put one'a your heifers back in tha field and patched a break in the fence."

"Thank you, John."

"Mary, this here farm is way too much work fer a single woman. Why don't you let me work it fer ya. We can work out some kind'a deal. I know we could work good tagether."

"Right now, I am just thinkin' 'bout my choices, John, but I will think about it."

And Mary did consider John's offer, but she knew it would be a mistake to be involved in business with John Williams. For one reason, she felt too vulnerable around him. And another was that she truly believed what Aunt Caroline had told her. John Williams would never change. Mary knew the best thing for her was to get as far away from John as she could. Not a easy task, if you wanted to stay in Fish Springs.

So Mary was relieved when Daniel Smith offered to buy her farm and cattle, allowing her to move back into her aunt's old house in town and at least putting a short distance between her and John.

Daniel took care of everything, making the move easy for Mary. He even put the small barn behind the house back in service, where she would keep her wagon and one horse. There were also a couple of acres of pasture beside the barn, where the horse could graze. Mary loved having fresh eggs so she would keep a few chickens and she planned on having a small garden.Then a week after she got settled in, she missed another period and decided to find out for sure.

"You're very much pregnant, young lady," Dr. Godfrey confirmed. "Congratulations! Looks like your Alfred gave you a gift you'll cherish for the rest of your life."

She cried tears of happiness as she thanked Dr. Godfrey.

The Elizabethton physician prided himself that the advice he had given Alfred had at least made this conception possible.

Mary was numb and ecstatic because she carried an unborn, but living human being inside her. God had somehow smiled on her, in her wrenching misery and grief, and given her this precious gift.

Noting his patient in a daze, the doctor became anxious. "Mrs. White, are you all right?

"I'm sorry, Dr. Godfrey. This was just so unexpected. I prayed for this child."

"And your prayers were answered. You'll need to take good care of yourself, for the sake of the little one. And my wife'll explain to you how to do that. I want to see you every other month. Blanch'll schedule your appointments. Also, because you're so far from me, I think it'd be wise to have a midwife to deliver your baby. There's a very good one near you. Her name is Dorothy Gouge. She's delivered lots of babies and I've worked with her on many occasions. Get in touch with her. Blanch has her address. And again, I'm so sorry for the loss of your husband. I only spent a short time with Alfred, but he seemed like a fine young man."

Mary thanked the doctor again and said she'd see him in a couple of months. And after getting instructions from Mrs. Godfrey, she headed home.

Her thoughts on the pregnancy kept her from dwelling on Alfred's death. It was a blessing that would help her to move on with her life.

And move on, she committed herself to doing.

When she arrived back in Fish Springs, she remembered she needed chicken feed and jars for the canning she planned to do later in the year. So she decided to pay a visit to the feed store.

Inside the feed store, a bulky black man with a thick, veined neck and arms as big around as the trunk of a small tree offered to help her.

"Thank you, Jacob," Mary said, when the soft-spoken Negro picked up her two sacks of feed, hoisted them over his broad shoulders and carried them to her wagon.

"You's welcome, Miz White, I sho sorry about Mista White."

As Jacob left, John rode up on his horse and dismounted quickly. He noticed Mary seemed happy for a woman who had lost her husband less than two months ago.

"Well I see ya got moved back into Aunt Caroline's house. Guess it's yourn now. I liked it better when you wuz across tha road, but as long as you're happy, I'm glad fer ya. It's nice ta see ya can smile agin', Mary."

"What I did works best for me, John."

"Tell me, how you're doin'," John said.

"I'm pregnant. I thought I might be, and the doctor in Elizabethton just confirmed it."

"Well, ain't that good news. I'm happy fer you, Mary, and I'm sure Alfred would'a been happy too.

"Yes, he surely would have."

"You know, Mary, a woman with a young'n on tha way shouldn't have ta be alone. You need a close friend. I'd like ta stop by and see you tonight, Mary. If I come over after dark, say about ten o'clock. Would that be okay?"

Mary couldn't believe what John was suggesting. "Of course it's not okay. John! What in the world are you thinkin'? Just because I've been nice ta you, you think I've got feelins' for you."

"Don't you, Mary? In truth, deep down don't you think 'bout how it could be between you and me—again."

"No, I don't." Mary pulled herself up onto the seat of the wagon and took up the reins.

"I know you have needs Mary, and I want'a be there for ya." John put his hand on the horse's bridle.

"Yes, I have needs, John, but I don't let them get the best of my good judgment."

"Come on, Mary! I ain't a bad person. I made a mistake."

"A mistake is something' you do one time, John. Not somethin' ongoing. You were not saved, and you didn't quit gambling or womanizing. Your whole life was a lie. There's givers and takers in this world, John Williams, and you're a taker. You take what you can get, with no lookin' back and no remorse, and I have nothin' for you." Mary glanced around, self conscious that someone could be in hearing range of her ranting.

"What say I stop by jist in case you change your mind."

"Don't bother! I won't open the door."

"Well, now, Mary, I 'member once before you tellin' me to not to come to the house, but I came. And I carried you into that hay field and we stripped off our clothes and made love. Don't cha 'member how much you enjoyed it, how you screamed you couldn't git enough of it, how good it was? You said you loved me. Why de'ny yerself'a that pleasure, Mary?"

"Because I am not a whore, John! That's why. I was eighteen years old back then, and what does a girl at that age really know? I may'a thought I loved you, and after the war I fell in love with the man I thought you had become. But then I found out who that man really was. You're a scoundrel, a liar and a cheater, John Williams! Aunt Caroline, bless her soul, tried to warn me 'bout you a long time ago."

"I can be the man you want me to be, Mary, iffen you will jist give me a chance."

"Goodbye, John." Mary snapped the reins and the horse headed out.

John mounted Charger, kicked him in the side and pulled alongside. "Jist let me stop by and we can talk about it. Jist gi'me a few minutes t'night , Mary. That ain't too much ta ask."

"You just don't get it, do you, John? I don't feel anything for you. If that don't discourage you, then I don't know what will, unless it's Aunt Caroline's old rifle. So stay away from me."

"Now Mary, you couldn't shoot me. Deep down you have feelings for me. We both know that. I can see now that I will jist have to prove to you that I am a changed man.

"I feel shor that in time you will see that. So I will leave you alone for now, but I won't give up on you, Mary White."

"Just stay away from me, John," Mary said as she guided the horse toward home.

"You love me, Mary!" John shouted. "You love me. I know you do."

Mary glanced back as she reached her house. She was relieved that John hadn't continued to follow her, but she couldn't get her mind off him. *What in the world's wrong with that man? He's so obsessed he frightens me. Any feelings I had for John Williams are long gone. Why can't he just get on with his life and leave me be?*

CHAPTER 20
Feelings of Joy

Fall was almost upon them, and now, Daniel and Polly had more acreage and more cattle they had bought from Mary.

"Mista Daniel," Isaiah said, "Da cows gonna need mo' hay fo' this winta. Dey's so many mo' of dem now, and we's got to feed'em."

"There's a man down in Valley Forge about eight miles from here, Isaiah. I think you went with me about two years back when I stopped by there and looked at a steer he had for sale. Name's Jake Edwards. He's kinda quare, but tomorrow you and me'll hook up the team to the wagon and pay'em a visit. I heard he had hay for sale. And you're right. We need more hay."

"Yas'a, we sho do, Mista Daniel," said Isaiah, tickled to be making the trip because on his last visit to the Edwards farm he'd noticed a cute young housemaid, a former slave girl. He hoped to see her again.

"Now you wouldn't be thinkin' about that pretty little gal again, would you, Isaiah?" Daniel teased his helper. "What was her name? Didn't Edwards call her Prissy? Why, I betcha she'd make some man a good wife."

"Ah, Mista Daniel, you's know, she could get any man. I not impotant 'nuf fo' her. 'Sides, she's there and I'm hea."

"Isaiah, don't talk like that! You're a good man—good enough for any woman you want!"

Isaiah smiled but he knew he had little chance with Prissy. He owned no property and had nothing to offer her but a dismal future. Prissy did have a roof over her head and three squares a day, but she toiled endlessly—cleaning, scrubbing, washing, gardening and cooking for Jake Edwards and his demanding wife Martha. Isaiah had it some better. He worked as a day laborer for Daniel and Polly and lived in a primitive but adequate cabin near their barn. With a muscular torso, big calloused hands and strong arms, Isaiah could more than hold his own as a carpenter, logger, blacksmith and farmer. Thus, Daniel and Polly relied on him heavily, provided him food and shelter and paid him a small wage, much more than what Prissy got from the slave-driving, heartless Edwardses.

"Isaiah, I have some things I need ta do in the morning. Just be here early enough to hook the team up to the hay wagon. We need to leave about nine o'clock," Daniel said to him from the back porch of his house. I'll see you in the morning."

"Yas'sa!" Isaiah replied. "I has da team ready ta go at nine o'clock, Mista Daniel!"

The next morning, after replacing a couple of cracked window panes—a job he had been putting off for weeks—Daniel waved good-bye to his wife and promised he and Isaiah would return with a full load of hay.

"Here's some lunch for you and Isaiah," Polly said, handing Daniel a small bucket.

"You always take good care of me, Polly. You're my angel."

"Well, some body's got'a do it." As she spoke, Isaiah pulled up with the hay wagon.

"Mornin', Isaiah. Are we ready?"

"Yes sa. We ready." Daniel climbed aboard, and Isaiah snapped the reins.

As they rode, Isaiah thought about the slender house girl. Even though it seemed far-fetched, Isaiah wondered what it would be like to be married to a woman like Prissy. He couldn't stop thinking about the pretty light-skinned Negro. She had perfect ivory white teeth, a slender waist, and big sensuous brown eyes. Her natural curves, from her breasts to her hips, would turn any man's head. *Oh, to see'er again! Just to lay ma' eyes on 'er.*

The cool crisp air and the fall beauty of the mountains—with their dazzling deep golds, reds, yellows and oranges—made for a pleasant trip. As they rounded a curve, Daniel anticipated seeing the small trickling stream that cascaded down the mountain and over a waterfall before ending in a pool near the road. It was one of his favorite spots along the primitive road to Valley Forge. And on this day a group of deer were there replenishing themselves with the cool mountain water. Three does lapped with four yearlings that had lost most of their spots. One big doe stared at Daniel while the others drank.

"Look up ahead, Isaiah."

"Yes sa'. I sees'em."

The big doe, her eyes locked on Daniel, stomped her foot and snorted, alerting the others of impending danger. The shy animals bolted across the road and down the mountain, their fluffy white flags dancing in the air.

"Ain't dat a pretty sight, Mista Daniel?"

"Sure is, Isaiah! I love watching deer! They're so graceful. You like venison, Isaiah?"

"Sho do, Mista Daniel. I sho do."

"Well then, if I bag one this winter, I'll bring you some."

"Yes sa, I sho would like some. I den't know you hunt deer, Mista Daniel."

"Only bucks, Isaiah. That way, they'll always be plentiful."

"Yes sa. Sho pretty out hea', Mista Daniel," said Isaiah, urging the team of horses onward.

"Good place for a man to marry and raise a family, Isaiah."

"Sho would be, Mista Daniel. Sho would." Isaiah smiled.

Their journey ended at about noon when Jake Edwards greeted them at his farm. Edwards was a short, heavyset, bearded man in his fifties with unsightly nasal hair touching his upper lip. The Carter County landowner with yellow, jagged teeth had a pipe in his mouth and was relaxing in a rocking chair on his porch when they arrived. Daniel thought he detected a slight smell of alcohol around him.

"Welcome back to Valley Forge! Been a while!" boomed Edwards, extending his right hand to Daniel but steering clear of having any contact with Isaiah. "So what brings you here? Smith, right?"

"That's right, Daniel Smith, Mr. Edwards. I need hay. I understand you have some for sale."

Edwards replied that he had a good amount of hay stored up in the barn.

"I remember now," the unsavory looking character said. "You come here a couple years back to look at a steer I had fer' sale?"

"That's right."

"Have your darkie pull your wagon into the barn. My man Tobey is down there—he'll help him load it. Come sit on the porch for a spell, Daniel, while they load the wagon."

"You have Tobey help you, Isaiah," said Daniel, reluctantly agreeing to sit. Something about him, Daniel concluded, was repulsive, even borderline rotten, but Daniel couldn't very well refuse to sit if he expected to conclude a business deal with the man.

"Yas sa, Mista Smith, I will," said Isaiah, heading toward the barn in the wagon.

"Is your man a good worker?" Edwards asked.

"Yes, Isaiah's the best and he's smart."

"Well, you're lucky. Good help's damned hard to git an' even harder to keep. I just wisht' we still had slavery, but the South lost the war, and nothing'll ever be the same again. In my opinion it's a buncha' horseshit.

"Prissy!" he yelled spitefully. "Prissy! Where the hell are you, nigga? I need you to fetch me something cool ta drink from tha house. And bring somethin' for Mr. Smith, too!"

"No need to be so harsh to the girl, Mr. Edwards," Daniel said. "Besides, after Isaiah and Tobey load that hay, we'll be on our way."

"Harsh an' hateful's all she understands, I'll have you know!" barked the snarling Edwards. "She's a triflin' no-good-for-nothin' nigga, and if it wuzzn't fer' me and my wife, she'd a starved a long time ago."

Isaiah, hearing Jake's loud, angry call for Prissy on his way to the barn, was uneasy. The long, ugly shadow of slavery seemed to hang over this place. *How can Prissy stand it here? These people be from da devil! They's work her ta death. She still be a slave! I bet dey beats her iffn' she dares to say anything back to'em.*

Isaiah pulled the wagon through the wide open door and stopped. Tobey, a massive coal black man in his forties, appeared from a horse stall where he'd been pitching hay.

"Isaiah, hey brother! Where's you been?"

"Workin', Tobey. Some us has ta work." Isaiah smiled as he answered.

"You stay hea'. I sho' you what real work is. I sho' can. You must need hay, b'ins you's in a hay wagon.

"I hep you," said Tobey, laying his pitchfork down for a few seconds and spitting on his calloused hands.

The two Negroes briefly caught up on what had happened in each other's lives the past two years. While they bantered, they heard Daniel and Jake Edwards arguing on the front porch.

"I guess we bes' get this dun and get on our way, Tobey," Isaiah said. "I don't think yo' boss and my boss like each other much."

"Nobody like dat Mista Jake Edwards. He be the devil himself. He be evil," Tobey said, lowering his voice and handing Isaiah a pitchfork.

As Isaiah gripped the pitchfork he noticed something worrisome out of the corner of his eye. There, hanging on a hook like a coiled snake, in a dark section of the barn, barely visible but for the light of a few errant sunbeams, was a rawhide bullwhip. About five-feet long, it had a short braided leather handle and tapered to a thin strand at the end. Isaiah knew such whips were used to control cattle, but Jake Edwards had sold all his cattle more than a year ago, according to Tobey. *Was dat' blood stains on da end a'bit?* But worse than that—and even more terrifying—two metal bars, each with two manacles attached to them, were near the bullwhip.

His heart nearly stopped, Isaiah tried to take in what he had just seen. *Surely,* he thought, *Jake Edwards not be shacklin' and whippin' his colored help. Surely not!* Or was he? Tobey had told him the man was evil. Daniel's faithful black worker could well picture, the more he thought about it, a shirtless Tobey, or even a stripped Prissy, being shackled and brutally lashed by Edwards—who conceivably still thought of himself as their "Masta." Isaiah had heard of slaves being whipped till the skin on their battered, bloodied flesh peeled off. *Maybe he jist wants his workers ta think he will woop'em if they doesn't work hard'nuf,* Isaiah thought, trying to reassure himself.

He put aside thoughts of slavery and cruel Mastas bloodying their blacks as he and Tobey climbed to the top of the hay piled high in the barn and began pitching it down into Daniel's wagon.

"Tobey, when I was hea' befo', a girl who works in da house waved at me from da poch. Is she still hea'?" Isaiah asked shyly.

"Prissy, ah yes. She ax me 'bout you."

"Whad'ya tell her?"

"I told her yo' name's Isaiah and yo' has a big mean, fat wife."

"What, you told—"

"HA, HA, NO, NO, NO. I told her you nice man, Isaiah."

They had about loaded the wagon when Tobey noticed Prissy approaching from the house.

"Ah, look who's comin' to da barn."

"What fo'? Won't she get in trouble?" Isaiah asked.

"No, she be bringin' my supper."

Prissy, wearing a blue sack cloth dress and a red bandana around her long, glistening black hair, pulled straight back into a braid, handed Tobey a small bucket. Her eyes sparkled and she smiled when she glanced at Isaiah.

"Yo' lunch, Tobey."

"Thank you. Prissy, dis man is Isaiah Washington."

Prissy, lovely as a mountain daisy, blushed. Finally, she asked softly, "Whe's you from, Isaiah?"

"Fish Springs. It's 'bout eight mile up de river. Have you been der?"

"No, Mista Edwards don't let me go no place 'cept to his sto'. He think he own me. He think I still his slave," said Prissy, her expression now sadder.

What Prissy didn't reveal had increasingly scared her nearly to death. For the lustful Jake Edwards, her employer, had recently begun making sexual advances on her. Prissy had pleaded with him to stop fondling her womanly privates. When he had persisted touching her and trying to kiss her, the young Negro ran as fast as she could to her room in the attic of the big house, all this while fearful that "the Mrs." would find out about what happened and furiously blame her for Jake Edwards' indiscretions. And once that occurred, Prissy had no doubt that "the lady of the house" would demand she be taken to the barn and brutally whipped. *So far, though, praise tha' Lord, he's not made me pleasure him,* Prissy thought. *But what'll happen tamara? And if I does dat, what happen to my soul?*

Back on the porch, Prissy's boss continued his tirade against hired help, but he paused when his wife emerged from the house. Stern faced, big bosomed and silver haired, she stared menacingly at her husband.

"Jake, didn't you hear me callin' you from the back bedroom? I cain't do all this work by myself. Where's that worthless, nigga' girl?"

"Martha, this is Daniel Smith."

"Mrs. Edwards."

The woman had the grace of a toad and barely acknowledged him. Instead, she shuffled back and forth angrily when Jake did not respond.

"Jake, you go get Prissy!? She took Tobey his lunch, and she ain't come back. She's s'posed' to be scrubbin' the kitchen floor! How long can it take to walk to the barn and back? Dumb nigga'!"

Thrusting his shoulders back and taking a big draw from his pipe, Jake gave Daniel a I-told-you-so annoyed expression. Then, flashing his crooked, unsightly teeth, he groused. "See what I mean? They'll take advantage of you, if you let'em. Giv'em an inch, an' they'll take a mile! Okay Martha, I'll go git'er. I'll be right back, Mr. Smith."

Meanwhile, Prissy had begun to open up to Isaiah.

"Mista Edwards bought me in Richmond when I was fifteen, and when we was freed, he wouldn't let me go. He say he gawn get his money wort' outta me. He say I owes money to his sto'. I got a few things but not what he say."

Overhearing this, her boss exploded in anger. "Prissy, why you tellin' that damn nigga' bout' my business? " His face red and contorted and his venomous eyes bulging, as if they might pop out of their sockets, he slapped her hard.

The young, thoroughly defeated Negro woman held her tongue and dropped her head. Her whole body sagged in contrition.

"Whad you tell'em, you worthless, lyin' nigga'? "

"I'm sorry, sir. I dent' mean..." Prissy mumbled contritely. A big welt began to swell up on her face where she bore Jake's fury.

His face still beet red with anger, Jake drew back to strike her again, but Isaiah grabbed him by the wrist.

Tobey stared wide-eyed at Isaiah, shaking his head as if to warn that Daniel's longtime helper had made the biggest mistake of his life.

"Boy, you dare ta raise your big ugly black paw against a white man? I'll see that you're put away an' castrated!"

Having heard Jake's outburst, Daniel arrived at the barn. "Mr. Edwards, what's wrong?"

"It seems yore boy here don't know where he belongs in tha peckin' order. He dares ta stop me from disciplinin' my nigga' help."

"Isaiah, is that true?"

"Yas sa, Mista Smith."

"Well, Isaiah, I think you owe Mr. Edwards an apology."

Isaiah said nothing.

"Isaiah? You need to tell Mr. Edwards you're sorry for interfering. Talk to me, Isaiah. Tell me what's wrong."

"I don't think he should hit her, Mista Smith. He hit her allfa hard. An he was 'bout ta hit her again. Dat's why I stopped'm."

"Hit her? Edwards, you struck this young woman?"

"Now see here, Smith! It's ain't none a' your damned concern how I discipline my workers! And I don't need your nigga buttin' in!"

"Prissy? That your name?" Daniel asked gently.

"Yes sa."

"Prissy, you know you don't have to work for this man."

"This ain't none'a yore' affair, Smith! Now you jist git the hell outta here and leave my hay be! Our deal's off!"

"He won't let her leave, Mista Smith," Isaiah said. "And he'll whup'er when we's go."

"You cain't keep'er from leavin', Edwards," Daniel noted. "She's a free woman."

"I can and I will! She ain't leavin' till she works off her debt at the store."

"What store?"

"My store in Valley Forge. I let my workers buy things they need on credit, but they have to work it off. And she ain't leavin' 'til she works off every God damned penny she owes me!"

"I've heard tell about stores like yours. How much does she owe you?"

"That's none of your damn business!"

At the end of his rope with this miserable wretch of a man, the six-foot-four-inch brawny Daniel grabbed Jake Edwards by his collar and yanked his face to his. Fuming with anger, Daniel demanded again that Edwards answer his question.

Shaken and red-faced, the hay merchant turned enemy reached into his pants pocket and jerked out a piece of paper. He unfolded it with his fumbling hands. "Thirteen dollars and ninety-seven cents."

"How much do I owe you for the hay?" Daniel asked.

"A wagon load is six dollars."

Daniel retrieved a wad of cash from his pocket.

"Here's six for the hay. Prissy, would you like to leave here?"

"Yes sa. I pray da Lord ev'ry day I kin leave hea'!"

Daniel faced the Negro girl's boss. "Here's fourteen to cover Prissy's bill. You can keep the extra three cents for your inconvenience. Prissy, go fetch your belongin's. You're goin' with us."

"My things are in my room in da big house. I'll get'em now."

Edward drew himself up like he was the one aggrieved. "Don't you ever set foot on my property again! You hear me? None'a you. You do and I'll git' Sheriff Nave after you!"

Daniel and Isaiah climbed in the wagon, and Daniel drove the horses out the back of the barn and around, then to the house. They rode past a disgruntled and defeated and angrily hollering Jake Edwards.

"You'll be sorry for this! I have friends in high places!"

The visitors from Fish Springs ignored his ranting.

Mrs. Edwards, snarling and clutching a broom, ran out the front door. "Jake, Prissy says she leavin'! You told me she couldn't leave. Jake, Jake!"

"She's leavin' Martha. And good riddance! She's a no good lyin' nigga, anyways."

With quick, light steps, Prissy burst out of the front door. She toted a threadbare coat over her shoulder and a worn cloth bag in her hand. Isaiah jumped down, took her possessions and threw them on the wagon. Then he hoisted her up to the wagon. She plunked down beside Daniel, and Isaiah sat next to her, cradling her protectively with his left arm.

"Nobody gonna' hurt you ev'r agin," Isaiah pledged. "I won't let'em."

Their eyes met and Prissy's tears of sadness turned to tears of joy.

Meanwhile, as the three of them drove away in the wagon—Fish Springs bound—Jake and Martha Edwards had at each other.

"Well, ain't that's just dandy! There goes my nigga' help! Who's gonna' scrub my damn floors, and who's gonna' cook our food and do our damned washin', Jake? Jake!"

"Martha, jist shut up."

On hearing Martha's cursing, Daniel and Isaiah grinned. And Prissy, now chirpy, put her hand over her mouth to keep from laughing.

"I'm sorry, Mista Smith," Isaiah said.

"There's no need to be. You did the right thing, Isaiah. No woman should ever be struck. Prissy, would you like to work for me?"

"Yes sa."

"I'm sure my wife Polly can use some help. Won't she be surprised!"

As they proceeded with their wagon full of hay toward Fish Springs, Prissy touched the big brown, rough hand that was next to hers. It gave her a sense of warmth and security.

And Isaiah?

Feelings of joy and excitement flowed through his body. Feelings he had never felt before.

CHAPTER 21
A White Christmas

After a mild fall, December descended on East Tennessee with a vengeance. So the woolly worm had it dead-on right when he put on a heavy coat. Mary was settled into the house she still thought of as Aunt Caroline's, but she was grateful for an invitation to spend Christmas week with the Smith family. John Williams had continued to take what seemed every opportunity to stop by with a bundle of firewood or the offer of assistance with small chores. His confidence that she must still have feelings for him made her all the more uncomfortable because there was just a tiny bit of truth hidden there.

Mary and Polly were busy in the kitchen early on Christmas Eve when Daniel and Charlie came through the front door dragging a snowy hemlock tree behind them. Mary was a little shocked; she had seen illustrations of Christmas trees in the magazines she and Aunt Caroline favored, but she'd never known of anyone having one in Fish Springs.

Polly took control immediately. She moved a big rocking chair from the corner of the room closer to the fire and directed Daniel and Charlie to set the tree up in the corner farthest from the crackling fire. A wash tub from the back porch and a few rocks from along the path helped hold it upright.

The tightly knit family now had their Christman tree—and a majestic, fragrant, tree it truly was. Its lush green boughs seemed to cry out to be decorated, and its top awaited an angel. The children clamored to make the tree even more beautiful. Prissy popped corn and everyone helped with the stringing. Pinecones gathered from the forest for kindling served as ornaments when Mary sprinkled them with flour to make them white. Peter and Izzy pranced about excitedly hanging popcorn strings and handmade ornaments on the tree. Mary added a string of glass beads that had belonged to Aunt Caroline and a white crocheted star with a carefully cut paper silhouette in the middle that resembled Alfred. Prissy surprised everyone with a corn shuck doll with wings added as the angel for the top. Daniel placed the angel, then watched from the doorway, arms folded over his chest and a big smile for everyone.

Meanwhile, Prissy busied herself in the kitchen baking cookies.

"Prissy! Yo' be there? "Isaiah yelled. He was shivering at the back door, bundled up against the fierce cold wind and snow, with an armload of firewood. He had pulled his old gray hat down over his ears.

"Don'chu track snow in on ma clean floo's, Isaiah," said Prissy, her hands on her hips as she opened the door.

"Ok, Prissy. I stomp it off," said Isaiah. He flashed Prissy a big smile while kicking the heels of his boots against the bottom railing of the back porch. "They's clean now."

Prissy bid him a merry Christmas and kissed him on the cheek. And when she put a spoon full of her cookie dough in his mouth, Isaiah smacked his lips with delight.

"I sho does like you, Prissy. You be my favorite wo-man," Isaiah said, just as Polly entered the kitchen.

"I sure like her too, Isaiah," said Polly with jolly bounce to her step, and humming a Christmas song.

"Merry Christmas ta you, Missus Smith," Isaiah said.

The head lady of the Smith household smiled and told Isaiah that she wished him the merriest Christmas ever.

On his way with the wood, he had to step around Izzy and Mary. The little one had curled up in the big chair near the fireplace and snuggled close to the woman she was becoming more and more attached to, and Mary worked on a tiny bit of crochet.

"Hey everyone, look outside!" Daniel exclaimed. "Look how hard it's snowing. We may be in for a good one. Maybe a foot or more! We'll have to dig ourselves outta here tomorrow morning, so we can make it to church for the Christmas service."

"It'll be a white Christmas!" Peter gleefully declared.

Polly, wearing a fancy red apron, entered the room with a tray holding glasses and a pitcher.

"Come and get it!" she announced.

"What is it, Mama?" Izzy asked, with an impish grin.

"It's eggnog, dear heart."

"Can I taste it?"

"Of course, dear," said Polly, pouring her daughter a sip.

"Mmm, more please."

"Boys, come and get some eggnog!"

After they drank their nog, the children resumed decorating the tree. It seemed every tiny object or bright bit of paper was going to end up on that tree. Daniel, meanwhile, excused himself and left the room.

In his office, Daniel spun the dial on his safe. When the mechanism clicked, he opened the thick black steel door and took out a bottle of whiskey from the back, where he had several stashed. Then he shut the door and spun the dial again.

He glanced smugly at his little liquid delight. The never-before-opened bottle of copper-colored whiskey bore a black label with a picture of deer antlers on its front. A yellow, tightly sealed cork served as a stopper.

Back by the fireplace, Polly had already poured three glasses of eggnog when Daniel returned with the bottle. Daniel and his wife gave each other knowing grins.

Then Polly, with a mischievous twinkle in her eyes, told Mary that on Christmas Eve they had a tradition of "puttin' a little touch of somethin' special in their eggnog."

Daniel poured a shot of whiskey into Polly's and his glass of eggnog. He held the bottle, tantalizingly, over Mary's glass.

"A touch of whiskey?" he asked her. "We won't tell anyone if you won't."

"Okay, just a touch. You know, I haven't had any alcohol since y'all took me and Aunt Caroline to the Snyder House."

Mentioning the Snyder House brought back a flood of memories for Mary, many of them on this Christmas Eve she thought of as best forgotten.

After Daniel reassured Mary that a swig of whiskey mixed with eggnog was good for the soul, the three adults sipped from their glasses. Mary especially savored the warm, smooth taste of the drink. Closing her eyes and smiling, she licked her lips. "Mmm, that's good!"

"This calls for a story," said Daniel.

But a knock at the door interrupted him.

"Who in the world could that be? And at this hour on a cold, snowy night?"

Hearing the knock, Prissy appeared from the kitchen and said she would get the door.

"Yes'sa"

"May I speak ta Daniel Smith?" said the snow-covered man.

"John Williams. What brings, John?" Daniel asked as Prissy headed back to the kitchen.

"I jist wanted to wish you folks and Mary White a Merry Christmas and leave these little gifts."

"Well, Merry Christmas to you, too, but come on in out of the cold, John, before you freeze your fool self to death!"

"I cain't stay," John replied, shaking the snow off his hat. "I need ta get back before this snow gets too deep."

When Daniel persuaded their surprise guest to at least warm up his bones a bit by the fire, John pulled a Mason jar of blackberry preserves from a sack. He said it was for Daniel and Polly. And the small bag of candy he retrieved from the sack was for the kids.

"And this is for you, Mary."

Knowing she should be cordial, for the sake of the children, Mary wished John a Merry Christmas and thanked him graciously for the tiny packet of red paper. She opened it to find a small gold cross on a chain. Mary wondered where John would have gotten such a gift, then chided herself for being uncharitable.

"Have a glass of eggnog before you leave, John," Daniel invited him.

Daniel handed John the eggnog, then offered to spice it up with a touch of whiskey but John covered the top of the glass with his big calloused hand.

"No thank you. I don't drink booze no more. I've been prayin' for the Lord ta fergive me for all I done wrong in my life, and I'm tryin' to git on the right path."

Mary wasn't sure if she should feel sorry for John or not. Because she and others had heard John's contrite tone and words before, and Mary, for one, was skeptical. *Still, he wouldn't drink whiskey. Maybe, just maybe, he really IS trying to change. But then again, he's been a liar all his life…*

After a few minutes of idle talk in which he warmed himself by the fire, John again wished everyone a Merry Christmas and said he hoped to see them at the Christmas service. Then he buttoned his coat, wrapped a red bandana around his neck to help protect against the wind and cold, put on his hat and walked out the door into the freezing night.

As the children scurried to the kitchen to check on the cookies, Polly said that while John's gift-bearing visit had been a surprise, even a shock, she herself wasn't certain he was sincere "or if he was just puttin' on an act for Mary."

"Maybe we should give him a chance." Daniel said. "Could be he's really tryin' to get his life back on the right track. After all, isn't that supposed to be the Christmas spirit? To give a man a second chance."

"John Williams has had lots of chances," Mary noted, "and he's let people down again and again."

"One thing's for sure," Polly said. "He's sweet on you, Mary."

"Well, he'll just have to get past it, because I'm sure not sweet on him. And for all I know, he got that little cross for one of his gal friends at the saloon and she didn't want it, so he brought it to me."

But after Mary spouted that, she thought about what Daniel had said about the meaning of the Christmas spirit, and she felt ashamed.

The children came back with a plate of cookies and gathered around Daniel for a story.

Later after Peter and Izzy had been put to bed, the others sat by the fire sipping their eggnog, except for Charlie who excused himself and scrambled to the kitchen for a more serious snack.

"Daniel, will you put another log on the fire, please? You know me. I'm always cold," said a shivering Polly, her hands clutched tightly to her elbows.

"Sure thing, darlin' and while I'm doing that, would you make your way through the snow to the wood pile and bring some more in?" As he spoke, Daniel giggled.

"No more eggnog for you, Daniel Smith!" Polly, half-way tipsy herself, said with a smile.

Hearing the request, from the kitchen Prissy kicked Isaiah, who was napping in a chair, on the foot.

"They needs some mo' wood on the fire, Isaiah."

Isaiah jumped up, put on his raggedy coat and boots and went outside. When he returned with an armload of wood, Prissy helped dust the snow off his clothes. Then he stomped the fluffy white stuff off his boots and carried the wood to the hearth.

Daniel thanked his always reliable helper and told him he didn't want him trying to go back to his own place on such a cold and snowy night.

"Have Prissy make you a pallet in the kitchen," Daniel said. "You need to stay here tonight. And, Isaiah, keep the fire going too, so it will be nice and warm when the children open their gifts in the morning."

"Yas'sa, Mista Daniel, I keep the fire gowin."

After Isaiah left, Daniel raised his glass to propose a toast, and he, Polly and Mary clinked their glasses together.

"Here's to Mary and a healthy new baby."

They sipped the whiskey-laced eggnog. Then Mary thanked Daniel and gave him a peck of a kiss on his cheek. Polly sipped her drink and smiled politely but said nothing.

Why's she kissing my husband and why's he sa' blamed happy about it?

Daniel looked at Polly and smiled.

Shame on me for havin' such thoughts. He's a good man who loves me and she's only showing her gratitude. Besides she's just a child.

Meanwhile, the wind had come back again, stronger than before, and it pounded against the windowpanes. Huge flakes of snow, mixed in with pelting icy sleet, continued falling. The sturdy old house, withstanding many a brutal winter in the Tennessee mountains, held strong against the elements, but Polly worried.

"It looks like we have a foot of snow and it's still comin' down," Polly said. "If we get too much more, we might not be able to make it ta the Christmas service."

"Let's toast to it," Daniel said.

"Shame on you Daniel Smith," said Polly

Daniel and Mary giggled, but this time Mary, sensing Polly's discomfort from before, kept her distance from the man of the house.

"Here's to two more feet of snow," said a smiling, eggnog-gulping Daniel. "And a healthy baby for Mary."

"You already said that Daniel," Polly said as Mary giggled.

"Oh, well m-may be she'll have twins."

"You know, Daniel, we ARE going to the Christmas service at church tomorrow," his wife reminded him.

"Not if we can't g-get there," he replied, downing another swig of nog.

"Daniel, don't you think we best put the presents out for the kids and get to bed? You know they'll be up at the crack of dawn. And another thing, you need to give Isaiah and Prissy their gifts."

"Yea, I s'pose you're right." Daniel blew out the candles, made one last check of the flame in the fireplace and followed his wife to their bedroom, where they had hid Christmas gifts for the children. Mary climbed the stairs to Izzy's room she was sharing for the week and slipped in beside the sleeping child.

Minutes later Daniel came back down the stairs and entered the kitchen just as Prissy was leaving to go to her room in the attic.

"Wait just a minute, Prissy. I want to give you a little Christmas gift. You too, Isaiah."

Isaiah rose from the pallet and the two humble workers stood facing Daniel. Isaiah had received gifts from the Smiths before, but not Prissy. She was in a state of disbelief. Daniel handed Isaiah a heavy sheep-skin coat. The big happy black man put the heavy coat on his large frame and smiled as if he'd gotten the best Christmas gift ever.

And when Daniel presented Prissy with a long quilted coat and told her to slip it on, tears welled up in her eyes and trickled down her light brown cheeks.

"I wants ta thank ya, Mista Daniel. I never had sech a fine coat. I's don't know what else ta say, 'cept me and Isaiah loves takin' care of yo' famly.

"Merry Christmas to both of you," Daniel said, reaching out and holding their hands.

"Merry Christmas to you and the missus, Mista Daniel," Isaiah said.

"And to all your chilluns', too," added Prissy, still weeping from joy.

Christmas morning the children rose early, rubbing the sleep out of their eyes and waking everyone else up. In her little-girl pink nightgown and with visions of gifts rushing through her head, Izzy announced, "Look everybody!"

"The tree is beautiful, Izzy," said Polly drolly.

"Not the tree, Mama!" Izzy shouted. "The presents!"

When Daniel entered the large main room he was glad to see that Isaiah already had a roaring fire going and the room was toasty warm for the kids and Polly. Mary came down the stairs with a robe wrapped around her.

"Can we open presents now, Mama?" an excited Izzy asked.

"Can we, Mom?" Peter pleaded.

"What do you think, Daniel?" Polly asked her husband, who the night before had consumed much more than his share of the eggnog and just now could kill for a cup of coffee.

"We can do that," said Daniel, heading to the kitchen for a cup of coffee that he knew Prissy would have ready for him. He'd hoped for enough snow to keep them from making it to the Christmas church service, but that wasn't the case. The road was now passable thanks to a brilliant red ball of a sun that had started to melt the foot or so of snow.

Isaiah and Prissy had been invited by Daniel to come into the main room to watch the kids open their gifts. So they readied themselves to take in the whole festive scene from two chairs near the door to the kitchen.

Izzy's excitement soared when she noticed a brightly packaged gift, bound with a red ribbon, with her name on it. Ignoring the new blue dress right beside it, she ripped the paper off a soft cloth doll with red hair, a porcelain face and a flowered dress.

"Oh, Mama, she's beautiful!" said Izzy, caressing the doll like a real baby.

"Santa knew you'd love her. Now remember, be careful with her 'cause her face is made of glass."

"I will, Mama!"

The boys, unable to contain their excitement, had already torn the brown paper from their gifts. Charlie got an oversized leather suitcase. Peter jumped up and down when he unwrapped a hunting knife with a pearl handle. It was in a black case that attached to his belt.

"Thanks, Mom and Dad!" Charlie shouted. "This'll come in handy when I head off to college!"

"Thanks for my knife too!" Peter beamed.

"I think there's something else under the tree for all three of you," said Polly. "It's from Mary."

"A book about all kinds of wild animals!" hollered Peter.

"And she got us candy, too," Izzy said. "I love candy canes! Thank you, Miss Mary."

The children threw their arms around Mary and told her again how much they loved her.

Mary hugged them back, then presented brightly colored knitted scarves to Daniel and Polly.

Daniel smiled and thanked Mary for the knitted scarf. Then Daniel and Polly exchanged their gifts, a wool shirt from Polly to Daniel, and he presented her a beautiful cameo necklace.

But that wasn't the end of the gift giving. The best had been saved for last.

"There's just one present left, and it's a big one!" Izzy hollered. "It's from Santa to Mary!"

Charlie set the gift wrapped in brown paper tied with a big red bow at Mary's feet, and she pulled the paper away.

It was a beautiful, finely crafted walnut cradle. It even had a little pillow and blanket in it for Mary's soon-to-be-born infant.

"Ain't dat beautiful, said Prissy to Isaiah, who thought, *You's what's beautiful.*

"I don't know what to say," said Mary. "Thank you all so much."

"You're surely welcome, dear heart. Every baby needs a cradle."

"I still have mine, Miss Mary. Mama's keeping it for MY baby," Izzy said.

"Merry Christmas, everyone!" said Daniel, raising his mug of steaming coffee.

CHAPTER 22
Fish Springs in Peril

It was a bitter cold February morning in Fish Springs and those who braved the outdoors did so at their peril. Dr. James Godfrey in a heavy coat and stocking cap rushed out of Sheriff Nave's office, climbed in his buggy and urged his horses to a run. A minute later, Nave himself came out and quickly headed toward the school house.

Three boys were kicking a ball around the yard in front of the one-room schoolhouse. Others bantered about rambunctiously or huddled on the front stoop. They could have gone inside by the potbelly stove, but chose their last few minutes of freedom in the frigid outdoors.

When their teacher tugged a rope ringing a big tarnished brass bell mounted on top of a pole, the kids dropped their playthings, gathered their books and ran toward the front entrance of their school. A few lost their footing and were gathered up by their classmates.

"Don't run up the steps please! I want you here in one piece!" the teacher yelled. Her straight coal-black hair was put in a bun and her skirt reached to within two inches of her dark ankle-high lace-up shoes.

Sheriff Nave reached the front of the school just as she ushered the last of the children inside and shut the door. He hesitated only a moment before striding up the steps, but he still eased the door open quietly. Old habits die hard.

"Miss Beasley, do you have a lot of students out?" the sheriff asked as he entered the school.

Looking at the half empty room, the stunned Miss Beasley did a fast count.

"I'm nine short, Sheriff. Do you know where they are?"

"Probably home sick, said the sheriff, walking to the front of the classroom.

"Doc Godfrey just left my office. He said a lot'a folks in Fish Springs are sick. He's not sure what it is yet. But it seems ta be spreadin'. He said we need ta get these kids away from each other and home.

"Peter's sick, Miss Beasley." Izzy raised her hand and spoke up.

"My brother's sick, too, Miss Beasley. He was upchucking all night and I don't feel so good myself. I think I'm gonna..."

Mikey threw up on the floor and started crying.

"Oh no! Ah pew wee!"

One red-haired frowning boy with freckles yelled, "He puked!"

"That's enough, children!" said Miss Beasley. She dabbed Mikey's face with a handkerchief.

"It's okay, Mikey. You can't help it."

"How many of you have sick family members?" Sheriff Nave asked.

When most of the children raised their hands, the sheriff gasped and uttered, "Oh my God!"

"Children, I need your attention!" Miss Beasley shouted. "Put on your coats and hats and go home. Stay there until you are told to return. Tell your parents there's a lot of sick people in Fish Springs. Taylor, can you walk Mikey home?"

"Sure, Miss Beasley."

"God help us," Miss Beasley mumbled to Nave as she watched her students file out of the school.

Later, at the other end of the community, Mary, six months pregnant, sat in Aunt Caroline's old rocker knitting baby booties by the fire. She had just thrown on two extra logs and it blazed warm. Near her was the empty cradle.

"Mary!" a voice shouted from the frigid outside. Lying near the fire, Blue raised his head ever so slightly and cocked it to one side. John's loyal canine seemed to have adopted his master's devotion to Mary, but unlike John, he was welcomed into Mary's house. He growled, annoyed that someone had interrupted his rest.

Mary went to the front door, pulled back the curtain from the glass, and wiped a peep-hole in the heavy frost with the end of her shawl.

Daniel, mounted on his horse, seemed to be hanging on to the saddle as he leaned toward Mary's porch.

She opened the door and shouted out. "Daniel, what's wrong?"

"They're all sick, Mary! Half'a Fish Springs!"

"What'a you mean, Daniel. What've they got?"

"Dr. Godfrey says it's the black measles. He said the solders had it in the camps during the war."

Covering her mouth with her hands and closing her eyes, Mary sighed and asked him if his family was all right.

"No, Polly and the boys have it, and Izzy seems to be coming down with it too."

"I'll get my coat."

"No!" he commanded sternly.

"But Daniel, I can help!"

"No, Mary! Doc Godfrey's been ta my place and he told me ta tell you not to leave your house for any reason. He said in your condition you cain't be exposed ta this sickness. You have to do this for your child. I can take care of my family. Now go back in and lock the door and don't open it for anyone. I'll send Isaiah to check on you every day."

She reluctantly agreed to do as he said. Then, as he galloped off, she wished him Godspeed with his family.

Back inside her house, with the door bolted, she put on an extra sweater, brewed herself some hot tea, sat back down beside the fire, and opened her Bible. And that night, before going to bed, she prayed extra hard—for Daniel and his family, for all the sick children and ailing elderly of the community and especially for her unborn child.

Back at the Smith farm, exhausted Prissy lay down on the makeshift bed on the floor in Izzy's room. She would normally sleep in her little room in the attic but was afraid that if the child cried out in the night, she might not hear her. From Izzy's room, Prissy would also hear the boys.

Daniel had delegated all the outside work to Isaiah—caring for the animals and keeping wood stockpiled on the porch as well as in the house by the fireplace. The head of the household kept a fire blazing around the clock. He made sure the house stayed toasty warm—for he had heard that the bitter winter cold breeds sickness. He slept lightly in a rocker keeping vigil over Polly in their downstairs bedroom.

Prissy, bone tired, had not slept more than a few hours in the last three days. Her day consisted of trying to get the children and Polly to drink water and take some kind of nourishment, be it soup or a biscuit soaked in warm milk or coffee. She put cool damp cloths on their foreheads, trying to get their fevers down. Daniel helped some with these chores but spent most of his time with his failing wife. Prissy also changed her patients' bedding when it got wet from their feverish sweating or when they soiled it. Getting them to the chamber pot in time was proving to be more and more of a challenge.

By far her most distasteful task was dealing with the lidded chamber pots in the corner of each bedroom. Under normal conditions, each of the family members was responsible for their own chamber pot—all but Izzy, that is;

she was not yet strong enough to carry the heavy metal pot all the way to the outhouse. But these were not normal conditions. So without hesitation the dedicated former slave girl took on the putrid task.

The slight but strong young woman would lug two pots at a time down the 300-foot path to the privy and pour the waste and vomit into one of the two holes.

Then she would tote the pots to a nearby stream where she rinsed them with water. If Isaiah were not busy doing other chores and saw Prissy headed down the path,, he'd jump in and lend her a hand—anything to spend a little time with the woman he was sweet on, and it made him feel good that she welcomed his help.

As Daniel and Polly's devoted housekeeper lay restlessly in the bedding on the floor, she prayed for Polly and the children. Then sleep overtook her.

She dreamed, not about sick, suffering adults or children, but about her own life as a little girl, when she lived with her parents on the Shirley Plantation in Virginia. The only child of her mother, who was a kitchen servant in the house, Prissy was happy playing beside her mother as she worked. As soon as she was well up on her feet, she was given small tasks to do, like carrying messages to members of the household. Mrs. Carter, the master's wife, enjoyed the pretty Negro child, dressed her in her own daughters' outgrown clothing and even taught her to read. Prissy's father was a field hand so Prissy's mother and father had to sneak out at night to be together. Prissy and her mother would watch every evening for the workers to come in from the fields so Prissy could see her father. Sometimes they could slip out with cold biscuits or other scraps of food from the kitchen to bring to him.

The master, Mr. Carter, disapproved of his wife "making pets" of the household servants, so Prissy and Mrs. Carter were careful that he didn't see her in a fancy dress or carrying a book. Prissy knew she was a slave, and that her life and her parents' lives were not like those of the "mastas," but in looking back, Prissy would have said she was a happy child.

But one day when she was about thirteen years old everything changed. Prissy and her mother were waiting beside the path as the workers were returning from the fields, when the master and several strangers rode up on horseback. When one of the strangers pointed to Prissy, her mother screamed out and fell to the ground crying. Prissy herself put up a fight—kicking and screaming and flailing her arms and fists, but it had been no use. Her abductors, seeming to enjoy themselves, laughed, grabbed her bare arms and legs and pulled up her shift.

Then they put her up on a horse in front of Arnold Yates, a young man who had become Prissy's new master. And when Prissy's father, a barrel of a man with bulging arms and wide shoulders, tried to intervene, he was tied to a tree and flogged. Etched into Prissy's memories—and now a big part of her haunting dream was that awful time when she was torn so cruelly from her screaming mother's arms.

The heart-wrenching dream had come back to her again and again, especially when she was dead tired. This time, however, her dreaming didn't last long, because two hours from the time she laid down her head, she was awakened by cries coming from Peter's bedroom. His bedding was soaked, from perspiration this time, as the fever had finally broken. After changing Peter's bedding, she sat on the side of the bed stroking his head till he fell back asleep. Although big beads of perspiration soaked his hair and the back of his neck, his body had started to cool down. Then she went downstairs to the master bedroom to check on Polly.

Daniel was standing over Polly. She was burning up with fever, bathed in a deathly sweat, screaming deliriously. Her hair was wet and matted, her teeth clattering, and her eyes fixed on the ceiling. She had bitten her tongue and now it bled profusely.

Daniel felt utterly helpless. He just held his barely alive wife, stroked her forehead and offered a silent prayer. As she took in the ghastly scene, Daniel gave Prissy a sign she'd best check on the children. Prissy nodded and left, but she would never, ever forget the sight of a wailing, miserable and dying Polly,

Later that morning, Mary was awakened by Blue's barking and a loud knock on her back door.

"Miz Mary! You be awake? "

"Is that you, Isaiah?"

"Yas'm, it's me, Miz Mary, but please don't open dis doe. Mista Daniel toe me ta talk ta you through da doe."

"Ok, Isaiah. I understand."

"Is you okay, Miss Mary?"

"I'm fine."

"I took care your horse and fed da chickens. I put yo a bucket a'water on da back poch and sa'mo fi' wood. You needs anything else, Miz Mary?"

"No. But thank you, Isaiah. "

"I be back tomorrow, then."

"Isaiah?"

"Yas 'em."

"How is Daniel and the family?"

"Mista Daniel, he fine. Prissy say da chillin gittin' better, but Miz Polly, she bad sick, Miz Mary. Mista Daniel real worried."

"Tell Daniel I'll pray for Polly."

"Yas 'em. I will."

"Is Prissy okay, Isaiah?"

"Yas em, she good. She hepping Mista Daniel take care of Mis Smith and da chillen."

"Take care of yourself, Isaiah, and thank you for coming."

"Yas 'um."

As Isaiah turned to walk toward his work wagon, he came face to face with John Williams. He had taken his hat off and his jet black hair was slicked straight back. He also wore a clean shirt, and his work boots, though old, had been shined.

"Scuse me sa," said Isaiah, stepping to the side.

John said nothing to Isaiah as he proceeded and knocked on the door.

"Mista Williams, you's will have'ta talk to Miss Mary through da doe. Mista Daniel tol her not ta open her doe for nobody."

"Boy, did I ask you anything? You jist need ta mind your own business," said John as he kept knocking.

"Yas'sa."

"Mary! It's me, John Williams! Can you let me in, please?"

"No! I can't, John!" Mary yelled from the inside. "Daniel told me not ta open my door for anyone! Daniel says the black measles is going around."

"I understand, Mary. I was just checkin' ta make sure you're all right."

"I'm fine, John! Isaiah's takin' good care of me, but thanks for asking. Do you want me to send Blue out ta you?"

"No, that old dog'll be better off with you, Mary. I'll pray for you and your unborn child, and remember, if you need anything, I ain't that far away." Then John turned and walked by Isaiah, who stood grinning.

"Right nice of him to come and see that I'm okay." Mary turned from the door and spoke to Blue. "I wonder if John'll really pray for me. Or is he just the same old John—schemin' and plannin' to get me back? Either way I'm standing firm, this time, on my convictions. I won't be hurt by tha likes of John Williams ever again."

She locked the door firmly. "I will be just fine on my own. I'll raise Alfred's baby and be true to his memory."

Being so worried about Daniel's family, it was all Mary could do to stay put and not go to them, but she realized that the head of the household, the man she dearly respected and admired, knew best. For the time being, at least, she would go nowhere.

John mounted Charger and rode away as Isaiah headed back to the Smith farm. Mary brought some firewood in and stacked it by the fireplace. Then she took the washbowl from the dry sink and threw out the dirty water. She refilled the pitcher from the sink with the fresh water Isaiah had fetched from the well and took the rest of the cold water to the kitchen where it would be used for cooking or drinking. All that done, she put another log on the fire and returned to the rocker. She thought about the Smiths. They'd done so much for her, always there for her, through the best and worst times of her young topsy-turvy life. Now, in their time of desperate need, she couldn't lift a hand to help Polly and the children. *And then on top of that, Daniel sends Isaiah to check on me. The least I can do is pray for'em.* And that she did.

A few days later, in the dim morning light, a heavy fog hung over the deserted Main Street through Fish Springs. At this hour, it was still so deathly cold that folks could see their breath in the air. In the stillness of the cold morning, the sound of a woman wailing could be heard in the distance.

At the Fish Springs Baptist Church the pews had been moved back to make room on the floor for the corpses. Twelve bodies were lined up and covered with sheets. A crying woman was kneeling at one of the bodies. Somber Preacher Ike Redford had his head bowed and his right hand on her shoulder. Nothing he did or whispered seemed to relieve her agony.

Out the window and through the dense fog, he saw a wagon pull to a stop. Two men climbed down and removed a sheet-covered body from the wagon. It was Daniel and Isaiah. They entered the church and laid the body next to the others—like cordwood stacked together. Ike closed the door, then went to the body, bent down and pulled the sheet back. The once sweet, smiling face of Polly Smith was now pale and stone-like.

Daniel was shutting windows on the side where he entered.

"I am so sorry, my brother Daniel," said Ike, fighting tears.

"Ike, it's freezing in here. These windows need to be shut."

"Wait, Daniel," Ike said softly as he embraced his friend.

Isaiah, with his eyes welling up, stood by Polly's body. Normally strong, his emotions had finally gotten the best of him; he couldn't stand to see his boss so devastated.

"It's cold in here, Ike. My Polly doesn't like to be cold. Ike, my Polly, my Polly . . ." Daniel cried.

Ike put a consoling hand on Daniel's shoulder. "It needs to be cold in here until we can get these poor souls buried, Daniel."

Daniel collapsed to his knees.

"But Ike, Polly don't like to be cold."

Ike dropped to one knee and held his bereaved friend.

"She's not cold, Daniel. She's in a better place. She's gone home to be with the Lord."

Tears streamed down Isaiah's face as he stood with his hands folded and bowed his head. "Lawd, Lawd, please ease this family's pain."

Polly Smith's death would be just one of the many such terrible losses from the epidemic in Fish Springs. The entire little mountain community reeled from the disease. It had come on all of a sudden, sickening mostly the elderly or very young.

People had become too sick to work or go to school. Runny noses, coughs and sore throats escalated to high fever, chills and severe body aches.

A general feeling of sickness caused some to retreat immediately to their beds. Many would not survive. And it fell to the living to bury the dead. So many died that bodies, in several instances, were buried without coffins. Gravediggers, many of them sick or feverish themselves, struggled with the frozen ground. It was almost two weeks before the ground thawed enough to begin burying the dead.

Daniel would not even consider burying Polly without a proper coffin, so Charlie got some lumber from the Butler sawmill where he was working at the time. He and his dad built a strong, thick pine casket for his mother. Polly was buried in the church cemetery, with just a plain white cross for now, beneath a huge red oak. It would become the resting place for all the Smiths.

At her funeral, Ike Redford and the deeply grieving family wept together and offered each other hope, and they reaffirmed their unbridled faith in the Almighty. Mary made her first foray back into the world for Polly's funeral. They solemnly swore to live their lives as Polly Smith would want them to. To be an everlasting example for her. To never forget her and to make sure her children grew up to be strong-in-their-faith-and-deeds Christians. To honor her and pray for her soul.

After about a month, the dreaded epidemic that sickened or killed many residents of Fish Springs ran its course. It was as if a deadly black plague had descended on the little mountain community, played havoc and slipped back into the depths of hell.

"It's the devil castin' his ol' evil spell," one of the community's naysayers opined. "People's been a layin' outta church and sinnin' and now hit's come home to haunt'em."

Daniel maintained his appearance of being a pillar of strength for his family. His children, devastated at losing their mother, clung ever more tightly to their father, and Mary came every day to help Daniel comfort and tend to them. The family cried, prayed and tried to console one another around the big oak table in the main room. Little Izzy especially took it hard; she couldn't understand why God had taken her mother.

In due time, the broken community of Fish Springs started pulling itself back together. The healing would take many months, even years, and some would never get over their loss. But life continued. Men returned to their chores on their farms and in the fields. Women again kept the home fires burning. They nurtured their children and supported their husbands. And for many, their faith in God seemed to grow stronger. For immediately after the crisis lifted, and for months after that, the pews in Preacher Ike Redford's church were crammed with people searching for answers and hope.

The one-room school reopened, and that helped take Izzy and Peter's minds off the loss of their mother. Charlie returned to work at the sawmill in Butler, where he planned to stay until he went off to college the following fall.

Daniel, on the other hand, had been so busy caring and worrying for his children that he had not properly grieved for the loss of his wife, friend and helpmate, of twenty years.

Polly had been the love of his life, the rock he leaned on especially when times got tough and had been his trusted confidante and cheerful companion in better, more uplifting times. He couldn't imagine life without her.

CHAPTER 23

A Force to be Reckoned With

Daniel Smith's family would never be the same, for Polly had been the glue that held them together. She had been the nurturer, the homemaker, the firm but gentle disciplinarian, the loving mother and wife that her three children and husband could never replace.

"Mom's with Jesus now," said Izzy, the most heartbroken of the children. "I know she ain't in tha cold, hard ground. I dreamed last night she'n a angel flew over our house."

Her brother Peter wanted to believe this but wasn't so sure. "I hear talk at school that when a person dies, they just rot and the worms get'em," he said. "They say all this heaven talk is just a lie, jest somethin' to give folks hope—"

"You shut your mouth, Peter!" older brother Charlie demanded. "Our mom's in heaven!"

"Now chillun'!" said Prissy, who'd been in the kitchen preparing a meal when she overheard the squabble. "You know's you fartha's not do'n so good. So pleaz try not to wake'm."

But Daniel Smith, sleeping in the darkened room with the shutters closed, hadn't heard a thing. When Prissy peeked in on him, all she could see in the increasingly foul smelling bedroom was an unshaven scruffy face and tousled hair, half-hidden under the quilts. She listened to make sure she could hear him breathing. She heard him inhale and exhale, but only faintly. Then after several seconds, he made a gasping sound. He was restless, withdrawn, so deeply depressed that Prissy and others in the Smith household feared he might even try to hurt himself. Daniel had been overheard in his sleep to mumble something about jumping off Cliff Hill, one of the area's highest, most potentially dangerous rock outcroppings, and joining his wife in eternity.

Had he been contemplating suicide? Or just having nightmares? No one knew, but they all watched him closely.

"Mista Daniel, you's okay?" asked Prissy. Since Polly's passing, she had taken over the household chores of cleaning, cooking and tending to Charlie, Peter and Izzy.

"I'm gettin' up, Prissy," he grunted. *But what for? What's the use?* he thought. "I don't rightly know what I'd do without you an' Isaiah. You two are the Smith family's brown angels."

Prissy smiled at the idea that her boss held her in such high esteem. But she worried about him. *When'll he come outta this and be back ta bein' his old self? When's them ole demons gonna' let go'a him?*

"I fix you some breakfast, Mista Daniel. I made some biscuits already and I made sho' da chillen lef you some."

"No thank ya, Prissy. I ain't wantin' nothin' to eat."

"Yas sa."

With a great struggle, Daniel rose from the bed, splashed water from his washbowl on his face and dragged himself to his chair in the main room by the fireplace. He hadn't bothered to change clothes. He had worn and slept in the same soiled clothes since the kids went back to school. He reeked of urine and even worse—but the now bedraggled, hungover head of the household didn't care.

His rear-end now in the big overstuffed chair, an unshaven, sad-faced Daniel asked Prissy to tell him about his family.

"They's all doin' good, Mista Daniel," Prissy said, trying to sound happy. "The boys is feedin' tha chickens an' pigs and pitchin' tha hay for tha cows. Isaiah's seein' to it dat they do it right, and Izzy's good as she kin be. She be a big hep to me!"

"Did Charlie head out to take Mary to the doctor?"

"Yas sa. I fed'm a big breakfast an' he lef'."

"That's real good, Prissy. Now I'm just goin' to have me a little nip'a whiskey. Can you get me a bottle out'a the safe; it's unlocked. Just bring one ta me please."

"You sho I cain't fix you a little sump'in ta eat, Mista Daniel?"

"No!" Daniel growled. "Don't want nary a thang' ta eat today, Prissy. Now just bring me that bottle. And while you're at it, pull them curtains over the windows. All this damned sunlight's hurtin' my eyes."

"Yes sa, Mista Daniel. I'll fetch da whiskey fo' you."

Prissy did as she was asked, but she knew, as she returned with the bottle, that her boss wouldn't last much longer like this. How's could he? *He ain't eatin' and all he wants ta do is sit in dat chaya' an' drink or lay in bed in a dark, cold room. It's like da life went straight outta m when Miss Polly died. The only thang dat might save'm is this be his last bottle.*

"Prissy, are you SURE this is my last one? I know I had more'n ten bottles in that safe!"

"I sho, Mista Daniel. I knows you had dat many, but you drank one up 'bout ever day."

The belligerent Daniel, ensconced in his chair, gulped the whiskey straight from the bottle and ended up spilling some of it on his filthy shirt. He scolded himself for not dispatching Charlie to the Black Bear Saloon. "Damn'it! If I'da known I was 'bout out, I cud'a got'm ta pick me up some in Elizabethton. 'Cause them folks at tha' Black Bear knows when a man's suffrin' and ain't fit fer nothin' but a drink ..."

Prissy checked on Daniel a few more times as he kept imbibing. She hated that he was growing more and more dependent on it, but the whiskey did have the effect of calming him down, at least for a while until, in his mind, he slipped back into some dark, gloomy place that had a hold on him. As he drank, his body would twitch. Then he'd close his eyes, and nod off, with the contents of the whiskey bottle threatening to spill all over his lap.

Satisfied that the weakened and tormented Daniel Smith was in his chair and could be left alone, Prissy went outside on the back porch. It was cloudless, unseasonably-warm. She shielded her eyes with her hands so that she could see more clearly through the bright sunlight. She wanted to make sure that Daniel's two youngest children were within sight. She spotted the two near the barn helping Isaiah with the hay. Prissy, now twenty years old and getting lovelier every day—a fact not lost on Isaiah—walked back into the house to keep working. For throughout the day and into the night, in the Smith home, there was food to be prepared, clothes to wash and rooms to clean—not to mention children, especially little Izzy, who always craved attention.

On the other hand, down the road a piece in Fish Springs, the burgeoning Mary White wanted anything but attention. She was now seven months along, prone to tire easily, and due for her regular visit with the doctor. Her unborn baby had taken to hiccupping and kicking, slightly bothersome but also reassuring to a woman who'd already lost her dear Aunt Caroline, a devoted husband and now a good friend and close confidante Polly.

She felt self-conscious when folks asked her how she was feeling, especially knowing that a more serious malaise had descended on the head of the household of the Smith family. She developed a stock answer for neighbors who'd drop in and check on her. "I'm all right. I ain't feelin' the best with this baby, but God'll take care'a me. And if you really want ta pray for somebody, pray for

Daniel Smith and his children. They're hurtin' somethin' terrible."

Not certain whether the neighbors genuinely cared about her or were just plain nosey, Mary acted cordial toward the well-wishers, told them what she thought they wanted to hear, and then pointed out—sometimes falsely—that her pregnancy nausea had come back. That way, she could be done with her visitors, some of whom surely would have lingered for hours had they not been given a reason to leave.

"She ain't a lookin' sa' good ta day," one busy body lady whispered to her equally inquisitive acquaintance as the two of them got back in their buggy and left.

"I still think she's mighty sweet on Daniel Smith," the second woman said. "You notice how ever' time we brought his name up, she'd change the subject…? And now him bein' sa sad an' all, why Mary'd be good fer'm, make'm feel like a whole man agin.'"

No sooner had the two supposed well wishers gotten out of sight, than Mary heard a knock at her door.

That'd be Daniel here to take me to the doctor in Elizabethton.

When she opened the door, she was surprised. It was Charlie, and before she could say a word, Blue was all over him, licking, yelping happily as if he'd once again been reunited with a long lost friend.

"Good morning, Miss Mary. Dad sent me ta take you to the doctor."

"Is your father okay?"

"Well, not really, he ain't sick or nothing', but I'm worried about him. All he does is sit in his chair all day in a dark room. He ain't right. He's drinkin' and he won't eat and he's plum sad all the time. And he ain't said hardly nothin' to me or Izzy or Peter. I'm embarrassed to tell you this, but he won't even bathe, Miss Mary. He's startin' ta smell real bad."

Charlie paused for a few seconds to collect himself and pet Blue on the head. He knew he had not honored what his dad had taught him about spreading family information. But Charlie couldn't help himself. Besides, Mary was more like family, and he hated to see his father suffering so.

"He told me yesterday I'd have to take you 'cause he didn't feel up to it. I had to lay outta work today. I hope I don't lose my job."

"Take me to your house, Charlie," said Mary, putting on a coat and tying a scarf over her head. As she did so, she squared her shoulders and thrust them back. Then she clinched her jaws and gave Charlie a stern I'm-ready-to-take-this-on look.

"Miss Mary, I ain't thinkin' that's a good idea."

"Nevertheless, that's where we're going."

"Yes, ma'am, but Dad might get mad, Miss Mary. He ain't hisself."

"Charlie, let's go right now! I mean it!"

"Yes ma'am."

"Stay, Blue!" Mary instructed when he started to follow them.

Being the young gentleman he'd been raised to be by his parents, Charlie helped Mary up into the buggy. He snapped the reins and headed back to his farm—fearful and anxious about what might occur when they arrived. Would his half drunk, grieving father humiliate himself, Mary and others? Would he begin slamming doors and throwing dishes and ranting and raving like a madman? That had happened a few days ago, with little Izzy within earshot, and Prissy had gathered her up quickly and taken her outside.

Charlie hated to think what might happen, but onward they rolled.

When they reached their destination, a grim-faced, determined Mary wasted no time. She strutted through the front door and straight to a startled Daniel still in his chair in the main room, near the fire, clutching his bottle of whiskey. Facing him sternly, Mary yanked the bottle from his hands and flung it into the fireplace.

The ball of fire from the explosion caused the cat Snowflake to dive into the air with his claws extended like he'd been shot from a cannon. The cat landed halfway across the room, then darted up the stairs out of sight. Turnup the dog followed, his tail firmly between his legs.

Embers were blown out onto the floor, and Charlie, not sure of what else to do, quickly gathered them up and dumped them back into the fireplace with an ash scoop.

Not expecting such an explosion, Mary was as startled as everyone else.

"Are you crazy? My God, Mary, are you tryin' ta burn my danged house down?" Daniel demanded through a fog of alcohol.

Hearing the commotion, even from outside, Peter and Izzy dropped what they were doing and dashed in through the back door. In no time at all, they appeared at their father's side and looked at Charlie for an explanation.

"WOW!" Peter gasped. "What was that?"

"What was that big bang?" Izzy asked.

Charlie quickly came up with an answer for the young ears.

"There must'a been a walnut in the fire that blew up," he said.

Then Izzy noticed Mary for the first time.

"Hi Mis—," but Charlie cut her off.

"Wait, Izzy," said Charlie, putting his finger to his lips.

The children stood obediently in silence.

Having Daniel's full attention, Mary realized now that she couldn't back down and that she had to be more assertive than ever. She looked him squarely in his drowsy eyes.

"Daniel Smith, get your behind out'a that chair and go clean yourself up! You're taking me to the doctor!"

"Mary?"

"And while you're at it, shave that mess off your face! And, Prissy, fix this man a hot cup of black coffee!"

"Yes M'am," said Prissy, a hint of a smile on her face for the first time in weeks.

She be a strong woman! Prissy marveled as she left to get Daniel's coffee. *She get Masta Daniel ta be hisself agin!*

"Mary, wait just—"

"I will not! And I'll accept no excuses!"

Trying to snap out of his stupor, Daniel focused as best he could on Mary. Then, through alcohol distorted eyes, he could make out, across the room, a blurry countenance. It seemed to be Charlie nodding his head approvingly as Peter and Izzy stood with hopeful expressions.

Ordered to get back on his feet and clean up, but still feeling the numbing effects of the whiskey, Daniel rose slowly from his chair and tried to take a step. When he stumbled and groped for something to hang onto, Charlie stepped up and kept his dad from falling.

"Peter, go fetch Isaiah, and ya'll start bringin' in water for the tub."

"Yes ma'am," said Peter as he ran out the back door.

"Mary I ain't thinkin' I'm up ta—"

"You hush right this instant. You hear me? You and I are goin' ta the doctor!"

When Daniel finally nodded and grunted that he'd get ready, it was the first time in a long while that he'd responded to anyone or anything—other than to bark orders about fetching his whiskey or leaving him be.

The change in his mood and demeanor, a glimmer of his old self, gave hope for his children. The idea that their father might yet snap out of the bleak hopelessness that had gripped him since they'd lost their mother made their day.

And they decided that Mary was a force to be reckoned with. Yes, without a doubt, she was the most beautiful young woman in Fish Springs—and possibly in all of the mountains of East Tennessee—but Mary was far more than that. The Smith children had learned firsthand that when she put her mind to something, she did it, and she didn't back down.

She even lent a helping hand with Prissy in getting Daniel bathed, shaved and dressed.

"No room for modesty now!" Mary retorted when Daniel objected to her peeling off his clothes. "Besides, I've seen a man's parts before. Ain't nothin' new ta me."

Bathed and dressed in clean clothes, Daniel began feeling better. And when he downed three cups of hot steaming coffee, along with a breakfast of eggs, grits, smoked bacon and biscuits, he improved even more.

It didn't hurt either, that Mary, cradling a cup of coffee, sat with him at the table. ***I just know Polly'd be glad she's here with me and the children. She's like an angel sent to watch over our family.***

As the two of them said little and kept an awkward watch over each other at the kitchen table, Izzy scampered down the stairs. She had Snowflake in her arms.

"Look at Snowflake's tail!" she said. "It's all curly and black—like it got burnt in a fire!"

"OOOh, poor Snowflake," said Mary, feeling guilty for the feline's scorched tail.

Daniel looked knowingly at Mary.

"He's okay, Miss Mary. Charlie checked him all over. He said his tail just got singed when that walnut blew up. His skin's not burned."

Mary, who would one day fess'up to blowing Snowflake across the room, tried to keep a straight face. Then she swallowed hard and told Izzy that she was glad her cat wasn't burned.

But the little one wasn't so easy to persuade. "Dad, do you think, for sure, it wuz' a walnut that blew'up?"

"All I can say is that some kind of a nut caused that explosion," Daniel said. As he spoke, he eyed Mary sharply. She stared back at him with raised eyebrows.

Later, as Daniel and Mary traveled the old dirt road toward Elizabethton, Daniel noticed a murder of crows in the top of a large poplar tree. They were perched high above one of last year's harvested cornfields, reminding him that a new planting season was just around the corner. The solid black cackling birds, with long bills and legs, also hinted of a place he didn't ever want to go again, a place of death and darkness, a place within himself that had threatened to be the end of him.

"Koww!" one of the creatures called out.

Glancing at her lapel watch, Mary knew she'd be hours late for her appointment. She hated that but also figured Dr. Godfrey would still see her. She knew from talk around Fish Springs that country doctors had to be flexible when it came to appointments with their patients living in the mountains. A swollen river or broken buggy wheel could wreak havoc on a patient getting to a doctor at the appointed time. So the unwritten code in and around Fish Springs was, As long as you got there on the day of your appointment, Dr. Godfrey would see you, even if it was after dark.

Neither one had spoken since leaving the farm. Finally, Mary broke the silence.

"Daniel, I'm sorry about the explosion in your fireplace."

"I'm just glad," Daniel responded, "that I only had three or four swigs left in that bottle, or you probably wouldda' burned the damned house down."

"Remind me to never take a bottle of booze from an old sot and fling it into a fire," she said.

"Deal. You know, Mary, I seen a side of you I ain't seen before. You can be right tough, even ornery. I like that in a woman."

"Not as tough as you might think. Because when that bottle blew up, it scared the living daylight out'a me."

"It scared the living hell out'a Snowflake," said Daniel.

"Poor Snowflake. I felt so bad about that."

"He's okay. Soon's the hair sprouts back on his tail he'll be good as new." Daniel couldn't keep from chuckling.

Then they laughed out loud.

Daniel stopped the buggy near a creek running alongside the road and put his arm around Mary, pulling her close. Not as lovers or mates but as two lonely souls who needed one another's friendship and encouragement.

And here and now, by this beautiful mountain stream, he had something to tell her. "Thank you for what you did for me Mary. That took a lot of guts.

"You wouldn't think it, but Polly could be tough too, if you made her mad enough. One time when we were first married, Polly made me an apple pie. It may have been her first and she was plum proud of it. While I was eatin' it, I told her how good it tasted, but the crust was a little too done.

"Lordy, I wore that pie until I got down to the spring to wash it off!" said Daniel, laughing hard.

"I never said nothin' bad 'bout Polly's cookin' after that," said Daniel, snapping the reins.

When his laughter suddenly turned to weeping, Mary leaned into him, trying to comfort him.

"I'm sorry, Mary! I just cain't believe she's gone. I can't get over her."

"You'll never get over Polly," Mary said softly. "Just like I'll never get over Alfred. But you do have to get on with your life and take care'a your family. They need you, Daniel."

"But how do I do that, Mary? It's hard losing someone you've loved for twenty years. Lord knows, you know what it's like to lose someone you truly love," he said between sniffles.

"You just keep goin', Daniel, keep tryin' to be strong for Peter, Charlie and Izzy. And you take it a little bit at a time. It's like crossing that stream," said Mary, pointing. "To get across, you take it one stone at a time, not tryin' to jump across all at once."

A little ways farther down the road, Daniel focused on what Mary said about taking it one stone at a time. And when they forded the creek, he noticed a school of horneyheads. There, below them, was a thick swarm of the dark brown little fish. Daniel had always argued that they were better to eat than trout.

Daniel nudged Mary's side and directed her attention downward, to the spawning mass of the delicious fish.

"Are they good ta eat?" she asked.

"Bettern' any fish in these mountains, Mary."

"Then, after I've had the baby and feel more like eatin', you ought to take your children fishing right here on this very spot and catch us a mess for dinner," Mary said. "Prissy and I'll do the cleanin' and cookin' if you and the kids and Isaiah do the catchin'. Deal?"

Daniel promised her he'd catch them their dinner after the baby was born.

And no sooner had he said that, a rider on horse back came into view. It was John Williams.

"Afternoon, Mary. Daniel," said John, tipping his western style hat. "Sorry about Polly, Daniel. I prayed fer both'a ya."

"Thank you, John."

"Are you jist out fer a ride on this beautiful day?" As he asked that question, John's eyes seemed to be locked on Mary's.

"Daniel's taking me to the doctor for my checkup, John."

"So when's your baby due?"

"'Bout two more months. None too soon for me."

"Well, ain't that somethin'," said John. "Guess you'll be right happy when that little'un gets born."

Then he wished them a safe trip, smiled, tipped his hat again and galloped off thinking, *I don't understand why Mary spends so much time with that old man. He must be twice her age. Maybe she jist feels sorry fer him, or maybe it's cause he's got sa' much land and money.*

As he rode off, the more John Williams thought about it, the more upset he became. So, he vowed not to dwell anymore on what Mary did or didn't do or who she spent her time with. *'Cause sure as the sun'll rise, she'll come back to me. She ain't staying away fer much longer.*

When the only thing they could see left of John Williams was the cloud of trailing dust created by his horse, Daniel said, "Sometimes I have to remind myself that he is the same John Williams, the rogue I knew before."

"I know, Daniel. I have the same problem." *It would be easer if he wasn't so blame good lookin'*, Mary thought. *The blue-eyed, handsome devil.*

"Mary, I need to tell you something. Before Polly passed she made me promise to watch over you. She didn't want you to be by yourself this late in your pregnancy.

"I want you to stay with us until the baby comes. The boys can double up and you can have Peter's room. I'll have Isaiah watch over your place."

"Thank you, Daniel, but I can take care of myself."

"No buts, Mary. I promised Polly. Besides, we enjoy your company. And you know how little Izzy loves havin' you around.

"And you know what else, Mary? Because'a you, this is the best I've felt in a long time. Thank God for sending you to us!"

"Okay, I'll do it, Daniel Smith, but only if you'll let me help Prissy with the cookin'."

"I would have to be a fool to say no to that."

"And one more thing, no more whiskey, Daniel Smith."

"Okay, as long as you promise not to burn my house down, Mary White."

CHAPTER 24
Fetching Mrs. Gouge

It was a beautiful April morning in Fish Springs. A shower the night before, along with cool temperatures, had created a mystical dense fog that hung over the mountains but the cloud-like haze had begun burning off quickly.

Water from the winter snow melt streamed down the craggy cliffs lining the Watauga River. March and April had brought a lot of rain. This boded well for the planting season in Fish Springs, but the fertile, loamy ground was too wet to work today, so Daniel busied himself catching up on his paperwork.

It was Saturday; there was no school and Charlie had the day off at the sawmill. In the barn lot, he brushed down his chestnut gelding. The horse, its coat a bright sheen from the brushing, stood completely still, as if it enjoyed Charlie's touch.

Peter lollygagged on the top rail of the barn lot fence watching Charlie, and Izzy was in a swing that Daniel erected for her in the towering oak tree in the front yard. At her feet lay Turnup. The dog paid her only casual attention, preferring instead to snooze and occasionally open one droopy eye and yawn.

Daniel Smith's youngest child, always on the move, always exploring and asking questions, decided it was time to see about Mary again, which she did about twenty times a day. Were it another woman being questioned and looked in on so often, Izzy would probably have long since been told to skedaddle. But Mary would never hurt Izzy's feelings so when the curious little one poked her head into her room, Mary was never brusque or dismissive. Instead, even in the depths of her fatigue, she always had a kind word for Izzy and blew her a kiss.

Mary had been a Godsend for Izzy, helping her through periods of grief over her mother's passing and helping her to learn how to be a little lady. Thanks to Mary, Izzy practiced table manners at every meal, picked up after herself—usually—and didn't interrupt when an adult spoke. The always-wanting-to-know-more little girl had even taken to reading. When Mary pointed out a few Bible verses about Jesus and little children, Izzy began memorizing them. She had become quite the little show-off with her knowledge of those parts of the Bible. And in the evening, before she went to sleep, she always wanted Mary, bone tired but still there for Izzy, to tuck her in. Then her dad would kiss his angel good night and promise her that Polly was looking down at her from Heaven.

On a beautiful Saturday morning, with the sun shining and a faint warm breeze caressing her face, Izzy was in her swing, suspended from the oak tree. She had been watching a family of scurrying squirrels, a few branches up, and was fascinated with how the bushy-tailed creatures frolicked about, grasping acorns, cracking them, then leaping, almost as if they had wings, to another tree limb.

She jumped from the tree swing and ran up the porch steps, jumped over Blue and entered the house, and she saw her father in his office near the front door.

"Dad, where's Mary?"

"She went upstairs to take a nap, so don't wake her if she's asleep, okay?"

"I promise I'll just peek in to make sure she's all right."

Mary's baby was due any time now, and the sooner the better, as far as she was concerned. She'd been here at Daniel's home for seven weeks, and though everyone made her feel welcome, she felt like she was imposing and just an additional mouth to feed. Plus, every day she seemed to have less energy, and in the mornings especially, she was nauseated. At times she wished she could just be alone and not trouble anyone.

Mary tossed and turned in the bed, unable to sleep. It was hard to get comfortable. As she lay there feeling pity for herself, an intense, deep pain hit her for several seconds, and then faded.

God almighty! What was that? And where'd it come from? Is this what I'll be feelin' from now on? Will there be another one?

She decided to keep this sudden, excruciating pain to herself. She would not alert anyone until she absolutely could not stand it. Mary closed her eyes, wiped the perspiration from her forehead, rested her hands on her huge, distended tummy and waited. *Either another deep pain will come out of nowhere and about kill me or I'll be so nauseous that I can't hold my head up. Not fair either way.*

She heard the door squeak against its hinges. She opened her eyes. It was bright-eyed Izzy peeking in on her, as she'd done countless times, day in and day out, the last few weeks.

"You can come in sweetheart. I'm not asleep."

"I'm just checking on you, Miss Mary. Do you need anything?"

"I'm fine, Izzy, but you can sit for a spell if you like."

"Can I ask you a question, Miss Mary?" Izzy climbed up on the bed and put her little hand on Mary's forehead as if to check to see if she had a fever.

"Izzy, you can ask me anything."

"Well I know there's a baby growing in there," said Izzy, touching Mary's tummy. "But I'm not real sure how it got in there. I think I know, but I can't be sure. Mom said we would have a talk about it real soon, but she's in heaven now and ever' time I ask Dad, he says we'll talk about it later."

When Mary, smiling, asked her how she thought a baby gets in a mother's tummy, Izzy had a ready answer.

"Well, Peter an' me wuz watchin' my rabbits, and my big one wuz runnin' around jumpin' on the back end of the smaller ones, shakin' his rear end back and forth.

"Peter said my big rabbit was a boy, 'cause he was plantin' seeds to make baby rabbits. I think he wuz right, 'cause not too long after that a lotta my rabbits had babies.

"Is that how it happens, Miss Mary? Do people do it that way too?"

Mary chose her words carefully. "Most'a God's creatures plant their seeds like that Izzy, but there's a lot more to it. Let me ask your dad if he'd like me to talk to you about it. Okay?"

"Okay, Miss Mary. I thought I wuz right!" Izzy, happy with herself, beamed.

When Mary, growing more tired by the second, praised her little protector and questioner as being a smart girl, Izzy hit her with another one.

"Miss Mary, Peter says Adam'n Eve didn't have no belly buttons, cuz they wuz made by God. Do you think that's true?"

"I just don't know, Izzy, and I don't think nobody really knows for sure," Mary drowsily replied. "But one day when we all git ta heaven, I 'magine we'll find out."

"Okay, Miss Mary. Now you just get some sleep. Your baby needs rest, too."

"Izzy! I think it's time to get your dad!" Mary exclaimed. Another sharp pain had just shot through her body.

Izzy stared at Mary, frozen to the spot..

"Now, Izzy! Please!"

Izzy bounded down the stairs as fast as she could, taking them two at a time."Dad!"

"What, Izzy?" said Daniel, his eyes locked on some documents on his desk.

"Mary said it's time!"

"Time for what, Izzy?"

"The baby's comin'!"

"Oh, it's THAT time!" her father responded. He got up and ran outside.

"Charlie, Charlie! Hitch up the buggy and go fetch Mrs. Gouge! And Peter, help your brother!"

Knowing without a doubt it was an emergency, the two boys sprang into action.

"I cain't git this halter on the danged horse!" Peter griped. He had tried nervously and too quickly to do something he'd done hundreds of times before.

"Here! Let me do it! Get outta the way!" Charlie hollered. "We ain't got no time to waste!"

Within a few agonizingly long minutes, Daniel's two sons were on their way to pick up Mrs. Dorothy Gouge, a round-faced woman with bangs of gray hair and a hint of a mustache. A midwife for twenty-five years, following in the footsteps of her mother, she lived in an old cabin on the road between Butler and Fish Springs. Charlie knew exactly where because Daniel, anticipating this moment for weeks, had shown him.

Mrs. Gouge, now getting up a bit in years but still as active as ever in midwifery, was always available if needed in an emergency. And, occasionally teaming with Dr. Jim Godfrey, she rendered her services regardless of whether people could pay.

In due time, Charlie and Peter would return with the woman who'd helped bring hundreds of babies into the world, including all three of Daniel and Polly's.

Daniel ran back into the house and paused at the staircase to gather his thoughts.

"Mista Smith, does you wants me ta do anything?" Prissy asked.

"Maybe heat a few pots of water, Prissy."

"Yas sa."

And then Izzy, bubbly as ever and unable to keep from jumping up and down, asked her dad what she could do.

Daniel knew his youngest had to feel like she was needed. "You help Prissy bring some water in from the spring."

"Daniel!" Mary yelled from upstairs.

Daniel attacked the stairs three at a time. "I'm comin', Mary!"

He burst into the room to find Mary gripping her sheets, her back arched in a contraction. She gritted her teeth and growled, for all the world like a bear. When it passed, she flopped back on the pillows, her face dripping with sweat.

"Oh Daniel, I'm so sorry." She panted and writhed in pain.

"Sorry? What? Why?"

"I didn't know it was labor. I thought it was just another nasty pain of pregnancy. Now I've waited too late and put you in this … this …"

She grimaced and Daniel was sure it was another labor pain, but even though this was only a little cramp, Mary knew it was a precursor of much deeper suffering and that frightened her.

"What can I do, Mary?"

"Just don't leave me, Daniel, please." For the next hour, every few minutes, Mary asked, "Where is Mrs. Gouge?"

Later Daniel responded. "She's on the way. She should be here any minute now."

"That's good 'cause I think this baby is…ooooh God!" Mary arched her back again and screamed, this time louder than the last. She squeezed Daniel's hand so hard that he flinched.

Almost in a state of panic, Daniel chided himself, realizing fully for the first time what he had gotten himself into. *Mary could die tryin' ta have this baby and it'd be my fault. I took on this responsibility, but now what? Mrs. Gouge was always here when Polly went into labor. Why didn't I stay when Polly was birthing? Oh God, where are my boys with Mrs Gouge?*

Mary screamed again. "Daniel I need you, PLEASE!"

Now totally panicked, Daniel ran to the top of the stairs. "PRISSY!" Daniel hollered at the top of his lungs.

"If you're calling your house maid, Mister Smith, she's at the well pumping water," Mrs. Gouge said matter-of-factly as she ascended the stairs.

"It's okay. I'm here now. Let's see where we are with birthin' this baby." Mrs Gouge spoke to Mary reassuringly as she entered the room and pulled up the sheet covering her.

"Oh yes, I think you are about ready," she said, patting Mary on the head.

"Thank God you're here, Mrs Gouge," Daniel said. "I didn't know what ta do."

"Most men don't. You can leave now, Mr. Smith, unless you'd like to stay and maybe learn a few things."

When Daniel didn't immediately respond, the midwife tossed a bundle of clean rags at the foot of the bed, the stains of previous use not entirely conquered by bleach, hot water and sunshine.

"Well I would, Mrs. Gouge but I think the children'll need me ta be with'em out there waitin'," said Daniel, as Mary screamed again..

"Just get the hell outta here, Daniel, and let Mrs. Gouge do her job!"

Mrs. Gouge smiled at Daniel and said she understood.

Six excruciatingly long hours later, while waiting for the newborn to arrive, Daniel and Charlie sat in the main room, talking about farming and using sharecroppers. Peter and Izzy lay on the floor playing checkers, and Prissy busied herself in the kitchen preparing the evening meal. Through it all, the old grandfather clock in the big main room ticked and tocked, ticked and tocked.

"I know this for a fact, son," said Daniel. "If you give your sharecroppers a fair share and you treat them with respect, they'll produce. Trust me on that, Charlie."

A door opened to the landing at the top of the stairs.

"Mary's doin' fine, and so is her new baby boy," Mrs. Gouge announced, almost as if she were giving them a report on the weather. "You may come up and visit a few minutes."

"That's what I wanted, a baby boy!" Izzy clapped her hands and squealed.

Shouts of joy and celebration filled the house. Mrs. Gouge raised her hands for quiet and they all obeyed. Then they all ascended the stairs. Daniel, last to start up, saw Prissy standing in the kitchen awkwardly, as if she didn't know what to do.

"You come too, Prissy. You're part of this family."

The former slave girl, her hands chock full of vegetables she was preparing to cut up and cook for dinner, cracked a big smile. Then she laid the food down on the table and joined the others.

They all marveled at Mary, completely spent but exultant, lying in the bed with her new baby in her arms.

"It's a boy," Mary said proudly to the group lined up at the foot of the bed.

"He's indeed a handsome boy, Mary," Daniel boasted. "And look at that head of hair he's already got!"

"He's not very big, is he?" Peter asked.

"All babies are little like that, Peter," Charlie said.

"He's not much bigger than a big potato. Hey, we can call him Tater!" Peter said, grinning.

"No he will not be called Tater, Peter," Mary insisted. "His name is Alfred Daniel White, and I want to call him Danny."

An ecstatic Daniel said he was honored, and then Mary asked Izzy if she'd like to hold the baby.

"May I?"

"Let Mrs. Gouge show you how."

Mrs. Gouge whose soft palms and long slim fingers seemed made for midwifery, took the baby from Mary, swaddled it and demonstrated to Izzy how to support the newborn's head with her hand "Just like this," she said softly, cuddling the infant. Then she gave the baby to Izzy.

Izzy smiled from ear to ear as she gently cradled the newborn.

"Isn't he beautiful, Dad?" Izzy said.

"He ain't beautiful. He's handsome!" Peter declared.

"He's both," Daniel said.

"Dat's a fine boy. Da Lawd done give you a precious baby," Prissy said. "Now, I'm gown get back ta makin' dinner. I has food on da stove. Can I's fix you anythin' Miss Mary?"

"Oh yes, Prissy. I'd love ta have some'a your oatmeal, with some'a that wild strawberry jam And is there any buttermilk?"

"Yes ma'am," Prissy responded, already on her way out the door. "I git it fer ya."

The baby's face, wrinkled and red, contorted as he started to cry.

"I think it's about time for this little boy to have some milk, folks," Mrs. Gouge noted.

When Peter asked the midwife if she wanted him to fetch it, Mary smiled and put one hand on her breast.

"I've already got it, Peter."

"Oh, yeah, I forgot. Let me outta here!" He covered his eyes and quickly exited the room as everyone laughed.

"May I stay, Miss Mary?" Izzy asked.

After Mary said it was all right for Izzy to remain, Daniel and Charlie left. Mary then pulled back the sheet exposing one breast and her tummy. Mrs. Gouge laid the warm baby on Mary's tummy, covering his body with the sheet. She gently guided his mouth to Mary's nipple, and little Danny stopped crying and began to suckle.

"That's so sweet, Miss Mary," Izzy whispered.

Mary closed her eyes and praised God for her healthy, perfect baby boy.

Meanwhile, John Williams sat at the bar in the Black Bear Saloon. He had been stewing since hearing a few days earlier that Mary would bring her baby into the world at Daniel Smith's home. But that hadn't been the worst of it, John concluded, because Mary and Daniel would most certainly be getting closer. Furthermore, John figured she would be depending on him—and his damned money—to help her raise Alfred's baby.

And then, who knows what else'd happen? When a woman's under a man's roof, they start lookin' at each other. And it ain't as if they're not already doin' that, John fumed.

Here I sit in this damn bar drowning in my sorrows and Daniel Smith's laughin' and gettin' closer to the woman I care about more'n anybody else in the world.

God, why's it always somebody keepin' me away from my Mary? First it was that old dried out prune Aunt Caroline. Then it was sorry, good-fer-nothin' Yankee Alfred White. And now it's rich old, connivin' Daniel Smith. Why'd she have to come ta his house to spit out that baby?

John Williams pledged to himself right then and there that no man, regardless of their wealth, would stand between himself and Mary White.

CHAPTER 25

Jumping the Broom

Charlie hooked up the buggy and returned Mrs. Gouge to her home the following day, but not before she taught Mary some of the finer points of breastfeeding and caring for an infant.

"Now remember, Mary, lil' Danny loves ta be touched and held. And he likes ta hear your heart beat. Makes'm feel safe and sound," the venerable midwife said. "And when he cries, that ain't necessarily a bad thang. He's a growin' his lungs."

By the time Mrs. Gouge departed, Mary felt confident she could take care of her baby. But it was reassuring to know that Daniel and his family, along with Prissy and Isaiah, were nearby just in case...

"Miss Mary, you's hungry? Gotcha somethin' for your lunch," said Prissy, setting a tray of food next to Mary's bed.

"Oh, thank you, Prissy. Can you stay a few minutes?"

"Yas'em."

"Would you like to rock little Danny while I eat?"

"I'd like ta do dat," said Prissy. She took the fussy infant in her arms and he squalled and kicked. But baby Danny fell asleep as Prissy rocked and hummed an old lullaby. It was a song she'd heard from her youth as a slave in Virginia. Always, it seemed, a baby was being born on the plantation. So she had learned early, from watching and listening to her elders, how to help keep a newborn quiet and satisfied.

"I'd like ta have me a baby some day."

"Well Prissy, all you need is a good man. I heard Isaiah was sweet on you. Are you likin' him?"

"Yas'em. Isaiah, he say he love me, Miss Mary. He say he wantin' me ta be his woman forever, but he don' ax me to marry him. I been waiten an waiten."

"Sometimes you have to help a man talk, Prissy. You have ta give'm a little push. I learned that from Aunt Caroline."

"How do I do dat, Miss Mary?"

"The next time Isaiah says he loves you, you say, 'will you love me forever?' When he says yes, you say, 'and I should never be with another man, like if we wuz married?' Then when he says 'that's right,' you say, 'Exactly what are you trying to say, Isaiah? That we should get married?' Then if he asks you to marry him, he'll think it was his idea."

Prissy covered her mouth to keep from laughing out loud as Daniel entered Mary's bedroom.

"What's so funny in here?"

"That's mine and Prissy's secret," Mary said playfully.

"Well … okay. So how's little Tater?"

"Daniel Smith, don't you dare call little Danny that. If you do, I'm going to start callin' you big Tater."

With that mild reprisal, Daniel assured Mary he very well knew her baby's name "but he's still the cutest little tater I ever laid eyes on!"

"Daniel!"

He apologized once more—this time profusely—and promised her he'd never again refer to baby Danny as "Tater."

Then Daniel told Prissy that he'd almost forgotten, what with so much going on the last few days, that he had a letter for her. It had recently come in the mail and there was no mistaking that the sealed envelope was addressed to her.

As she examined the envelope and wondered about its contents, Prissy nodded when Daniel informed her that there'd be six people for dinner that night, not counting little Danny.

"Yas sa."

"Daniel, remember I'm goin' home tomorrow," Mary said.

"We'll see," he said. "You're still plum weak, Mary, and nobody' wants you to leave. And besides, I think little Danny likes it here."

After Daniel had left the three of them to themselves, Prissy eagerly opened the envelope and unfolded a one-page letter. Mary offered to read it for her, but Prissy thanked her just the same and told her that she had learned to read as a slave.

"Well, good for you," Mary said with a hint of surprise.

"I kin writes too," Prissy said proudly. "I cain't spell too good but my mama knows what I says."

"So you learned to read and write during slave times, Prissy?"

"Mrs. Mary Carter teached me when I lived at the Shirley Plantation. It be in Virginia, Miss Mary."

"Was she a school teacher?"

"No, ma'am. She be the wife of Mr. Hill Carter. He be the owner and masta of Shirley Plantation. Mrs. Carter teached some of us slaves how ta read and write."

"She musta been a special person."

"Yas'em, she wuz. She learned my mama too. Dat where my mama be now, wit my daddy. My mama writ' me in a letter a couple years ago dat Mrs. Carter died of 'monia. It made me real sad."

When Mary said she was sorry that such a good woman had passed, Prissy nodded. Then she opened the envelope, unfolded the letter, written on a stained, yellow piece of stationery that had seen better days, and read.

When she finished she stuffed it back into the envelope.

Mary detected a hint of a smile. "Good news, I hope?"

"Yas'em it was. My mama say she and my daddy had a real weddin' wit a preacher and rings 'cause dey wornt 'loud to have a weddin' when dey was slaves; all dey could do is jump da broom."

"Oh, Prissy! That's wonderful that they had a genuwine' weddin'! There was so many thangs that were awful about slavery."

"Yes, dey wuz, Miss Mary. I ain't never liked dem years I wuz a slave. Dat wasn't good times. An' I wuz even one of the lucky ones. I wuz a house slave on the Shirley Plantation, not like the others dat had ta work in the hot fields hoein' corn and 'bacco and pickin' cotton. I wuz borned on the Shirley Plantation an' liked it 'cause I'z there wit' my mama and daddy, but when I got my monthlies I wuz taken away by my new masta.

"Masta Yates, he be very bad. I'member once my seein' Masta Yates almost whup a thirteen-year-old girl to death cuz she wouldn't do what he say. Dat scared me! Those wuz bad times when people got whupped ... And then, I 'member bein' taken to Richmond and bein' chained up on the slave block and bein' sold to Jake Edwards. He be a mean, mean devil too! He hit me and spitted on me and put his hands on me and and say awful thangs to me. I ain't never had no good times 'till I wuz here with Mista and Missus Smith and their family."

Prissy told Mary that some of her fellow slaves had warned her that all white people were evil. "But I finds out, Miss Mary, that they wuz wrong, 'cause some white people's good and some's bad, just like us colored folks."

With Prissy on the verge of tears, her listener decided to change the subject.

"Prissy, have you written your parents about Isaiah?"

Patting the baby on his back so he would burp, the beautiful Negro smiled. The sound of little Danny belching loudly was music to her ears.

"I done tol mama 'bout Isaiah. Dat I hope he'd ax me to marry him. Mama say she hope so too, and dat she wuz glad I could have a real weddin' wit' a preacher and rings and dat I wouldn't have to jump the broom like she and Daddy did."

"I'm happy for you, Prissy. Now don't you go a darin' ta give up on Isaiah; you try what I told you."

"Yas'em I will. I likes talkin' ta you, Miss Mary. I best go git cookin' on dinner now," said Prissy, gently handing Danny back to Mary.

"Come on big boy," Mary said. "Prissy's babied you long 'nough. Time to be back in your momma's arms."

"He be a good child, Miss Mary."

After mother and newborn had napped, Mary carried her baby downstairs and sat for a while with Daniel.

"Daniel, Prissy said somethin' about her parents havin' to jump the broom insteada' havin' a weddin' durin' slavery times? What'd she mean?"

"The slaves were treated real bad, Mary—almost like animals," said Daniel. He explained to her that even if they were fortunate enough to have good-hearted, kind masters, slaves were still chattel. And they weren't allowed to have a wedding in a church with a preacher and witnesses.

"Instead, in the slave community, when a man and woman wanted to have a marriage-like relationship, they'd jump the broom. It was a kind of public ceremony where people could be there and declare that a particular slave man and his woman was settlin' down together as a couple. They weren't legally married but people knew they loved each other, and they accepted it. Not that white folks wanted to accept anything a slave wanted, but some of 'em went along with the idea of jumpin' the broom, 'cause they figured happy slaves'd make better workers."

Daniel went on to explain that after the Civil War, when the slaves were freed, they could have traditional style church weddings, just the same as white people, with rings, vows and a preacher pronouncing them man and wife.

"How you knowin' all this, Daniel?"

"I ain't all that smart. I just do a lotta reading, dear, and Prissy and Isaiah told me a little of what it was like to be a slave. Isaiah said his friend Tobey told him Jake Edwards made him work outside during that terrible cold spell a few winters back. His feet got frost bit and they had to cut two of his toes off. Isaiah told me poor Tobey never could walk right after that. Tobey's evil master told him what happened was a good thing, because now he wouldn't have to hobble him to keep him from running away. "

"I don't know how some people could be so mean."

"I know Mary some people just don't have any feelin's."

Mary hesitated looking down at her hands in her lap, so long that Daniel wondered what she was thinking. "Daniel, I need to leave in a few days. I will be packing my things and moving back home."

"You're practically family, Mary. You ain't needin' to go nowhere," Daniel protested.

"Oh, but I do Daniel. Surely deep down you know that. As much as I love the children, they can't become too dependent on me. Besides you know how people talk and we can't subject the children to that."

The last few days spent with Daniel and the children seemed to fly by. It would be hard to leave the Smith home; Mary had felt so comfortable there. Leaving things like, when she needed a break from motherhood, Peter and Charlie would offer a helping hand. The infant seemed as if he couldn't get enough of the two gangly boys. Things like teaching Izzy how to carry a melody and sing some new songs. And the time when Izzy asked her to teach her how to dance, the two of them would act like a couple, their cheeks pressed against one another, moving to the rhythm of a Tennessee mountain tune.

But it just wasn't right, Mary reasoned, she and Daniel enjoying each other's company and her enjoying his family when she wasn't really a part of that family. Then there was the very good advice Mary had given Prissy—advice she needed to consider herself.

Meanwhile a few gossiping tongues in Fish Springs again wagged. "She ain't nothin' but a concubine," one old widow asserted."And you cain't tell me that Daniel Smith ain't gittin her in bed. If he ain't, it's jest a matter'a time. He's a bustin' at the seams to git her 'tween tha sheets."

"Now remember, Mary, we want you to come to dinner Sunday week, but me'n the boys'll be checking on you plenty between now and then. You take care'a little Tater. Uh, I mean Danny!" yelled Daniel, as he and Izzy drove off.

It was a tough, somber ride home for Izzy, who for the first time in weeks didn't have Mary to lean on, learn from or play with."I miss little Danny!" she wailed. "Why'd they have ta leave us, Daddy?"

Daniel, too, had a hard time accepting that the young woman who'd brought so much love and tenderness to his family—and who had likely saved his life—

now had left them.

"She'll be back, Izzy. I promise. We've just got ta let her have some time alone with her baby."

As the buggy rolled slowly back to his farm, Daniel imagined how life would be if Mary were there all the time. Just thinking about it made him happy, even mildly excited, but then reality set in. *How'd that ever work? And why on earth'd she ever give up her own place and move in with us? What would folks think?*

Well, a body can think and dream. Ain't nothin' wrong with that, long as a body keeps such foolish thoughts to hisself.

Sunday week finally came around and dinner at the Smith home, with special guests Mary and Danny White, was a big hit. The children were all over them, hugging Mary, peppering her with questions, and playing with little Danny.

And at some point in the afternoon, Prissy managed to get Mary to herself. "Isaiah ax me ta merry him, an' he thinks it wuz his idea."

"And you said yes?"

"Yas'em I did," said Prissy, giggling.

"And when is your wedding?"

"In October, Miss Mary, after da crops is in, and Mista Smith goin' let us have de weddin' 'ception here. I doesn't know who gown ta marry us but we find somebody."

Mary threw her arms around Prissy and wished her the best "'Cause you an' Isaiah deserve some good times in your life. You'll make a great married couple!"

And so, nuptial plans were made. The two loyal, devoted Negroes who had worked so faithfully for Daniel Smith would soon be husband and wife.

But it wasn't just a matter of course. Because even though the war had vanquished slavery, old prejudices died slowly in Fish Springs and elsewhere in the South. So slowly that a few days later, when Daniel tried to talk Preacher Ike Redford into marrying Prissy and Isaiah in the church, Redford said he couldn't do it. The normally unflappable clergyman feared such a ceremony, performed at the Fish Springs Baptist Church, would cause a big uproar. However, when he did offer to marry them anywhere else, Daniel opted to have the wedding at the Smith house. That was, if Isaiah and Prissy so desired.

"I'll marry'em, Daniel, but you got to remember, the deacons'd never stand for 'em havin' a Christian weddin' in our church," said Redford looking down in shame.

"Then those deacons must not be Christians," Daniel snapped back angrily.

As it happened, Preacher Redford's services were not needed. For Isaiah had heard about the Reverend Horace Leftwich, a former slave who had recently founded the Colored Baptist Church in Elizabethton, and after a visit from Isaiah and Prissy, the reverend agreed to come to Fish Springs and marry them at the Smith farm. When Preacher Redford heard that the Reverend Leftwich would be performing the wedding at the Smith's, he let be known that he would like to meet Leftwich, the Negro preacher he had been hearing so much about. So Isaiah invited Ike Redford and his wife to the wedding.

It was against such a background that Leftwich promised he'd be there as a minister on Isaiah's and Prissy's special day. And what a glorious, memorable wedding day it was.

On a gorgeous Saturday in October, with the East Tennessee mountain foliage at its peak brilliant colors, and under a sunny, clear blue sky, the couple were married outside on Daniel's big porch. Most of the well-wishers were farm workers and sharecroppers, except for an elderly couple from Virginia. They were Prissy's mother and father, and Daniel had paid their transportation to come to the wedding.

And the bride? She screamed with joy the day before the big celebration when she opened the front door to see her parents. It had been six long years since the old couple had seen their only child. They all cried. Then they laughed. Then more tears and laughter and hugging.

It was a day none of them would ever forget.

After the wedding, there was backslapping, hand shaking, dancing and singing, banjo picking, and eating fried chicken and cold watermelon cooled in the spring. There was also a little jug sipping, but that was done discreetly.

Ike Redford finally found a time when the popular Reverend Leftwich wasn't surrounded by wedding guests and the two sat down at a table for a chat.

Sipping on his lemonade, Leftwich told Ike how he had been brought to Tennessee by Lt. William McQueen of the 13th Regiment of the Tennessee Calvary. He shared with Ike that the church he founded was one of the first black churches in Northeast Tennessee. He said his church was a dancing, clapping, shouting group of congregants, most of them former slaves who rejoiced in finally having a place of their own to praise and worship the Lord. And it had been no easy task to establish the Colored Baptist Church. He had been met at every juncture with those who opposed such a bold idea.

"Why tha' dickens cain't them uppity niggas just keep worshippin' like they always has?" one staunch white Baptist had argued. "They's thinkin' they's too good ta sit'n tha back like they always has."

In the end, Reverend Leftwich, who from his pulpit ranted against racial injustice, lynching, lying, stealing, adultery and all manner of abominations, had prevailed. With the help of a few dozen freed slaves, he'd built his church, with his own calloused, strong hands, from the ground up. And the crude but serviceable little sanctuary fast became known in Elizabethton, to the dismay of many white Christians, as a divine refuge or uplifting haven for Negros seeking to connect with God.

Between sips of lemonade, Leftwich also told about the incidents he had witnessed before coming to Tennessee during the Civil War, including the fall of Fort Sumter in Charleston, S.C., in April 1861; it was the bloodiest conflict in American history up to that time, and the beginning of the War Between the States over the bitterly divisive issue of slavery.

Ike Redford was quite impressed with the Godly Negro preacher and suggested that perhaps someday he could come to Fish Springs Baptist Church and give a sermon.

"I'll look forward to that day," Reverend Leftwich replied.

The talkative, friendly black clergyman wished much happiness for Prissy and Isaiah and climbed into his buggy for the trip back to Elizabethton. But before leaving, he let it be known that all were invited to visit his church, the Elizabethton Colored Baptist Church, later to be called Phillippi Missionary Baptist Church.

This had been the happiest day in Prissy's life, a dream come true.

She had her man, a good man who loved her and wanted to spend the rest of his life with her. Her prayer had been answered. She had also prayed fervently to one day be reunited with her mother and father. Thus, another prayer and dream had come true.

Mrs. Carter, who had taught her to read and write at Shirley Plantation, had been right after all, Prissy thought. *Not all white people be devils. Some white folks is good. What's inside de man or woman's soul is mo' impotant than de color of dere skin. And they's no better folks den Miss Mary and da Smiths.*

CHAPTER 26
Maybe I'm Just an Old Fool

Isaiah moved Prissy into his little shack. It wasn't much but at least they were together. And even after the longest, hardest days of work, they couldn't wait to be in each other's arms. Nights in that respect were too short; for they both delighted in taking each other to new heights in bed.

"Isaiah, you sho' da answer to my dreams! I like's what you be doin'!" Prissy squealed.

Isaiah smiled, tickled his bride where she loved to be touched, and swore to her that he'd never, ever stop making her feel good, even when the two of them grew old and feeble.

"I's sho' like bein' your man! I loves ya, Prissy!"

When the two former slaves woke up each morning, their bodies spent, they nevertheless felt refreshed, energized, blessed. And more than ready for another day's work. Prissy would hug her husband and give him a lingering kiss before reporting to Daniel's house where she did the cooking, house cleaning, picking up and straightening up and tending after Izzy and the boys. Once her main house chores were complete, she followed Mary's lead with Izzy, playing and singing with her and answering, the best she could, her endless questions.

"Now Prissy, you've done enough for today. You ain't never gonna satisfy these youngins'. You just get your sweet little self out of here and get supper ready for your husband," Daniel implored her one afternoon.

"I's fine, Mista Daniel. I's loves these chil'uns. I'll fix Izzy's hair and be on ma' way."

When the Christmas holidays rolled around, Daniel and his family recognized the occasion, but without great celebration.

Mary agreed to spend Christmas day with Daniel and the children but only if she was allowed to help with the decorating and helping Prissy make cookies. Prissy and Mary tried to make it festive, decorating the house with branches of holly, with their bright red berries, and boughs of pine. The fresh evergreens created a mountain woody smell throughout the house. Mary added some special red candles from the general store. Prissy baked cookies and cakes with lots of cinnamon and spices. The fragrance helped focus everyone's mind on the specialness of the holiday season.

"Doesn't everything smell wonderful, Daniel?" Mary poured Daniel and herself a glass of eggnog, but Daniel was having a tough, sad time of it. Mary understood what the holidays could be like for people who had recently lost a loved one. She still thought of Alfred every day, but she not with the deep mourning she felt when his loss was fresh.

Daniel tried to hide his pain. He didn't want to put a damper on Christmas. He had to be there for his children. He knew that's what Polly would have wanted. He also knew she would not have wanted him drinking whiskey to help ease his pain, but the temptation was great. However, he had promised Mary that he would stay away from the bottle.

"Your family needs you, Daniel. Don't ever forget that!"

"You're right, Mary. It's just that, sometimes when I think about Polly, I can't believe she's gone. And the thought of it seems to pull me down."

But with Mary's help and encouragement and support from his children and Prissy and Isaiah, Daniel gradually gained strength. By early spring, he had come so far that his depression had lifted. Not that he had forgotten Polly, but he had somehow gotten past dwelling on her death to remember the happy times. There was a lot to get done in March and April—making the always rocky but fertile Tennessee ground ready for planting, getting all horse drawn farm equipment in good working order, ensuring that the livestock got sufficient water and food, and repairing and rebuilding fences. All of it more than kept Daniel busy.

And that was a good thing.

Because Daniel let Prissy off on Sundays, Mary took it on herself to cook Sunday dinner for Daniel and the children. While she and Izzy prepared the meal, Daniel and the boys entertained little Danny.

It was a routine Mary cherished, but Daniel worried that his family was becoming too dependent on her.

"Now you just hush, Daniel Smith!" said Mary. She was in her food-stained apron with her hands on her hips. It was a Sunday, and she and Izzy had begun clearing the table. "You know I love all of you, and I'm proud to do anything I can."

The family had just downed a splendid meal of fried chicken, mashed potatoes and gravy, corn bread, green beans and stewed tomatoes. Charlie leaned back, smacked his lips and patted his stomach. And when he and Peter and Daniel thanked Mary for the tasty vittles, she gave a lot of credit to Izzy.

Clearing the dishes off the table, she mentioned an apple pie that she and Izzy had made. It was cooling in the pie safe, Mary noted, and it had been all she could do not to munch on it. "So who wants apple pie?"

She didn't have to ask twice.

Peter yelled "Yea, apple pie!" and, as the sweet aroma from the pie wafted through the room, the slicing and serving began.

Daniel couldn't take his eyes off Mary as she served the pie. Her apron did little to conceal her beautiful shape and he felt more than slightly aroused. *What an unbelievably gorgeous woman she is! Oh, how I'd love to touch her, to feel her warmth against my body, to taste her lips...To go to sleep with her and wake up with her...*

That night, he couldn't sleep. He tossed and turned in the bed and tried to get the sight of Mary out of his brain, but it was impossible. He dreamed of brushing up against her softness, as he'd done by accident just a few days ago when he had turned around and accidentally bumped into her in the kitchen. But then the fantasy progressed to touching her, kissing her, holding her body closely to his, sharing sweet romantic intimacies with her.

It caused Daniel to remember a time in his youth when he and Billy Nave were pulled aside. They had been overheard talking about pleasuring themselves. They had shared that salacious tidbit during what they thought was a private conversation at Bible class. The hard-nosed Reverend Ross Potter, a bearded preacher at Fish Springs Baptist Church, had angrily thrust his finger at them and chastised the youths that it was a lustful sin to sexually satisfy oneself. He barked at the two embarrassed boys that they would only escape Hell through "purity of mind and spirit and the grace of Jesus Christ as the son of God."

"What if I jist done it once?" asked Billy.

"It's still a sin, and if you keep doing it, it's a worse sin!" the pugnacious preacher warned.

Daniel smiled when he surmised that if there was any validity to Reverend Potter's statement back then, *right now I'm surely on a steep slope to hell.*

One part of him was embarrassed for getting in such a romantic frenzy over Mary, but another—more alive—part was excited, because he had not had feelings like this since he fell head over heels in love with Polly twenty-five years earlier.

They had met at a church social during a summer break from college at the end of his second year. Polly, from Virginia, had been visiting a cousin in Fish

Springs. Daniel was instantly infatuated. She had been a slim, vivacious pretty girl, with long light-brown hair and the face of an angel. By the end of the summer he was hopelessly hooked.

Daniel told his parents he wanted to make Polly his wife. They loved her, but cautioned him it was either school or Polly. They couldn't support both of them. So ended Daniel's formal education. His father had tried to convince him to finish school before marrying Polly, but who, when they fall deeply and irrevocably in love, has any sense of good judgment?

And even though his feelings for Polly mellowed in the years that followed, in their place developed a deeper, more mature kind of love. It had been a good, solid marriage. She had taken care of him, had been his constant, faithful, devoted partner. And he had cared for her, his beloved wife, with all his heart, body and soul. They had built a life together, and, while it had not always been easy, they had been a wonderful example for other married couples in Fish Springs. People cast their eyes enviously on Daniel and Polly Smith and they saw two who seemingly were made for each other—that would be together always, walking their final steps and taking their last breaths on this earth as husband and wife.

Her death had taken a lot of the life out of him, and during those darkest, most bleak times, Daniel had thought it might even be possible for a suffering man to die of a broken heart.

But now, Daniel reasoned, it was time to move on. It had been over a year since Polly had passed. Time to get back to living life as it was intended to be lived, hopefully with Mary. Time to laugh together and make memories together and enjoy life to the fullest.

But how, he imagined, could he possibly win Mary as his wife? After all, they were so far apart in age—she in her early twenties, he in his early forties. What could she see in him? And what, really, did he have to offer her except maybe security? He was older, slower, set in his ways, grumpy and had far less patience than the strikingly beautiful, selfless Mary. And she seemed always to be so outgoing, helpful and friendly—to the point of being a mother to his children. Even on Mary's worst days, when she suffered during her pregnancy from nausea and fatigue, she had always given her all to Izzy, Charlie and Peter. And when Daniel lost Polly, triggering his severe depression, Mary had been there for him, with him, encouraging him, listening to his ramblings, not ever giving up on him.

Daniel told himself again and again, that of all people in the world, Mary would be a fool to even consider marrying him. However, his strong feelings for her, his deep desire to wrap her in his arms and never let her go, wouldn't go away. *But maybe that's not all bad. People might claim it's bad or sinful, but let'em say what they will.* Daniel Smith just plain and simple wanted to have Mary as his wife! He wanted to hold her, to love and cherish and take care of her every day, to share his bed with her, and he desired her to do the same with him.

A couple of weeks later, after the worship service at Fish Springs Baptist Church, Mary and Danny were back for their Sunday meal with the Smith family. And emboldened Daniel decided then and there that he'd make his move.

He wanted Mary alone and he realized the best time would be when he was taking her home. That wouldn't happen until she and Izzy finished washing and drying the dishes.

"I guess me'n Danny need to be gettin' home," said Mary, drying the last plate. "It's gettin' late and the little guy needs to be in bed."

"Get the buggy hooked up, boys," Daniel instructed his sons. And when Izzy pleaded with him to let her go with them, he said it'd be better for her to stay home because he had some important business to talk to Mary about. Daniel's youngest sniffled, as if she were crushed, but her dad didn't give in.

"Next time, Izzy. Now get on back in the house and see after your brothers. I'm leaving you in charge while I'm gone."

"Yippee! I get to be the boss!" she squealed.

Later, as the horse-drawn buggy bumped along the rutted dirt road, and as an owl hooted in the distance, little Danny giggled. The ride caused him to bounce on Mary's lap and he seemed to like it when his mom took him by his hands and lifted him up for a kiss.

"Danny really enjoys a bumpy road, doesn't he?"

"That's because he has a soft mommy to bounce off of. Isn't that right, Danny?"

The little one responded with indecipherable but cute baby talk. His mother kissed him again and this time wrapped both her arms around an increasingly sleepy child.

As he drifted off to sleep, she gave Daniel her full attention.

"What was the business you wanted to discuss with me?"

Daniel didn't, at first, answer, parsing his words in his mind carefully as he just kept his eyes on the road ahead and his hands on the reins.

After Mary insisted that he speak up, he blurted it out.

"Oh, ah well, Mary. It wasn't really 'bout business. I just didn't want Izzy along. I'd like for you to consider somethin'."

"Consider what, Daniel?"

"Well, the children and me," Daniel stammered. "Well, we love havin' you and little Danny around, Mary, and … uh, I think it's good for Danny too. I surely believe it'd be a good and blessed thing, you know, for both of us if we got married."

"Sounds like cut and dried business to me, Daniel. Is that the best you can do?"

Daniel swallowed hard. "Can I start over?"

"Yes, you may, and please say it better—like you truly mean it and it's coming from your heart, not from some business ledger."

Embarrassed but now hopeful, Daniel pulled the buggy to a stop by her porch.

"Mary, I love you! I'm crazy about you! I can take good care of you and Danny! I'm askin' you to marry me. Don't give me an answer now. Just think about it. Sleep on it, and then give me your answer tomorrow. I will see you after I drop the kids off at school.

"I know there's a big age difference and you might worry about what folks would be saying," he groveled. "But I love you, and the children love you. I can give you a good, full life, I promise. And I can be a strong, loving father for Danny. I've been prayin' about this day and night, and I think the Lord wants us to be man and wife."

"That's much better, Daniel. Now take my hand and walk me to my door, and don't wake the baby."

At the door's threshold, she gave him another order, that being to look her squarely in her eyes and to listen carefully.

"I will consider your proposal, Daniel Smith. But I'll say this now. I love you, too."

Then she stood on her tiptoes, tenderly kissed him good night, went inside and shut the door softly so as not to awaken little Danny.

And there, under the moonlight and star-filled Tennessee mountain sky, Daniel stood, in shock and with his heart pounding.

He tried to take stock of what had just happened.

"She loves me. She's going to say 'yes', because she didn't say 'no,'" he mumbled and stumbled, somewhat awkwardly back up into his buggy.

"Then why didn't she say 'yes' now?

"Because I told her I'll come for her answer tomorrow?

"She could love me and still not want to marry me.

"Or maybe she loves me like a father.

"Maybe she thinks I'm too old, or that I'm a fool.

"Maybe I'm just an old fool."

CHAPTER 27
Coat Tail Trailing

Mary was snuggled in her big, soft feather bed with her baby. Danny studied his mother's face, touching her mouth and nose and ears. And when Mary smiled, he giggled and made sputtering sounds while flapping his arms like a baby bird. She had been trying to get him to say mama but so far his best effort had been a "baba."

Mary gently positioned Danny in his cradle, kissed him and rocked him to sleep; then she brushed her long, shining blond hair and captured it in a braid. Finally, she put out the oil lamp and climbed back into her bed. She had also recently gotten into the habit of hugging a pillow as she drifted off to sleep. It didn't replace having a warm, loving bedfellow, but it gave her a sense of security and comfort.

The vision of the pale moon through a wavy windowpane put her in a romantic frame of mind. *Wouldn't it be lovely to not be alone? To be held. To be caressed.*

Taking in the night song of the whip-poor-will, she thought longingly about Aunt Caroline. Her aunt had shared an enchanting old Indian story that when a whip-poor-will sings, it means that a lonely, forlorn soul is departing from this earth, and the bird is trying to capture the soul before it's gone forever.

Was Daniel such a forlorn soul? *Why can't things stay the way they are? Why complicate it? I promised myself that I'd never marry again. I've made it on my own. I like my life. I'm comfortable in my little home. But then again, Daniel's probably got the finest house in Fish Springs. And wouldn't it be nice to live there with him for the rest of our lives? I like my time alone—most days. I'd hate to give up the quiet times I spend at home with Danny ... But then again my happiest days are the ones I spend with Daniel and the children. I know I'll be a good mother to Danny, but a son needs a father too. Danny'll grow up just fine without brothers and a sister, but wouldn't it be nice to have them? And then there's Daniel himself, a pillar in the community, a Godly man of strength and character. A man who'd lay down his life for his family. The kindest most caring man I've ever known, and handsome too. A little old maybe, but not that old. I believe I truly love the man. And I know he loves me. So what else is there to say or think about? I'd have to be out of my mind to not accept his proposal!*

Mary sat straight up in her bed, stretched her arms out and pumped her fists. "Yes, yes, Daniel Smith, I will marry you! Of course, I will! Why on earth wouldn't I?"

Meanwhile, about a mile away at the Smith home, Daniel bided his time in a rocker on the porch smoking his pipe. The children were all asleep in the darkened house. One of the horses whinnied in a nearby pasture, and the mournful howling of a wolf could be heard down in the valley. Daniel was too apprehensive, too unsettled to sleep. He fretted about the outcome of his proposal to Mary. *Maybe I didn't give her enough time to decide. Why'd I rush her so? But if she declines, I pray she'll still be my friend. Because it'd be unbearable not to have Mary in my life. And the kids would surely have a hard time dealing with her absence, especially Izzy.*

Daniel heard a rumbling as he made his way to his four-poster bed, the same bed he had shared with Polly for so many years. The bed where they'd conceived their children, the bed where they'd shared their most innermost thoughts, dreams and desires. But now it seemed so cold and empty.

Daniel turned down the quilt and eased himself into the bed. He glanced at his pocket watch before putting out his lantern. It was two a.m. Sleep didn't come easily, but it did at last overtake him, and for a few hours Daniel Smith was at peace.

But shortly after dawn, storm clouds clustered together and rain pounded the roof. Lightning crisscrossed the sky, and thunder echoed off the mountains.

Daniel was sleeping soundly, until lightning struck close and he sat straight up in bed, startled awake from the ensuing boom that shook the house.

Daniel's first thought was, *What time is it? It's so light out.* Looking at his watch, on the night stand, he was relieved to see it was only ten after seven.

Daniel pulled on his trousers and splashed water on his face from the washbowl.

Hearing him shuffle about, Prissy first knocked, then peeked into his bedroom.

"I has your breakfast 'bout ready, Mista Daniel."

Prissy left and Daniel proceeded to get dressed. Then looking at his watch again, he realized it wasn't running. He had forgotten to wind it.

"Have the kids left for school?" Daniel asked, dashing into the kitchen.

"Yas'sa but I made'em wait 'till da storm passed. Then Charlie took'em in da buggy, so's day wouldn't be too late. Day left jist a few minutes ago."

"What time is it Prissy?" Daniel asked nervously..

"It be almost nine o'clock, Mista Smith. Is you okay?"

Daniel, normally up at the break of dawn, was anxious to get going. Mary was expecting him to show up around eight o'clock.

"I overslept Prissy and I need to be on my way."

"Mista Smith, I has you some hot coffee and some ham and biscuits. Dey's in the main room on da table and I be frying you up some eggs rat now. You need's ta eat some breakfast befo you leave."

Then glancing down, Prissy chuckled. "Mista Smith, yo sox don't match."

And sure enough, her oversleeping, anxious, boss had on one brown sock and one blue sock. The scattered man chastised himself and headed back to the bedroom to fix the problem.

Hurriedly he slipped on matching socks. Then, while Prissy was finishing his eggs in the kitchen, Daniel rushed to the main room, gulped his steaming, hot coffee—burning his tongue but saying nothing—devoured some ham and a biscuit and dashed out the door.

"I has yo eggs, Mista Daniel jist the way yo like'um!"

"Mista Daniel?"

Not seeing Daniel when she returned to the main room with his eggs, Prissy peeked into his office.

"Where you be, Mista Daniel?" Then, looking out the front window, Prissy spotted Daniel, his arms flapping and his coat tail trailing on his galloping horse, splattering water as he dashed through puddles left by the storm.

"Lawdy, Laudy, wot be da matta wa dat man? Where he be gwine in such a hurry?"

Daniel held Burney, his rough riding but trustworthy equine, at a fast pace, then slowed him to a trot as he neared Mary's house. He didn't want to appear as anxious as he felt. He dismounted at the hitching post, landing *Drat!* in a mud puddle and ascended the porch steps. He tripped over too-lazy-to-move Blue and knocked. It seemed forever before Mary opened the door.

"Why, Daniel, come in. So you decided to show up after all."

Removing his hat and trying to brush the mud off his boots, he stepped meekly inside. "Sorry I'm late, Mary. I came for your answer."

"Answer to what, pray tell, Daniel?" Mary said coyly.

"The answer to my proposal of marriage."

"Oh that. Well, of course," she said.

"Is that a yes, Mary?"

"I will marry you, Daniel Smith. Will you have me as your bride?"

"Yes!" he hollered gleefully as he lifted his bride-to-be from the floor and twirled her around the room. Easing her back down, he planted a soft kiss on her lips. Daniel dropped his hands to the small of Mary's back and pulled her to him. It was all Daniel could do to refrain himself from taking things further. He felt a part of himself, his core manhood, suddenly responding with vigor. He wanted her in the worst way, but there would be precious time enough for that later, so he reluctantly dropped his hands, like a gentleman, and kissed her softly and longingly one more time.

"You kiss and hug darn well for an old man. You're pretty frisky!"

"I love you, Mary White!"

Things might well have gone further at that moment, but Danny started fussing from his cradle and the smell of scorched oatmeal from the stove intruded.

"Oh my, I'm sorry, Daniel." Mary grabbed a quilted pot holder and rescued Danny's breakfast, then rocked Danny's cradle to soothe him.

Looking down at his feet, Daniel apologized for the mud he brought in and told Mary that he needed to get back and eat the rest of his breakfast Prissy had fixed for him.

"Ok, Daniel, but come back as soon as you can so we can talk about our wedding plans."

They walked to the porch. Then Daniel wrapped his arms around his soon-to-be-bride again, like he never wanted to let her go and kissed her, at first softly, then more passionately.

Taking this all in from his wagon, loaded with bags of feed, was John Williams. He pulled his horse to a stop close enough to see Daniel and Mary kissing, like they couldn't get enough of each other. They hadn't noticed him because they were too interested in each other. It was about more than the bedeviled man could bear. He had almost yelled "NO!" but held his tongue and gritted his teeth. Angry to the point of almost flying into a rage, John snapped the reins when he saw Daniel mount his horse and ride away.

Trying to calm himself down, he pulled to a stop in front of Mary's and knocked on the door.

"Hi, Mary. I was jist checking on Blue. If he's a bother ta you, I can take him home."

"He's no bother, John. I like having him around. He can stay, if it's okay with you." As Mary spoke, she straightened her clothing and buttoned the top of her blouse. It had come unfastened during her ardent hugging and kissing with Daniel. Mary wondered how much John had seen.

Mary's unbuttoned blouse enraged John even more.

"Wasn't that Daniel Smith I jist saw leaving here? And if it was, you seem ta be spending a lot'a time with'em."

"That's none of your business, John."

"Mary, I know Daniel was a big help ta you, b'in all alone and having that young'in an all. But for a friend you seem ta be gettin' awful close to'em."

"He's not just a friend, John. I love Daniel Smith."

"My God, Mary! That old man's old enough ta be your pappy."

"Daniel and I are going to be married, John."

"Mary, Mary! That old man? Do ya know how crazy that is? Don't waste your life on him. Do you know what I sacrificed for you, Mary, jist ta show you I could become'a better person? Don't do this, Mary. I know Daniel Smith has a big fancy house and more money'n and land than I do. But he can't make you happy like I can, Mary. And you KNOW that. Not that old man. You and I were meant ta be together. I love you, Mary. I been praying about it a'lot and that's what God wants. Please, Mary, don't marry him! For God's sake, he's got two sons that could be your brothers!"

She expected as much from John Williams. Mary didn't say a word. Instead, she slowly shut the door in his red, contorted face and went back to tend to Danny.

As John, feeling defeated and rejected—and once again outbid for Mary's affection—left, he called for Blue to follow. When the old dog refused, he dragged the canine, yelping, down the stairs by the collar, picked him up and threw him in the back of his work wagon.

"You ain't coming back here no more even if I haf'ta chain ya!"

John Williams was in agony as he slapped the reins on the horse's rump and drove away. The livid loser mumbled as he left. "That old son-of-a-bitch Daniel Smith is coming between Mary and me. I wish he would die."

CHAPTER 28
Together Forever

The day after Mary accepted Daniel's marriage proposal, she told him about John coming to see her and how he had tried to convince her not to marry him. John, she said, likely would spread rumors about himself and her. So she made Daniel promise not to confront him. "You know the truth and that's all that matters."

Daniel agreed but vowed to himself. *I'll keep that promise but if I ever hear another lie about my Mary, somebody'll damn sight wish they'd kept their mouth shut.*

Mary and Daniel made plans for a June nuptial. It was to be only for the family. No elaborate big church wedding. No fancy reception afterwards. It would be a short and simple but meaningful ceremony—with just the two of them, their children and Preacher Ike Redford and his wife Betty.

A few days before her wedding day, Mary shopped at the dry goods store. There were those last minute items she wanted to make their upcoming big day one they'd never forget. a few bags of candy for the children; a new dress for herself; a fanciful derby for her soon-to-be husband.

On encountering her at the store, Preacher Redford smiled and tipped his hat.

"Mary, how are you? You must be countin' the days."

"I am, Ike, but I think Izzy's more excited than me. She asks me every day, 'How many more days left before the wedding?' And it's been a labor of love, Ike. I didn't just fall in love with Daniel. I fell in love with the whole family."

"Speakin' of Daniel, I heard somethin' he might be interested in. He had told me he was looking for a good ridin' horse to use when checking on his sharecroppers. A friend of mine up at Ripshin Mountain has got a really good Tennessee pacer, a true beauty of an animal, goin' up for sale. And you know, Mary, that's the smoothest, ridin' horse there is. But he's not cheap. Tell Daniel to come and see me about it."

"I have a better idea, Ike."

As the day of their wedding approached, Mary worked on the final plans. Everyone would gather at home for a meal served on tables, decorated with flowers, set in the shade of the front yard. Mary thought it would also be nice to have some old-time mountain music. So she asked Daniel to round up Jacob Miller, who had played a dulcimer at church.

"If he could play "Greensleeves," Daniel, that'd be perfect. It's one of my favorites."

The children, Izzy, Charlie and Peter, seemed to get more excited with each passing day. The wedding couldn't come fast enough. Daniel's brood didn't mind at all that Mary was young enough to be their sister. And cute little Danny, now with a thick swatch of hair on his head, could well be mistaken for Daniel's grandchild. Some folks in Fish Springs even gabbed that the soon-to-be newly weds had long ago consummated their relationship. True, Mary had been married to Alfred when she got pregnant, but gossipy tongues swore that Daniel, even while he was with Polly, had always seemed to be overly sweet on Fish Springs' loveliest young woman.

Not true, but no matter. All that was important to Daniel and Mary was that they all be together as a family.

The day before the wedding Mary was on the porch snapping beans with Danny on a pallet at her feet when Izzy approached and stood looking at her feet.

Mary knew instantly there was a problem when Izzy didn't immediately start playing with Danny. "What's tha matter, Izzy?"

"They said you can't be my mom."

"Who said that?" Mary wiped her hands on her apron and brushed away a tear from Izzy's face.

"I told'em I wuz getting' a new mom 'cause you wuz marryin' my dad. Patricia Hancock said you wouldn't be my mom, and I couldn't call you Mom, 'cause you'd be my stepmom. Do you think my mom in heaven'll mind if I call you Mom?"

"No, Izzy, I don't think she will mind at all. Your mother knows how much you loved her, and you can keep her in your heart forever. Polly's probably lookin' down right now with the angels smilin' and blowin' you a kiss."

"I miss my mom, Miss Mary."

As tears began to dribble down Izzy's rosy cheeks, Mary put her arm around her.

"Ma Ma Ma Ma," little Danny jabbered.

"He said Mama!" Izzy said. She clapped her hands and jumped up and down with joy.

"Yes, I love you too, Danny," said Mary, as she cuddled and kissed him.

A day later, on a bright, sunny Saturday, Daniel and Mary recited their wedding vows on the front porch of what was now their family home. Dressed in their Sunday best, they swore before God, their children, Jacob, Prissy and Isaiah and Preacher Ike Redford and his matronly wife Betty to be faithful to one another and to support each other for the rest of their lives.

It was a solemn, short ceremony—just the way they wanted it.

Nonetheless, Mary looked radiant in her dazzling new pale pink dress. Lace and crystal beads accentuated the neckline, and thanks to Izzy, her necklace of freshly picked Flame Azalea seemed perfect for the occasion. Daniel wore a spiffy, new pinstriped suit. He had picked it out at a men's store in Elizabethton. Noting to Reverend Redford that he himself didn't wear jewelry, he slipped a gold wedding band on his bride's finger.

"Mary, you're as beautiful as a mountain wildflower!" said Betty. Then she bent down and hugged Izzy, who was holding Danny's hand. "And Izzy, you're the prettiest girl in Fish Springs."

"Thank you!" Izzy, a bundle of irrepressible happiness, beamed.

"And Danny, you're the handsomest boy," Betty added.

The little one made an undecipherable response.

Preacher Redford put his arms around Izzy. Then he held and rocked Danny.

Daniel thanked Ike and then gingerly put his hand on his son Charlie's shoulder. "Charlie, I want you to know that you've been the best, best man a dad could ever have."

"Aw-shucks, Pop, when we eatin'? I'm starved!"

"It just so happens that Prissy, with Isaiah's help, has prepared a delicious feast, and it's waitin' to be eaten. So get ready to fill your bellies, everybody."

And a scrumptious, delightful meal it was. Laid out splendidly in the yard on a long table fitted with a white tablecloth, it was a feast that the wedding celebrants bragged about for a long time. Prissy had outdone herself in the kitchen, baking a turkey with all the trimmings. They could also fill their plates with baked dressing and gravy, cranberries, smoked venison, baked rolls and all kinds of delectable vegetables from the garden. They washed it all down with a big pitcher of lemonade made with the cold water from the spring.

As folks ate and made merry, and as little Izzy curtsied and sang and frolicked to her heart's content on the front lawn, Jacob played his dulcimer, charming them with some old mountain ballads. And Daniel and Mary danced slowly to "Greensleeves" as Prissy watched over little Danny.

"This is one of the happiest days of my life," Mary whispered, her body snug against Daniel's on the porch where they moved to the music. "Daniel Smith, you are my love, my husband, from this day till we die. And don't you ever forget that."

"You've made me feel like a man again, Mary," Daniel whispered back.

Mary held him a little tighter, her eyes locked on his. Then they closed their eyes, rubbed the tips of their noses together and lightly kissed.

The romantic interlude was broken when Charlie yelled that everyone should have a piece of wedding cake.

The groom grinned at his beautiful bride and said, "We'll continue this later." Then he took her by her hand and led her to the cake.

As was customary, Daniel and Mary were served the first piece. And Prissy couldn't have been happier when she witnessed Mary placing a fork full of the frosted cake into her new husband's wide-open mouth. Then Daniel did the same with Mary—feeding her the cake and kissing her.

Daniel craved right at the moment to be near his bride, to hold her and love her like no man in these Tennessee mountains had ever held and loved a woman. It was their glorious first day as man and wife, and it couldn't have been sweeter.

In no time at all, the after-wedding eaters had devoured most of the cake. Prissy, her head bound with a red kerchief, began cleaning up and heading from the table back to the kitchen.

Mary said sternly. "Young lady, you get right back out here."

"Yas um," said Prissy, a startled look on her face.

"You get you and Isaiah a piece of this cake before it's all gone."

"Yes um, Mrs. Smith. I do dat."

On hearing the sound of approaching horses, Daniel looked out at the road and saw a beautiful black horse. It was tethered to another horse, but not nearly as striking an equine, on which was mounted a dignified looking man.

When the man pulled to a stop in front of the house, Daniel asked what it was he could help the stranger with.

"Would this be the home of Daniel Smith?"

"Yes sir. I am Daniel Smith."

"I'm Ed Grindstaff, Mr. Smith." The immaculately dressed horseman dismounted and extended his right hand to Daniel's.

Daniel, puzzled, nevertheless obliged him and shook hands.

Taking off his hat and tugging at his big belt buckle, Grindstaff said it was his pleasure to inform Daniel that he was the new owner of a fine Tennessee pacer. "It's tied there behind mine. There ain't no finer animal in the whole country. He's the best breed'a ridin' horse on God's green earth!"

The horse was indeed a thing of beauty, with its long neck, sloping shoulders and wide, alert eyes. Its feet were white, as if it had on socks. The rest of its perfectly sculptured body was a gleaming coal black. Its ears were proudly erect, as if ready to take in even the slightest sound.

Daniel stood there, speechless—his mouth agape.

Finally he found his words. "Who am I to thank for such a wonderful gift?"

"Well, that'd be a lovely young woman by the name of Miss Mary White, who, I understand, became Mrs. Mary Smith this very day. I might add I was conjured into my rock bottom price by our friend Ike Redford. I've known him since we were young men living in Elizabethton. Ike drives a hard bargain."

Mary and Ike were thoroughly satisfied with themselves. The horse had first been Ike's idea, but Mary had tapped into her savings and made it the ultimate wedding gift for Daniel.

Mary put her arms around Daniel.

"Mary, I hardly know what to say except this is the finest gift anyone's ever given me. I don't deserve it, but thank you, darling, from the bottom of my heart. My God, that's a good lookin' horse!"

"You're welcome, sweetheart." And then she and Ike flashed each other big grins of satisfaction.

Daniel strode over to his new horse, hardly able to believe that such a beautiful animal could be his.

As he began petting the horse, the expressive animal stared straight into Daniel Smith's eyes. And as Daniel thanked Mary again and again for his surprise wedding gift, the others joined in admiring the stunningly beautiful horse.

"He's a mighty fine horse, but I wonder what you have to feed him?" Charlie said.

"And why's he so danged high steppin', like he's the high and mightiest horse in the country?" Peter added.

When Grindstaff untied the horse from his ride and walked him into the yard, the two boys couldn't wait to stroke the handsome jet-black animal.

He neighed loudly, shook his head and kicked his front left hoof up slightly. The sons of his new owner continued to stroke him.

"He's a seven-year-old gelding, well trained, very gentle, very bright. His name is Blackjack. He was my brother's horse, Mr. Smith. And when my brother, may he rest in peace, was killed in the war, I could not bring myself to sell him—until now. I've been around a lot'a horses in my time, but this one's extra special. Ain't seen nary another one like'm!"

"He ain't the fastest horse, but he's the smoothest," the horseman said. "And one more thing. you'll want to train'm to the way you ride. Soon enough, he'll know what you want him to do."

Daniel asked the horseman whether the animal needed any special care.

"It ain't that he'll need special care, just good care. Good hay, plenty of fresh water, a little sweet feed, keep him shod, and brush him down after ever ride. Just use good common horse sense, Mr. Smith."

"Good enough, Mr. Grindstaff."

"Lift me up, Charlie," Izzy said.

As Charlie held Izzy up so she could pet the horse's muzzle, Ed Grindstaff, mounting his own horse, continued, "I think you'll find him to be a very good ride. Enjoy him, Mr. Smith. And congratulations to you on your wedding to this lovely young woman."

Daniel welcomed the horse man to stay and have some wedding cake but Grindstaff declined, saying he needed to head back to Ripshin Mountain. He then bid farewell to everyone and went on his way.

"Now that there man knows all about horses," Preacher Redford noted. "He's bred'em, he's raised'em. He understands'em and they understand him."

As Redford spoke, Daniel nodded.

"I ain't never seen nobody like'm," an amazed Charlie said. "How'd he get ta be so smart 'bout horses?"

"I don't know, son, but I know I'll need help making sure he's fed an' watered and cared for, the way a horse like him deserves. Can you help me, Peter?"

When Peter nodded that his dad could depend on him, Daniel patted his son on the back and stroked Blackjack's neck.

Later, with all the food eaten, the dancing done and the toasting and celebration complete, Mary and Daniel set about getting to know each other as man and wife. They started with a short romantic trip to Elizabethton, where they would stay at the Snyder House Hotel for two nights, and forgetting, at least for a while, about any responsibilities or worries at home.

The latter proved easier said than done for Mary—naked and frolicking with Daniel in a large tub of sudsy warm water in their hotel room. She fretted about her little one.

"I hope Danny will go to sleep for Prissy tonight, Daniel?" Mary said anxiously.

Her husband lathered her back and gently massaged it in the soothing water.

"Prissy'll be fine with him, my love, and remember Izzy's helping too," said Daniel. "She's a good little mother. After all, she's—

"Mary! My Lord, that feels good! "

"You're going to be doing it to me now," she teased, gripping Daniel's hand and pulling it under the sudsy water. She leaned back, closed her eyes and when she couldn't bear any more, her body trembled with excitement. Their lips came together and her tongue found his.

They were more than ready for an inevitable act of pleasure.

They dried each other off. Then Daniel scooped up his bride and carried her to the large hotel bed, laid her down and made her most intimate fantasies come true.

Later, they enjoyed a glass of wine poured from the bottle they'd received as a wedding present from Preacher Redford. But after only two glasses, anticipation was tugging at both of them. She begged for him and Daniel again obliged her with pleasure.

After their little honeymoon, Mary and Daniel returned to Fish Springs and eagerly began their married life. One of the first things they had to sort out was what furniture Mary would, with the help of Daniel's sons, move from her home to Daniel's house, hereafter called "the family home."

From Aunt Caroline, she had inherited a finely crafted cherry highboy and a walnut waterfall dresser, among other assorted pieces. The newlyweds decided that those would fit in well in the family home.

But whose bed would they sleep in? That was a more delicate question. The bed in Mary's house, the one she had shared with Alfred White? Or would Daniel prefer to keep his own four-poster rope bed with a canopy, the one he and his beloved Polly had slept in and borne their children in?

In the end, they decided that Mary's bed would remain in her house, which she rented out, thinking that someday one of the children might want to raise their family in the old home place.

Daniel's bed would be their marital bed. It was put to heavy, thumping use. So much so that a few weeks after the union Daniel had to have a furniture repairman from Elizabethton tighten up all its joints and re-rope it. As the man was leaving, Daniel handed him an extra dollar and said, "You will not speak of this repair to anyone."

The craftsman took the coin, dropped it in his vest pocket, smiled and replied, "What repair?"

After a few weeks, things at the Smith farm took on a normal routine. Being the height of the growing season and harvesting just around the corner, Daniel made many visits to his sharecroppers on Blackjack. The smooth-gaited horse made his trips fast and pleasurable, and the more time Daniel spent with him, the greater the depth of affection and bond between Blackjack and his owner. Daniel swore, with each passing day, that Blackjack could almost read his mind—as if the horse knew, without even pointing him in the desired direction, where he was supposed to go. Daniel took to letting him nibble sugar out of his hands. And while the horse devoured the sugar, his master would lovingly scratch him behind his big, always-alert ears.

On arriving back home in the late evening, Daniel would turn his treasured ride over to Peter, who'd be sure to give Blackjack a good brushing, fresh water, and sweet feed. The pampered horse was the envy, Isaiah said, of all the animals on Daniel Smith's farm.

After Peter had tended to Blackjack's needs, he'd turn him loose in the barn lot with a couple of forks of hay to munch on as the sun went below the mountains and cool air from the river replaced the summer heat.

CHAPTER 29
Prayer on a Coon Hunt

Dawn was breaking over Pond Mountain when Daniel walked out the back door and hollered at Turnup to hush. The little watch dog was bad about barking at every critter that came near the farm. Daniel was up early and on his way to the barn, where he would saddle Blackjack and ride out to check on some of his sharecroppers.

"You ready boy?" Daniel said, reaching into the stall and stroking Blackjack's neck.

He unbuckled his saddle bag that was draped across the wall of Blackjack's stall and flipped open its cover. He started to drop in a couple of hard boiled eggs and a biscuit, but one of the eggs slipped from his hand and bounced on the straw covered floor, rolling several feet away. Daniel walked over and picked up the egg but when he turned around, he stopped stock still, frozen in shock. A three-foot-long rattlesnake was slithering from his saddle bag.

The rattlesnake surely would have sunk its venomous fangs into his hand had he reached in the bag. Stunned, Daniel watched as the Timber rattler dropped to the floor shaking his black tail, posed for an attack. He grabbed a shovel from the next stall and, with one hard whack, he took the snake's head off. *I guess that fella somehow found my saddlebag when he was lookin' for a nice place to spend the night*, Daniel reasoned. It struck him as strange, though, that this particular snake seemed to be missing his rattles.

That evening, about a mile closer to Fish Springs, John Williams walked out the door of his cabin with his Winchester rifle strapped to his back, carrying a lantern he had just lit.

"Come'on Blue, you lazy hound!" John untied the yawning, stretching dog from a porch post. "Full moons'a wastin'."

"John, where you goin' this time?" Madge, his girlfriend from the Black Bear

Saloon, angrily asked. She was sitting on the porch in the dark because of the heat.

"Me'n Blue gonna do a little coon hunt'n, babe. We'll be back shortly."

Madge looked at him with skepticism. "You sure that's where you're goin', John? When ya come in this morning, you said you'd been fishin'. Funny thing, though. I didn't see no fish."

"So they waddent bitting, Madge. What's the big deal?"

"You sure you ain't slipping off ta see that Mary you was sweet on?"

"I tol you a hunert times. She married Daniel Smith, you stupid bitch ... I'm outta here."

"If I'd a knowed you was gonna be goin' off, I wouldent'a let ya bring me over here, John. You said we was gonna spend some time ta gether. What am I s'pose ta do while you're gone?"

"Read that book I gotcha, 'bout presidents. Maybe it'll smarten ya up some," he said, as he crossed the road.

"I love you, John!" Madge hollered.

"Okay. Madge, I love you too," John replied, barely audible.

As man and dog made their way through a hay field toward the river, he held his lantern high to light the way. *I shore as hell don't wan'a step on a rattler or a copperhead. I could end up like Alfred. That would shorly ruin a good coon hunt.*

They crossed the Watauga River on a rickety old footbridge, then walked upstream along the bank on the other side. A cool breeze whistled down from the mountains and through the trees. In the distance he heard the howling of a red wolf. Closer, crickets and owls and other creatures of the dark made their own particular brand of nature's music. Blue, his floppy black ears swinging, trotted ahead . The dog constantly sniffed and surveyed the ground except when he and his master had to push their way through brambles and nearly impenetrable thickets of dog hobble.

With the moon at full, and the sky clear, it was a perfect night for treeing an old crafty coon. And so what if Blue found no prey that night. *Nothin' could be better'n bein' out in the woods with your dog, even if I'm givin' up time bein' with old Madge. Come ta think of it, I'd rather be coon hunten anyway.* John chuckled.

As John and Blue walked up river, John babbled an old Tennessee mountain song. His father had sung it when he took John coon hunting as a young boy.

"Once I had an old coon dog as blind as he could be,

"But ev'ry night at supper time, I believe that dog could see.

"Somebody stole my old coon dog, I wish they'd bring him back..."

Sad but true. It was the only good memory John had of his father.

Weaving along and covering every inch of ground for a scent, Blue suddenly picked up the pace and bolted up a weed-strewn path alongside the river. John hoisted his lantern higher and strained his eyes to trace where Blue was headed.

Something had caught the canine's attention, because the dog's nose was glued to the ground and his tail sliced the air.

He didn't act like an old dog. He seemed to feel no pain or tiredness and cared about only one thing—the hunt. He was in his element. He stopped, his nose pinned to the ground for a few seconds. Then he bounded upriver, baying as he went.

"Git'm, Blue!" hollered John, his excitement building. "Best damn coon dog in Tennessee!"

When John reached the spot where Blue had detected the scent, he knelt down and in the light of the lantern inspected a raccoon's footprint in the sandy soil. The stalker muttered to himself, "Coon, a big'n, probably a big ol' boar coon."

Now in a frenzy, Blue charged ahead, still baying.

"Git'm, Blue!" John yelled.

As he ran, trying to catch up with his dog, John became aware of Cliff Hill jutting out over the river. It's was a scenic but potentially treacherous place he knew well from when he was a boy. He and Alfred and a few other friends would climb part way up Cliff Hill and jump into a deep, clear pool below the cliff. One time they even climbed to the top, contemplating jumping, but then came to their senses.

John, panting, stammered. "That damn coon's goin' up Cliff Hill for sure!"

He knew that the sides of the hill could be scaled, but the easiest way up was from the backside. Blue was nearing the top from the side, baying at the ascending coon.

"I'm comin', Blue! Stay with'm, boy!"

Breathing faster every second, his heart pounding, John scampered around to the back of Cliff Hill. It was a good distance to the backside of the cliff, but worth it, he figured, because it wasn't as steep or dangerous as the practically vertical rock face.

Holding the lantern in one hand and pulling himself up with the other, his rifle slung across his back, John clung to small trees and thick vines as he inched upward. He lost his footing in the soft, loose, ground but regained it each time. Briars and thorns punctured his hands and scratched his arms and pulled at his trousers, but he continued his climb, pausing repeatedly to catch his breath and raise the lantern to see ahead. He would wipe the sweat and pesky gnats from his eyes, then start out again. The top of the cliff couldn't be much farther, he figured. And Blue's barking and baying had reached a fever pitch—a telltale sign that he had treed his prey.

It won't be long now, John thought. *That ol coon'll be a good supper fer me and Madge tomorrow night.*

Meanwhile, Madge sat in a rocker by an open window, reading by the light of a lantern. She heard the sound of Blue baying spiritedly in the distance. She put her book down, leaned back and closed her eyes.

Back across the river, John slowly continued to make his way up the back side of Cliff Hill, pulling himself up with the help of saplings and tree branches.

"I'm comin', Blue!" he screamed to the relentlessly baying dog.

Finally at the top of Cliff Hill, John stopped and took a few deep breaths and held his lantern high. There, low and behold, was Blue—standing up and baying nonstop at the base of a twenty-five-foot sourwood, his front paws clawing the tree's trunk.

"Okay, Blue, I see'm!" *Ain't that barkin' dog music to a man's ears? We 'bout got'm, but I got to be careful, 'cause that ole' coon's sly, and I'm afeard' he'll git away.. And he can escape in the blink of an eye.*

John hung the lantern on a tree branch, took the Winchester strapped to his back and leaned against a tree. He cocked his rifle, drawing a bead on the ring tailed, black masked coon that seemed to think he had found refuge by climbing to the highest part of the tall thin tree. Unfortunately for the coon, his choice of refuge silhouetted him against the full moon. Taking careful aim, John squeezed the trigger. It was a perfect hit to the raccoon's head. The dead animal, its sparkling white eyes still wide open, tumbled a couple of feet into the highest crotch of the tree.

"Ain't that jist' my luck!"

John carefully laid his rifle down in the thick undergrowth of pachysandra where he stood. Then he reached up to the lower branches of the thin sourwood and shook it as hard as he could. But the coon only slipped deeper and more tightly into the crotch.

"Blue, this here's the biggest coon I ever kil't and thar' ain't no damn way I'm leavin' here without'm!"

The determined hunter began climbing, and, as he closed in on the dead coon, he glanced down. John was about twenty feet from the edge of the cliff. Scary, sure enough, but the drop off still seemed to him not to pose a threat. For John believed that even if he slipped and fell, he'd land far enough away from the cliff's edge.

I'm 'bout thar. Jist a few more feet.

As he reached for the huge coon in the swaying sourwood, the tree began bending at a weak spot in its lower part, perilously toward the cliff, farther and farther out.

"Oh God, no, no!"

In a crackling snap, the tree broke. John, screaming and clinging desperately, fell with it, and slammed hard against the rocky, root-rutted ground, and right over the cliff's edge.

He frantically grabbed a handful of small vines and let go of the tree that plunged out of sight into the dark abyss below.

"Oh help me, Lord! Help me! Don't let me die! I'm too young! I know I'm a sinner, but I'll be a Christian from now on. Please, God, help me! I need more time!"

The scraggly vines which John clutched started giving way one by one, and the desperate man grasping them began to lose hope. He sensed he could die—alone, miserably and painfully.

But one of Fish Springs' most wayward residents—and at this time, one of its most desperately repentant—made one last ditch attempt to save himself. With all his strength and determination to live, he lunged to grab a much larger muscadine vine and got hold of it.

Straining his exhausted body, he pulled himself up to and over the dangerous cliff's edge. It was still several feet up to level ground, so holding onto the large vine, he got himself to a standing position; then he breathed a sign of relief—confident that he'd be able to walk those last few feet.

John Williams stopped to praise God for saving him. He leaned back, looking up and feeling secure grasping the thick muscadine tentacle. "Thank you, Lord! I'll be a better man, a God fearin' Christian, I swear! I reckon you got plans fer me after all!"

But then, with a sickening pop, the vine snapped, and and the defiant man who had lived on the edge all his life, his mouth agape but silent, plunged backward into the darkness.

With his time running out he remembered the deep pool under Cliff Hill he had jumped into as a teenager.

That same deep pool might be the last hope and salvation of a man who was used to having his way and overcoming all kinds of odds.

I ain't gonna' die. I still have a chance.

He pulled his knees up to his chest and wrapped his arms around them. Then he braced for a hard hit on the water.

"Lord God, please save me!"

John tilted forward as he fell, and in the eerie, beautiful moonlight, in the last split second of his life, he saw the jagged rocks below.

Early the next morning, a Saturday, Daniel and Mary were traveling the dusty road into Fish Springs, on their way to the dry goods store. Prissy was tending to the kids, allowing Daniel and Mary to have a little one-on-one time together.

"What a gloriously beautiful day this is, Daniel!" said Mary, as they rounded a curve near John Williams' farm.

"Daniel, who is that out in the road in front of John's place?"

"I don't know, dear. I don't recognize'er."

"Wait. I do. I think that's John's friend from that saloon in Elizabethton.

Seeing Madge desperately waving her arms, Mary asked Daniel to pull to a stop. "Something's wrong Daniel," she said.

The buxom red-headed woman from the saloon seemed beside herself with panic. "Ain't you John's neighbors … the Smiths?"

"Yes, I'm Daniel and this is my wife Mary."

"I thought you'ns was. I'm so afraid that somethin's happened ta John. He went coon huntin' last night cross the river, and he never come back! I waited all night."

When she started shaking and crying, Mary climbed down from the wagon and put her arms around Madge.

"His old hound dog Blue's been howlin' all night. He ain't come home either. I'm afraid something tarble happened to my John! Can'ya please help me find him?"

"Of course we can," said Mary.

"What's your name, dear?" Mary handed her a hanky.

"Madge. Madge Carter."

"We need to help Madge, Daniel."

Daniel nodded in agreement. "Mary, why don't you stay with Madge here, and I'll ride down to the river and see if I can find John."

"Thank'ya, Mr. Smith. I hate to be so much trouble but I'm worried ta death." Tears continued to trickle down her cheeks.

"It's no trouble, Madge. I'll be back shortly."

As Daniel pulled away, Mary, with her arm around Madge, walked her to John's porch where they sat down on a bench together.

"You're a nice person, Mrs. Smith. John tol' me you was a real lady, too."

"Well, that was right nice of John to say, but I have my faults just like most folks. You just call me Mary, Madge."

"Okay. You're really pretty, too, Mary," said Madge. "I don't know why John stays with me. But he does. And he treats me as good as most men have. Even better'n some. I'm lucky ta have him, Mary, 'cause there ain't really nothing special bout me …" Madge's face knotted up as she started to cry.

"Now you just hush. You are beautiful! Why, I would give anything to have gorgeous red hair like yours."

"Thank you, Mary. John plum likes my red hair, too." Madge ran her hands through her long red locks. But mentioning John's name unleashed a flood of tears. "What if something really bad happened to John?"

"Why don't you and I say a little prayer for John, Madge? Maybe the Lord can help us."

"I ain't much in'ta praying, Mary."

"Well then you just put your head on my shoulder and close your eyes and I'll say a prayer for both of us. Okay?"

"Okay."

A few days later folks gathered at Fish Springs Baptist Church, this time to pay their respects to one of their lesser admired neighbors. For it was not lost on some who'd known John Williams that he had not always led a pure life. Many had heard of his carousing, drinking and gambling. They had heard, too, that he had a long-standing, deep hatred for former Yankee soldiers, regardless of his professed reconciliation for those he'd fought so savagely against in the Civil War.

"He hadn't darkened tha door of a church that I know of since Mary Clemmons married Alfred White. I think he jist came before 'cuz he wuz courten' her," one old regular at the feed store opined.

But to Preacher Ike Redford, John Williams was a man, weak and sinful like many others in Fish Springs, but also created in the image of God.

"God loved him just as much as he loves you and me!" he reminded those who would pass judgment on the deceased. "And one of these days, brothers and sisters, we'll all meet on the other side. We'll all be together in Heaven!

"So judge not, lest ye be judged!"

Mary and Daniel, who had sat in their usual place during the service, stood up to leave but were approached by Ike.

"May I have a word with you, Daniel?"

"Sure, Ike," said Daniel as Mary left and stepped outside to offer her condolences to Madge. Most of her red hair now covered with a black shawl, she said she would never forget Mary's kindness on that terrible day and would always consider her a friend.

"And I will consider you my friend, too, Madge," said Mary, hugging the grieving young woman.

Seeing Joshua and his friends, Mary approached the group.

"I know y'all were very close to John," she said. "I'm sorry for your loss."

"Yep, we shared everthin', Mrs.Smith," said Ben. "But you'n don't haf'ta worry none. We ain't tellin' nobody nothin'."

Joshua glared at Ben, his hand twitching like he could choke him.

Mary fumed. "I don't know what John told you but if it included my name, it was a lie!"

As she spoke, Daniel walked up. "Is everything all right, Mary?"

"Yes. Daniel everything is fine."

"Are you sure?"

"I'm quite sure, Daniel. Can you take me home now?"

As they walked away, Daniel looked back at John's friends with a less than friendly glare. Then they pulled away in their buggy, and Joshua grabbed Ben by his collar.

"You stupid son-of-a-bitch! Do you know how close you came to getting your plow cleaned?"

"What! By that old man?"

"That man ain't so old, an he would'a whupped your ass all the way ta the river. If you don't b'leve me, ask Butch Hale what happened ta him when he made a remark ta Daniel Smith's first wife."

Several weeks after John's death, his brother Jerry from Oregon made it to Fish Springs to liquidate John's holdings. On his arrival, Daniel let him know that he would buy the farm, the equipment, and all the livestock if a price could be negotiated. In due time, Jerry quoted Daniel a price for everything, with the exception of John's horse Charger. Jerry knew John's friend, Joshua Arnett, had cared for Charger when John went off to war, so he gifted the fine animal to Josh. Daniel bought everything else, selling off some of his timber and even using some of his life savings. Jerry returned to Oregon with a bag full of cash, and Daniel and Mary added another 200 acres to their spread.

With so much land now and wanting to reward a longtime faithful worker, Daniel turned to Isaiah. He decided the former slave had acquired sufficient knowledge to become a bountiful sharecropper, and Isaiah jumped at the opportunity. And Prissy? She couldn't have been happier. They would move into John's former cabin. It was in far better condition than Isaiah's crude little shack, and they would sharecrop the newly acquired 200 acres.

Very few former slaves lived in such serviceable cabins—even if John's former abode did need a little loving care.

CHAPTER 30
THE GIFT

A year had passed since Prissy and Isaiah moved into John Williams' old cabin to sharecrop the fertile, mountainous land. Another planting season had just begun. Isaiah steadfastly worked, bearing the heat in the unrelenting sun, bending his back, plowing and planting till his hands were blistered.

When Prissy wasn't working as a housekeeper for Daniel and Mary, she was right there beside Isaiah, and their efforts paid off. The land yielded a generous bounty of potatoes, beans, cabbage, corn, tomatoes, squash, cucumbers, watermelons, even tobacco.

One a sweltering day, Daniel paid Isaiah a visit. He found his loyal worker cooling off on his porch. Exhausted from plowing, Isaiah was catnapping when Daniel arrived on Blackjack.

"Aftanoon, Mista Smith," said a startled, half-awake Isaiah.

"Afternoon, Isaiah. It's awful hot today."

Isaiah invited his boss to "sit a spell on da poch in da shade."

"I will. Thank you." Stepping up to the porch, Daniel noticed evidence of recent carpentry work. "I can see you replaced some boards on your porch, Isaiah."

"Yas sa, I work on da cabin whin I has time."

"John Williams didn't care much for making repairs. So how'ya liking this little cabin?"

"I likes it a lot Mista Smith, and Prissy do too. She love it."

Daniel smiled and told Isaiah that he had something for him. He handed him an envelope and asked him to open it.

"What be in dis, Mista Smith? Is dey somethin' me an' Prissy in trouble for?"

When Daniel assured him it was nothing bad at all, and in fact, might be something very good, Isaiah opened the envelope and unfolded a single piece of long paper.

"I heard that you're learning to read Isaiah."

"Yas sa, I can read some. Dat wo-man from Valley Forge beens teachin' me some thangs 'bout da words. Her name be Miz Clarinda Jenkins, and Prissy teach me ta write my name. Dat Miz Jenkins nice wo-man. Her man, Mista Hugh Jenkins, walked all dey ways from Knoxville to Valley Forge when da war ended. He done fight fo' the Union. They say dat he walked mo' than one hundred miles! Now they's namin' a mountain for'em."

Isaiah studied the document, running his big, rough fingers over certain words. "It say 'deed,' Mista Smith?"

"Yes, it's the deed to this cabin, and a five-acre plot it sits on."

"Is you gown ta sell it to me, Mista Smith?"

"Well, yes. I'm selling it to you for one dollar."

"Fo one dollar?" Isaiah seemed mystified. "Mista Smith, you gown sell me this cabin an' land fo' one dollar, fo' sho?"

"For sure. It's yours. The dollar just makes it legal for you to say you bought it from me. It ain't nobody's business what you paid me for it."

"What does I have ta do, Mista Smith, fo you ta give me this cabin?"

"Nothing, Isaiah. You've been working for me going on sixteen years now. First as a slave, then as an employee, now as a share cropper, and I hope we have many more years of working together.

"You've earned this cabin, Isaiah," Daniel added. "You're a loyal worker and a good man and I hope that you and Prissy'll raise a family and live here for many years. Whaddya think?"

For a few seconds, the stunned beneficiary of the cabin was speechless. He took a handkerchief from the pocket of his frayed workpants and dabbed the sweat from his forehead. His eyes, watering up, betrayed his emotions. He looked upward, as if thanking the Almighty for this incredible gift.

"Thank you, Mista Smith! It's fo' sho' Prissy wants chillin and so does I. This be a fine cabin ta raise'm in. You sho' know how to make a man happy. And you sho' is a good man yo'self."

"You deserve happiness, Isaiah. Oh, and by the way, I haven't told Prissy about this. I thought you'd like to do that.

"She gown be very surprised!"

"I have to go to Elizabethton tomorrow on business and I thought you could go with me and we can record your deed. I can help you with it. What say I pick you up about eight o'clock?"

"I be ready, Mista Smith."

"Well, I guess it's almost dinner time, so I'll be on my way, Isaiah, but I'll send Prissy home in a bit. You have a good eve'in'."

"Yas sa. You too, Mista Smith."

As Daniel headed home, Isaiah held the deed in his hands as if it were a treasure, and he envisioned breaking the joyful news to Prissy. He harkened back to that wretched, dark time in his life when money-driven, Godless white men in Africa threw a net over him and stole him away from his parents. Isaiah had thought for sure that he would die, especially when the slavers forced him, along with 400 other Africans, into the dank, wretched hold of a schooner that would land six weeks later at Jekyll Island, Georgia.

Manacled and chained under the deck of that ship, *The Wanderer,* a third of the slaves had not survived the voyage across the Atlantic Ocean. Some had died from dysentery or scurvy. Fearing that the whites would eat them, others jumped overboard, preferring suicide to cannibalism.

But Isaiah had stayed alive. He had withstood the branding with a red-hot iron, the miserable stench of human vomit, excrement and urine, the screaming and pain and anguish. He had endured sleeping with hundreds of other poor, suffering, naked, half-starved Africans in pens under the deck. He had lived to promptly be put on the trading block and sold in Charleston, South Carolina. Always, it seemed, white people had been bad or evil. His first owner had been that way, whipping him, cussing him, never happy with anything he ever did.

But Isaiah's feelings started to change after he was bought at the age of seventeen from his previous owner by Daniel Smith. He soon discovered that Daniel was unlike his other slave owner. He actually treated him kindly, but Isaiah had still resented the fact that another human owned him.

So when Daniel, incurring the wrath of some of his hardened racist neighbors in Fish Springs, freed his slaves two years prior to the Emancipation Proclamation, Isaiah couldn't help but wonder if "Mista Smith" still felt some lingering guilt at being a slave owner?

But that was all in the war-scarred, hate-mongering past. *Today, I be truly a free man! One who owns land!* Isaiah thought.

He couldn't wait to share the life-changing good news with Prissy. *She soon ta be dey happiest colored wo-man in Fish Springs!*

Daniel couldn't have predicted what glorious effect his gesture would have on Prissy. Because early the next morning at the Smith home, when Daniel came downstairs to the aroma of frying bacon, Prissy had a big smile. He had never seen her so happy. She grinned widely and practically danced as she set a heaping plate of scrambled eggs on the table.

She had arrived there an hour earlier, after the mile walk from her newly acquired cabin, to prepare breakfast for the Smith household. But today breakfast would be memorable—very much so. Her faced glowed, she had an extra bounce in her step and she merrily hummed a Negro spiritual as she straightened her apron and pulled back a chair for Daniel. Still humming with one hand on her hip, she poured steaming hot coffee into her boss' mug on the table.

Earlier, wanting to have Daniel and his wife to herself this special morning, she had fed the older children and hustled them outside to do their chores. Peter would slop the hogs, and Izzy would feed the chickens and gather the eggs. Charlie, on a summer break from college, handled the heavy work of mucking out the barn. Danny played happily with beads tied to his high chair.

"Where'd them fresh flowers come from, Prissy? And where'd that big smile you're wearin' come from?" Daniel questioned her before taking a gulp from his mug.

"Dey's from our land, dey land dat you gives ta Isaiah and me," she replied chirpily. "You be da' bes' man in all'a Fish Springs, Mista Daniel.

"And my smile's fo you. You made it. It's fo' sho,' you made it," said Prissy, as she headed back toward the kitchen..

As Daniel chuckled and filled his plate. Mary, seated at the other end of the large harvest table, noted that Prissy had been smiling all morning.

"It was a wonderful thing you did, Daniel Smith," said Mary, raising her own cup of coffee to her lips. "Deeds like that make me proud and honored to be your wife."

"It was the least I could do, Mary. You know, I harbor this guilt that I suppose I'll take to my grave. Slavery was so unjust. So bad! When I got to know Isaiah as a man, and not just part of a work force, I started to feel awful. Then when my children came along, I thought what it must feel like to have your kids torn away from you and shipped off to another part of the world. Imagine the horror of that!

"Peter's about the age that Isaiah was when he was taken from his parents. My God, how terrible that must have been for them, and Isaiah, too."

A tear ran down Daniel's cheek that he wiped off with his napkin. "I cain't never make it right, Mary, but I sure as hell can try."

"You're a Godly, good man, Daniel Smith, and I love you."

Finishing his breakfast, Daniel heard the big grandfather clock in the main room chime one time. It was seven-thirty, time to be on his way to pick up Isaiah for their trip to Elizabethton.

As he hurriedly spread butter on one last biscuit and rose to leave, Mary asked him if he would consider taking Izzy with them.

"Why?"

"Well, she told me the other day that you always took Peter everywhere because you loved him more than her. Of course I know that's not true. But eleven-year-old girls need some time with their dads, too."

Daniel said he couldn't have her thinking that way and that Mary should get Izzy ready while he ate that last biscuit.

And you'd have thought that Daniel had gotten his daughter an early Christmas present, judging from her joyous reaction when Mary came to the barn and told her she could go with her Dad and Isaiah to Elizabethton.

"Yippee!" she yelled, while flaunting the good news to Peter.

"Miss Mary, can I go to Elizabethton with Dad?" Peter asked.

"Not this time, Peter. This time he's taking Izzy. Now come on, Izzy. Let's get you cleaned up and dressed for the trip."

But Peter, thirteen, wasn't so easily deterred when minutes later his Dad drove the buggy to the front of the house and Mary brought Izzy out in a pink dress with white trim.

"You sure are right pretty this morning, Izzy," said Daniel. He helped her onto the buggy seat and gave her a hug.

"Thank you," said Izzy, bustling with excitement, her hair done in dog ears with pink ribbons.

"Dad! Can I go, too?" Peter shouted.

"Not this time, Peter."

"But Dad, I—"

"Son, you asked me and I gave you a answer. End of discussion."

"Yes sir."

Daniel pulled away and headed toward Isaiah's cabin as an animated Izzy waved and hollered goodbyes.

She talked nonstop all the way to Isaiah's cabin, then half way to Elizabethton before finally running out of questions. But the silence lasted only a few minutes.

"Dad, I think Millie's fixin' ta empty out," said Izzy, holding her nose. She was sitting between the two men and looking at the mare's tail standing up.

Daniel pulled back on the reins slowing the mare to a walk. He sensed the worst was yet to come because just a few seconds earlier, gaseous, smelly fumes engulfed the buggy.

"Peweee, Millie!"

"We got lucky that ... " Daniel started.

"Nuh-uh!" said Izzy, as Millie raised her tail and did indeed empty out.

"That wasn't very nice, Millie," she said, still pinching her wrinkled up nose.

"No it wasn't," Daniel added. He put the mare back in a trot and looked over at a grinning Isaiah.

Daniel noticed that Izzy was fixated on Millie's rump. He could sense the wheels turning like windmills in her little head and anticipated getting another question.

"Dad, why don't you hook Millie ta the back of the buggy, and she could push us to Elizabethton. Then if she emptied out, it'd be behind us?"

"Well for one thing ... "

Daniel stopped and thought about it. *Why wouldn't that work? The horse could push the buggy and the driver could steer it.* Daniel glanced at Isaiah, whose eyebrows were pushed up into his forehead. He was flashing a huge smile.

"You know, Izzy, that's about the best idea I've ever heard. Don't you think so, Isaiah?"

Izzy smiled proudly.

"Sho' do, Mista Smith. I sho' do."

The more he thought about it, the problem they had just encountered had been the very same unpleasant one that had plagued buggy and carriage drivers and passengers for centuries. And it had just been solved by a little eleven-year-old mountain girl from Fish Springs, Tennessee.

An hour or so later, when Daniel and Isaiah stood at a counter in the Elizabethton courthouse, Izzy patiently sat waiting on a bench nearby.

On the other side of the scratched, worn counter was the clerk, a short, pudgy man wearing a monocle. His hair was slicked down with oil and parted in the middle.

At this moment, the clerk seemed befuddled—even incredulous.

"I want to make sure I've got this right. You, Mr. Daniel Smith, are selling this house and the five acres it sits on to Mr. Isaiah Washington for the sum of one dollar. And this here's that man?"

As he asked that question, he pointed at Isaiah. "Is that correct, Mr. Smith?"

"That's correct," Daniel said.

"One dollar, Mr. Smith?"

"Well, it needs a lot of fixing up."

"Then put your mark here, boy," said the disgusted looking clerk.

"I can sign ma name sa," said Isaiah proudly.

The clerk brusquely pointed to the place where Isaiah was to sign without acknowledging his statement. He seemed anxious, to the point of being rude, of getting the transaction done and having the Fish Springs men out of his office.

"That'll be fifty cents," said the officious clerk. He stamped the deed and a sheet of paper that he put in a tray. Then he handed the deed to Daniel, who handed it to Isaiah. Daniel reached into his pocket to get the fifty cents. But Isaiah had already laid the money on the counter.

"You have any more land you'd like to sell, Mr. Smith?"

"None that you could afford, Clerk."

Daniel, Isaiah and Izzy left the office and entered the long courthouse hallway.

After shaking hands, as if to seal the already done deal, the two men agreed to go their separate ways for about the next half hour or so. Isaiah would take Izzy to the dry goods store to buy candy, while Daniel tended to some business in town.

"Thank you, Daddy! You know I love candy!" The happy little girl put the change her father gave her in the coin purse she had hanging around her neck.

"You're welcome, Izzy.

"Isaiah, I should be finished by the time ya'll get back."

"Okay, Mista Smith. Yo' take yo' time."

"Take care of her, Isaiah."

"I's will, Mista Smith. I promise."

Later, as Isaiah and Izzy crossed the main street through town, the big Negro took the frilly, happy-go-lucky eleven-year-old by the hand. Not because he needed to; it was just what he had always done, and Izzy never balked as it seemed natural to her also. They entered the dry goods store and Izzy scampered ahead, finding the candy counter. Big, fat jars of candy sticks, and drops in an assortment of colors and flavors covered the counter. Izzy could not reach any of the goodies, so a young woman asked if she could help.

"Yes, please, I want all the candy I can get for twenty-five cents, but I don't want any of that kind," said Izzy, pointing to the reddish brown, horehound candy drops.

The store employee did as she was asked, placing a few pieces of the sweet treats from each jar into a small bag.

"Is all this for you?"

"For me, my step mom, my brothers, my father and Prissy, and Isaiah, if they want any," Izzy replied.

"Are you sure your step mom doesn't like horehound candy? A lot of grown-ups do."

"Oh, okay. Maybe two pieces."

Izzy paid the clerk, then began gazing at the many pretty dresses hanging from the racks, while Isaiah stood nearby watching her. There were yellows, reds, blues, pinks—all sorts of garments in dazzling colors. Izzy wanted to touch each one of them.

After several minutes, Isaiah spoke up.

"Izzy, we best start back. We doesn't wana keep Mista Smith waitin' too long."

"Okay, I'm ready, Isaiah."

Isaiah and Izzy made their way down the wooden sidewalk. At the corner, he took her by the hand to cross the now muddy road, created by a momentary light rain. Isaiah also told Izzy to raise her long pink dress to keep it from getting dirty.

Taking this all in, from the other side of the road were two young men—one of them tall and thin, the other, short and husky. In their mid-twenties, they leaned against a store front. Hank, the tall thin one, anger in his squinted, snake-like eyes, was focused on the large black man with the little girl in the pulled up pink dress.

Hank spat out a stream of tobacco juice and nudged the other. "Duke, check out that nigger holding the little white girl's hand."

As they approached the other side, Isaiah noticed that the two men watching them were law men. Each of them had a tin star attached to his vest, which made him feel less threatened. But that feeling diminished when Isaiah and Izzy reached the other side and stepped up on the wooden sidewalk; the two young, full-of-themselves deputies stepped in front of them, blocking their way.

"Where you be going with this darkie, Missy?" Hank asked.

"He took me to the store so I could get some candy."

"And what did this nigger make you do to get that candy?"

Puzzled as to why the deputy would ask such a thing, Izzy looked up at Isaiah.

"You doesn't has ta say nothin', Izzy."

"I dent ask you a damn thing boy!" Hank growled.

Then he and his husky partner grabbed Isaiah and threw him against the store front, each one holding an arm, while the stronger one, Duke, began choking their captive. The muscular ex-slave thrust his arms forward, hurling both men off the sidewalk into the muddy street.

"Oh! you done done't now, nigger!" Hank screamed. "You assaulted an officer of the law! You're under arrest! Your black ass is goin' ta jail!" As the deputy spewed his threats, he pulled a revolver from a leather holster strapped to his side and pointed it menacingly at Isaiah.

"And if we find out you tauched this little girl, we're gonna hang yo black ass from the biggest tree in Elizabethton," Duke snarled. While the lawman handcuffed Isaiah, little Izzy, totally terrified by now, stood by crying.

"It's okay, little girl. You're safe now," said Hank, grinning.

"It be all right, Izzy. Yo daddy be comin' fo'us," Isaiah said.

"You shut your damned black mouth, boy!"

"Let's go, nigger!" The impatient lawman pushed Isaiah down the sidewalk toward the sheriff's office.

But just as the deputy shouted that hateful epithet, Sheriff Nave himself rode up on his buckskin mare. And on seeing Isaiah in cuffs and one of the deputies standing beside Izzy, the chief law enforcement officer of Carter County, Tennessee, quickly dismounted.

"What did'e do, boys?"

"He done assaulted us, Sheriff," said Hank. "We was bein' diligent like you tol' us, and we saw this here nigger walking down the street holding this little white girl's hand. Something jest didn't look right."

"And he had jest got her a bag of candy," Duke added.

The sheriff stared dubiously at his deputies.

"What's your name, young lady? You look familiar." Nave bent down to be at her same level.

"Izzy Smith."

"Would Daniel Smith be your daddy? The one who lives in Fish Springs?"

"Yes sir."

Sheriff Nave raised up and, glaring at his deputies, mumbled nervously under his breath. "Oh shit."

And just then, as the sheriff had begun putting two and two together, Daniel pulled Millie to a stop at a hitching post about fifty feet away, tied the reins, hustled to frightened, crying Izzy and put his arms around her.

"What the devil's goin' on here, Sheriff?"

"Well, Daniel, it seems that your boy here assaulted my deputies."

"I doubt that, Sheriff. What happened, Isaiah?"

"Dey had me pushed agin' dat sto', Mista Smith, and one was chokin' me. I couldn't breathe an' I got real skead, so I throwed'um in'ta tha street."

"Sheriff Nave!" Daniel barked angrily to the man in charge of the two rogue deputies. "Can you take those handcuffs off of my man so he can take my daughter to my buggy? I'd rather she did not hear this conversation. Isaiah will not run away. You have my word on that."

"Uncuff'm, Hank."

Hank removed the handcuffs, then following Daniel's instructions, Isaiah took Izzy, and the two walked back to the buggy and climbed in to wait.

"Okay, Sheriff. I want to know why your deputies had my man pushed against the wall."

"Well, I'm sure they had a good reason, Daniel."

"Hank?"

"Well, Sheriff," the deputy said sheepishly. "He done over step't my authority. I asked the girl what she had to do to get that candy, and the darkie told her she didn't have to say nothin'. So Duke an' me was 'bout to find out the truth. That's why we had him up against the wall."

Sheriff Nave stared disgustedly at Hank for several seconds. Then he spoke emphatically.

"Both of you know you can't go around ruff'in up suspects without due cause!"

"But Sheriff, he's a nigger," Hank said meekly.

"God damn'it, Hank! That don't make any differ'nce! Times is changed. Cain't you get that through your thick heads? Now git on over ta the Black Bear. I saw a couple'a scalawags goin' in there. Go check'em out."

"Sheriff, you tol us ta be diligent, and —"

"Just get the hell out of my sight—NOW!"

Hank shut-up and left with Duke.

But Daniel wasn't satisfied.

"I'm not happy about this, Nave. My man being roughed up, and not only that—my little girl was scared half to death."

"I'm sorry 'bout that, Daniel, but you need to look at our side too. I told my men to be diligent, and if somethin' didn't look right, to check it out. I know you probly' heard 'bout the darkie they hung down near Bulls Gap after he raped a twelve-year-old white girl. Now you and I both know most darkies'd love to git a twelve-year-old white girl alone."

"Come on, Sheriff!" Daniel interrupted.

"Ok, a few."

"So, I'm sure there's a few white boys who'd like to get a twelve-year-old girl alone too," said Daniel.

"Yea, an' if they rape one, we'll hang'um right up next to the niggers."

"I doubt that."

"Listen, Daniel. I only want to keep all our citizens here in Carter County safe. Haven't I done a pretty good job at that so far?"

"Yes you have, Sheriff Nave, but that don't make this right."

"Well, maybe not, and I'll have a long talk with my men. But as long as I'm sheriff, I'm gonna do ever' thang in my power ta see that nothin' like what happen to that twelve-year-old girl happens in Carter County.

"Now I know you have a big spread over there in Fish Springs and I'm sure you pay your fair share of taxes. I'm working for you, Daniel Smith, and I'll do the best job I can. Okay?"

Nave reached out to shake hands with Daniel.

But Daniel, still bristling from how the deputies had accosted Isaiah, at first did not extend his hand.

"What do you say, Daniel? Can we put this behind us and be better men for it? I promise I'll have a come-ta-Jesus meetin' with my deputies."

"Okay, Sheriff," said Daniel, shaking hands.

"Give my best to your new wife, Daniel."

Daniel nodded and started back to his buggy while Sheriff Nave mounted his horse. When Daniel was almost to the buggy and Nave rode by, Daniel called out.

"Oh, Sheriff! One more thing!"

"What's that, Daniel?"

"My man here, Isaiah Washington, he's also a landowner here in Carter County, so I rec'in you'll be working for him, too." As Daniel spoke, he cracked a big smile.

Apparently not seeing the humor in the situation, the sheriff didn't respond. Instead, he grimaced, slapped his horse on the rear and galloped off.

Daniel climbed in the buggy, put his arm around his little girl and pulled her close.

"Are you okay, sweetheart?"

"Yes sir, but I was afraid those men were goin' to hurt Isaiah."

"I know you were afraid, but Isaiah wasn't hurt. Right, Isaiah?"

"I be just fine, Izzy."

"Why were those men so mean, Dad?"

Daniel was careful with his choice of words. "They thought they knew Isaiah, but they didn't know him at all. They didn't know that Isaiah is a good man. What they did was very wrong, Izzy. I'm sorry you were frightened."

"They should'a asked me, Dad. I could'a told'em that Isaiah is a nice man."

"Yes, I'm sure you could, Izzy. You ready ta go home now?"

"Yes sir. You know, Dad, a little piece a candy'd be good 'bout now."

"Sounds good to me. How 'bout you, Isaiah?"

"Yas sa. Sho' would," said Isaiah, as the three of them headed back to Fish Springs, the unpleasantness behind them.

A few minutes into the ride, Daniel sensed something seemed to be bothering Isaiah.

"Mista Daniel, I sho' cause yo' a lot'a trouble."

"You didn't cause it, Isaiah. You were a victim of it. Life'll never be easy for you. Some folks still think the old ways are the right ways. It takes a long time for people to change. And I'm afraid some never will. They're just too plum full of hate and poison to ever accept that our country's now different and that all men are created equal.

"But Isaiah, just remember this. Be yourself. Hold your head up high. You're a good man. You're a citizen of Carter County and a house and landowner. You should be proud."

"Yas sa. I is, Mista Daniel. I sho' is."

And then after a few minutes. "And da sheriff works fo' me. Wait'll I tell Prissy dat."

CHAPTER 31

The Bible

"Isaiah, yous home early." Prissy was sweeping the kitchen, as Isaiah entered their now homey cabin.

"Too hot ta work. I gwine start early in da moning befo' sun up." Isaiah usually toiled from sunup to sundown, but on this extremely hot, humid day at the peak of the July dog days he knocked off early.

"Isaiah, I get yous some cold tea from da spring box. Den afta yous cools off, would you nail dat loose boad down in da kitchen I toad yous bout?"

"Sho', Prissy. I do anything fo' my woman."

"Yous so sweet. I get yo' tea."

After Isaiah cooled off with the tea, he got his hammer and a handful of cut nails and located the loose board; it was about eight inches wide and two feet long with each end resting on a log floor joist. He noticed that neither end was nailed. The hammer in his grip, Isaiah started to nail one end down, but curiosity got the best of him, and he stopped and lifted the board.

"Lawdy lawdy, what has I found?"

"What you find, Isaiah?" Prissy had paused from peeling potatoes in the dry sink.

"It's a box hid under dis flo'."

The open top box was on a flat stone, its opening right below the old creaking floorboard.

"What be in it, Isaiah?"

"I sees in dis wooden box, two jugs, a tin box and a Bible."

With Prissy drying her hands at his side, Isaiah opened the old, tarnished tin box.

"Lowd, look at all dat money!" Prissy said excitedly. Her husband counted out four dollars in U.S. coins.

"We can sho' use dat," she said.

"Hoad on, Prissy. Dis not be our money. Dis was John Williams' money."

"I know, Isaiah, but he daid."

"Don't make no difference, Prissy. It done b'long ta his family."

Prissy's excitement diminished, replaced with a pride she felt for Isaiah.

"You's right, Isaiah. I knows you's right."

"We do jus' fine wit' out dis money, Prissy."

Isaiah kissed his wife tenderly and patted her shoulder.

"I needs to take dis box to Mista Smith. You gawin with me?"

"Sho."

"I'll hook up da wagon, Prissy."

Meanwhile, at the Smith house, Mary, Izzy and little Danny had found refuge from the heat in the shaded porch swing. Old Blue snoozed contentedly at their feet, while Turnup rested in the shade of an oak tree.

"Say Ma Ma, Danny, say Ma Ma," Izzy coaxed him.

"Ma Ma," Danny managed.

"Say Izzy, Izzy."

Danny eyed Izzy, smiled, flapped his arms and uttered, "Eee, Eee, Eee!"

"I think you'll have to wait on that one, Izzy," said little Danny's laughing mom.

Later, Daniel and Mary relaxed on the porch. Daniel sat in a rocker, smoking his pipe, while Mary sat in the swing with little Danny. Charlie, Peter and Izzy were on their way to the barn to check on a new calf, born the night before, when Isaiah and Prissy pulled their wagon to a stop by the porch.

"Aftanoon, folks," said Isaiah. He flashed a big smile and tipped his crumpled, sweat-stained hat.

"Afternoon, Isaiah, Prissy," Daniel said. "Everything okay, Isaiah?"

"Yes sa. I jus' needed ta bring you somethin', Mista Smith. I was gowin to nail down a loose boad in my kitchen and dis box was under da flo'."

Isaiah took the box from the back of the wagon and set it on the porch.

After briefly perusing its contents, Daniel retrieved a jug from the box, uncorked it and took a big sniff.

"Looks like you found where John Williams hid his hooch. You keep it, Isaiah. Do you drink?"

Isaiah looked at Prissy then at Daniel, studying the question.

"No sa, he don't drink," Prissy said.

"That be right, sa. I don't drink," Isaiah agreed.

"Well, I'll take it. I'll find someone who would like to have it," Daniel said.

He winked mischievously at Isaiah when Prissy wasn't looking.

"Dere's dis too, Mista Smith."

Isaiah handed Daniel the tin container, which he opened.

"Money, how much money is it, Isaiah?"

"It be fo' dollars, Mista Smith."

"You found this money, Isaiah. Why don't you keep it?"

"Well, hit not be rightly mine, Mista Smith."

Daniel studied for a moment. "I tell you what. I'll send John's brother four dollars of my own, but you take this money in the box. I'm sure Prissy'd like a new dress."

"You sho' is a nice man, Mista Smith," said Prissy, grinning.

"Dere be a Bible in da box, too," Isaiah said.

"It must be a family Bible. I wonder why he hid it. I'll send it along with the money," Daniel said.

"I guess we be gwin to tha sto' now. Thank you, Mista Smith." Isaiah looked at Mary and tipped his hat. "Mizzus Smith."

Mary nodded. "Prissy, I want to see you in that new dress. Okay?"

"Yes'em. I sho' it ta you, Miz Smith."

As the horse ambled away, Prissy reminded her husband of what their boss had declared. "Isaiah, you gwin buy me a new dress, ain't cha?"

"Yeah, Prissy, I heard'm. I gwine buy you a new dress."

"You so sweet, Isaiah. I love you."

Back on the porch, Mary told her husband that he'd just made two people very happy.

"Well, it was worth four dollars just to see the expression on Prissy's face."

Mary asked Daniel if she could see the Bible. Handing it to her in the swing, he sat down in a rocker and lit his pipe.

"How many men would've done what Isaiah did and not put that money in their pocket?" he asked.

Her attention on the Bible, Mary responded. "Two that I know of—Isaiah and you."

"Well, I'm not so sure about me."

"This was Fannie Williams' Bible," Mary said. "Why, she must have been John's grandmother. It lists marriages, births, deaths."

Intrigued, she turned a page and read an entry aloud. "John Williams, age thirteen, was baptized in the Watauga River on July 28, 1852 by Reverend Ross Potter."

"Yeah, I remember Reverend Potter. He moved to Nashville around that time to pastor a large church," Daniel mused. He took a drag on his pipe. "You probably wouldn't remember him. You were just a little girl."

Intensely focused on a page of the Bible, Mary barely heard her husband.

Noticing her shocked expression, Daniel asked what was wrong.

"Oh, my God!" she wailed.

Daniel laid his pipe on the porch rail and went to his wife. She seemed devastated by something she had just read, so much so that she was now crying, causing little Danny to start bawling as well.

"Oh, Daniel! When'll it end? When'll it ever end?"

"What, Mary? What end?"

Mary handed him the opened Bible, then picked up little Danny and rocked him.

"Read it to me, please. I just could not read it all," she said, struggling to regain her composure.

Daniel, sitting back down in the rocker, read aloud from the open Bible.

To all whom it may concern. This is to confess that the vicious snake that done killed Alfred White did not drop out of nary a tree upon his head like old man Moss Campbell said. With my bare hands, I caught the snake, a timber rattler with 19 rattles, in my hay field. I done cut off his rattles so it couldn't warn its victim. I took the feed sack off the seat of Alfred's wagon that held his lunch and the horse feed and replaced it with the same kind of sack holding the rattler. I snuck behind some nearby bushes and stayed real quiet like and watched as Alfred opened the sack and reached inside. The snake struck his hand sa hard it almost knocked poor ole screamin Alfred down. Then it wrapped around him, bitin' him somethin' fierce in his face and then his neck. Alfred tried to throw the devilish creature off but it woren't no use. I heard him scream and saw him fall plum to the ground and die. Then I put Alfred's lunch and horse feed sack back on the wagon seat and fetched away the empty sack. I swear ta God I am writing this of my own free will and expect to be branded a damned murderer by all who read this confession.

I done this evil thang alone. I wanted ta get rid of Alfred White so I could have Mary White for my wife. She's pregnant with my child, a child made from the love between Mary and myself. So you see, I had to kill Alfred White. He wuz always a thorn in my side.

I know what I did was a terrible God awful sin and some folks will think I will burn in everlasting hell. But I pray ta Jesus that He will forgive anyone who repents and asks to be saved, which I now do.

John A. Williams

10th of October 1868

Daniel stood up and laid the Bible, with its yellowed pages, down on the porch rail and rubbed his sweating forehead with a handkerchief. Mary sat tearfully in a daze, her hand over her mouth.

"Oh my God!" said Daniel. "Mary, I think John Williams put that rattlesnake in my saddle bag!"

"He tried to kill you too? You think he put that snake in your bag the night before?" She spoke between sniffles.

"More likely he was hiding in the barn and when he saw me coming, he snuck that snake into the bag, then left. Because I remember when I came out of the house Turnup was barking his head off—probably at John.

"You know, Mary, as I remember it John fell off Cliff Hill that very night. Strange how some things happen.

"What an evil man!" he said. "I had doubts about the way Alfred died, but at the time, Moss Campbell's explanation made the most sense."

"Why would he lie about me being pregnant with his child?" Mary asked. "As God is my witness, I only gave myself to John one time, when I was an innocent eighteen-year-old girl."

"I know that, Mary. And I believe you with all my heart."

"He had to cover his lies, Mary, the rumors he had spread, even if the Bible wouldn't be discovered until years later. The only reason he wrote the confession was because he wanted people to think he was so smart that he'd gotten away with the perfect crime. John Williams never felt guilt for anything he did. He was so evil that he could write a lie into the Holy Bible. He thought people would believe everything that he wrote in the Bible. I don't think I would have tested the Lord like that."

"How could I have been so stupid, Daniel?"

"You weren't stupid, Mary. John was sneaky bad. He slithered through life, just like that snake he found. He had us all fooled."

"Daniel, you need to take this confession to Sheriff Nave, so the truth can come out."

Daniel did not answer. He stood in silence gazing out at the Tennessee mountains. Then he slammed the Bible shut.

"Daniel!"

"No, Mary. It ends now. What good could possibly come from this confession? It would make several men look like fools, and think what it would do to Madge, John's girlfriend. Some would believe it to be true because it was written in the Bible and that would hurt you and little Danny. You've had enough heartache in your young life. No. It ends now. You deserve happiness without this cloud hanging over your head.

"I'll write the truth under John's confession. Then I'll lock this Bible in the bottom of my safe, and, so help me God, you and I'll never speak of this matter again. After we're dead and gone, if this confession is discovered, so be it."

Mary didn't speak. Her expressive eyes, locked onto her husband's eyes and soul, said it all. One long embrace and lingering kiss later, the two returned, with little Danny, to the inside of their home.

And never again, for the rest of their lives, was John Williams' confession mentioned.

Epilogue

From that day on, Daniel and Mary lived a happy and prosperous life and their marriage grew stronger each year. Daniel frequently boasted that his lovely wife was irresistible and kept him young and vibrant.

They eventually became some of the largest landowners in Carter County, Tennessee. Daniel raised little Danny as his own, and Mary bore him three more sons. Charlie earned a law degree and started a practice in Elizabethton where he raised his family. Peter worked the farm alongside his dad, and, going from farm to farm checking on sharecroppers. He married and raised a family in Mary's old house.

When Izzy was a young woman, she was, as Mary had been, referred to as the prettiest girl in Fish Springs. She married the young preacher that replaced Ike Redford when he retired from Fish Springs Baptist church.

Daniel died in his sleep in March of 1902 at the age of 91. But folks always said that even at that age he had a young man's energy and outlook. Fish Springs Baptist Church overflowed with mourners, and during the eulogy resident after resident of Fish Springs bestowed praise upon him.

Mary, still as beautiful as a mountain wildflower, asked Prissy to say a few words, and with Isaiah's encouragement she found her voice. Mary wrote her words in the back of her Bible.

"My name is Prissy Washington and I worked for Daniel Smith for over forty years. Me and my husband Isaiah and our three children have had a good life because of Mr. Smith. He made sure we had everything we ever needed. Mr. Daniel Smith was the kindest, most caring man I ever knowed."

An ensemble of hearty amens reverberated through Fish Springs Baptist Church.

Meanwhile, daily life in Fish Springs continued. People worked their crops, attended to their dwellings and barns, and cared for their animals. Men hunted meat, plentiful in the lush mountain forests, and women made clothing, quilts, crafts and prepared the food. When they weren't doing their chores, little boys played war with sticks, and little girls played house with their rag dolls. Kindness, sweetness, smiles, handshakes and hugs prevailed in church services, but outside of the Lord's House gossip, jealousy, lying, envy and suffering were also a part of the fiber of life in Fish Springs.

It was a sleepy little backwoods mountain community that some 46 years after Daniel Smith's death would find itself totally underwater, and even then, as historians tried to make sense of its past, would be a place full of contradictions, many of them below the waters of Watauga Lake.

In the late 1860s, however, Fish Springs and its people, along with their mysteries, triumphs, failures and secrets, very much still existed. Several mountain streams fed the lake that would one day submerge the off-the-beaten-path community. But that was still decades away.

This photo from Spring 1925 illustrates the connection in the Williams and Timbs families. In the back, from left to right: Robert L. Williams (the source of the story), Fannie Peters Williams, Wallace Timbs, Avery Timbs, Novella Timbs Peters, Bertie Williams Timbs. In the front row from left: Retha Timbs Hamm, Charlie Timbs, Lawrence Timbs, the author's father.

Larry C. Timbs, Jr interviewed his aunt, Novella Timbs Peters (Eighty-nine in 2013. Babe in arms in the photo above.) She remembers her grandfather Robert L. Williams as a gentle, good man who went to church every Sunday. "He never was seen to lose his temper and was always good and kind. He got up every Sunday morning singing 'Rock of Ages.' He used to say if his kids or grandchildren did anything wrong, he'd get a switch after us, but I don't ever remember him using it on any of us. He just threatened.

"He chewed Brown Mule chewing tobacco and he loved a bottle of beer. Every time he got home from town grandma would smell his breath and say, 'Now you've been drinkin' that beer again!'

"And he'd say, 'Now Fannie, even the Apostle Paul says wine is good for the stomach.'

"And she'd say, 'Don't pull that Bible on me!' "

Aunt Novella thinks he worked as some sort of timekeeper for the railroad, but she's not sure; she was only 14 when he died. He always carried a pocket watch--maybe because he worked on the railroad, Aunt Novella said.

"He was very religious. He always gave the blessing over the communion at Campbell's Chapel Christian Church near Piercetown where he was an elder."

For more Fish Springs stories, visit the authors' website:
www.fishspringsnovel.com

The Snyder House was the first hotel in Elizabethton, operated from about 1850 to 1900. The hotel is featured in Chapter 8, "Roast Duck and a Glass of Wine." Photo from the Murrell Family Collection, from the Archives of Appalachia.

The authors, Michael Manuel (left) and Larry C. Timbs Jr (right) with Lawrence Timbs (center) the author's father and author of the original story.

Author Bios

Michael Manuel finished high school on the Mississippi Gulf Coast and attended The University of Southern Mississippi. He and his wife Joyce live on a mountain, with their two cats, overlooking Watauga Lake near Hampton, Tennessee. They like to hike on the Appalachian Trail just below the house and kayak on the lake. The Manuels each have a daughter. *Fish Springs: Beneath the Surface,* is his first published novel. Michael says, "Life is good."

Learn more about the novel and Michael's current projects at:

www.fishspringsnovel.com

Author Bios

Larry C. Timbs Jr, a Vietnam-era USAF veteran, is a retired associate professor in the Department of Mass Communication at Winthrop University in Rock Hill, S.C. He has a Ph.D. from the University of Iowa.

He is a former general manager and editor of community newspapers in Kentucky and Illinois, and has published many travel articles in the *Charlotte Observer.* He also published frequently in journalism trade publications.

Growing up in East Tennessee, he heard many colorful stories about Fish Springs from his father, Lawrence C. Timbs, and his grandfather, James Avery Timbs (both natives of Fish Springs). He edited his father's 1981 self-published book, *Tragedy at Old Fish Springs.*

He lives in Johnson City, Tennessee. *Fish Springs: Beneath the Surface* is his first novel. He blogs at:

http://larrytimbs.blogspot.com

Authors note: My father, Lawrence C. Timbs, pictured above, died at the age of ninety in Elizabethton, Tennessee, on January 25, 2012. But not before he knew the story told to him by his grandfather would be kept alive in our book, *Fish Springs: Beneath the surface.*

Acknowledgments

of author Michael Manuel

Many thanks to my neighbor and friend George Simmons for telling me about a little known book, *Tragedy at Old Fish Springs*, written and self-published in 1981 by Lawrence C. Timbs. This is the book we re-wrote as *Fish Springs: Beneath the Surface.* Thanks to my friend Connie McCall for bringing my attention to a screenwriter's workshop, where I met movie producer Belle Avery; she convinced me I could write this book and encouraged me to do so. Thanks to my friends John and Darlene Morrissey and Dr. Bryston Wineger and Ella, for their encouragement. To Ella, for lending me the phrase, "Dear hearts."

A heartfelt thanks to my family--my sister Marcia, brothers Fritz and Chip, and their wives Lois and Betty, for their never ending support and encouragement, and also Betty's editing of the Screenplay for *Fish Springs*. Thanks to my lovely daughters Leigh and Gwen for being there and listening. To Joyce, my lovely wife, an avid reader, for her intelligent feedback and tolerating my obsession with writing, thank you. I love you.

Thanks to Dr. Jim Godfrey for his feedback and encouragement of my writing. To Betsy Sullenger who works in the film industry—thank you for helping me with my early screen writing, which ultimately led to this book. Thanks to my friend Roberta Herrin, Ph.D., and Professors Daniel Koch and Andrew L. Slop from the Department of Appalachian Studies at East Tennessee State University for their knowledge of the Civil War and life in Appalachia during that period. Thanks to the following people for photographs for our cover, as well as historical facts. Herman Tester, Dawn Trivette Peters, Glenn Elliott and the ETSU archives.

Thanks to Peter and Pari Ford for their many hours of typing and editing the first drafts of this book and for Peter's computer skills that were invaluable.

A heartfelt thank you to my friend and co-author Larry C. Timbs Jr. Larry, a retired journalism professor, came on board after the first draft to edit the book. But I soon learned that he was a gifted writer and a master of words.

Together, I believe we created a novel that captures part of the heart, soul and lore of Appalachia.

A special thanks to Ingalls Publishing Group. Thank you, Bob Ingalls. You are a true gentleman. You made our dreams come true. Thank you, Barbara Ingalls for creating a publishing company that caters to Southern fiction writers and stories of Appalachia. Thank you, IPG senior editor Judy Geary, for your hours, days and weeks of editing and your expertise of historical facts and researching. You are the best.

To Lawrence C. Timbs, a native of Fish Springs who passed away in January 2012, you left us too soon to see your story told again. We based our book *Fish Springs: Beneath the Surface* on the riveting tale told to you by your grandfather in 1938. Your son and I sincerely hope we made you proud by helping keep the story alive. We know you have been with us every step of the way, and we like to think that you are smiling down from heaven on our novel.

For more information about the current projects of the authors and the novel, visit the authors' website:
www.fishspringsnovel.com

For more information about more great stories by Southern authors of historical fiction, mystery, romantic suspense and adventure, from
Ingalls Publishing Group
visit the publishers' website:
www.ingallspublishinggroup.com

Acknowledgments
of author Larry C. Timbs Jr.

Thank you most of all to my parents, Lawrence C. Timbs and Dixie Nadine Jenkins Timbs. I was truly blessed to be the oldest son of two very gifted storytellers and writers. Whatever natural talent and determination I have as a writer stems from them.

My editors, professors, writing coaches and mentors in English and journalism also have shaped me as a writer. I won't list names here for fear I'll leave someone out. But I learned from them that everyone is hungry for a good story. It's just a matter of creating it and telling it the right way. I hope that has happened with *Fish Springs: Beneath the Surface.*

Michael Manuel, my co-author, also pushed and inspired me. But for his prodding and encouragement, I'd have never been a part of *Fish Springs*. It isn't always easy writing a novel with someone else. Disagreements inevitably make the process challenging. But in the end, we found common ground as writers, and I believe the result was well worth all that we went through—the hundreds of emails and phone calls, the give and take, the back and forthness that took place between Michael and myself for several years.

Michael, who fittingly lives on top of a mountain just outside of Hampton, TN, never let my dad's story die. Because of him, *Fish Springs* now has a much wider audience, maybe even a worldwide audience. Thanks, Michael, for helping keeping a part of my dad alive.

Thanks also to the following people for making me a smarter writer about Fish Springs: Lucille Brown of Mountain City, Tennessee; Novella Timbs Peters of Elizabethton, Tennessee; Clint Howard and Betty Howard of Mountain City, Tennessee; Patsy Howard Robinson of Johnson City, Tennessee; Wallace Timbs of Elizabethton, Tennessee; Mark Rodenhauser and Bessie Meeks of York, South Carolina; and Francis Stewart of Butler, Tennessee.

Lastly, thanks to all those salt-of-the-earth folks I grew up with or befriended in

East Tennessee. And thanks to my extended family—aunts, uncles, cousins, grandparents. Many of their stories of the mountains and how they told them to me—their "mountainese" language—have made their way into Fish Springs. Some of the stuff you hear you just can't make up! It truly pays to be a good listener.

For more information about the current projects of the authors and the novel, visit the authors' website:
www.fishspringsnovel.com

For more information about more great stories by Southern authors of historical fiction, mystery, romantic suspense and adventure, from
Ingalls Publishing Group
visit the publishers' website:
www.ingallspublishinggroup.com

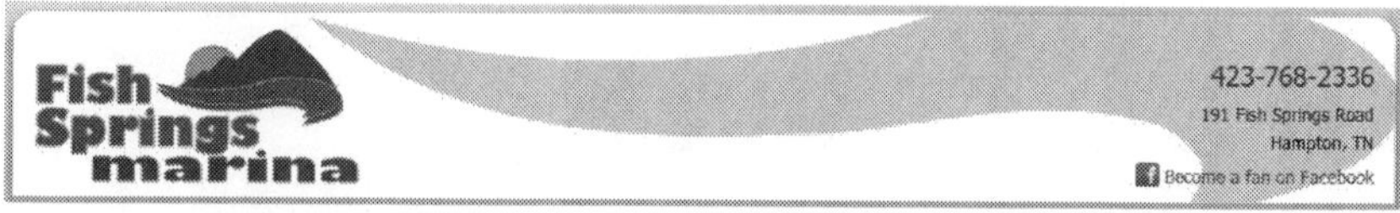

$25 off a daily or hourly pontoon rental at Fish Springs Marina www.fishspringsmarina.com

Take advantage of the coupon below to spend the day on beautiful Watauga Lake—TVA's highest elevated reservoir in Tennessee. The remote lake is nestled in the Appalachian Mountains and framed by the Cherokee National Forest. Watauga Lake is one of the cleanest lakes in the U.S.

Spend a day on this spectacular mountain lake with this coupon (redeemable year around) for $25 off a boat rental at Fish Springs Marina, the oldest continuously family-owned marina on the lake. What you save on a boat rental more than covers the cost of the novel, ***Fish Springs: Beneath the Surface.***

And when you return from your boat adventure, visit the full service store at Fish Springs Marina. It's chock full of fishing supplies, souvenirs and refreshments.

- -

$25 off a daily or hourly pontoon rental at Fish Springs Marina

191 Fish Springs Road, Hampton, TN 37658
For reservations call 423-768-2336 or visit
www.fishspringsmarina.com

Coupon cannot be used for any other goods or services
Coupon expires October 31st 2017